William M. Baker

The Making of a Man

William M. Baker

The Making of a Man

ISBN/EAN: 9783743407985

Manufactured in Europe, USA, Canada, Australia, Japa

Cover: Foto ©Andreas Hilbeck / pixelio.de

Manufactured and distributed by brebook publishing software (www.brebook.com)

William M. Baker

The Making of a Man

THE

KING OF A MAN.

By the Author of

MAJESTY, MYSELF, "BLESSED SAINT CERTAINTY,"
"A BLESSED GHOST," ETC. ETC.

Deus et ipse evolventes.

BOSTON:
ROBERTS BROTHERS.
1884.

University Press:

JOHN WILSON AND SON, CAMBRIDGE.

CONTENTS.

THE MAKING OF A MAN.

CHAPTER I.

"CONFOUND you! De-de-double confound you!" and then the oaths grew too hot to be repeated by one who does not care to scorch his own lips therewith.

You would scarcely have thought, as they rang heartily out on the foggy air, that they came from a man who had once been a clergyman, and might any day become one again. Any one can tell by the report of a cannon whether the cartridge is blank or shotted, and there was in the profanity a sincerity and force of moral meaning which savored, shocking as it may seem to say so, of prayer meeting and of pulpit. If you had known Mr. Thirlmore during his popularity as pastor of the Church of the Holy Oriflamme, and had gone into the long, low stone stable from which the oaths now came, you might have hesitated to acknowledge that swearer and preacher were the same.

He was a man whose height was lost in his admirable proportions; and he used to have the art of dressing, when he cared to do so, with a sort of ministerial magnificence whose intense blackness, in contrast with his linen, set him off as purple does a king. On this Decem-

ber dawn he was clad in the shaggiest of woollen jackets,
dirty gray in color, which reached below his stalwart
hips.   It was loosely held together by buttons each larger
than a dollar; his red undershirt showed at the broad
bosom as he stooped or rose at his currying.   His trousers,
of a thick and corded brown material, were stuffed into
heavy boots.   Upon his head of black and dishevelled
hair was the most shapeless of felt hats, of a storm-beaten
yellow; his hair and his hat were liberally coated, as was
his whole person, with dust and hay sifted down from
the low loft overhead.   The stallion upon which he was
at work, currycomb in hand, had trodden upon his foot;
and consigning the animal to the worst its Maker could
do to it here and hereafter, he had contributed what he
was able toward that doom by striking its jaws with a heavy
fist.   Then he limped out into the passage-way which ran
between the range of stalls on either side, and leaned
against the partition, nursing his hurt foot with a hand
which had been badly jarred by the blow.

As he did this he saw that Tamerlane, the horse, had
turned his shapely head, and was looking at him with an
almost human apology in his intelligent eyes.   Thirlmore's
anger passed rapidly away.   " I can stand almost anything," he often remarked, " from a horse, a bull, or a dog;
but any creature that walks on two feet had better not try
it," and so it was now.

" I know you did n't mean to do it, old chap," he said,
as he let down his aching foot.   " Look next time before
you stamp, and we will call it square."

Taking advantage of the place in which he stood, he
stretched himself into a yawn, his long arms almost touching the cobwebbed floor of the loft overhead.   Then he
laughed aloud, and with sincere enjoyment.   Every colt

and horse, every ox and blooded cow in the range of stalls, had ceased eating and was gazing at him with large inquiring eyes and suspended jaws. As he gave himself another deliberate stretch his hat fell off his head, revealing his full and dark brown beard, his finely formed forehead ; the husk of a cocoanut or of an autumnal ear of corn is not in more unison with itself than were his stable surroundings and rough garb with the genuine nature of the man.

"Eat ahead all of you," he said cheerily. "I love to hear your jaws going. I wish I could get that much enjoyment out of *my* fodder ; " and he went into the stall again. Laying his arm along the neck and his hand between the assenting ears of his pet, he rubbed the moist cool velvet of its nose with the other.

"Good friends again, Tam? So we are. Eat away, old fellow." It was long past the hour of breakfast ; but he stayed, taking pleasure in the satisfaction his horse took in its chopped food, more pleasure than he would do in his own meal, then waiting on him in the house.

"How would you like to swap places with me, Tam?" he asked. "I'm willing, and I'll give you my wife to boot. But don't you turn into a woman ; " for the horse had stopped feeding to whisper its general consent to anything, and to rub its head upon its master's nearest shoulder.

He put his arm about Tamerlane's neck. "What Cæsar was it, Tam, who made his horse consul? He was a first-class emperor to do so. I must go in to my grub, but I would much rather stay with you. We'll take a gallop together after awhile. Take care of yourself, pard."

When he opened the door and saw what the weather had become, he closed it behind him, as carefully as a mother might have done the door of her nursery. As he did so, an imported Jack within began to express its hitherto silent admiration of its owner, at first in a subdued whisper, and then with head thrown back and open jaws, pouring its whole heart into a tremendous bray. Cold as it was, Mr. Thirlmore stood still until the last sound had subsided into a whistle. "Hurrah for you, Senex," he laughed; "I like a fellow, whoever he is, to put his soul into it, whatever it is! I should have accomplished more with my braying if I had been half as much in earnest."

It was a miserable morning. The day was still undecided as to whether it should rain, clear up, come down in sleet, or take it out in wind. Nevertheless, the muggy air lay like an incurable disease upon what seemed to visitors to be the bleakest of farms. It had been picked out as such by an old uncle of its present owner, who had come before he died to love it even more than he had done the Grampian austerities of his poverty-stricken childhood. Situated in one of the most out-of-the-world regions of New England, far from town or railroad, it was destitute of even such life as would have been imparted to its barrenness by the most meagre of rivulets. The property was a confusion of rocky hills, broken here and there by reaches of meadow, a jungle of underbrush, or the clinging and shivering together of a few forlorn trees, pine and spruce, hackberry and oak. Instead of the gentler yielding to exigence in curves and slopes the hills broke angrily everywhere into angles, through which the rusty granite protruded like bones, a lean covering of soil barely hiding the underlying unchangeability of rock. In all directions, the rounded bowlders dotted the only arable intervals of the farm like the scattered seed of hills yet to be.   There was over a thousand acres in all, but if you did not know that there was no other way of reliev- ing the soil from its ever-increasing product of stones, you would have wondered what the manifold reaches of wall were intended to fence out or to fence in, and would have been glad to get away.   But then you were not born upon it as was Mr. Thirlmore, nor had you come back to it, as he had done, from a world to whose yet rougher surfaces he had found it even more difficult, vigorous as he was, to adjust himself.

When he left the stables he went toward the house. This was a rambling structure of stone, a story and a half in height, the heavy roof closing down upon the lower rooms like a perpetual frown.   It clung to the southern side of one of the largest of the hills, and had been added to from time to time, as the needs of its occupants de- manded, with as little reference to symmetry as to the bowlders lying about it.   Its present owner had returned to it at thirty years of age, from one of the wealthiest circles of one of the most carefully cultured and every way cared-for of cities, to find that it still held its own as it had done in his boyhood.

His wife was waiting for her husband at the breakfast table ; she would have waited if he had come hours later. She hastened out on the stoop to help him off with his hat and coat.

" I would n't bother myself about them.   In an hour or two they will be as wet again," he said, as she shook out the sleet and snow, and went to hang them before the kitchen fire under care of Maggie, the only servant.

" It is no bother, Theo," she said gently.   "Maggie has got up a splendid breakfast this morning.   I hope you are hungry.   I am."

"I wonder," her husband thought, as he went in without looking at her, "what in the mischief is coming over her."

"Do you know, Theo," Mrs. Thirlmore said, after the coffee had time to do its beneficent work on her husband, "I enjoy this weather, it makes indoors so cosey?"

"Yes," he assented, and meditated within himself: "It must be the farm. I thought it would kill her. A man can count on what a sheep, say, will do, but who can tell how a woman will act? It must be the farm, and she is taking it that way. But, great heavens! what will she do when she comes to know?"

For the simple fact was that Mr. Thirlmore was on the verge of another and, if possible, worse ruin. The popular preacher had indulged for so long and so largely in oratory that it had unfitted him for the stern practicalities of a farm as unproductive as his. For years he had made from the pulpit the most glowing of prophecies, the most delightful and magnificent of rhetorical promises in reference to this and that. He had indulged so long and so sweepingly in the exaggerations of sentiment that he could not get down all at once from the platform to the solid soil of business dealing. His imported stock did not bring in returns as rapidly as he had expected; dogs and rot had got among his sheep, murrain had slain his Devons, dishonest neighbors had robbed his pens of their Berkshires. He was being brought to book in a sharp and sudden way wholly unknown to the arabesques and spirals of eloquence. Rich friends who had admired and rewarded him munificently as a preacher, lost interest in him as a farmer. The day of reckoning was very near.

Now, Mr. Thirlmore was in some senses the manliest of men. Bravely and unwhimpering, he had worked with almost desperation, neglecting no chance, leaving no stone unturned. It was the severest test of his endurance that he had hidden everything from even his clear-sighted wife. But, now, he could do so no more.

" I am sorry for her," he thought ; but the sharpest of his pangs was that Tamerlane must go. " I have half a notion, old chap," he confided to him more than once, " to blow out first your brains and then my own."

It is doubtful whether there had ever been a time in his wedded life when he would have looked to his wife for suggestion, encouragement, support. He was not a man of that kind. In common with everybody who knew his wife, he acknowledged that she was a superior woman ; it did not occur to his mind to ask whether hers might not be the transcendent womanly superiority which had precisely that sweetness and succor of which his need was never so great as now.

CHAPTER II.

THE uncle of Mr. Thirlmore, Donald McGregor, emigrating from Scotland when a boy, had worked his way up in a commission business in New York until he had made himself, by unfaltering and persistent pluck, senior partner and a man of wealth. He had brought his sister Elspeth over from Scotland as soon as he could. She had kept house for him during many months, but had fallen in her brother's opinion by marrying a thriftless half farmer, half country-store keeper named Thirlmore. Donald held possession of the farm, which had fallen to him by the bankruptcy of Mr. Thirlmore, till he died, but he had allowed his sister to live there. She was by nature an excellent but hard woman, whom the iron mould of poverty had made harder still. She had one son, named Theodore after his father, and it was strange that the sole weakness of her life — her marriage — should result in a son who was the one hope and strength of her last days. When death, the only power strong enough to do it, had plucked the farm out of Donald's grip, it became hers by an ownership as thoroughly incorporating every acre into herself as if it were a thumb or a lung. In a word, and like almost all emigrants to America from Scotland, brother and sister were still Scotch, Scotch to a degree obsolete in Scotland itself.

As such she had ideas as clearly defined and as unchangeable as her native hills, where all that softens the outlines is not trees but heather. These she carried out all the more steadily for never putting them into words. Her first thought was to make her son as vigorous of body as possible. To this steady end she saw to it that he had as much plain but wholesome food, as much thick, seasonable underclothing, as much hard work on the farm, and in all weathers, as was in her power. Although she never mentioned it to herself, far less to him, she took pride in her well-developed vigorous boy ; but the intense sense of ownership was the chief fibre of her affection for him. As her next intention, she had seen to it that Theodore was thoroughly instructed at the district school near by, going over his lessons with him every night herself. Then his uncle came in, and Old Orange, of which college he was trustee, did all it could for his nephew ; for the old man had devoted himself so exclusively to business that, as his head grew gray and his conscience aware of a balancing of accounts elsewhere, he sought to live his life over again, this time in the ministry and in the person of this large-framed Thomas-Chalmers-like nephew of his.

Both brother and sister knew — the sister a little the more devoutly — that their charge had a soul as well as a body and mind. These three parts of every man were, in their estimation, as completely separable as so many silver dollars. Theodore's body and mind were those portions of him which had to do with this world. The soul was that part of him which entered upon its functions after he reached the next life. His mother had done her duty by so training her son in body and mind that it should not be her fault if he did not master for himself the thoroughly fenced-in world which he now occupied. It was even more essential that she should so deal with his soul that it should perform *its* duty when it arrived in the hereafter.

To this end she carried him through a certain course of religious instruction. It was her custom every summer to cook and can an abundance of fruit, and to put it carefully away in the cellar, hermetically sealed, to be opened when winter was come. So was it in her care for Theodore's soul. She had a complete set of receipts brought with her from over the water, and on Sundays she so applied these as at last to believe that, when the time came to test in another life the result, it would be found that her boy was as thoroughly qualified for the other life as he had already been for this.

One failure there seemed to be in her work. A year or two before this history begins she had died. Almost from infancy she had trodden her path of life with firm and even step, and she went on into the other world with as steady a going. But, somehow, she had so effectively sealed up the soul she had canned, she had so hidden the key of the cellar, deep within him, in which was her completed work, that neither he nor any one else could get at it for daily use.

"There is no nonsense about Thirlmore; you don't catch *him* indulging in sentimentality," was the remark often made of Mr. Thirlmore during his splendid career as a popular preacher. Yet these friends were compelled to confess there was a lack, a painful lack in him. What this lack was it puzzled people to say.

Yet Thirlmore, as has been said, had been a man of mark. After undergoing a full course in college and theological seminary, he had taken charge of the Church of the Holy Oriflamme in a leading city, and had crowded that church for years as the most conspicuous preacher of a city in which such pre-eminence meant much. Strange to say, his church, at what seemed to be the very noon of its prosperity, had suddenly collapsed. Could it have been for lack of that part of him which lay locked up awaiting its opportunity of use after death?

"You are in every way a fine speaker," his wife often remarked to him, from almost the outset of his popularity. "You have a noble presence, an excellent voice ; you are rich in rhetoric and illustration ; at intervals you interest people, thrill them, make them laugh, flush them to hot indignation at the wrong-doing of other people. You can do everything, Theodore, but make your hearers weep — for themselves, I mean. As you know, I am far enough from being a fanatic, but you fail in this one thing ; you do not so seize upon any one individual as to compel him to halt and give his own case a careful consideration ; and this is because you do not get at and face your own inmost self. Some day you will lose your popularity without anybody being able to tell why. It will be suddenly gone from you like a silk umbrella, of which the owner says : 'Was it stolen from me? Did I mislay it? I can't imagine what is become of it.'"

"Do you think so?" he said in an indifferent way at the time ; but it was little he cared. When the crash came Mrs. Thirlmore uttered no word except of encouragement. And then they removed from the city and settled down upon the farm.

When Mrs. Thirlmore married her husband she was a Miss Peace Van Dyke, the granddaughter of an old and very dull country pastor near Old Orange. She was of a slight but graceful figure, of gentle manners, and she spoke in a low voice. Her features were singularly refined, and the marble of her almost transparent complexion made her seem, especially in her simple home dress, like one of the virgins of Phidias. Her eyes were what held you; not so much because they were unusually large and of a steely gray, but because they listened so intently to all you said, and for hours at a time; that is, if you had anything to say which she thought worth hearing, otherwise she paid no attention at all. The chief thing about her when she married was that, with insatiable hunger, she wanted to know; no man could have a zest for knowledge so persistent, because it could not be so feminine as hers. If ever a woman read, inquired, studied, observed, reflected, — did everything to fill her mind with all the knowledge there was attainable, and to expand it for the reception of more, — she was that woman.

In this way she came to marry Mr. Thirlmore. During his stay at Old Orange he was often at her grandfather's house. He stood so high in college, was so successful in his oration as valedictorian of his class, was called so soon to an important church, that it was impossible a girl like Peace Van Dyke should not fall in love with him, even if he had not been the handsome fellow he was. It had always been with her, and in everything, a matter of intellect rather than of heart, and what she thought was love was really pride in him. During quite a long honeymoon she was passionately, not so much in love with as interested in him. Then came a slow but a very steady disillusionment in regard to her husband. She became conscious of the fact that it was not for herself but for her pride in him that he had married her; naturally — and as a matter of course — he would tire of it. As he did so she came to realize but too well that she had greatly overestimated his abilities.

Her mind was such that when she knew anything at

all she knew it with singular clearness, and stated it to herself with entire frankness.

"Why is it," she now asked of herself, "that I find him so much less than I had supposed? He seems to be the leader of a church which is apparently in the rush of a strong current, but really he and his people are in a whirlpool instead; all the enthusiasm and noisy foam come from the violence with which they are carried round and round in the same small circuit of sentiments rather than thoughts, while he is really standing still. Is it possible that I am outgrowing him? And then he is too thoroughly satisfied with himself to strike out of his unconscious repetitions into broader things. Now, is it because he is so much more — animal than I imagined? Is it possible," she slowly came to ask herself, "that I was the Titania of a midsummer night's dream, and that he was all along," — she shuddered and — laughed. He had said and done things now and then which she, in her intellectual over-refinement, had shrunk from with horror.

It did not draw them closer together, their life in the city. She had all opportunities there of reading, hearing the best thought upon every topic on the platform, and in association with those who, in an intellectual sense, were the best people. She had travelled in Europe; her mind had grown all the more that, having no children and slackening in her affection for her husband, her heart had lent its juices to the development of mind; she had enjoyed it amazingly for a time, but she had grown tired. After journeying east, west, north, south, over the surface of all there was to know, she grew so weary, — and with bodily as well as mental weariness, — that she was glad to retreat with her husband to the old farm.

"I 'll be shot if I can explain it!" Mr. Thirlmore pondered as he sat at table that morning. "Something is coming over her, and it is just like her to keep it to herself, to endure it without flinching. I dare say it is the farm. She has to take to something, and horses, cows, sheep, dogs are no more to her than so many troublesome beasts about a place. It is queer she does not take a fancy to a thoroughbred cow, horse, or something, she is such a thoroughbred herself. I wish I could love her. It might make the time pass more comfortably for both of us. She is wonderfully sharp. I shall never forget what she told me, and from the outset, about those confounded people."

What she had said, expressed in various forms, was this: "The men and women who crowd to hear you are those who have broken away from and despise their own fathers and mothers, so far as religion goes. When it has become the habit of their lives to laugh at these, do you suppose they will continue to be faithful to you? And then they have so many things to be enthusiastic about, you will win only your brief hour of their attention. Theo, I wish you could be absolutely sure about something, could grasp after and hold men by — by the roots of their nature, by — by whatever is deepest in them." Mr. Thirlmore had but a hazy memory when it related to men and women, but he recalled what his wife said, and the look on her face as she added, "What is it, Theodore? What is the deepest thing in us? Can't you tell me? I wish I knew!" — her face, so finely attuned to what she thought and felt, had expressed such keen desire.

"I would n't be sentimental, Peace," was all he replied to her at the time.

It recurred to him as they sat at breakfast this morning. But it did not interfere with his appetite — he rose so early, had worked so hard. "Yes, it must be living on the farm which is changing her," he thought, over his griddle-cakes and hot coffee.

She made a pretence of eating, but it was merely to keep him company. If any one had observed her very closely as she sat, her eyes lingering almost timidly upon him as he ate, such an one might have known that her appetite was chiefly for her husband himself. As to him, whether she ate or not was a matter of small moment. He had been absent on business some days. As they did not share the same apartment he had not seen her before during that time; but it was sincerely a matter of indifference to him. Yet, as he turned matters in general over and over in his mind, he struck yet again upon a question that had grown wearisome to him.

"How will she take it when she knows — and she must know soon — that I am dead broke?"

CHAPTER III.

HEZEKIAH GRUMBLES.

BEFORE Mr. Thirlmore was through with his breakfast he was told that some one was waiting to see him. It was Maggie who made the announcement. Many years before Maggie had been imported from the Isle of Man as an inseparable member of a flock of sheep which she had herded all her life. Maggie was almost as broad as she was long, her hair cut short into a mop of sunburned tow about her head. Hers was a square face of animal honesty; and she had such a droop of the head, such a forward thrust of the muscular shoulders, such an amble of gait, as to resemble, with the hair hanging about her patient eyes, not a Shetland pony merely, but one which has long tugged at the drawing of a well-loaded van.

"Is it a man or a woman who wants to see me?" demanded her master. Maggie's sleeves were rolled up tight to her shoulders when the knock came at the door; she had time to unroll but one before answering it.

"It is a man, sir," she now replied, tugging to draw down her other sleeve over an arm which was purple from the wash-tub.

"And not a gentleman? Then I'll see him."

Maggie glanced from her mistress to her master. "It is a mon who is a gentlemon," she said in her dogged fashion.

"Then I won't see him. Tell him so. I am too busy." Mr. Thirlmore took another egg; but Maggie lingered, held by the eye of her mistress.

" I had hoped people would let me alone," the master
of the house growled over his plate like a dog over his
bone. " Why should anybody want to see me? I don't
want to see anybody."

" It may be one of your old members from the city.
You have devoted friends there, Theodore."

" Do you think so?" His wife was venturing upon a
topic of which he was evidently tired.

" I am sorry, dear, you will look at it in that way," she
persisted in a lower tone, and with a manner which would
have puzzled the attention of a close observer, so eager
was it, yet so submissive. " You have many friends, Theo,
who rate you too highly to let you alone. They value
you too much to give up their hopes or to allow you to
bury yourself."

" Do they? Well, I am sorry for them. Maggie, ask
whoever it is to excuse me." But the girl was looking
at her mistress and did not move. Mr. Thirlmore proceeded to break and eat his egg; his hunger was satisfied;
the egg was only an excuse not to leave the table.

" Confound whoever it is," he grumbled; " there is
not a man, woman, or child I want to see."

Mrs. Thirlmore winced a little. It was like him to
care nothing for the presence of the girl; but it mattered
little to Maggie what he said or did. Never had she met
a handsomer man than her master. She was vaguely
aware that he had been a great preacher in the city, and
yet she had not an atom of reverence for him or of fear,
so well had she come to know him. King Saul must have
been somewhat the same kind of man to his servants, —
very big, nominally king, but no more in their eyes than
a badly spoiled boy who was at times very much in their
way. It was this pale mistress of Maggie, finely featured,

low spoken, always on the alert, holding so much in reserve, of whom the girl was afraid, even while she admired and loved her as she had done no mortal before.
A twelve-inch box in which is condensed electricity
enough to drive a steamship across the Atlantic, would
seem, if we knew nothing of its contents, to be no more
than any ordinary box hardly worth a glance. But you
cannot so conceal force of any kind when it is within a
man or a woman waiting its hour. In a way wholly beyond description the lurking element will suffuse the flesh
containing it; though the face be finer in texture than
glass the hidden attar of roses will sweeten it. No pore
so small but it will breathe out and betray the inmost soul,
provided the soul be more than the body.

"It may be," Mrs. Thirlmore suggested at last, "that
some one has a valuable dog or horse to show you."

"To tempt me to my ruin? Most likely it is a rascally
book-agent, or some villain with a patent stump-puller
which cannot drag up a radish." But he ate faster; his
wife, alive to every movement, observed this; she was
watching as keenly as only a wife can watch his chances
and her own.

Maggie had gone back to her wash-tub, and, having
finished his repast, Mr. Thirlmore strolled at last into the
front room. As he did so, a man, tall and ungainly, in the
rough clothing of a farmer, rose to meet him. He had a
large and plain face, red and yellow from out-of-door work.
It was evident that, wet and dry, cold and hot, he had
borne for a long time all that weather and sturdy toil
could do for him. As the master of the house came in he
stretched out to him a large hand.

"I'm afraid you don't know me," he said, with a
questioning smile.

Thirlmore uttered no word of recognition, but he knew his visitor perfectly well. One glance at the freckled face, framed in its yellowish red of hair and whiskers, had been enough. Those light blue eyes, surmounted by flaxen eyebrows, with almost imperceptible lashes to the eyelids, once seen could never be forgotten. Such loose-jointed legs and arms, such downright ugliness, one does not behold more than once in a lifetime ; especially when so much genuine honesty goes with it, such open-hearted good-humor over it all, like midsummer and the smell of clover upon the roughness of a last year's hayrick. True, their visitor had added, since Mr. Thirlmore saw him, years to his age and many pounds to his weight ; but he was only so much the more of what he had been. And yet Mr. Thirlmore had no responsive smile upon his face in answer to the greeting of this old acquaintance. He took the extended hand as he would have done the hindering bough of a tree as he walked. "How are you?" he asked, but he did not seat himself or ask the other to do so.

"I knew you would not know me." It was said pleasantly, but there was a creeping something, half confusion, half anger, under it which made the face of the visitor ruddier than before. Mrs. Thirlmore herself was not quicker to understand this insolent ex-idol of the city church. The visitor shifted his hat to his right hand, as if about to go without another word. Something unseen prevented.

"It is so long," he said, "since we were in college together ! So many things have happened to both of us —"

But with the word he flushed again. He might be thought to refer to Mr. Thirlmore's downfall, which had made

more noise than the success which had preceded it. Both
felt it. On the whole the speaker was not sorry that he
had said it. The two were more on a level afterward.

"I 'm not surprised that you do not remember me," he
went on. "Though we were classmates we seldom spoke.
My name is Grumbles, Hezekiah Grumbles. You may remember it by the fun the fellows used to make of it. I 'm
the man who never could do anything at the blackboard.
You can't help recollecting Professor Rodney, and how he
would stick me up at the board like a bug with a pin
through it. I don't blame him — not a bit. I could not
get the hang of the Differential Calculus then; and I know
now that there *is* such a thing, but that is all. The Professor and the rest of you had your fun out of me; but it
was death to the frogs, as Æsop says. I hailed from Scrubstones then. That is where I live now. But that is n't
what I came to see you about."

"I remember." Mr. Thirlmore was evidently trying to
draw his visitor up out of the wells of oblivion; but he
did it very slowly, indifferently. He did not say aloud,
"But what in the mischief do you want with me?" though
he might as well have done so. But Mr. Grumbles held
to his purpose.

"Yes," he said with a bright face; "I was the dunce of
our class. But that does n't matter. We all knew you.
You had the valedictory, you remember." He was on the
edge of adding, "And you did it splendidly!" but why
should he give plum-cake to a man not yet recovered from
a surfeit of pudding? "You married near Scrubstones,
you know. Everybody knew Miss Peace. Of course," he
spoke more rapidly, "we were proud — all of us — of your
call to that city church. I 'm told you had great success.
The only time I was in the city I went to see it."

It was not pleasant to dodge around the preacher's subsequent failure, but the visitor had an object in view. "And you must not be in too great a hurry," he had cautioned himself.

"How is Mrs. Thirlmore?" Since the other said nothing, there was no better question to ask. "I hope you have a house full of children. I have. Ah, excuse me," and the simple heart of the farmer overmastered for a moment what the sun had done in his face. "Bragging over him," was his self-rebuke. But the other disclaimed the children as he would a handful of popped corn, and Mr. Grumbles hurried on.

"I wanted to see you about an important matter. Not relating to myself;" he added, with a dignity as natural as the coming and going of school-girl blushes.

"The way of it is this." Still the master of the house remained standing, still he did not offer the other a seat. His bearing, too, was such that there was hardly another man alive who would not have let the insufferable ex-preacher go to perdition before he would have taken a step farther to carry out the purpose which had brought him to the house. Hezekiah Grumbles was not a poet. It was very much more in his line to plow and to hoe, to reap and to haul rails ; yet never did poet have nobler inspirations than that which had driven him to see his classmate that day. Never did Homer or Milton carry out an epic purpose more steadily than he was now carrying out his. It did not, except in a wholly subordinate degree, relate to himself; it was this which so lifted him from his substantial feet and hurried him on with a zeal which would have been lacking from any errand solely his own.

"The way of it," he said "is this: Ever since I left college — I did n't graduate, you may remember ; bless you, I could n't graduate; my grade was n't over forty, and of course that would n't begin to do. I can't say I wished the Church to send and make a preacher of me, but, bless my soul! all the churches and Old Oranges in the world could never have turned *me* into a parson. Visit the sick, — that I might have done; but, preach, — no, sir, not much! Oh, well, ever since I left college I 've been at work on the farm."

Mr. Thirlmore put on his hat. His visitor understood him. But he could not dash so suddenly into the business in hand. " It is not every man," he said it with a sense that it was the wrong thing to say, "who can farm *and* preach like you. As to me, I 'm at Scrubstones still. I was born there among the pumpkins, between the plow-handles. But that — I see you are in a hurry — is n't what I 've called to see you about. What I wanted to have a talk with you on is this."

If you make a cast in plaster of Paris you must be quick about it, so swift is it to take a set of its own. It was a peculiarity of Mr. Thirlmore, that under the attempted handling of his friends he not merely took a set in advance of all they could do, but the set was always in exact opposition to what the others desired. The more they would, the more he would not. It was so now. Whatever this fool wanted with him, he resolved not to do it. He had no idea what it was, but his own *no* was already and unalterably decided.

" Let me tell my wife you are here," he said, more than indifferently. He would turn the farmer over to her, nor would he come in again until she had rid herself of him in some way. Mr. Grumbles knew it, and here was an advantage he had over the other. Dull as he was he could, in virtue of not having his eyes fastened on himself, see things more swiftly, more clearly, and at farther distances than the gifted orator. He did not lack for brains. Like a gnarled oak, his fibres had taken a twist to farming instead of to rhetoric; but especially had he taken a bent toward caring for others more than for himself. He was as large-bodied a man as his classmate; but he was all angles and awkwardness, while no elm bore its well-proportioned height more symmetrically than did the ex-preacher: it had been a large part of his impressiveness as such. The essential difference between the two was that the farmer was as unconscious of himself as he was of the jack-knife in his pocket, while the other never for an instant forgot himself. Paris running away with Helen was not more keenly alive to the lovely lady in his arms. But it made matters easier for the farmer. Not being bothered with the weight of himself he had so much the more strength to manage the man he had come so far to see.

"It is a tough job. I knew that before I left home," said Mr. Grumbles to himself, "but I think I can do it. He was the tallest tree in the woods, and he has had the biggest kind of a cut down; but I've rolled some big logs in my day. Aurora Ann was right; it is worth trying anyhow."

But the unconscious object of all this had pulled his slouch hat firmly on. "Mrs. Thirlmore will entertain you," he said. "I have a thousand things to do. You must excuse me." And he left the room.

"I will be glad to go with you." His friend was ready for that also. "I'm like you in that, I love out of doors. You can eat," he continued, accompanying him, "sleep, die, in the house. When you've anything really to do you must go outside. A house is a good enough place for women, I tell Aurora Ann, and for young children, especially girls. A man's place is elsewhere. You are always in the way of the women inside. The chairs, glasses, and things get in your way ; the walls cramp a man up somehow. If I am not breaking something, I am always thinking I shall."

"Ah, this is what I like," he went on as he stood on the stoop. "If it is slushy under foot, snowy overhead." He drew a deeper breath, rubbed his red hands one in another. "What I intended to say, Mr. Thirlmore," he added, with a change of manner, "is too large for indoors. You are a heavy man ; not more than I am. Suppose we step toward your barn."

Yes, so it is, when a man has fully intended to do anything great he is like Niagara as it nears its cataract : he draws along with him upon his quickening course whatever chances to be near. There was a conscious quickening of the current in Mr. Thirlmore's veins as they walked on together.

"Well, to what species of animal do you belong?" he exclaimed as they neared the stables. Interested as he had always been in dogs, he had never seen one of the breed which now came waddling toward him. It was of a jet black color ; its hide, coarse and close, resembled the horsehair covering of old-fashioned sofas. The body was as long and large as that of a mastiff, flat-backed and terminating in a tail which stuck out and up like the bowsprit at the wrong end of a vessel, and at the other end in a broad head, with large and hanging ears, which reminded one instantly of Daniel Webster. But the deformity of the animal lay in its legs ; one would have sworn that three-fourths of them had been chopped off, leaving mere stumps. An uglier beast it is impossible to imagine, looking like nothing so much as an enormous leech, gorged and glossy. Mr. Thirlmore would not have done it if a sudden

elevation had not almost intoxicated him in view of what
he knew, and yet did not know, that his visitor was about
to say to him.

"Out, damned spot!" he quoted; and with a foot beneath the brute he lifted and hurled it so far that its flight
to the other side of the yard would have disabled if not
killed it, had it not fallen into a dirty drift of snow.

"Doggon your likeness! what did you do that for?"
Mr. Grumbles faced upon him in such a rage, his face so
wrathful, that the other threw up his hand to ward off what
might come next. "What was he doing to you?" It
was some time, and not until he found that the dog was
unhurt, that the farmer cooled down enough to explain.
The dog was his, and it had persisted in waddling desperately along after his master from Scrubstones. It was a
turnspit, under such ban, since the coming in of cooking stoves, for its preternatural uselessness, in addition
to its ugliness, that the breed was almost perished from
the earth.

But Mr. Grumbles had forgotten his ugly charge in a
sudden qualm. "Bet you a dollar," he said to himself,
"but I've gone and done it. After coming so far to see
him, too!"

"There's just a suspicion of weakness in old Grumbles,"
Lieutenant Van Doren had more than once remarked
of his old friend. "He is too everlastingly good. A
man must have a bit of a Nero in him to be worth anything;" which was remarkable doctrine for a person of the
Lieutenant's antecedents, as we shall see.

Weak? His wife had moments when it was necessary
that she should drive this estimate of her husband out of
her soul, as with a mop handle. No physician understood
medicine as he did farming; nor an anatomist the bones

and muscles as he did pork or beef, dead or alive. Like his father before him, he sold butcher's meat, and from the same old wagon, to his neighbors ; and he would have his price, or would bring the meat back to make soap of. And yet the scales were a pretence and a mockery, when it was to his blind old friend Mr. Sudkins that he sold, so far were they from stating the facts of weight or quantity.

"It is like measles," he now apologized for his mild profanity; "it will break out now and then ; not very often. I beg your pardon."

It did not occur to Mr. Thirlmore to ask pardon for his act. "What do you call the dog?" was all he said.

"He hasn't got any name, he's so despised. The boys, who stone him, call him Seal, Tadpole, and worse names than that. He is so miserable, such an outcast, that at our place we call him Wretch. I don't know where he came from. One hot afternoon I found him all starved and perishing for water, by our well. He looked as if he had been hooted, stoned, and run down. When he looked up in my face, as much as to say, ' Please, master, don't kick me ; I can't help it ; let me die ; I won't be long about it !' I couldn't help being sorry for the poor brute. I do suppose Aurora Ann is as kind-hearted a woman as lives, but the trouble is, he *will* go into the kitchen. ' He can't help it,' I tell her. ' It runs in his blood to be at the kitchen fire basting meat. A hundred generations of his ancestors did it before he was born. He thinks his solemn duty, the thing he was made a turnspit for, lies there.' ' May be so,' Aurora Ann says, ' but it don't run in my blood to let him ; ' and what with being chased out every day with a broomstick and now and then a ladle full of hot water, his temper is soured.

Children he looks on as his natural enemies ; he will growl
and show his teeth even at ours.   In that way he 's come
to stick close to my heels as the only friend he 's got in
the world.   That is why he followed me from home.
Come here, Wretch, poor fellow ! " and, keeping an eye
upon Mr. Thirlmore, the grotesque brute sidled up to his
sole friend and laid a nose in the hand held out to him.
" Is 'nt he an odd fish ? " his master continued ; " look
at him ! " What with his vast but mutilated size, his capacious brows, his large and mournful eyes, his crouch of
hopeless woe — " he is like greatness in ruins, ain't he ? "
Mr. Grumbles asked.

Then a sudden flush dyed the farmer's face.   " Good
heavens ! " he said to himself.   " What a donkey I am?
He may think I 'm hitting at *him !* "   What he said aloud
was : " You know how I was laughed at in college as a
dunce.   Wretch and I can sympathize together.

" But, now, Mr. Thirlmore, we must get to what I came
to see you about.   It won't take very long."

CHAPTER IV.

A RARE WOMAN.

AS has been said, Mrs. Thirlmore was the granddaughter of an old clergyman long settled in a country parish, but if ever the egg of a sea hawk was hatched beneath the motherly wings of a barnyard fowl it was in her case. Her grandfather upon the mother's side was no other than Maximilian Rodenstein, so famous in his day as that Professor in the University of Göttingen who first dared advance views which since then have become so common. Whether, as·was asserted in his biography, the Professor was an intimate from his childhood of Spinoza's attic in Amsterdam is not certain. One thing is sure, and that is that, like Spinoza, he was a Jew. Now a Jew, as a rule, is like a lump of lead when the mission of Christ is in question ; the heart and mind of Oriental fervor chill into a passionless incapability of even thinking much less feeling upon that subject. So intelligent and energetic in reference to anything else, there was instant paralysis with the Professor when the Messiah was mentioned ; not heat or hate, not vituperation or violence, not argument, objection even, but sudden palsy to him was lodged in the name Christ. There are trees which, petrified upon one side, are full of life on the other. Strange to say, Professor Rodenstein, dead as a hammer to Christ, was equally so to Moses. If glass-grinding Spinoza had such effect upon him, then that pallid atheist was as powerful to impart death as was Christ to bestow life.

For who so successful as his pupil in preaching atheism ?

It was little the government cared for that, but when he carried out his principles and struck at the Kaiser, seeking to demolish all human as well as all divine government, then the State hastened to act. So swiftly was he dealt with, that one bleak December day the savage old iconoclast found himself landing upon the New York wharves with small possessions beyond a trunk full of his destructive books, a meerschaum, and his daughter Cara, a girl of sixteen. Because his means were so low, and it was the nearest to New York of the better known institutions of learning, he settled himself as a teacher in German and all manner of radicalisms in Old Orange, the last place in America for such an experiment, because the most orthodox. Here he took a small house and managed to secure scholars enough in German to keep his pipe and his stomach filled, with a little over for Cara. When he had grouped his pupils around him and had hastened through with the lesson, he was very sure to begin a fresh utterance of ideas, concerning which he was vastly more zealous than Jenner had ever been with regard to vaccination, or Harvey for the circulation of the blood. It was little the youths about him cared for his queer notions; but his grotesque earnestness interested them.

"De government of de king like de idea of a God is," he insisted between puffs of his pipe, "necessary to de races in dare — what you call it — dish clout? No, swaddling clothes. Here in America you have outgrown de first humbug, not as yet de second. Outgrow it you must, as de leetle boy gets too big for his fader's coat. Look here, behold!" To the dismay of his two or three listeners, he would throw open his greasy dressing-gown, pull apart vest and shirt, and smite a hairy hand upon a hairier bosom. "De mammal of de man, it is dare; but

is it not extinct? Has it any use now? So it is wid de
religious faculty. It has what object outside of itself?
Nein! It is extinct. You can, you Americans, imagine
such a ting as loyalty to a Kaiser? No. In a little whiles
you will not understand how a man can believe in God any
more, my friends, dan dey do in Mumbo Jumbo or Thor,
in Zeus or Jupiter. Each had his turn. Effery king from
Nimrod down to Kaiser Wilhelm, effery god from de
fetich down to de present Deity, each had his turn and
is gone — gone like dat," and he eyed with triumph the
wreaths of smoke curling overhead from his bearded lips ;
" and dey all — gods, kings — proceeded from de restless
mind of de man himself, as does dis smoke from my
mouth. Forty — twenty — years from now men will no
more haff faith in God or ruler. ' De *faculty* of belief will
be dead. I, Maximilian Rodenstein, swear it! What is
you laughing at?. Haff you not de brains to understand ?"

It so happened that the Professor brought with him a
perpetual contradiction of himself in the person of Cara, his
daughter, a blooming *fräulein*, rosy and plump, given to
good humor and the showing of beautiful teeth through
coral lips, in a laughter which was but the expression of
perfect health. Tired of tobacco smoke, metaphysics, and
outcry against all things human and divine, she allowed
herself to be fallen in love with by the only son of a country parson. He was a handsome fellow, who was perishing for a little variety upon the pale damsels and doleful
routine of his daily life ; so the two ran away and were
married. It would have killed good old Mr. Van Dyke if
he had not been driven thereby to take a fresh hold upon
his Maker. Having no Maker, the enraged Professor first
dashed his meerschaum to shivers upon his hearth and
then blew out his brains. Not very long after, the bride-

groom was killed by the overturn of a wagon-load of stone which he was carting, and the poor young wife followed him soon, after giving birth to twin daughters. An excellent Miss Rachel, the only daughter of the old clergyman, devoted herself to the babes ; and in the sure evolutions of nature the children became the living images, the one of her mother, the other of her atheistic grandfather. But the latter likeness was in mind, not in body. It was as if the dead professor had revived in her only so far as his intellect, and the peculiarities of his intellect, were concerned. She grew up from a frail and pallid child into a young woman of slight yet elastic build, graceful, erect, of an intellectual loveliness which ripened with education into a refinement of feature and manner, a fascination of clear and questioning eyes, a modulation of voice and of bearing, which was as much more than beauty as beauty is more than prettiness.

Now, imagine such a girl growing up in the home of an aged pastor in a country parish. At variance with all religion from before her birth, as it were, the dull reiterations of a life in which religion was the chief thing deepened and decided her hereditary disposition ; and all the more that she was of so sinewy and elastic a build, — for this, too, she derived from her German parentage. She possessed absolute health. It was in vain that grandfather and aunt strove to instil religious sentiment into her. As mere information, she grew to have it all, to her finger tips. No one could be more familiar with the history and doctrines of Christianity than herself. She could repeat the catechism perfectly, knew almost the whole New Testament by heart; but it was and remained as purely a matter of mind and memory as the multiplication-table. Christ and his apostles were as much to her as

Alexander the Great and his soldiers, — as much and not a particle more. She listened with childish wonder to the fervors of song, to the pathos of the prayers. Even as a child her eyes were dry when all others wept. If there had been anything like wilful perversity or temper in it, her good aunt could have dealt with her, but there was nothing except a profound indifference.

"She is a good child, an obedient child," Miss Rachel often said; "but where religion is concerned, it is as though she were deaf, dumb, blind, paralyzed. It is dreadful!"

As she grew older, the sole results of her aunt's perpetual and tearful pleadings with her were to quicken her indifference into a strong, though silent, aversion. Yet it was as if the old atheist had dropped in the dust behind him whatever was coarsely masculine, and had risen in her into a feminine, wonderfully refined, purely intellectual repetition of himself.

Then came, as has been said, her marriage with Mr. Thirlmore. Following upon that his pastorate which, like himself, seemed as if curiously ordered to confirm her character along lines laid before her birth. For a time he was the preacher of whom it was invariably remarked to guests at the hotel or to friends on a visit, "It would never do for you to be in town on a Sunday and not go and hear Thirlmore!" After awhile came disaster. Not in the shape of bronchitis; physically, there was not a sounder man, not a finer specimen of what life-long health can do for one, than Mr. Thirlmore when he resigned. His congregations were never so large or, seemingly, so enthusiastic. There was no call pressing upon him from elsewhere. None the less, and as in an instant, he ceased to be pastor there or anywhere.

Mr. Adair, the most advanced preacher in the same city, had his say about it from his pulpit, as he had concerning whatever conflagration, defalcation, explosion, ocean disaster, or political revolution that befell, — in short, concerning any and every event. "It is the law of electric action," he observed, the Sunday afterward, and to a congregation which packed his church in expectation of what he would say in regard to it. "It is a law of that divine mystery which we label electricity — that it is instantaneous in action. It appears suddenly, burns intensely, ceases suddenly ; " and a very striking discourse he made of it, illustrated as it was to be not long afterward by his own instant extinction as a public instructor, although for reasons of another kind from those which extinguished Mr. Thirlmore.

"I hope his people settled with him up to date," Mr. Adair remarked, while being congratulated upon his sermon. But that, no one knew then or after. There was no one to speak authoritatively upon the subject, so utterly had the Church dissolved into the smallest of mist and passed away.

It had not been necessary that Mrs. Thirlmore should believe in anything in particular, beyond her husband, to enable her to perform her whole duty to him and to his Church while it lasted. Apart from the Sundays, with their crowded congregations and eloquent sermons, the life of the society lay in its social gatherings ; and she exerted herself the more at these, as her husband considered his part of the work done when he came out of the pulpit. If one were to try and sum up the life of Mr. Thirlmore down to the hour of his return to his farm, it would be done in the one word *disgust ;* with this distinct understanding, — that he was not in the slightest degree

disgusted with himself.   He had, in fact, a higher estimate
of himself than ever; and considering his unimpaired
qualities and his enlarged experiences, he was right.   As
to his wife, she was more intensely herself than before;
with this distinction, that, as her husband could not but
observe, something had befallen which had wrought a
change in her; and this change showed itself chiefly in
her attitude toward him.

"I know him perfectly," she mused these days, "and
I cannot rate him higher than before, since he is no other
than he has always been.   But I take more interest in
him than I did.   Ah, how much more!   It is odd," and
she could not repress a smile, "that so large a baby
should have so feeble a mother; but was ever mother so
determined?   We are, in all probability, to live, he and
I, for who can say how many years; and what he is to be
depends upon every day that is going by, and upon — me.
What a godlike hero I imagined him at first!   How long ·
ago it seems!   Had I worshipped him less I might have
loved him more; now that I have come to know him so
well, now that he is little more even to Maggie than a
suffering infant, God knows how I love him!"   Tears
sprang to her eyes.   In some strange fashion her husband
had of late been born to her like a babe, and hers was the
passionate love of a mother for her first-born.   More than
that, this infant was a child of whom his proud mother
knew with certainty that he would secure a splendid manhood.   His past life, she thoroughly believed, would be
forgotten in what he was to become, and what that was
to be depended — no conviction of hers was deeper than
this — upon what any day, every day, was bringing him.
Yes, and upon what she might be to him.

The last thing must be added.   During the height of

her husband's popularity she had yielded to such an
emptiness of soul in regard to her husband, religion, and
everything besides, as prepared her for something worse.
It so happened that she was thrown a good deal in the
society of a man of genius and charming manners, a Mr.
Guernsey. In her desolation and desperation she had
found, as she thought, the one being she could love, who
would be to her the God she had lacked, and everything
else. Very narrowly had she escaped the destruction of
such a fall. Then came her sudden withdrawal to the
farm. There, and during her agonies of shame and re-
morse, she had the most remarkable experience of her
life. It is sufficient to say of it, that one day she found
herself prostrate in her room in something more like
prayer than she had ever before attempted. She arose
exhausted, and confusedly conscious that as wonderful a
process was begun as if she bore the first beginnings of
another life within her. She did not try to understand
it, did not try to do more than yield herself to whatever
might come of it.

If we do have guardian spirits, the angel to whom
Mrs. Thirlmore was given in charge might have said:
"In this woman is surely one of the most difficult of
immortals."

But it is precisely nothing at all that we know of guardian spirits. Mrs. Thirlmore we do know, and how completely she devoted herself to her husband. He was as
ignorant of it as possible ; but to him she gave herself as
to the one supreme object of her life.

"And this I know," she thought, "that in doing this
I find such a use in living, such peace, joy, confident
hope, as assure me that I, too, am just born ; that we
have our best days before us yet."

CHAPTER V.

OTHER DAYS.

WHEN Mr. Thirlmore went so reluctantly to receive his visitor his wife went with him. Not in person; but all the more she accompanied him there, as of ~~old~~ she did everywhere.

They say that a sea-hawk poised in the air can detect a fish many a rood below it through intervening air and sea. It is also said that its telescopic eyes are microscopic, as it darts down and strikes its talons in its prey. Now, the old German grandfather had whetted his eyes to astonishing sharpness by long and exclusive prying in one direction only. Whatever keenness of insight his granddaughter was gifted with by inheritance had been made sharper by all that befell her before, as well as after her marriage. If, like her unbelieving ancestor, she ignored whatever she could not see, all the more did she devote herself to what she could see. There were years during which she gave herself to books, after that to people, as they clustered in admiring crowds about her; but from the beginning of their acquaintance there was no object to which she gave such attention as to her husband. A cow-boy on the western plains, a sailor at sea, comes by long use to a perfection of sight almost incredible; and what Peace did not see in her husband, was not worth the seeing. With all her quietness, it was only his Maker who read him, mind, heart, soul, as she did. For, in common with many others, she had a fixed impression that, with all his present weakness and even shallowness, there was that in him which would some day repay her.

"Thirlmore is sure to come to the front again. Yes, and ten times the man he was when he left!" So people were always saying of him. This unformulated promise is something which belongs to a man of his sort as insepara-bly as his insolence, arrogance, the drawl in his speech, the nonchalance of his manner. Feeling this more deeply than any other, what his wife was saying to herself when Hezekiah Grumbles came to see them was this: "It is a long time since we were cast up on this rocky farm by the wreck of the church. It takes time for a man of his kind to get over his hidden bruises. Now he is strong and well, rested and ready. He is like one of those bowl-ders near the top of that hill, underwashed by the rains; he cannot lie still much longer, and whichever way he goes will be with violence and for what is left to him of life."

She did not in person go with him to see the visitor. Not only was he but too sure not to do what that visitor desired, but for her to add her voice would but confirm him in his perversity. Since the downfall of his reputa-tion, the only way left him to assert his manhood was to say to whoever might come, "No." But how eagerly did she follow with her eyes the two men as they left the house!

"Of all men alive, what can Hezekiah Grumbles want with my husband? Yes, it is the same battered hat, the same yellow, ill-fitting old overcoat, the same copperas-colored trousers, — just such as his father used to wear. I have known them as long as I can remember."

What a flood of memories the sight of Hezekiah Grum-bles let loose upon her! As she stood peering through the foggy air after him and her husband, a certain Sunday afternoon came back to her as if it were yesterday. It was too stormy to go to church, and Aunt Rachel had drawn her nieces to her as she sat, one on either side, her arms around each; and her talk was of Christ. She was the most devout of women; and as she told the girls, then about fourteen years old. the story of the arrest of Jesus, his trial, his mockery and death, her own heart melted within her; Revel, her other niece, wept too.

"What is the matter?" Peace had asked, wondering at them. "Do you think it was good in him to let people spit in his face and treat him so? I don't like that kind of goody people. I like Joseph, but not after he breaks down and goes to crying like a baby over his brothers — he a great ruler, too. What I like is Daniel defying Belshazzar, Peter striking out with his sword — men who are not afraid, who strike back —"

Then her thoughts shifted back to her husband. What was Mr. Grumbles saying to him? "Something worth his hearing, I hope. He cannot keep on at this life. He must have something to do. Something must happen, and soon. If he should be struck down by a long and dangerous illness! He might go West, or to mining, building railroads, farming on a grand scale, raising cattle by the ten thousand, — work requiring a strong man."

It was a long time before the two men returned. The snow had begun to fall heavily. She could hardly make out their faces. But something had taken place; she could see that in their bearing, in the frank tones of their voices, as they stood upon the stoop, stamping and shaking off the snow and wet.

"I'll let him lie there, if you please," Mrs. Thirlmore heard Mr. Grumbles say, as she opened the outer door to welcome them in. He was down on one knee in a corner of the porch, compelling Wretch to coil himself up on the floor. " Now, you villain, remember," he said to him with lifted finger, " there is no kitchen to this house, none for you ; stay where you are." Then the farmer, seeing how the animal shivered, cast his rough great-coat over him and, with another warning, followed his companion into the building.

" This, my dear," the master of the house said, presenting his friend, " is an old college classmate of mine, Captain Hezekiah Grumbles, whom you have known of old. He dines with us ; and he is the best and stupidest old chap you ever knew. Make yourself at home, captain ! " Mr. Thirlmore's whole aspect was changed ; he stood erect and strong ; his cheeks were flushed ; there was a light in his eyes, a frank energy in his tones. But his wife was too thoroughly mistress of herself to do more than accept and enter into her husband's mood.

" Go upstairs, old fellow, and have a good wash before dinner," the host insisted ; and in a little while their visitor reappeared, very sleek as to his abundant hair, very shiny about the protuberances of face and forehead. As he went into the front room, there was a shriek from the back premises, a rush of feet, a clamor of exclamations, and slamming of doors. The visitor turned of a guilty red as Maggie made her appearance.

" Oh, madam ! " she panted, " there 's a thing come into me kitchen ! It looks like a hotter, except that it is the picture of a worrum—a big, black, horrid worrum. It frightened me, and it is not easy I am frightened. Get out, you baste," and Maggie opened the outer door an inch to see if the animal was safely without. Whereupon Mr. Grumbles, hot and cold with confusion, told the story of the turnspit.

"Let him come in here, at least a moment," said Mrs. Thirlmore, who detested dogs only less than cats. To the astonishment of her husband she stooped over the ill-looking brute as, encouraged by his master, he wriggled his slow and gruesome length into the hall, humiliation in every wrinkle of his statesman-like brow, unfeigned apology in every writhe of his queer legs and stiff, upstanding tail.

"Maggie is right. He looks like an otter. See how beautifully ugly he is, Theo ! You poor thing !" and she snapped her fair fingers near his penitent eyes, even touched his entreating ears. All on a sudden there had come upon husband and wife a gentleness, a gladness, almost a loving kindness.

"I never knew her to touch a dog before," Mr. Thirlmore said to his friend, returning from bundling his follower up in his overcoat again, his wife having disappeared to wash her hands. "If she is going to take things that way, Grumbles, she will never consent to my going, never ;" and again he asked himself, "What in the mischief is coming upon her?"

They had a good deal of fun over Wretch and the tale of his woes before they sat down to dinner, and afterward. But not in vain had the mistress of the house spoken to Maggie in private. How he contrived to smell out his way, who can tell? But to Maggie, seated by the kitchen fire peeling potatoes, there was the advent at a back door of the black tip of a nose, then the noiseless corkscrewing through the narrow aperture of the snake-like body, and Wretch was in the room again. Advancing very cautiously, holding in the air each foot in turn before putting it down, glancing from under heavy brows to the left and to the right lest broomstick or mop-handle should be in motion, with eyes fixed at last upon Maggie with steady regard, the turnspit yielded to the ingrained instinct of the centuries, and having made his way to the right-hand corner (he had never been known to take the left-hand) of the fireplace, he so placed himself against the bricks that when, to Maggie's horror, he had reared aloft his stalwart body, it was supported against the wall ; then with his forepaws held out before him in the fashion of begging poodles, he said to the girl as plainly as possible, " I am here, ready and willing to do my ancient duty ; do yours, and give me the wheel for the basting."

The eyes of the Manx girl grew larger and larger as she gazed stupefied ; but in a little while, and without a motion or a word, she went on with her potatoes. Her mistress had interceded for the turnspit, and Maggie would not have murmured had it been a unicorn, or a bushel of frogs slimy from the nearest swamp. Her broad and honest face brightened as she sat, for from the front room came the music of a laugh. Till now she had rarely heard that sound from her mistress.

CHAPTER VI.

HOME AFFAIRS.

AS if by common consent nothing was said at dinner of the errand which had brought Mr. Grumbles to the farm. Both of the men had the aspect of those who are about setting out on an expedition, and there was a certain informality and appetite as of wayfarers picnicking by the roadside, for a minute or two. Mrs. Thirlmore asked no questions. Except for the subtile something in the classmates which speaks without words when there is anything of moment on hand, she knew nothing; but it was sufficient that a determination was being reached which would change the lives of all of them. The swift-witted woman felt instinctively that what was resolved upon would bring her greater misery and yet greater joy than she had ever known; she felt it and was more than willing. After dinner her husband went out to attend to his farm affairs, their visitor consenting to stay until the next day.

"I know it was all very dull to you," he assented, as the conversation reverted to Scrubstones. "But you were always, if you will let me say it, like a quail in a trap. You belong, ma'am, to the kind of people who never feel as if they were going to be there for more than a day or so longer, wherever they are."

"That is true. I always have been like the patriarch, dwelling in tents, feeling that I was a stranger and a pilgrim; although — " Mrs. Thirlmore added thoughtfully — "it was not because I was looking for heaven. I never

had an idea in my life of any life after this. It may shock
you, but to me death always has been the end of all. I
never think of any other world, — never wanted any other.
The fall of the curtain, the putting out of the lights, the
play ended, — that is the way; was the way, at least."
For so clear-eyed a lady she seemed embarrassed for a
moment.

"It is odd, how people differ," Mr. Grumbles reflected
aloud. "There is my wife, Aurora Ann; if she was not
compelled to do our marketing, shopping, and the like,
she would never go off our place, unless it was to church,
or to see some sick body. That's the way with me; it's
little I care for anything except Scrubstones. I was born
there, raised there, never was away from there except
when I went to College; and that was a fool's errand.
You see, madam, there's always plenty to do. If you
are not grubbing out stumps or rocks, you are plowing,
fencing, sowing, harrowing, reaping, wagoning in the crop,
hauling wood, — something always on hand. You go to
the table hungry and you eat ; you are tired out at night,
and sleep like a log; you get up in the morning and go
at it again. There's a grand, slow sort of satisfaction
in keeping steadily on. That is what the globe does, you
know, turning round and round; and the sun goes on
burning, burning, in the same old way."

"And our Maker, he keeps on repeating himself."
The lady said it rather to encourage her visitor; it was
the rarest of things for her ever to give a thought in that
direction; the whirling upon itself of the original fire-mist
was as often before her mind as that. To one of another mould it is impossible to explain how the idea of a
Creator or a hereafter affected her mind as vaguely, as
rarely, let us say, as the dance of the aurora; but no,

there is, however mysterious and evanescent, a brilliancy,
a celestial loveliness, and therefore an interest about those
fantastic fires which appealed to her more strongly.

"We are contented, we country people," Mr. Grumbles went on, " because we are so stupid.   But, seems to
me, we are happier."

" Like beavers and dogs," the lady interjected, in
thought.

" For what do you bright and restless people get, after
all," Mr. Grumbles ventured, " for all your rushing up and
down, hither and thither?   I ain't a preacher, but if
you 'll allow a text without a sermon, I would remind you
how the smart ones are forever saying — "

Mrs. Thirlmore was listening attentively, yet he hesitated, blushed, was silent.   What he set out to say was
this : " Yes, you smart ones are always complaining,
'Who will show us any good?'   We believing block-
heads say instead, ' Lord, lift Thou up the light of Thy
face upon us.   Thou hast put joy and gladness into our
hearts more than when their corn and their oil increased ; ' " but he thought best to keep it unuttered.   If
the truth must be told, much the best of what this cum-
brous rustic thought he left unsaid, even in the bosom of
his home, so doubtful was he of his own wisdom.   Yet
his thought left a glow upon his face, which his companion
interpreted more by her heart than anything else.   She
looked at him with new interest.   Was it not he who had
come all this way to do what he could for people who
had as completely dropped him from heart and mind as
if he were a crow that had once flitted across their path?

Her visitor had done ample justice to Maggie's cookery,
and was now seated in a wide-armed rocking-chair, before a good fire in the sitting-room, with a wider display

of legs and lumbering feet than the companionship of
ladies generally allows. But Mrs. Thirlmore cared little for
etiquette to-day. She seemed to be fairer, fresher, more
gentle, and happier than for a long time. There was a
sudden re-birth of girlhood in her face as she sat, sewing
in hand, making herself comfortable on the other side of
the old-fashioned fireplace, while the wind howled without.
There was no concealing the definite fact that Mr. Grumbles was not handsome. The tones of his voice, too,
were husky as autumnal corn is husky ; the overflow of his
shirt collar, the breezy ends of his yellowish neckerchief,
the undulating expanse of his waistcoat, and the super-
fluity of his coat in collar and skirts, adding, with his now
again disordered hair, to the same rural result. Colorless
as his eyes were, the lady observed this in them, — which
was lacking from those of her gifted husband, — that,
whatever was the topic of their varying talk, his eyes
were wholly given to her. The ex-preacher had looked
from his pulpit and yet seen nobody in particular. To
him, an audience of less than two thousand people was
inappreciable.

"Why," Mr. Grumbles was asking of himself, as if Mrs.
Thirlmore were a blooded animal, "should long and narrow hands always go with feet of that dainty kind. She
must be of racing stock, she is so spare and sinewy. I
wonder if there is a thing those splendid eyes of hers fail
to see. People in the city always said that she was the
smartest of the two, — or so I 've heard. She is no more
like my Aurora Ann — " He flushed to find, as he thought
this, that it was of his wife Mrs. Thirlmore was asking
him. On the point of telling her about his errand to
the farm, she insisted upon his talking of Aurora Ann
instead.

"When I get to speaking about her," he said, "I don't know when to stop. Do you know, ma'am, she was nothing at first but our hired girl? Bless you! it was she who carved the beef, chopped and stuffed the sausages, milked the cows, made the cheese —"

"I remember," laughed Mrs. Thirlmore; "when your father drove up to our house on Fridays he was always telling us about Aurora Ann."

"Only our hired help," Mr. Grumbles said with pride. "They took her from a drunken old stepfather who beat her. That was when she was a child. She came to do our work. *She* never thought of marrying me, and I'm certain I had no more notion of it than I had of marrying one of the cows; but then, you see, I'd seen her at the washtub, scouring the milk-pans, scrubbing the floor, helping with the hay, digging potatoes, loading up the manure wagons, — there was nothing she didn't do. When I went to college — it's the oddest thing in the world — would you believe it, I couldn't think of my Latin and Calculus for thinking of her? It was so much easier, you see! She was all over the farm at once, was so powerful strong and so willing, too, always a-laughing and singing. Sensible people as my father and my mother were, do you know, ma'am, they wouldn't hear, at first, of my marrying Aurora Ann? And she wouldn't. She was peeling potatoes, I remember, when I asked her, and she up and threw the pan of water all over me. Lucky it was not very hot. She thought I was making fun of her; but I was in dead earnest. Father and mother, they had to chime in and just persuade her. I do believe," laughed Mr. Grumbles, "that she took me as she did pulling turnips, leading the heifers to pasture, or anything of that sort; it was so much work to be done."

How could he stop while Mrs. Thirlmore listened with so much interest to the story of his marriage; of how the children began to come; of how Aurora Ann nursed his father and mother through their last illness. "But I must tell you about my errand with Mr. Thirlmore. You see —" Mrs. Thirlmore was not in the mood as yet for that.

"No," she insisted, "tell me about your children. You lost your little — Lucy, was it?" Mr. Grumbles' face brightened, then grew sorrowful.

"Thank you for remembering her name; only," he said, "we did not call her Lucy much. She found a little cooter under the steps —"

"A cooter?"

"Some call them turtles. Cooter is the common name. She took such a fancy to the thing the children got to calling her their cooter, until that was all the name she went by."

The ungainly farmer had drawn his chair nearer to her, his eyes were full of his pitiful story, his huge hands assisted his narration, his voice was tender as that of a woman as he told how diphtheria struck his child down when apparently in perfect health, and how she died hugging the little turtle in her arms. "Aurora Ann stood back and left her to the doctors. You had better believe, ma'am, she did not do that with the rest, for they all had diphtheria, — Squash, Snap, Pop-corn, Owl! Oh, it is a shame; ma'am, a shame! the way we allowed the children to nickname each other! Always some foolish reason for it. Aurora Ann she rolled up her sleeves, went to work with all her soul and saved all the rest, except poor little Coot — Lucy, I mean."

The tears were flowing down his cheeks now. He had

forgotten to bring a handkerchief, but Mrs. Thirlmore noticed almost as little as he did that he had to use his hands instead, wiping with them now one cheek and then the other. But at this moment she was called from the room by Maggie. Mr. Grumbles had been led on to tell her his sorrows. Had he been in conversation with her husband, had Mr. Thirlmore been in the room at the time, nothing could have induced him to mention the matter.

CHAPTER VII.

NEW PURPOSES.

WHEN Mrs. Thirlmore left the room, Mr. Grumbles, seated by the fire, his head sunk upon his bosom, fell into deep thought. He had come many miles to the farm to tell Mr. Thirlmore things of great importance. Before their conversation was ended, the ex-preacher had, in his turn, told his classmate something, — something about which Mr. Thirlmore would not have talked but for the errand which had brought his friend thither. What he had thus told him made that errand far more important than it would otherwise have been, and Mr. Grumbles was greatly confirmed in the business which had brought him, and rejoiced that in the very nick of time he had taken it in hand. But Mrs. Thirlmore knew nothing either of what her husband had imparted to their visitor, or of what had brought that visitor to see them. It was a proof of the new feeling awakened in Mr. Thirlmore toward a man whom he had hitherto known only to despise, that he had intrusted to him the duty of breaking the double news to the unsuspecting wife.

"That of all men I should have it to do!" he now thought. "And how shall I go about it? If Aurora Ann was here I'd get her to do it. She would — Aurora Ann!"

Mr. Grumbles was smitten with a new idea, and at that moment the lady of the house came back. Her visitor looked at her wistfully. "Such a superior woman as she is, too!" he thought. "How could a plain fellow like me — If she was a professor, now, I could begin by

reminding her of a Providence. She does n't believe in
Providence. She is scientific, they call it, and believes in
evolution instead. Ah, now I 've got it ! "

" I am glad to know you have so excellent a wife," Mrs.
Thirlmore began, taking up her sewing and setting it
down again.

" You ought n't to start me about her," said the other ;
" but since we are talking about her I must tell you one
last thing. Do you know, madam, I think she makes a
body understand — what do you call it ? natural selection ?
survival of the fittest ? evolution ? I pick up something
about such things from the papers. So does Aurora Ann.
We had scientific lectures last winter in our church. Our
new minister delivered them, tc raise money toward new-
roofing the building. He don't let us treat him as we
used to treat your old grandfather ; you 'll be glad to hear
that ! What I mean by Aurora Ann's making matters plain,
is this. I 'm not tiring you ? "

" Not at all," and it was plain that she meant it. Mr.
Grumbles went on : —

" I told you how our people took her in when she was
a poor little thing, dreadfully abused. Well, I was their
only child, and they had the more time to see she went
to school of winters, while mother taught her everything
about the house. As I told you, it was astonishing how
she learned. You see she was kept in splendid health by
hard work, living in the open air, and the like. Then she
would read some, as she could snatch a book up while the
things were cooking. We had good preaching, too. But
it was the troubles we had which helped her most. We
were not rich ; then father and mother, they lay sick one
after the other and died, — my father first, because he was
the strongest ; that is always the way. Then our little

girl died: the others were sick. I broke a leg rolling logs. It does not matter what, there were always changes going on. You believe, ma'am, that things happen so as to develop people as well as plants, animals, and the like, don't you? I believe that God makes them happen that way; but we both of us agree to the happening. What I want to say is, that out of it all my Aurora Ann has come to be, from a poor, hard-working house girl, about as fine a woman as you ever saw. She never is sick. She knows everything. She can do everything. The neighbors come to her about everything. Our children worship her. Only last week our minister told me the church could n't live without her. She is a 'mother in Israel.' She is a hundred times more than my mother ever was."

"Don't you agree with us"—Mrs. Thirlmore smiled—"that you are an advance on what your old father was? And that your children will be an improvement on you both?"

"Perhaps so. But when I talk so about my wife, it is," Mr. Grumbles said, gravely, "because I want to ask if you do not think—say, in regard to Mr. Thirlmore and your-self—that things work the same way?"

He was looking at her with something in his manner which made her heart sink. She stopped sewing, her face grew pale. "If you have anything to tell me," she said with trembling lips, "I am ready to hear."

The eyes of her companion were very tender. "Excuse me," he said. "Aurora Ann has not a bit of your education, your intellect and all. It may be because she needs it more, but"—he stopped; but he added to him-self, "she takes all her comfort from believing that she has a Father behind all, who *makes* things so happen as to change us all into something higher and better."

Then he said aloud : "But you know best, and Mr. Thirlmore did ask me to tell you something."

Mrs. Thirlmore was sitting very still and pale, her hands holding each other, her large eyes fastened upon Mr. Grumbles. "Tell me," she said, in a low voice.

Her visitor did so. He made it as easy to her as he could, but she saw through all his comforting phrases. Her husband, counting upon what would come of his early training upon a farm, upon his hosts of city friends, above all upon his own hearty determination to succeed, had gone deeply into debt. He had failed of help where he had counted most upon it, his losses had been many —

"In a word," she said, with lips gone suddenly very dry, "my husband is a ruined man. He will be sold out, and very soon." She glanced about the room, she rose and hurried to the window, she went to the door. "You will excuse me," she began, growing stronger every moment, even as the result of becoming weaker.

"Please," Mr. Grumbles followed her, "he is not on the farm. He rode away a little while ago. He did it on purpose. In an hour or so he will be back. There is something else I had to say — "

He walked to the fireplace, took a book in his hand, while she went out into the hall. There she paused a moment, her hand on the rail of the stairway. She would go upstairs. But to whom? for what? She thought of Maggie at work in the kitchen. Whom else could she go to? To somebody she must go ! Maggie? That would not do. Almost mechanically she went upstairs to her room ; fell upon the bed, her face in her hands, vaguely remembering how it had been with her there in another great agony; her lips began to move with inarticulate supplications.

When she entered the room again Mr. Grumbles was surprised at her calmness. Evidently she had been weeping. She was very gentle. "You said you had something more to tell me. I want to know everything before my husband gets back — everything. You need not fear for me."

"Why, my dear madam —" Mr. Grumbles had risen to his feet, was standing before her rubbing his hands in each other, a broad smile upon his homely face. "Can you forgive me? What a miserable mess I have made of it! Aurora Ann as good as tells me every day what a stupid fellow I am. What is there to trouble you so? Nothing at all. Suppose Mr. Thirlmore has lost money, is it his fault? And what is a little money to a man like him? He is young and strong, worth a hundred ordinary men. He will get it all back, and ten times more. But I am, I can't say how glad, for coming here just at this time. Everything seems to fit together like — like machinery. Let me tell you the rest."

And then he proceeded, with a bright and happy face, to tell her what it was had brought him from Scrubstones. From his first word she listened to him with breathless attention. She would not sit down again. It seemed to her as if a year had passed since dinner; everything before belonged to her childhood; she had risen to the level of the occasion. Beneath everything there was within her a new throb of joy and gladness. She felt wholly competent to whatever would befall; was conscious of growing stronger every moment. What he told her she had not thought of before; she wondered that she had not done so long ago, as the very thing her

husband should do, now especially. She had been a baby
not to have thought of and suggested it herself. As Mr.
Grumbles proceeded, his whole person in a glow of awkward enthusiasm, to develop his plans, it seemed to her
as if nothing could be better. She accepted, assented to,
entered into it as if it were rather a matter undertaken
and happily ended long before.

" He said he had not thought of going into the army
before," Mr. Grumbles remarked in the end, " but I do
not see how he could have helped it. Was there ever a
thing more natural for a man like him to do? He did
not want me to see at first how gladly he went into it, but
anybody else could see that. And it grew upon him like
wildfire. Tamerlane helped me. We had let him out
into the meadow, and he kept near us, pretending to be
nibbling at the grass till we got through. It's a silly
thing for me to say, ma'am, but I almost believe the
horse understood every word ! He was as quiet as you
please till I was done. Then he began tearing round
and round us like mad, kicking up his heels, spattering
us with mud, whinnying. Then he would rub his nose
against his master, as if to say, 'That's the doctrine for
me,' and raced about until Mr. Thirlmore got to be like
a boy himself, whistling to him, clapping his hands together, laughing. The idea of a man like *him* burying
himself on this farm, when so much is going on ! Aurora
Ann agreed with me from the first. We had Tamerlane
go through all his tricks, finding a pocket-handkerchief,
kneeling down, rolling in the snow, galloping off, coming
back. The Lord taketh not pleasure, the Bible says, in
the legs of a horse, but your husband does. The two were
like boys on a lark together. How they do love each
other ! I don't believe Thirlmore cares a corn-cob — ah,

excuse me !" Mr. Grumbles' face grew red at his blun-
der, then redder yet on having called her attention to it.

"He does not care for anybody, — outside his family, I
mean ;" and he hastened to add, "the last thing we saw
of Tamerlane he had reared his forehoofs up on the top of
the stone fence, was snorting and pawing to break out and
be gone. *He* understands !"

It was not of the horse Mrs. Thirlmore was thinking.
She had fifty questions to ask, objections to raise.   It
helped Mr. Grumbles in what he said that her heart was
with him in it all.   There was much to be said ; but when
they were through it was because they had exhausted, for
the present, the entire topic.

"It is very good in you," she said, at length, "to take
such an interest in my husband.   You hardly knew each
other in college, and you have scarcely seen him since."

Mr. Grumbles scratched behind one ear, rumpled his
already disordered hair, thrust abroad his legs only to
draw them in again in his confusion.   "I declare to you,
ma'am," he said at last, "that it is a puzzle to me, that very
thing.   I don't suppose he ever thought of me twice in
his life.   But did you ever read the life of the great Napoleon, ma'am?"   She had done so, and saw now what
was coming.

"Don't you think," Mr. Grumbles ventured hesitatingly,
"that Napoleon was, upon the whole, one of the most —
we all know what a genius he was, but don't you think he
was —   There was his way, for instance, of treating his
wife —"

Here was another of his perpetual blunders, but the
Josephine of this emperor did not falter.

"You mean," she said, "that Napoleon was the most
selfish man that ever lived.   Who doubts it?"

" Just so. Now," argued the farmer, " he cared as little for his soldiers as if they were so many insects. We 've
got a book at our house, full of pictures, which tells all
about him. He was very selfish — "

" And yet," Mrs. Thirlmore said for him, " there were
millions of men, better men than he, who gave their lives,
would have given their souls, for him ; and it is so with my
husband." It was true, how could she help knowing it?

" It is strange," Mr. Grumbles meditated aloud, " but
I never had but one feeling for Mr. Thirlmore. There in
college I would say to myself, ' You fool, what do you
suppose he cares for you?' but I went on just the same.
Now, there 's reason in the roasting of eggs ; and the way
I put it up is this : I had the feeling toward him I had and
have because he is a Napoleon. That is, he has grand
qualities I don't have. He is capable of doing magnificent things. In a sense, one is loyal to such a man as
one is to God. And when the time comes that you can
put such a man on his track towards doing what only such
a man can do — "

The wife, her head softly to one side, was looking at her
companion, the hover of a new light in her eyes, the coming and going in her cheeks of a something which had
once on a time fled from them seemingly forever.

" When I see men," Mr. Grumbles reasoned, " con-
tinuing to believe in their Napoleon even after he has
been driven to Elba, — the more on that account, — I
say to myself : I tell you, old fellow, it is because your
emperor is going to do something great yet. Has he not
the same qualities, the same splendid possibilities?"

" It is very kind of you, sir." Ugly as he was, the wife
could almost have kissed him.

" Not at all, ma'am. Look at Marshal Ney. He had

the boundless enthusiasm for his emperor that so many
people have, Yankee fashion, for your husband ; and yet,
when you dive to the bottom of things, he went in heart
and soul for Napoleon, because he knew that he could
advance himself thereby. It is selfishness, ma'am ; pure
selfishness. For it is myself I am thinking of. My wife
loves me as much, I suppose, as a woman can love so
ugly a chap, and she is eager to have me go. Squash is
old enough — our Henry, I mean — to do almost a man's
work on the place, and the other children are coming on.
Aurora Ann is well and strong, and, as I tell her, always
has been master on her farm, and always will be. Yes,
she is more than willing ; and I am going, that is certain.
Now, whom could I go with and under so well as with your
husband? Madam, for one, I believe in him ! " with a
glow of confidence.

" What comes next," he went on, glad to see the color
rise in Mrs. Thirlmore's cheeks, " is this. My wife is
dreadfully anxious you should make your home with us
while he is away. We have a large house, if it is old. If
you say so, we will be glad to have your hired girl come
with you ; there will be plenty for her to do when you
don't want her to wait on you."

" Oh, no, Mr. Grumbles, we could not think — " Mrs.
Thirlmore began. She had gotten bravely over her first
shock. Her eyes hardly left the window. She was listening to every sound without. When would her husband
come back?

" Let me be frank with you," her companion was saying.
" I told you how Aurora Ann had improved ; but there is
a vast deal yet that she has to learn. If ever there was
a lady who could help her — help her — evolve," — it was
said with all gravity, — " you are that lady. It would be

the greatest favor in the world to us. We would do all we could to make you comfortable. We keep ever so many cows. We would do all — "

There was a sudden light in Mrs. Thirlmore's eyes, her face grew paler ; she had heard an approaching step. Mr. Grumbles snatched hat and overcoat off the rack in the hall and slipped out by the back door as the master of the house entered at the front. His wife knew perfectly how far she could go, how easily she might spoil everything by a word too much. Perhaps it was because he had so much of it to go through with from the pulpit, because he was rather sick of the practical results of excess of sentiment there ; certainly Thirlmore was not given, by disposition or training, to indulging out of the pulpit in anything like demonstrations. In any case he wanted most of all to be left alone, as far as possible by everybody, just then. Nor was she a woman whose largest self lay in her heart. Moreover, the two had been separated for so long, — she because she had been sorely disappointed in him ; he because he knew this, and because he had never really loved her, or anybody. But as he stood upon the front porch, a new sensation had almost mastered her. She was in the act of springing forward, of throwing her arms about his burly form dripping with wet, of whisperng, " Oh, Theo, I am so glad ! " and kissing him. It would have been the first kiss in many a long day, and who can say what effect it might have had? There is power in as small a thing as that. We know what the Delilahs, Omphales, Cleopatras have effected with the Samsons and Hercules and Mark Antonys of the world, by the least touch of their lips. In this case it might have hastened results by whole years ; who can say?

But Mrs. Thirlmore was too deeply concerned as to

the results to risk it, and intellect was so far the owner
of the baby impulse of her lately-born love. "Take care,"
she reminded herself, "you may ruin everything; and he
is worth waiting for." .Her purpose died out in a brighter
smile than usual, leaving her all the sweeter for it. She
was the happier thereafter. There was a flush as of newness in her raiment, and girlhood in her cheeks, a fresher
glint, one might almost swear, in her eyes, by reason of it.
Except for that, matters seemed to flow in their usual
routine.

It is said that in tropical lands the first to perceive the
coming on of an earthquake or a cyclone are the animals.
Tiger and elephant, horse and cow, they abandon their
food, rush hither and thither. No one said anything to
Maggie; but that very night, after going to bed, she sat up
therein in the dark, drew an old soda jar from beneath
her mattress, poured out its handful of coins — the savings of years — upon the blanket before her. Then she
counted them slowly over, with vague hope that they might
have increased, somehow, in number. After that she put
them back, replaced the jar, and went into the depths of
such sleep as is known only to animals, and to beings
of her kind.

"She may need 'em," Maggie said.

CHAPTER VIII.

LIEUTENANT VAN DOREN.

MAY, 1861. Flags fly on every public building, State and Federal, throughout the city. Flags upon every private residence, shop-front, stable. Flags upon every steamship and sailing vessel; on sea, harbor, river, lake, bay. Flags on every carriage driven by; on every booth for the sale of gingerbread and ale; on every soda fountain, peddler's cart; on the horses plowing in the field, the horsecars, railway trains, — everywhere and always flags, flags, flags.

By what figure can it be illustrated, this universal, unanimous display of the national bunting? Let one suffice. Suddenly, unexpectedly, the Republic has been smitten full in the face, and in sight of the whole world; the colors displayed are the red wrath of a great people flushing its cheeks in reply. As soon as may be, the wrath will grow redder in the flash of cannon, the blaze of burning cities, the flow of oceans of blood.

How could Hezekiah Grumbles go on contentedly with his spring plowing and sowing? Lifted as upon the rising of a wind which is to quicken into the great tempest, the newspapers filled the land with their flying leaves, each day's issue more significant of what is to come. Nothing else is thought of. Neighbors drew up at the front door or at the field fence for a talk upon the overwhelming theme of the hour, with some dim sense of reproducing, as they did so, the pictures they .have so often seen of the coming together of good patriots during the days of Lexington and Concord.

"And what does your good wife think of it?" was the question of almost every man of them before they parted. There was not a farmer's wife for miles around but put on her sun-bonnet and ran in to see what Mrs. Grumbles had concluded that Mr. Grumbles ought to do. Aurora Ann, stout of body, florid of face, strong of opinion, sweet and sensible of soul, was almost as much of an authority outside her household as she was within it.

Hezekiah Grumbles was slow to think, to feel, to speak, — very slow, indeed, to act ; but he was content to know that Aurora Ann was quick enough for both. She is more energetic than ever in kitchen, wash-house, and dairy, driven by a patriotism which ferments within her more vigorously for every paper she reads, and every speech or sermon she hears. Squash and Snap, Popcorn and the youngest little girl, misnamed Owl on account of her large and solemn eyes, wonder and thrill as they hear her drop startling words as to the possible use of old linen as lint, and of a more stringent economy of pork and butter in view of "heaven only knows what dreadful times the war may bring upon us !" And all are graver at table as the talk turns upon troops that are marching southward, bridges that may need to be burned, neighbors "who may have to go ;" while Squash, the oldest boy, shakes his head gravely when examined as to whether it may not be his duty to enlist "before it is all over."

It was largely because Mr. Thirlmore lived so secluded a life upon his out-of-the-world farm that he had been so little interested in the rising storm. How his notes were to be met was the subject which most interested him of late, and he had experienced sincere regrets that he had

not had time to breed horses which would bring large
prices for cavalry purposes. And this was the juncture
at which Captain Grumbles called upon him. For he was
a captain. When all Scrubstones selected him for command of its first company of men, the idea seemed to him
to be wild, absurd.

"What do *I* know about soldiering?" he demanded
of them and of his wife. But it was not for nothing that
the copiously illustrated volume of Napoleon had been
lying about the house all these years, nor that the family
had long ago been seduced by a highly conversational
book-agent into the buying of a history, whereof every
other page was a picture of "The Wars of the Republic
upon Sea and Shore." The most splendid object in the
parlor was a gorgeously colored chromo of the battle of
Buena Vista, its rearing horses and blazing cannon ; and
it wears a new interest now even to Owl, who climbs with
dumpling legs upon a table to examine it, with her "big
buddy" Squash to explain the pages.

The truth is, the neighbors in electing Mr. Grumbles
came as near as they could to electing his wife, and she
gave him small room for refusal. Meanwhile all Scrubstones grew more and more enthusiastic as the public
meetings increased, and the fife and drum made their
inspiring rounds. Concerts were held in which native
talent turned from "Old Hundred" and "Hebron," and
put such soul into "Hail Columbia," the "Star Spangled
Banner," and on Sunday, "My Country, 't is of Thee,"
as brought tears to the eyes. Sewing circles dropped the
heathen for a time and went to work upon uniforms and
flags ; while the demand for stockings, shirts, and underclothing put every housewife on her mettle, ancient gossip
perished in the talk of the day, and speculation upon the

awful because utterly unknown future took its place. The rising tempest was to sink great navies, to dash armies together, to fan the fires of many a blazing city; but its breezy beginning thoroughly penetrated into and dispersed the malarial dulness of every home in Scrubstones, inspiring men, women, and children with that new life which their new nature was to put on, as it strode through war to the leadership of the race.

"It was I," Captain Grumbles told Mr. Thirlmore, the day he called upon him on his farm, "who first suggested it; but people jumped at the idea at once, for who was there in or near Scrubstones except you that was fitted to be colonel of our regiment? I was hard at work studying my military tactics, but I went to the city to see what could be done. You have swarms of friends there. Even those who did not like you as a preacher said it was a splendid thing. We can get all the money we want, and more men than we know what to do with, from among your former people;" and the farmer grew eloquent as he dwelt upon the enthusiasm he had witnessed. "The Congressmen, Senators, Governor, all are eager for it. 'He is the very man for it, sir!' the Governor told me there in his office. 'The clergy will not be exempt, and Mr. Thirlmore has a fine voice, a commanding presence, great personal magnetism. Do you think,' the Governor asked, 'do you think he would not prefer to go as a chaplain?'"

"Stuff!" so Mr. Thirlmore exclaimed.

"'And you think Dr. Thirlmore would *not* like to go as chaplain?' that was the way the Governor put it in the end with a laugh. 'Not a bit of it,' I said. 'I suppose not. I suppose not,' and he rubbed his hands together and laughed. 'You can consider it as good as

done ; the President has sent me commissions in blank,'
he said. ' Let him get the men ; his commissions will
be ready. I will speak to General J. Mandeville Gilmore
about it to-day,' said his Excellency."

" Gilmore ? Gilmore ? that old peacock ? " Mr. Thirlmore demanded.

" Well," the other assented a little ruefully, " he *is* a
vain old soul ; but he was at West Point, you know, and
the way he has dropped the presidency of his railroad
and gone into military matters again is wonderful."

Thereupon the farmer, all aglow from his experiences,
went into a description of the warlike preparations which
had turned the city into a great camp, Scrubstones following on after it with equal fervor. Mr. Thirlmore had
almost nothing to say ; he had worn his garb of indifference and disgust at everything too long to put it off at
a moment's notice. Captain Grumbles was not dis-
couraged. He had addressed himself to his work of
persuading his friend as he would have done to a job of
hauling rails or reaping a field of oats, and proposed to
go on until he had succeeded.

The ex-preacher assented to nothing, would promise
nothing. He was interested enough not to repulse the
other when he tried by adroit questions to learn how
Mr. Thirlmore was succeeding on his farm. It was as
he supposed ; the result so far had been a crop of debt
sufficient to swamp the whole undertaking. It encouraged Grumbles to push matters.

" I intrude," he said, " on no man ; but if you will let
me say so, how can you stave off the sheriff? Even if
you save your farm, — and it is a mighty rocky one, —
every hoof will be sold from under you ; and then what?
Have you any opening to compare with what I propose ?

Promise, at least, to come to Scrubstones and give us a talk. There will be no trouble as to your commission. See here. I 've brought you my copy of the Tactics. Look it over. I have found it pretty tough, but a man like you will learn in a week all it can teach."

A good deal more took place between the two men before they returned to the house.

" He does not like to let anybody think he has any influence over him," Captain Grumbles reported to his wife, upon getting back next day to Scrubstones. " I could see that his wife would have to be more careful than any one, but she is the sort of woman who, without stirring, can do more than most women. You are not at all alike, you and she, Aurora Ann ; no two women could be more unlike. But you are just the two smartest and strongest women I know ; and oh, how I hope she will come and spend a little of her time with you when Thirlmore and I are gone ! "

As has been said, Captain Grumbles dined and spent the night with Mr. Thirlmore. It was after midnight before they got to bed, there was so much to be said.

" Do you remember," he suddenly asked in the med-ley of conversation, " a man named Van Doren, a queer genius there in the city ? He was a fanatic at the time, and was down upon all churches and ministers."

Neither the husband nor wife could recall him. Under any other circumstances they would have resented the familiarity with which their visitor conversed ; but circum-stance was everything. Captain Grumbles was as modest as a man need be, but he had also a genuine self-respect which kept him on a level with any one. Moreover, he had an object in view.

" Van Doren," he went on, " saw me when I was in

the city, and told me about himself. He used, he said, to go and hear you preach, and then hold you up to his little circle of fellow-fanatics, and in his tracts, as a man of sin, a high-priest of the synagogue of Satan, and all that, — a specimen of the Pharisee whom Christ would come, in a day or two, and destroy. A lank young fellow he was then, long-haired, sallow, with big eyes, bitter tongue, bold as brass — "

"I remember now," Mrs. Thirlmore said, quietly. "He came to our house, Theo, not long before we left the city. Do you not recall how he stood in our parlor one day and denounced us both, and how I tried to make your dog run at him?"

Her husband did remember, but very faintly.

"He came to see me when I was in the city," Captain Grumbles went on, "and told me about it. It is the oddest thing, he has whirled about and taken the greatest fancy for you. There is quite a reaction in your favor since you left, and he is now one of the loudest of your friends. He had a first-class row in the little group he had drawn about him on Sundays to study Scripture together; some other fellow wanted to be leader, or some new doctrine was sprung upon him. I don't know how it was, but he has given up his preaching and got some sort of office in the Commissary Department. He was a deal of help to us in engineering matters, he is so small and glib and swift. I tell you all this in case he should come to see you. I begged him not to, but he said he had business with you. One has to put up, you know, in such times as these with all sorts of people. But that is enough about him."

"I did not know," Mrs. Thirlmore said to her husband after Captain Grumbles was gone, "that a man could change so entirely. He was a dull and plodding farmer.

But now he has had all these months of oratory, brass bands, and incessant excitement; he has been made captain, has worn a uniform, has seen himself in print, has been drilling and drilled, and all the while his wife, more enthusiastic than he, has been behind him day and night, urging him on. I dare say he is a duplicate of old Israel Putnam. He, you remember, was a stupid old farmer; but the Revolution of '76 so stirred him up that he dashed down the rocky sides of a mountain on horseback when duty led that way. The truth is that even George Washington, but for the Revolution, would have been little else than a heavy old planter, eating hearty dinners, and managing his negroes. There is an amazing power in circumstances."

"An exasperated old cow," remarked her husband, "is the most dangerous of animals. Grumbles is a good fellow in his way, but I am glad he is gone; he was boring me to death."

"Of course, Theo, you will know what is best to do," Mrs. Thirlmore said after a while, beginning to speak in a manner which for her was almost timid; "but I hope you will think of this offer. I am not speaking of any duty you owe the country."

"I should hope not!" Duty was a thing her husband specially despised.

"As long as the war lasts," his wife went on, "it will be the one path to success. If you will, you can rouse the whole country with your eloquence —"

"I could blaze away as eloquently, as you call it," her husband said, "on the other side. The war is got up by scoundrels on both sides. There's not a straw to choose between them. Henceforth I intend to look out for my own interest purely, exclusively. If I go into any hurrah it will be to get myself out of debt, and to secure the mastery again of the drove of donkeys we call men and women."

"Well," his wife said, with eyes patient under their kindling interest, "you happen to be on this side ; a grand opportunity lies before you. You can exert a wonderful power if you care to do it. And then it will open your way to public life, — Congress, office, whatever you may prefer. Please think of it, Theo."

She was coming slowly out of the valley of the shadow of doubt, disappointment, death. Her one clear intention now was in utter forgetfulness of herself to save her husband. As the days went by, she ceased to be a questioning child ; her eyes grew more direct, her tones more decided. Captain Grumbles was not the only man, nor was his wife the only woman, who was lifted into a larger, more authoritative life these days.

A week or two after Captain Grumbles had come and gone, Mr. Thirlmore, while mending a gap in one of his stone fences, was hailed by a man riding by on the road.

"I am out on government business," he said. "We are buying beef for the army. We pay good prices. Have you anything you care to sell ? "

Mr. Thirlmore had quite a lot of beeves which he would dispose of, — that is, if he could get what he asked. In the end the man dismounted, went to pasture and barn, examined the stock, agreed to what was asked, and closed the matter of pay and mode of delivery to the satisfaction of the other.

"No, thank you, I won't go in to dinner," he said, in reply to an invitation. "I do not think Mrs. Thirlmore would care to see me," and he mounted his horse to go.

"I see you do not remember me," he said.

Mr. Thirlmore looked closely at him. He was a fresh-colored young man, alert of eyes and tongue, with closely cropped hair. In his neat military garb and gold-laced cap, with a ready smile, an open face, a clear, almost curt manner, he seemed to be the very man for his office of commissary. Gathering his reins in his hands, gauntleted in new yellow buckskins, he continued, —

" I am glad you do not recognize me, — glad I am so changed ! Oh, yes, I used to be a sort of man-hater, down upon everybody who did not think as I did. The fact is I was a printer and preacher, and had overworked myself, taking too little exercise, eating too little, thinking too much. I thought I was a saint, and really I was a dyspep-tic, or hypochondriac, on my way to suicide or the lunatic asylum. Have you a moment or two to spare? I have but a word or so more to say."

Mr. Thirlmore had brightened and broadened during the days following upon Captain Grumbles' visit. His mind had struck out upon a new track, he was beginning to crave a part in the fervors of a people stirred to its depths. He had made a good thing of his beef, and re-plied carelessly : " Go ahead. I am in no hurry."

" I hope you have forgotten it," the other said, brightly ; " but I was the chap who forced himself one day into your house when you lived in the city, to denounce you as a false pastor. You won't be angry with me, will you, when I say that I don't believe in your way of doing things any more than I did then ? "

" Oh, go on, say what you have to say ; what do I care ? " Mr. Thirlmore said.

" I think it is worth hearing. It is this. I was a sincere believer in prayer, and I hope I am now, but not in that way. I thought I was a special favorite of heaven ; that

I should get what I asked for if it was a good thing, and if I prayed long enough, and hard enough. When I was so weak and sick that I could scarcely crawl, and I had to go to business or starve, I used to think, as I stood in the wet or bitter cold, Providence is so loving and tender it will surely send the right street-car along quick. Does it not know what terrible pains I am in? After awhile I came to realize that Providence did nothing of the kind. No car would pass for a long time; or when it did come it was so packed I had to stand, or could not get on at all, — and that when I was almost dead. So of everything, and almost always. At last I came to see that one need n't beat out his brains against the iron fact, that Providence did not vary its regular working for me any more than if I were a tadpole, or a drunkard staggering home to thrash his wife. I had gone to God so long, so steadily, that I forgot all but Him. He did everything. When He did not help me I was like a heathen who beats his idol with a stick. Ah, what revulsions into blasphemous bitterness I used to experience. I need n't go into the story of how I came to my senses, but I know now that Heaven does nothing for a man; not — one — thing," with emphasis, " except along the line of its regular movement; yes, and through a man's own hard hands, as a rule. Except in a soul-sense, there 's no manna in these days; not a wafer, and not one raven with bread in its beak. Just so far as I am sensible, strong, energetic, I get things; otherwise I don't. Fear God *and* keep your powder dry. That 's so !

"That is all. I wanted to apologize to you this far. I tell you, sir, God despises a man who lies at His feet singing all the time, or crying like a baby for what he ought to be up and working for. Stand on your feet ! that 's what he said to Daniel ; and Daniel *did* stand on his feet, did n't he ?

I know this is queer talk for a commissary and beef buyer,
but look at it ! Christian people have been praying about
slavery, for instance, for how long? Now God seems to say
' Oh, hold your tongues, draw your swords and go for it !
Fight !' A fellow can be a Christian without being a pul-
ing fool, can't he? Look at Cromwell ; look at Havelock ! "

" You *will* preach still ! " Mr. Thirlmore said, but there
was something so cheery and vigorous in Lieutenant Van
Doren, that it was impossible not to like him.

" Do I? Well, I buy beef too. We hope to see you in
the army soon. My regards and repentance to Mrs.
Thirlmore. Good-by ! " and sitting strong and erect in
his saddle, and on a bay which met Mr. Thirlmore's hearty
approval, he galloped away.

CHAPTER IX.

GENERAL J. MANDEVILLE GILMORE.

AFTER Captain Grumbles was gone, Mr. Thirlmore said as little to his wife upon the business which had brought their Cincinnatus to the farm as could be helped, nor did she discuss the matter with him ; but both were conscious of being slowly lifted upon the incoming tide in national affairs, and aware, both of them, that good fortune lay in taking it at its flood. When by himself in his library, or oftener still in his stable, the ex-preacher made a thorough study of everything he could get relating to military matters. Such books were the Bibles of the hour.

"By the right flank, wheel ! By the left flank, march ! Charge ! Halt ! " Mr. Thirlmore one day, secured from intrusion by the raging of a sleety storm about the stable, in which he was going through the manual, paced up and down the corridor between the stalls. The oxen took but a languid interest when facing in front of them he seemed, with extended hand, to be more personal than usual in his remarks. They would cease for a while the working of their ponderous jaws, gravely consider his words, and then go on again as if understanding so far they were ready for more. Not so with Tamerlane. He was of a dark, rich brown, some sixteen hands high, with a small head, high shoulders, clean limbs ; and his owner always called special attention to the eyes of his favorite, they were so large and deeply set.

" More human than those of many a woman," he would
say. " Was the ear of any Venus more delicately curved
than this," he would often ask. " And Tam talks with his
ears as no woman ever did with hers."

Any one could see how deeply interested Tamerlane
was that day; his ears were on the *qui vive* to every
command ; he held in his breath at the end of a complicated order, to let it out again in that peculiar assent
which flutters a horse's nostrils but has no synonym in
our language ; he pawed his eagerness to be out and obey-
ing what his master so peremptorily commanded. Maggie
was but as a draught animal compared to him, that was
evident.

As Mr. Thirlmore that day drilled, wheeled, and ma-
nœuvred his imaginary troop hither, thither, up and down,
the empty space opened before his hand ; the narrow
walls parted ; an army stood before him in glittering ranks
obedient to his command. The air was alive with flags ;
the sun sparkled upon helmet and sword ; the country
awaited breathless for impending defeat or victory. For
the first time since his downfall the wearied and disgusted man realized that an audience of three thousand
in a church is not the grandest gathering one can face.
Here something was to follow upon his words more than
laughter, tears, vague resolutions, or empty applause. Here
those who listen, listen to act, to march, to charge, to
struggle hand to hand, to die if need be.

" Ah, this is something more than talk, talk, talk !"
His heart swelled within him, his eyes moistened. " This
is genuine, this is worth a life of preparation."

And so it was that he endured almost with gladness
the day of the selling out. Notices had been posted for
weeks upon the doors of blacksmith shops and cross-road

taverns, upon the walls of the little railroad station and
the trees and fence-posts of the neglected graveyard,
that a great sale would take place; and in due time the
red flag of the auctioneer upon the gate of the farm
announced that the financial revolution had come. The
people hastened to the spot from all the country around,
crowding after the man, on his slow rounds through field
and pasture, through poultry yard and wagon house,
sheep-fold, barn and stables, and then into the house,
outdoing the frogs of Egypt in penetration and perti-
nacity. Not a square inch of the farm escaped the tramp
of dirty and eager feet.

"What am I offered, gentlemen and ladies, for this
celebrated bull, this imported sheep, this wonderful cow,
— an unfailing fountain-head, as you have all heard, of
milk; this blooded colt, this beautiful brand of Spanish
fowls," — and so on and on, until not an animal, imple-
ment, cupboard, or bedstead had been neglected.

Mrs. Thirlmore had quietly refused various invitations
to stay with friends in the city. If it had been wise to
do so, she would have liked to be near her husband
during the out-of-door sales. She feared he might quarrel with some unlucky critic of mare or hog, of hayrick or
patriarchal ram. It reassured her to see him, as he towered head and shoulders above the heads of the country
people, stunted as they were by hard work and by worse
weather. His farm and all upon it were to him already
things of the past. He had so planted his feet in the
future that the crowd was almost silenced by his mere
presence. He had succeeded at considerable sacrifice in
retaining the ownership of Tamerlane. As if from fear of
the possibility of losing him also in the general wreck he
kept, during most of the out-of-door sales, upon his back.

Two or three times Tamerlane was obliged to enforce, with his master's cordial consent, the divinity which should hedge a king, by lashing out with his hoofs at the intrusive crowd until it learned to yield him respectful room.

When the devastating swarm reached the house, it was rather as if Mrs. Thirlmore were holding a reception than assisting at an auction. There was that in her face and manner, in the few and low-spoken words which she uttered, which had power to hush and shame the motley rabble. The rudest rustic removed his hat when he saw her; the neighbors, young and old, married and single, ceased disputing over quilt and blanket, over table and looking-glass, and sank clamor into whispers, when they saw her passing by. There was coffee and cold meat in the kitchen. Maggie had stopped crying, and in dogged silence, her head lower than ever, was trying to serve the throngs. But the hungry rush upon the tables, the reaching of greedy hands around other people and over their heads, the rapid eating of whatever anybody could seize upon, and as if for dear life, — all this ceased so suddenly that Maggie looked up astonished, to find that her mistress had come in; then her head went down, and her tears flowed again. It was a harder pull than before. The face of her mistress, if pale, was smiling. Whenever the wife could do so unobserved she stole a look at her husband, rejoicing in his manliness more than she had ever done in the highest flights of his eloquence in the midst of quite another crowd elsewhere. Both felt that this swift and terrible destruction of their home was but the transition to a something beyond, so much greater and better, that if they had time or mood to put it into words, they would have said, "What are these hungry bidders,

after all, but the maggots which feed upon what is dead
and done with for ever and ever !"

And now their life on the stony farm was past almost
as utterly as if it had never been. Its sterile acres were
rented to a neighboring farmer, of whom the saying ran
that his hands were hard enough to squeeze oil out of
the very bowlders. What Elba was to Napoleon was it
henceforth to its former possessor. For he had entered
heartily upon his new life. He had given weeks to the
business of speech-making, in and around Scrubstones
especially, and had good success in raising recruits. He
had gone faithfully through a course of private instruction and assisted at the drilling of his men, greatly aided
therein by Captain Grumbles.

One thing confronted Colonel Thirlmore at the outset,
and that was General J. Mandeville Gilmore, his superior
officer. A West-Pointer, and seasoned by his campaign
in Mexico, the General could not have reached his present rank if he had not possessed some qualities which
compensated in a degree for his enormous self-conceit.
He had made an excellent railroad president ; but now
that war had come, he resumed brass buttons, sword,
and stars with the eagerness of a boy.

" I go because I must," is the comment Colonel
Thirlmore made to his wife upon their invitation to dine
with the General.

" It is *so* bad that it simply amuses me," laughed his
wife. Her husband did not laugh for some subtile reasons. Had the General drank, gambled, or played the
coward, he would have been less offensive to him.

When they entered the parlor Mrs. Gilmore met them
with effusion. She was a small, slight little lady, with a

thin and sallow face, ornamented on either side by a
cluster of spiral curls which were in perpetual motion, as
was her tongue.

" The General is so glad to meet you," she said. "A
superior man himself, he cannot endure inferior people
about him. It was like death to him to be associated
with those stupid railroad directors. Now that he is in
the army again he is once more himself. This is our
daughter, Morgana."

Miss Moxy, as she was always styled, was a girl of twenty,
and an evident advance upon her mother. She was of
a larger pattern, not exactly plain, yet could not be said
to be pretty. She had been educated in Germany and
Paris, had read and seen nearly everything, was accomplished in music and the languages, had lived all her life
in society, and had the unspeakable advantage of her
mother as an example to be avoided. It was not without
its effect upon her that her father was rich and that she
was an only child. Lieutenant Van Doren, on the staff of
her father, seemed to be on intimate terms with her. He
was present, and was so bright and ruddy of face, so almost
joyous of manner, that Mrs. Thirlmore could hardly bring
herself to believe that this handsome commissary officer
was once a long-haired, pallid-visaged Plymouth Brother,
who one day compelled her husband and herself to listen
to his denunciation, for which he hastened now to make
the fullest apologies.

But if a man ever bore his entire self upon his exterior
it was General J. Mandeville Gilmore, who now entered the
room. He was a large man, whose ruddy face so contrasted
with the almost orange yellow of his hair and beard as to
make him the striking object he so evidently knew himself to be, and to constrain his wife continually to say:

" He is, you know, the very image of the Duke of Argyle. *His* hair is orange, you remember ; only the General is much the finer looking man of the two."

On this occasion his dress-coat, white vest, gold chain, diamond breastpin, and extraordinarily large signet ring set him off wonderfully well ; as with white handkerchief open in one hand, he came in with such an unfolding of his plumage, as it were, such a manifest exhibition of himself as could not fail to impress. He had a way of turning himself full upon the person he addressed, his whole body turning with his face when he spoke, which reminded one of a wax model, — say, of the Father of his Country on its revolving pedestal.

" I am exceedingly happy to see you, madam," to Mrs. Thirlmore. " More than delighted to meet you again, Colonel Thirlmore, and to welcome you to the army. How are you, Van Doren? " and he made the round of the room, for there were quite a number of guests present, bringing his full front to bear upon each in turn, as if he were a battery of cannon, moving slowly because consciously under view.

Seated at last at the table, Mrs. Thirlmore was near enough to her hostess to be entertained throughout the meal by the variations rung by her upon the one theme in life which Mrs. Gilmore seemed able to discuss, — her husband.

Language was inadequate to express her pride in him ; it was adoration — infatuation. Her eyes, even in the busiest moments, seemed never withdrawn from the god of her idolatry, as he loomed at the other end of the table, a flowing napkin under his chin. He informed his guests from time to time about himself, what he liked, what he abhorred, what he had done, what he meant to do.

Whatever the topic, and by whomsoever introduced, it invariably recurred to himself.

"It reminded me," Mrs. Thirlmore said afterward to her husband, "of that child's toy, a jack-in-the-box; there is no touching anything, but up starts General J. Mandeville Gilmore. What a pity that a grown man should be such a perfect fool." This was a singular remark to be made by one who had too light an estimate of people in general to dwell with any pleasure upon either their virtues or defects; but Peace seemed for the moment to have caught the spirit of exceeding frankness which characterized this remarkable trio. Miss Moxy had been seated near her, on the other side, and Mrs. Thirlmore glanced from time to time at her face in the few pauses made by her voluble mother. There was a sullen look in her fine eyes, a flash now and then of sarcasm like lightning from a cloud. It seemed a pity that lips so rosy should have learned what threatened to become an habitual curl of contempt.

"You see," she said to Mrs. Thirlmore, "what a devoted wife my mother is. But she has a rival in her affection for my father; a rival who leaves her far behind, I assure you."

"You mean yourself?" Mrs. Thirlmore said it the more sweetly because she did not mean it.

"Myself? Not quite!" There was a scorn in the eyes and the accents of the young girl which would have surprised a woman of less quickness than Mrs. Thirlmore.

"No. There is one person who loves my father far more than she can ever do," and the well-moulded chin indicated who was meant. "My father loves himself with a love passing that of woman!"

There was so much bitterness in the tone that it reminded Mrs. Thirlmore of what she used to hear when she lived in the city, of the phenomenal selfishness of the General.

"Yes, he is a wealthy man," people would say; "but it is upon himself that his money is spent, while his wife and daughter are little more than underpaid servants in constant attendance upon his highness. No wonder Miss Moxy grows soured, and says the most dreadful things; but his wife, little goose, is intoxicated with her illustrious spouse. To be his wife is glory enough. It is a good thing that Moxy is so bright and strong; she is afraid of nobody. She has a little money of her own, — that accounts for her stay in Europe. If it were not to help her poor mother, she would have left the house long ago."

So ran the tongue of gossip, and who can say whether it lied or not? Nothing cared the General for what was said of him; to self-conceit such as his the hide of the rhinoceros is as tissue paper, and the armor of Achilles as gauze to whatever shafts may fly. And so the dinner ran its course, — its courses, rather, for the *pièce de resistance* was always the same. What with the wife at one end of the table and the husband at the other, soup, fish, fowl, the meats, the entrées were General J. Mandeville Gilmore and him only. The cloth might be removed, but the General remained; the guests had him for dessert; they drank him and what he did in Mexico in the wines. What he accomplished in railroad matters came on with the coffee; and with the cracking of the nuts, the revelation of what he proposed to do in the impending destruction of the followers of Jeff Davis. Meanwhile, and all along, the General would cast an occasional

glance as of one sitting for his portrait, to the other ènd
of the table. How could the touches of the faithful
artist there be otherwise than incessant and minute,
seeing that he was the one inspiration of a soul otherwise
wholly feeble and devoid of energy !

Through the long meal Mrs. Thirlmore was almost
afraid to glance at her husband, so fearful was she lest his
disgust should take shape, audible or visible. But he
had too important an object in view ; his ships lay in
ashes behind him, and he would not allow himself to
seem more than politely bored.

" For one," he said, as he went home with his wife,
" I have dined more than is desirable upon my beloved
commander. I knew it was going to be bad ; but, great
heavens ! " —

CHAPTER X.

MARCHING AWAY.

IT befell that, with the exception of General Gilmore commanding, no one was so conspicuous along the decorated streets, on the day of the departure of the troops, as Colonel Theodore Thirlmore. Many months of energetic preparation had gone before, and, of late, the messages from the Secretary of War urging the soldiers to the front had come thick and fast. To-day, the hour of leaving had arrived. A platform had been erected in a central commons of the city in which Colonel Thirlmore was for so long the most prominent pastor. From this, the Governor of the State, accompanied by many distinguished men, reviewed the regiments. Every door, window, house-top, along the route of the march was crowded with eager faces, while great multitudes lined the sidewalks and surged along the ways. For the fires of '76 were fairly kindled by this time, and there was scarcely a heart which did not beat responsive to the drums.

General Gilmore's open carriage was drawn up beside the central platform, and Mrs. Thirlmore was seated therein with Mrs. Gilmore and Miss Moxy. Lieutenant Van Doren came and went during the afternoon and seemed to find it convenient to keep his station on the side nearest the General's daughter. Of the sentiments of the swift-footed, bright-faced officer toward Miss Gilmore Mrs. Thirlmore had no doubt, but she was by no means clear as to those of the young lady in return. Even in the hour of parting with her husband she could not fail of interest in young people such as these.

"I am so glad, so very glad to see General Gilmore like himself once more," Mrs. Gilmore was saying. She was wide awake to-day and every curl was a-tremble with excitement. She sat down, stood up, looked here and there in expectation of the coming event; but it steadied her that she had always the one theme.

"The General," she went on, "insisted on carrying his army ways into his railroading. — that is, as much as he could. But bless you, Mrs. Thirlmore, he never felt at home except in his uniform. I tell him he would never unbuckle his sword if he could help it; would never take off his cocked hat, plumes and all, if he had his way, not at table nor when he goes to bed; and he has been perfectly miserable all along since the war with Mexico. Fifty times he has said to me, 'What hope can we have of a war with anybody? Fighting those savages at the West, poor wretches, is as glorious as if you were fighting so many fleas. Mexico is whipped for a century to come.' When there was that stir about Cespedes, you know, in Cuba, he had some little hope. You can't tell, my dear madam, how anxious he was that it should come to blows with Spain. Even then he complained it could be nothing better than a little affair of the navy. The General despises the navy. For a commander to go about in a ship is, I think, as if a general should carry his fort about with him. It does look cowardly, now, does n't it? And all these years he has been hoping and praying it would come to a fight somehow. The General did have some faint idea at one time, when the Fenians were up, you know, that they would get us into a war with England; but it was the eternal quarrelling between the North and South that

encouraged him most.   For years, whenever Congress was
in session, the first thing the General would say at breakfast was, ' Where is my paper?'   Then he always turned
first to the debates.   Sometimes the Northern Congressmen would burst out against the men from the South, or
the men from the South would blaze out at the Senators
and things from the North ; and the General would be *so*
interested !   Whenever words grew hot he was as pleased
as a child.   ' Good for you !' he would say, whether it
was Sumner that was speaking, or Butler.   He did n't
care who said it, or what it was, so that it looked as if it
would end in a fight.   For years, madam, oh, for years
and years, he has said to me, ' Melinda, it must come to
a war yet, and the sooner the better !   It is a shame, a
burning shame, that a man like me should live and die
in this miserable mousehole of a railroad office.   What
chance has a man to show himself?   He might almost as
well be dead and — ' "

"Mother, mother !" Moxy could contain herself no
longer.

"In a moment, Moxy.   No, madam, you cannot imagine how eager the General has been all along."   Mrs.
Gilmore refused to look at her daughter, as, doubly excited by the scenes of the day, she rattled on : " When
there was all that squatter trouble in Kansas he would walk
the floor up and down, up and down.   I don't think " —
confidentially to Mrs. Thirlmore — " that the General cared
a straw as to the merits of the question.   If he had been
South he would have been just as hot to fight on that side.
It was his being so cruelly laid aside that hurt him.   All
the mention of him was now and then about his railroad ;
and what did that amount to?   And how he brightened
up when things began to look alarming ! — those times, you

know, when people were talking about Fremont, and free soil. Those mornings the General would throw down his paper and say, 'All right, Melinda!' and he would take another egg, a fresh cup of coffee, and tuck his napkin under his chin. 'It can't be long, now, my dear,' — he would say, and eat — oh, as much again! How he used to hate his poor railroad! 'If I was only going about hurrying troops to the front,' he would say; 'but those crowds of wretched passengers, and boxes and barrels of flour, codfish, and things — bah! I despise such a life!'"

"Mother, for goodness sake, mother!" Mrs. Thirlmore could not but pity the poor girl. There was quite a crowd near by, and it seemed to be much interested, as the whisper ran around that it was the wife of General Gilmore who was speaking. People came up closer to listen. But it was in vain that Moxy laid a beseeching hand on her mother's arm. The little lady had got fairly going in her one well-worn path, and nothing could stop her.

"You know," she persisted, "that the General likes to have the very best things for his table. I tell him he is an awful epicure, he is so particular about what he eats, and how Moxy and I prepare it for him. As things got darker and darker he got so that he could eat almost anything. Since Lincoln was elected he has gained, oh, ever so many pounds! For months and months he has had his resignation of his railroad written out and ready. You would n't believe if I were to tell you how often he has been on to Washington, to be on the spot to report for service. He wanted to be in the eye of men, you see. Because he has drawn up a plan — hush! it is a great secret — by which, when he is placed in chief command, he will finish the war in, oh, ever so short a time; though he says that he supposes the Government will be compelled to experiment with a list of boobies at first ! "

" Mother, you must not tire Mrs. Thirlmore any longer. You may imagine," Moxy whispered, turning in disgust to their companion, " how tired I am !   One would think it was enough to be with my father, and to hear him talk about himself all the time !   To hear of nothing else when he is away is more than flesh and blood can stand.   Look ! They are getting ready to photograph something on the platform."

In the confusion of the moment, before the platform was as yet occupied and the troops arrived, Lieutenant Van Doren, who had come again, stood beside Mrs. Thirlmore.

" I wanted," he said in a low voice, " to say that I suppose I shall be closely associated with Colonel Thirlmore. I need not say how uncertain everything is as to our movements, as to where we shall be and what we shall do ; but if I can serve your husband in any way I will with pleasure.   I thought this might be some small comfort to you when we are gone."

The way in which this was said conveyed more than the mere words.   The wife understood him perfectly, and he knew that she did by her manner of thanking him.

" You are greatly changed.   I should not have known you," she said.

" I hardly know myself," he replied, modestly. "As to that, I hope I am changing all the time ; there is plenty of room for it.   What I mean is that I am happier than I ever was before, and if I can serve Colonel Thirlmore I shall be glad.   I am one of a good many who have great faith in him.   You will see ! " and his laugh was like cheerful music to the wife.

Mrs. Thirlmore was slow in her preferences, but there sprang up in her a strong liking for this healthy, hearty, genial man.

" I think," she smiled roguishly, " I can guess as to one person who did much toward the change in you," and she glanced at Moxy Gilmore, who was talking busily with a gentleman on the other side of the vehicle.

" Yes," Lieutenant Van Doren said frankly, " that is so. A little, or rather a goodly degree, of sarcasm has an excellent effect. I was so crusted over with — at best it is but another sort of selfishness — with my ascetic, emotional species of saintliness that nothing less corrosive could have cut through it. As to that, General Gilmore too does me a world of good, and every day. So does Mrs. Gilmore. A man has two things in this world to help him, — perpetual circumstance grinding on him from outside ; freedom and force of will within him. Between the two, you can out of almost the poorest material make yourself into almost anything."

"You are as glad as if you were setting out for Europe — " Mrs. Thirlmore laughed.

" I am always setting out for a higher something in myself. But it ruins the journey for me to be thinking about it. I leave that to — to the General. Good-by, madam. When I see you again, I hope I shall be so changed that you won't know me," and, lifting his hat, he moved on for a parting word or two with Miss Moxy.

Meanwhile the long line of troops was on its way through the city, and at the head of the columns rode General Gilmore, a little in advance of his staff. He was really a noble figure of a man ; but his weakness was so well known, and he bore himself with an aspect of such consummate self-importance, that everywhere he was greeted with half-derisive cheers mingled with laughter. No pea-cock could be more unconscious of it. In his new and gorgeous uniform, in the superabundance of waving plumes, gold lace, silver mountings to bridle and saddle, glittering buttons and all, the General sincerely regarded himself as the most illustrious of warriors, the terror of the Con-federacy, the hope of the Union, the hero of the future; and he showed it in every line of his face, for when a man is filled from top to toe with one overmastering sentiment it must overflow. And so he rode slowly along, accepting the homage of the city as merely the nearest expression of that of the entire land, of the whole world; he had not a thought beyond that.

It may be his knowledge of this which kept Colonel Thirlmore in check as he followed. He was mounted on Tamerlane; was a younger and really nobler-looking man than his superior officer. People recalled his career in the pulpit and greeted him with cheers of extra sincerity; but he had seen so much of late of General J. Mandeville Gilmore and his supreme conceit, that he bore himself with becoming modesty.

Tamerlane had no such sentiment. He divided with his rider the admiration of the people, and he knew it. That he approved of his master's decision in going into the army was very evident. It will not do to say that he was as well informed as any one as to what the excitement and marching was about, yet there were too many present who really comprehended almost as little as he the causes which had brought it to pass; and, in the end, who of all those multitudes knew so much more than Tam of what had taken place? Meanwhile, not General Gilmore himself could manifest more pride than Tam, as he arched his neck, champed his bit, stamped now with one forefoot, and then with the other. Beneath his cool exterior, Colonel Thirlmore's heart swelled to the flying of flags, the excellent music, the roar of the people, to the pressure above all of coming danger. All men knew that the South was up as one man, was more skilled in the use of weapons, was by temperament hotter for fight than the North ; and there were whispers of treachery even among the highest in authority at the North. It was a gallant bearing the city wore that day, but who can say — !

Mrs. Thirlmore's attention was drawn from General Gilmore, as at last he ascended the platform, to his wife. The little lady had risen to her feet, her lips were parted, her curls electric with excitement, her eyes were fastened upon her husband in ecstasy of worship. There was to her at the instant but one man living. "Oh, is he not," she panted to whoever came near her, "the most magnificent man ever seen? When he gets to the front I have no more fear of the result — "

"Oh, mother!" her daughter broke in, "how *can* you? Papa is already the most conceited being alive. I am ashamed of you; and, oh, I am so ashamed of him!" she said with a fervor which, from long trial, had become almost fierceness. "See how he looks around! Don't you hear the people laugh? That an old man can be such a fool! Don't think, Mrs. Thirlmore, that I cannot see it as well as you. Go away, Mr. Van Doren; I cannot endure it!" and there were tears of mortification in the eyes of the girl.

But a group was swiftly formed, — the Governor and his aides, a prominent clergyman in his gown, General Gilmore planted in advance of all. For a moment the camera was levelled. Then prayer was offered for the Republic and for those who went to die for it, if so it must be.

There was a roll of drums, a presenting of arms, an address was delivered, the kettle-drums struck up, the bugles blew clear and shrill, the line of march to the railroad was begun ; there was weeping, cheering, and then the measured tramp of feet dying in the distance ; the regular throb. of the drum diminished into silence, the shrill fife itself ceased to be heard. The vast multitudes dispersed to their homes, and night and sudden silence came down upon the city. In a thousand households women were weeping, and men were without anything to say in the shame of staying behind, while the ladened trains roared southward toward battle and, alas, toward the first terrible defeat.

Mrs. Gilmore seemed, poor little lady, as if she would weep her soul away as they drove off. Her daughter did not cry; she was too much taken up with sarcastic observations upon the events, and more particularly upon the people, of the day. Mrs. Thirlmore understood very well why Moxy was so exceedingly severe upon Lieutenant Van Doren. Had she not caught sight of the softened face of the lovely girl when that commissary lifted his jaunty cap from his happy and hopeful brows in the act of parting with her? He knew Miss Moxy too thoroughly to indulge in the ghost of a whimper. The girl saw everything ; saw that the eyes of Mrs. Thirlmore were upon her at the instant, and it created a loving bond between the two from that hour.

Mrs. Thirlmore often thought of it afterward ; the last look which she exchanged with her husband was while he was standing on the platform, his eyes upon General Gilmore, who was never quite so much of an Olympian Narcissus as then. The glance of husband and wife met ; there was a smile upon her lips, it was too absurd ! She fancied that a sudden shame came to her husband's cheeks; was he learning something more than war of his vainglorious commander?

It was hard, very hard, upon this wife, newly awakened to what her husband, herself, and their married life had missed, to know as she did that he was not sorry to leave her. She did not grieve over it, because, heart and soul, she was resolved upon winning him to herself. Winning him to herself not merely by making herself more to him than she had ever been; great changes were to take place in him, too. Eternal separation by death might come, but nothing short of death should prevent her. The peasant girl of Syria, bearing upon her head the water-jars to and from the well at Nazareth, knew what was to be born of her, yet fainted not, and whispered no syllable of it. May it not be said, with all reverence, that to this woman too was revealed a miracle to come? Surely it was a trust not in herself, which made her rest in a future which was to be hers because given to her.

7

CHAPTER XI.

MRS. Thirlmore had a sister living in the city, the wife of Dr. Steven Trent, the celebrated physician. They were twin sisters; but while Mrs. Thirlmore, as has been said, was the duplicate of her German and atheistic grandfather, her sister was the very double of her mother, the only child of the atheist aforesaid. The likeness of these, to the parent in the latter case, to grandparent in the former, was amazing; the radical peculiarity of the old German was but intensified by the sex of his granddaughter, while Mrs. Trent was a rosy matron, plump and overflowing with good nature, — her joyous mother over again and redoubled.

During their brief stay in the city before Colonel Thirlmore departed for the war, Mrs. Thirlmore made her home in the large and handsome house of her brother-in-law, Dr. Trent. But the sisters were too unlike. The divergence of their characters had but widened with the lapse of years. Mrs. Trent dearly loved her sister, as she did her husband, her little girl, — everybody who was dependent upon her.

"My sister," Mrs. Trent told her husband, "has, ever since she married, drawn herself away from every one. I cannot make out as yet what effect the downfall of her husband and their life upon that desolate farm have had upon her. Now that her husband has gone into the thick of the fight —"

"She is like Volumnia," said Dr. Trent. "You know

that Shakspeare makes her seclude herself from even her dearest friends, while Coriolanus is away at the war. It is nature, or Shakspeare would not have done it. She is a wonderful woman, my dear, and a remarkable process is going on within her. In her husband also, for that matter. For one, I await the result with the greatest interest."

And thus it was that Mrs. Thirlmore accepted the urgent request of Captain Grumbles and his wife, and for the time made her home on the old farm at Scrubstones.

Though nearer the city, it was almost as rocky a region as the farm from which she came. When she stepped from the train at the Scrubstones station, she found Captain Grumbles' son Henry, misnamed Squash, waiting for her. He was a youth of fourteen years, or so ; and there was a certain gnarled knottiness about him, a ridgy roughness of person, which, with a grayish yellowness of complexion, justified his name, for he was like nothing so much as the vegetable. It was little he had seen of the world. For years he had been trained by his energetic mother to rise with the dawn, to work long and hard ; and he was graver of manner, more scant of words, more stooping in neck and shoulders than Mrs. Thirlmore liked to see. Maggie, the Manx girl, who came with her mistress, he seemed to understand ; but he gazed open-mouthed at the lady. To him his stout and red-visaged mother, broad of shoulders, vigorous of hands, was the model of her sex ; and here was a woman of whom he had heard so much, and who was as much unlike his mother as it was possible for two persons to be.

" Why, I could have picked her up," he said the same day to Snap, his younger brother, " and put her in the wagon with one hand and never winked. But she 's got mighty fine eyes, — her face is like that marble woman we saw in the art shop when we went that day to the city."

"The woman Pop would n't let me stop to look at," Snap interjected, "because she had n't no clothes on? I remember."

"Yes; and this one is sort of marbly too; not stony, I don't mean, but a little cold and keep-you-off like. But did you ever hear such a nice voice? It 's like — like the wind through the pine-trees, only not so much of it. That 's what it 's like. When she saw me, she came up to me with such a smile, right up to me, and said: 'Is this you, Squash? I hope we shall be good friends.' But she 's so fine, somehow, I 'm afraid of her. She 's more like you, Snap;" for Snap, who had been named Guernsey, after an old friend, was a smaller, slighter boy than his brother, — so narrow, in fact, in proportion to his length, that he did resemble the vegetable after which he was named.

Except "Yes, ma'am" and "No, ma'am," Squash had little to say as he drove Mrs. Thirlmore and Maggie home. The region was well known to Mrs. Thirlmore, for she was born in her grandfather's parsonage not far off, and had grown up there; "and yonder," she said to her driver, as the wagon wound along through the hills clothed with pine-trees, "yonder, on the top of that hill, is where I taught school when I was a girl. Is the little house still standing?"

"Why that is where I went to school," said the boy, glad of a bond between them. "When I was a little boy, like Snap, I mean. I work on the farm now. Snap goes there. So does Pop. Owl, she is too little and too fat to go anywhere."

"Why do you call him Pop?" Mrs. Thirlmore was struggling against a profound depression which had fallen upon her since her arrival, and was rousing herself to resistance.

"Hoh! It is n't a him; it's a her; did n't you know that? She is a girl, Pop is; but her full name is Popcorn. In the big Bible father has got it written Peace; but we call her Pop, she is always hopping about so. Now and then she is like corn when it bursts open; she says and does things so sudden-like."

"Peace? That is my name!" Mrs. Thirlmore said with new interest.

"Oh, yes, I know; she was called after you. Mother told me so yesterday. She says if we nickname her any more she'll — "

"I'm so glad. I did not know it; I know I shall love her."

"Well, maybe so. You see she's mighty sudden sometimes;" but Mrs. Thirlmore felt a new spring of affection opening within her. What had she done to cause these people to care for her? Up to the visit of Captain Grumbles she had dismissed them from her mind as entirely as she had done the cats of her childhood.

"Owl is named after mother," Squash was saying. "*Her* name is Aurora Ann. You just see Owl's eyes, and you'll know why we call her that. And then she has such a round and fuzzy head, and she is so fat she has to move as slow as you please. Yonder is our Hans. He's our working-man; he saw us coming, and is holding the gate open for us. He don't talk much, but he is a good man. We're mighty glad he's living with us, specially now father's gone."

The red-wheeled wagon had made its way as of its own volition along the oft-traversed road among the rocky hills. The day was a dull one, and now and then the road was so carpeted with brown needles fallen from the pines on either side, that the wheels were soundless. To Mrs. Thirlmore it was as if she were entering the realm of dreams. For many weeks she had been busy with the breaking up of her old home, and with getting her husband ready for his start. Then came the days of strong excitement in the city. But now the troops were gone southward; and in the reaction from all this she was coming back to the dull, old-fashioned country, in which her life was passed before she knew her husband and all he had brought to her. How well she remembered having seen when a child the two-story mansion, with its confusion of one-storied additions, which was now lifting itself upon the right hand. There was the garden in the rear. On the opposite side of the highway from the house was the orchard, a large one. Stretching away beyond the garden were the fields, between them and the house the great red barn with its ricks of hay, the pigeons flying in and out, or preening their wings upon a ledge in the gable-end of the barn. The yards seemed to be well supplied with hens; a flock of geese were coming in a line up the road; and in the distance she heard the gobble of turkeys, and the shrill potrack! potrack! of a procession of guinea fowls issuing from behind the barn.

At the gate stood the laborer whom Squash named Hans. He was a square-built, stoutly-framed, somewhat coarse-featured man of about sixty years of age. Clad in the heavy jeans, corduroy trousers, and thick-soled boots of a laborer, the only thing noticeable about him was a mixture of gravity and gentleness in his face.

"He is not an Irishman?" Mrs. Thirlmore asked carelessly.

"Irish? Our Hans? Hoh! I guess not! He is a

Swede. But he don't smoke, or drink whiskey. Do you know what a Swedenborgian is, Mrs. Thirlmore?" Squash demanded.

"I believe so."

"Well," and it was said with pride, "Hans is a Swedenborgian. I can't say I know much what a Swedenborgian is," the boy said frankly; "but, whatever it is, Hans is one! I can't get him to talk much about it; but he likes it, and he is all right, and he's got the queerest way of swearing you ever heard.

"That funny-looking dog with him is named Wretch. He looks like a big black caterpillar, don't he? Oh, yes, I remember now, he followed father when he went to see you all. Isn't it funny? He wanted to go with father to the war. You see, he thought father was the only friend he had. But he's taken up with Hans since then. Hans lives all by himself in what used to be an old seed-house, behind the barn, and Wretch stays with him now, for mother she won't have him in her kitchen. Yonder she is. Do you know my mother, ma'am?"

Mrs. Thirlmore could have almost laughed. The boy turned gravely around on the front seat and looked steadily at her for a reply. Evidently, to know or not to know his mother was a matter of the first importance.

But his mother was already at the side of the wagon. She was more like an English farmer's wife than one of the hard-driven, lean, and overworked drudges so often seen upon American farms. Of unusual height and what might be called strapping make, her cheeks glowing as from perpetual cookery or experience of the harvest field, she bore in her whole manner an aspect of the authority which comes to one in virtue of good sense energetically used. With this there was a kindliness, an unclouded cheerfulness, an open-faced sincerity, which won the heart of Mrs. Thirlmore, as it did that of all who came to know her.

"She is what the old English writers call a notable housewife," Mrs. Thirlmore said on the instant to herself; and there was a confused minglement in her mind of the wife of Bath, John Gilpin's wife, the wife of the Vicar of Wakefield, and a passing flash of what Shakspeare may have meant by his "Merry Wives of Windsor." To the visitor it was an entirely new type of her own sex, in almost every sense the opposite of herself.

The children were grouped about Mrs. Grumbles, — they always were, as a rule. Hezekiah Grumbles was deficient in no sense as a husband and father, but he was referred to by the children only in the absence of their mother; and her absence was of all things the most to be deprecated by father and children. Then and afterward, Mrs. Thirlmore could not help observing that the children kept their eyes upon their mother in coming in and going out, in speech and in silence, whatever was said and done, and where nothing in particular was on foot, — it was a curiously significant thing, which interested the new comer greatly.

But now Squash glanced from his mother to Snap. Pop, a bright-faced, red-headed little girl, looked to her brothers, to even Owl for explanation; for never had any of them seen their mother defer to any one as she now did to this fine-featured, large-eyed lady who was just arrived. The way in which their mother spoke to her surprised them one and all. There was almost a flutter of confusion in Mrs. Grumbles' face and manner; she half advanced to kiss her guest, but drew back and gave her a cordial hand instead. She seemed to be almost afraid of her visitor. It was as if some Dame Durden of olden times was receiving Queen

Elizabeth ! The mouth of every child there opened. Their mother do this ! They looked at the new comer with an awe which would turn easily into dislike — hatred.

"And this is my little Peace? Your son has told me about it. How kind in you to name her after me ! Come, dear !" And Mrs. Thirlmore took the hand of the child and stooped to kiss her ; but Pop justified her name by breaking away and flying to the door of the house, in which she stood defiant, while little Owl took with solemn eyes the kiss instead. The other children laughed.

"You must excuse Pop — Peace, I should say," Mrs. Grumbles remarked, when all of them were seated in an hour or so later at the supper table. "She will learn better. We have all of us much to learn. I'm sure I have. I for one should be glad to learn." There was the same embarrassment in the honest face of the good lady. The children looked up from their plates astonished.

"You learn ! and from me, my dear madam !" and the guest glanced over the well-ordered and abundant table. "It is I who have everything to learn from you. That is why I came. Everybody knows what a housekeeper you are, Mrs. Grumbles. I cannot remember the time when I did not hear of it, — at the parsonage, you know."

Dame Grumbles was evidently pleased ; but she too had heard, and much more, about her new friend, — of her city life, her trip to Europe, her surmised unbelief and all, — than this refined lady dreamed of.

"The state of the case is this," Mrs. Thirlmore said frankly : "You know, Mrs. Grumbles, what an energetic woman my aunt was, and how hard she tried to make everything move smoothly for my poor old grandfather. She would let my sister Revel and myself do

hardly anything; our business in life was to keep clean
and to keep quiet. As soon as day dawned, I had to be
up and at my lessons; then I went to school. At night
I was so tired with the walk to and from school that I
was glad to get to bed. Before I was really grown up I
began to teach : you know how far the parsonage is from
the old school-house. Then I married and went to the
city. What could I know about housekeeping? The
Irish girls we chanced to have did as they pleased.
You have never tried them?"

"I? No, madam! We do our own work about the
house."

"So I thought;" for Mrs. Grumbles repudiated the
Celtic idea with a horror which was amusing. "You can
imagine what a time I had," laughed Mrs. Thirlmore.
"When we went to our farm—it is a shame to say it,
but I left everything to Maggie. She is from the Isle of
Man; a good girl, as I hope you'll find. What chance
have I had to learn anything? But I am going to try now.
When my husband comes back, I intend to astonish him
by keeping his house as it never was kept before. That
is why I am here, Mrs. Grumbles. Everybody says there
never was a housekeeper like you. I couldn't be at a
better school. If you will only let me look on and learn.
But I shall try your patience dreadfully. You will help
me, won't you?"

In the press and hurry of events Mrs. Thirlmore had
not formed any very definite plans. Except that Colonel
Thirlmore insisted upon paying liberal board for herself
and for Maggie, no thought had been given to the ac-
ceptance of the urgent invitation of the Grumbles family
other than that she should make her home for the present
with them. It was the inspiration of the instant for her

to put herself under the good woman of the house; but she was all the more sincere and eager about it. She had, for the present, had enough of the city, — of lectures, concerts, and books. The face of Mrs. Grumbles was fairly radiant; the children looked from her to their guest with pride, — even Pop could have kissed her.

"Let me see," said the new arrival, as supper proceeded, "what is it that I want to learn? These delicious waffles, to begin with, my husband is so fond of them; but I have no more notion than a child how to go to work to make them. And how do people cure hams, — like this, I mean? And I never milked a cow in my life."

A murmur of pity ran around the table. The mother was watching her guest very closely. Had there been the least condescension in her manner, or in her heart; had she not sincerely meant what she said; had there been the slightest affectation or insincerity on the part of this fine lady from the city, — she would have detected it on the instant, and rejected her and it with scorn.

"This farmer's wife," Mrs. Thirlmore was saying to herself, "has an unerring instinct for the right color and taste of butter, for the grade of her cream and of the cow yielding it, for the degree of acid in apples or in cider. I dare say she can tell from the honey what her bees have been feeding on. She has the same keenness of estimate as to her children, her neighbors, and of myself. If there is a speck of decay in a fish or a joint of meat, or in me; if there be ever so tiny a bit of mould in her jellies, or a moth in her blankets, or insincerity in any form in my nature, — those sharp eyes will find it out."

"You must have greatly enjoyed," Mrs. Grumbles said, "living so long in such excellent society as you have had in town." There was a touch of the old awe of the far away and wholly unknown in her tone. To this Mrs. Thirlmore made some general reply; but while she did so, she was adding to herself, " Most women in that fine society habitually count upon nothing in others but genuine selfishness, feigned interest, polite falsehood, because they are conscious of these in themselves. I am glad I 've got back to nature, to simple truth."

" See what I 've come to be taught," she laughed, and made a memorandum of it with the end of her spoon on the table-cloth. " I must learn how to make butter, cheese, preserves, sauer-kraut — "

" Sausage," suggested Squash. " Oh, but you ought to taste the sausage mother makes ! "

" And souse," Snap contributed.

" And cracknels, crullers, rice cakes, doughnuts, cookies, pumpkin pies, mince pies, gingerbread, cocoanut candy, cream cakes — "

Pop rattled it off so rapidly and without taking breath that everybody laughed.

" She knows how to mend my socks, and — and — " Owl hesitated, " gives me, — castor oil."

The shudder with which Owl said it, her eyes open at their most solemn size, accompanied the burst of laughter round the table. Mrs. Grumbles was protesting with uplifted hands, but Squash declined to look at her.

" And, oh, Mrs. Thirlmore," he burst out, " she knows what is good for chickens when they 've got the gapes. Why, there was our cow Catty; mother gave her a bottle full of — " but a peremptory look silenced him.

Every one was in a good humor. Mrs. Thirlmore began to speak of those who had just gone from them to the war. Little red-haired Pop was looking at her intently, waiting an opportunity to say something. "What is it, dear?" the guest asked at last.

"And sometimes she puts us in a dark closet," Pop hastened to add. "She had to whip Snap once; she did it with her slip —"

"Children!" It was not said in a loud voice, but Captain Grumbles would be fortunate if his command was as instantly obeyed in the ranks.

"Vulgarity! Of course," Mrs. Thirlmore communed with herself, "and I have much to teach them if I stay. But there is more than what was on my list which I must learn. Let me rest a little first; rest. And where is *he* to-night? — where?" She uttered it aloud.

"Mrs. Grumbles, where do you think they are to-night? Suppose we look at my map after supper, and see."

CHAPTER XII.

AN AD INTERIM.

"I DO not see," Mrs. Thirlmore wrote to her husband about this time, "how a sculptor could have a rougher or more unshaped block of marble upon which to work than I have in the person of Captain Grumbles' oldest son, misnamed Squash. So far as parents go, he could not have better; his material is of as sturdy a grain as could be wished. He is very fond of me, I really believe, and it is a great help to have the marble yield itself so eagerly to chisel and mallet. There is a pleasure peculiar to itself, also, in dealing with a fellow-creature in this way, the material glows so under one's hands. There are such sublime possibilities too. Shall I make him a Minos or a Mercury? an Apollo or an Antinous?"

It was of Squash in an exceedingly subordinate sense that she was thinking. The one hold she had upon her husband now was by letter. Very well, by letter then; and ah, what care it would require! She would interest him; make herself necessary, essential to him! A poet can move and melt, can mould and make, whosoever reads; but hers was an inspiration beyond that of any mere poet. Although their correspondence might be simply, to begin with, as between friends, she felt a woman's divine power within her, and she had no fear!

And the country lad was as good a subject to begin upon as any. Far from being jealous, the boy's mother was proud to see that such a relation could spring up between Squash — who, like all first-born sons, had had a hard time of it from childhood — and a lady whom every day she admired and secretly feared more and more.

"We are not enough like each other," Mrs. Grumbles said to Mrs. Sudkins, her nearest neighbor, "for us ever to be intimate friends, as you and I are, for instance. There are things I talk about with you which I would no more think of mentioning to her — She's had advantages which you and I have n't had. But, law me, there is the best of understanding between us; that is, we don't have anything we try to hide from each other; that is, except " — but here the good lady stopped, with an increase of color which Mrs. Sudkins did not understand.

"It is a something in her fine friend she don't like," that lady said, and not without pleasure, to her nearest gossip. But she was mistaken. It is a thing which must be manfully told, and now as well as at any other time, that the estimable wife of Captain Grumbles, although she could read, could barely write. Mortally ashamed she was of the deficiency; only less than if she had murdered a baby did it weigh upon her : and yet will any one please say how she could help it? A dreadfully abused step-child, she found refuge when very young in the house of hard-working Mr. and Mrs. Grumbles, the parents of her husband. She was sent faithfully to school ; a fitful attempt was made to teach her at home of evenings. But the learning of the old people, in books at least, was very limited, and "there's so much to do every day," she said to her conscience, "and I am so beat out when night comes ! All I do is to get the ink over everything when · I try to write, and my fingers are so stiff from washing the floor, handling the hoe — never mind, I'll learn some day."

But the day never came. It was this which made her refusal almost fierce when the son of the old people asked her to marry him. After she yielded to pressure and was married, she made, in deepest secrecy, an honest, desperate attempt to teach herself. But there was more work to do than ever ; the children began to come, the old people died, household cares crowded her to the utmost. As Squash came to be a school-boy, the dreadful secret necessarily revealed itself to him ; but the sole effect was to give him an increased contempt for schooling. " If *she's* got along so well without it, so can I," was his reasoning many a day when playing truant, or giving his soul to blackberrying, nutting — to anything rather than to books. Then as Snap grew older, the family skeleton was cautiously revealed to him, and by him to his sister Pop, as in due time it would come, as she was able to bear it, to Owl, the youngest.

Mrs. Thirlmore was swift to divine it ; and it touched her to the heart the way in which the children guarded the secret from her. Mrs. Grumbles " was so busy " that her husband and the children were accustomed to read to her whatever was of interest in the papers. There was always some book in course of being read of nights. It took a long time to get through a book, but she derived the full benefit from it. Her reading, apart from this, was pretty much a thing of the past ; and Squash was singularly prompt with his pen, when any writing had to be done, " now that father is away." But all agreed, Captain Grumbles only less than the rest, that since *she* could do so well without it, education was by no means what it was popularly considered to be. Their guest came to be almost of their

opinion when she saw how admirably her hostess contrived without it.

And so the days passed by. Mrs. Thirlmore came to
enjoy the early rising ; her appetite adjusted itself to their
food and to their hours for taking it. Beginning half in
jest, she came to feel a sincere interest as to how the last
cheese would turn out, or how many eggs this or that hen
or guinea fowl would contribute. It amused her to see that
Pop was not much more interested than she herself was in
the hatching out of chickens, or in how many young turkeys the speckled mother would lead proudly out from
under the barn. And there was always some wonderful
baking on hand. With the cordial permission of Mrs.
Grumbles, she would borrow a check apron and try what
she could do in the way of cup-cake or Sally Lunn, en-
joying more than any one her deplorable failures ; while
her successes were a joy so sincere as to make her half
ashamed.

Very slowly and cautiously she seduced the three oldest
children into an interest in some new invention or some
story from history suggested by the warlike news of the
day. She would read of nights the briefest and most
striking episodes in the biography of one hero and another.
Little by little she managed so to engage the attention of
the older members of the household in the " Idyls of the
King " that, at last, to her surprise and their own loudly-
expressed sorrow, none were left to read. It was by very
gradual approaches that Squash and Snap, as pitted against
Pop, undertook the elements of Latin ; and the victorious
progress of the red-haired and impulsive child amazed her
teacher, aroused the boys to the very desperation of en-
deavor, and delighted the mother beyond measure. There
was a little botany now and then of sunny days ; a very

little geology, until the house was cumbered with speci-
mens picked up in field and forest; a merest amusement
of experiments in chemistry. But when Mrs. Thirlmore
showed what could be done with galvanic battery and
electrical machine Mrs. Grumbles became as Owl in her
interest and delight.

"But, oh, my! you ought to hear her at the piano," was
the boast of Squash to his comrades when out fishing or
after squirrels. "She's got her piano, you know, in her
own little parlor, and you should just be there when her
hands get to flying over the keys. Sing? I should rather
think so! Mother has got so she can't live without hearing her play and sing for us of Sunday afternoons. She
doesn't cry, but mother does. We don't see how we
could have lived without her all this time!"

But beyond anything that Mrs. Thirlmore said or did
was what she herself was. As a rule, the household did
not speak so loud by half as before her coming; and
many a word dropped from their vocabulary forever, for
the simple reason that she did not use it. Squash and
Snap blushed if caught with their caps on in the house,
and the meals ceased to be merely the rapid disposal of a
sufficiency of food. Less was said in contradiction of each
other or in the way of criticism of the neighbors, and
laughter was none the less sincere that it did not make
the rafters ring as of old. Mrs. Grumbles paid more attention to her toilet, was less energetic in admonition of
her children; the bath-room came into greater use. Once
or twice the guest begged for the making of a ruffle or
a cap for the mother, of a little sack for Pop, or a frock
for Owl.

"What is coming over you people?" Mrs. Sudkins demanded at times; but she dared not say anything deroga-

tory to Mrs. Thirlmore. Mrs. Grumbles would not allow
that, as she had learned. It is wonderful what silent
power is possessed by some women; yet a drop of nitro-
glycerine is not more widely diffusive in its way than is
the merest particle of attar of roses.

And so the days, weeks, months passed by. Maggie had
been sad at first at her forced idleness; then sullen; then
so urgent, that Mrs. Grumbles was obliged to add a half
acre or so to her kitchen garden, a half dozen to her number of cows to be fed and milked; and not until the Manx
girl had a little more than she could do, her head down,
her shoulders braced as of old to a steady pull at her work,
was she content.

"I did ·think," Mrs. Grumbles almost complained,
"that I knew what it was to work; but there's an amazing deal I am learning from Maggie. She finds such a
perfect pleasure in work, for work's sake, that it does me
good to see her. She is like Hans in that."

Mrs. Thirlmore lived, for health's sake, as much as
possible out of doors. Wherever she went she could
hardly fail to come upon the broad-shouldered laborer,
feeding the stock, chopping hay or turnips, digging potatoes, ploughing, or cutting wood with a slow and steady
stroke. He knew but a few words of English, was always
cheerful of aspect; but there was a self-contained, almost
mechanical movement about the man which arrested the
attention of Mrs. Thirlmore.

"He never goes to church, with or without us. I
notice," she said to Mrs. Grumbles, "that, when the
weather permits, he takes a book on Sunday afternoons
and walks off into the woods by himself. Except that he
is so kind to the children, he is more like an automaton
than a laborer. It is as if he sought to make as much of

a mere machine of himself as he could. Has he been with
you long? "

Mrs. Grumbles, who was seated that Sunday afternoon
by the piano, at which her friend had been playing fit-
fully, and singing as the mood seized her, changed color
a little, began to speak, hesitated, attempted again, was
again silent.

" Mrs. Thirlmore," she began at last, " I promised to
say to no one a word about it ; but as there is no one
here but ourselves I will tell you. Why not? " And with
the relish peculiar to such a disclosure she told the story.
There was, it seems, a well-born and rich merchant who
had lived several years before in Upsala, a town in Sweden.

" I never knew his name ; I doubt if I ever shall," Mrs.
Grumbles said. " The way of it was this. Our minister
went to Sweden on a vacation. They did not think of
such things as that when your dear old grandfather was
alive, did they? I doubt if he ever was out of his pulpit
in his life, except to exchange with some other minister,
or when he was sick. We do things differently these days ;
and so we women of the church made up a little purse
and sent our Mr. Kellogg over the water. His throat was
threatened, you see. He happened to have a college
friend who had married on his travels a Swedish lady in
Upsala, and lived there. One day she happened to ask
Mr. Kellogg if he had ever met such a person, and then
it all came out. The rich merchant had a run of terrible
trouble. First, he lost money in the Dannemore iron mines,
which are famous for making the best steel in the world,
they say. And he did not lose money only. He was the
treasurer of the company, and Mr. Kellogg did not understand exactly how it was, but it was supposed that he had
made away with the funds. On the top of his misery his

wife died, broken-hearted, poor thing. They think worse of such things there than they do here," Mrs. Grumbles added with grave simplicity; and then she went on to detail how one child after another had died of scarlet fever. "For a time they thought the man must go to a lunatic asylum. Nothing could be proved as to the missing money; so at last he was released and disappeared.

"How strangely things happen! Our Mr. Kellogg's friend told him the story, and then said that there was one man in Upsala who knew to what part of America the miserable man had fled; and when he came to find it out, it was to this very neighborhood. Of course this made Mr. Kellogg curious to know how the broken man looked; and sure as you live," the good lady added, with intense enjoyment, "it was our Hans! Mr. Kellogg made us promise not to tell anybody. Hans has no idea that we know. Our minister, Mr. Grumbles and myself, and now you, are the only people in America that have heard anything about it. Strange, is n't it?" and she went on to say how silent the refugee was, how grave and quiet. Since his coming, he had worked as steadily as he was doing now.

"And Mr. Kellogg says," Mrs. Grumbles added, "that he was a member of their Congress, a kind of nobleman, and ever so rich, and no man more respected. What I think is, that he has taken up his life for good as a laborer with us. He tries to bend himself down to it, as if he was a kind of threshing machine. Whenever there is anything to throw him out, he has a way of saying," and she repeated the words with painful accuracy, "'Debt can ikky war langy new.' Odd, is n't it, ma'am? The children think it is a kind of swearing. Do you think so? I don't."

It was the merest accident in the chain of accidents, but Mrs. Thirlmore happened to have picked up enough of the

cognate tongues to make it out. "You are right," she said.
"What he says is about the same in Danish and Swedish.
It is ' *Det kan ikke vare lange nu,*' and it means, ' It is
but a short time now, it cannot be long ; ' that is, he hopes
that some day soon his reputation will be cleared up, and
that he will be able to go back again to Sweden."

"Do you think so? No, ma'am ; no," she said at
last, reflectively. "I don't believe it is that. Taking his
way of saying it, and the kind of man he seems to be and
all, what I think he means is that it can't be long that he
has to live in this world ; anyhow, it won't be many years
before he will go where he will be with his wife and children once more, and where people will know he is innocent.
For he *is* an innocent man, ma'am ! I know that as well
as I know my own name. Don't I know an honest man
when I see him? Yes,"—and she clasped her large hands
in her lap, the tears began to gather in her eyes, — "that
is what he means ; it won't be long ; only a little while,
and then—heaven ! "

It was some moments before Dame Grumbles spoke
again. "I dare say," she remarked, "that there are city
people who notice our ugly old house in riding by, and say
' What a stupid place that is, and what dull, old-fashioned
folks live there ; what can they find to think about?'
Sometimes it reminds me of what I have heard of the
rocky, desolate, out-of-the-way regions where nobody would
live if he could help it ; and yet when they bore down with
their Artesian wells the oil comes spouting up, so rich and
plentiful. Look at Hans ; and I suppose if you go anywhere, where people seem to be the most uninteresting, if
you could only get deep down under things, into the history and hearts of the poorest and meanest, you would
find that there are, as if it were, lakes and oceans of what

is more valuable and interesting than oil, or gold and silver. It is n't dull, if we can but get under the surface. Don't you think so, ma'am?"

Her companion was thinking of Hans, and could only assent. Mrs. Grumbles' interpretation of what the Swede said seemed to her an absurd idea; but, cautiously so as not to be observed, she looked at Hans thenceforward whenever she saw him at work. With his slow, set way of laboring, there was also something set in his aspect, — set, resolute, but by no means sullen; almost cheerful. One Sunday afternoon, in strolling through the woods, she saw him seated, book in hand, upon a rock, his back against a towering spruce. He was looking fixedly toward the west, and his solid face was aglow with the splendors of the setting sun. She had but a rapid glance as she stole by unperceived, but she fancied there was in the worn countenance of the man a peace and solemn gladness; and as she passed she heard the words, in a low and reverent tone, —

"*Det kan ikke vare lange nu!*"

CHAPTER XIII.

TORN IN TWO.

"HAVE I made it clear to you, my dear?"

"Clear? Oh, yes; it is as clear as clear can be. Clear as the sun, moon, and all the stars. But you cannot change me; I must stand up for my own side."

Dr. Doubleday looked at his daughter and sighed. "I was so proud," he said, "of your intelligence. We know, Myrtle, that you are the beauty and the belle of the Blue Grass,—so they say."

She really was very beautiful, of an Oriental kind of beauty. Her features were regular, her eyes of a dewy largeness and languor, which matched perfectly with the roseleaf lips, the fulness of every curve, the slow sweetness of her voice. There was but the faintest hint of red in her cheeks; but the creamy pallor, especially if she was excited, which happened pretty often these days, reminded one of the fact that what is crimson comes with increasing heat to be white. There was an audacity also about Miss Myrtle which, at its worst, never broke the bounds of that wholly indescribable grace which belongs to but two classes, — women like her and babies of six months old.

"You are your mother over again, my child." The care-worn father could not help looking proudly upon a daughter whom he knew to be, if only he would acknowledge it, ten times the beauty that her mother had been. "I had hoped," he added with a sigh, — sighing was coming to be as natural to him in these woful days as breathing, — " you would grow to be like me, in striking under the surface and reaching to the fundamental facts. From the first of this miserable struggle between North and South I have done my best to put things clearly before you. How often have I told you, Myrtle," and he counted off his points with the long forefinger of his right hand upon the digits of his left, " that the tide of history has run so far with ever-increasing volume against slavery — and how can you suppose it will be halted and turned back because the South chances to be OUR South? — that a successful separation between North and South would necessitate near four thousand miles of frontier between the two, and that this would make a standing army indispensable upon both sides ; and," his forefinger resting upon the tip of the third finger of the other hand, " that there could be nothing but war."

" That the adoption of secession as a radical right," his pretty daughter replied, telling the argument off upon the rosy tips of her fingers, "must result in the perpetual practice of it among the Southern States ; that the success of the Confederacy would end in a Babel of wrangling States like Mexico, to the arrest of everything like civilization and religion ; and so on, and so on. Yes, you 've been over and over it all, till I know it better than twice two are four. All the same I am, always must be, a true-hearted Southern girl. And you? With all your twisting this way and that, you are a rebel too, and you know it ; " and she seated herself at her piano, and dashed into " Maryland, my Maryland," with a will.

Dr. Doubleday was sadly put out. He was as tall and thin almost as an aspen tree, and its leaves are scarcely in more continual tremor than was he in these perilous times. "Two things are my nature," he often said to his daughter.

" I am thoroughly informed, intensely convinced and satisfied as to the wrong of secession ; and my conscience, as you say, is the severest of masters. I am very unhappy, my child."

Everybody knew that. He was the best educated man in the Southern State in which he lived. All denominations agreed to the fact of his being the ablest preacher therein ; and not in the rhetorical or flowery sense only. His forte lay in a depth and lucid vigor of statement which compelled even uncultivated men to listen. He was by no means a brave man. " If I were not from South Carolina I should be mobbed. As it is I can hardly hold my church together. Was ever man so situated ? " he would say to his daughter as he paced up and down his study. He often walked his chamber all night long, and yet would be first of the family down to breakfast in the morning, in order to read the paper ; yet when it came he was feverishly unwilling to see what was the latest news.

" Why is it he is so haggard ? " her friends often asked Miss Myrtle. " He paces up and down the sidewalk like a ghost." They would have liked to add, " Does n't it give you the shivers, dear, to hear him pray on Sundays ? "

" As you well know," he often told his daughter, " I am silently scowled at by the Union men in town as at heart a Secessionist ; while the boys yell ' Yankee ' and ' Abolitionist ' after me as I walk the streets. Some of my parishioners, one or two of the church officers even, have left my church forever ; and the richest refuse to come even to prayer-meeting, because I won't pray for the President of the Confederacy. One side say, ' Why don't you come out flatfooted for the Union ? ' the other side say, ' Be true to your section, or go North where you belong.' "

The common opinion, although the Doctor did not quote it, was that he was trying, as the phrase runs, to carry water upon both shoulders. It was not that he was torn as between the wild horses of the conflicting factions; his agony arose from the fact that while intellect and conscience dragged him Northward, every sympathy of his soul pulled him Southward. It was this inward bleeding to death which was killing the man.

"Blondin took but an occasional trip," he bemoaned himself, "over Niagara; under me Niagara never ceases to roar. It is worst when I rise on Sundays to pray!" Assuredly it was, so eagerly was he listened to by both parties present. Time and again he was assured as he went to church that he would be certainly arrested, possibly shot, if he prayed or if he failed to pray for or against the Southern cause, according to the leanings of his informant; but it was the deadly division of the poor preacher within himself, and against himself, which caused him to enter upon every service with a careful balancing of petitions which would have been comic were it not so tragic.

"And these are the supplications," he groaned, "wherewith I must mock thee, O Thou heart-searching God!"

He wiped the moisture from his brow at the thought of it. The days of fasting and prayer for the Confederacy, the days set apart for the thanksgiving for the victory of Bull's Run, and the like, were a terrible strain upon him. The vestry of the church was crowded week after week with ladies sewing for the army. "Anyhow *you* are true to the South," was his frequent remark to his energetic daughter. But it took all the grace, beauty, and audacity of the spoiled belle to keep matters straight for her father, vibrating as he did between expediency

and deepening detestation of secession. An unhappier
man did not exist than Dr. Doubleday.

"Yet I should be ten times more miserable," he often
thought, "if Myrtle had not succeeded in preventing me
from flying to the North, as I once determined to do.
Oh, that I were blind, or that I could sear my conscience
and go in with the rest. Heaven knows, I try to look at
things as my people do. Knowing what I know, conscientious as I must be, I cannot — cannot!"

The sorely beset pastor had an opportunity of trying
the experiment of a change of situation, for now there
was a sudden move upon the board.

The little Southern city in which Dr. Doubleday lived,
was near the border line between North and South. It
was and is one of the most charming towns of its class,
and is too well known by every one to be further designated. Most unexpectedly a brigade of Federal troops
under General J. Mandeville Gilmore was thrown into it
one Monday afternoon. It so happened that there was
no immediate danger of an assault by the Confederate
forces, and before the following Sunday Mrs. Gilmore
and her daughter had arrived from the North and established themselves at the hotel, which, for the present,
was taken possession of by the General and his staff as
headquarters.

"If we could have imagined such a thing!" Mrs.
Gilmore exclaimed with horror, during the first week of
their coming.

"Do you think we had a right to expect anything
else?" the more sensible Moxy demanded.

Had they been lepers, they could not have been more
isolated from all society. It was very plain that there
was not a soul in the place who proposed even to recog-

nize their existence, except, indeed, with scorn and contempt, unless in the case of a Northern shopkeeper or so.
Not a bookseller or milliner, not a confectioner or hair-
dresser, but declined their custom, and without thanks.
The colored people of the town, rejoiced as they were at
the approach of freedom, caught the profound aversion
and hostility, " and actually treat us," Moxy said, " with a
sort of condescending patronage ! But," she always added,
" if *I* were a Southerner, I should do the same ; for we
are an invading army, nobody can deny that. But to carry
on so at church is simply dreadful ! "

By reason of his ability, as well as popularity, in the
day before the war, Dr. Doubleday's church was the
largest, handsomest, and best attended in the city. Many
of the men connected with it were now away, — a few in
the Federal, but most of them in the Confederate, army.
A handful of families had left the church because the
pastor did not pray from the outset as definitely as he
should have done for the Union ; a much larger number
of families had withdrawn because he did not pray as
unhesitatingly and as vigorously as he ought for the Confederate cause. Thus it was that many pews were unoc-
cupied ; barely enough members, in fact, were held to
the church by life-long attachment to it, or to its pastor,
to keep up a show of worship.

For these a horror was in store upon the first Sabbath
after the arrival of the Brigade. By the connivance, it is
to be feared, of the undecided and unhappy minister,
and before any one could intervene and prevent, General
Gilmore had taken a whole block of pews upon the left
of the pulpit. The large and handsome building was
not half filled the first Sunday after the Federal occupation, when to the dismay of most of those present, the

abhorred General came walking up the aisle with Mrs.
Gilmore and Moxy, followed by his staff.   A shudder ran
through the congregation.   Some got up and left the house,
and not as silently as they might.   The choir, suddenly
shorn of its proportions, broke down.   Myrtle would have
fled first of all, but for her father.   She was a good Secessionist, but she was a better daughter.   She saw the deadly
whiteness of his face as he supported himself in the pulpit by a hand clutching either side of the Bible, and her
voice grew full and strong.   She had always been the soul
of the choir, as she was the pride and pet of the church;
but now she excelled herself.   Her tears, her soul, had
entered her song; and with each hymn and chant she so
more than made up for the flight of the deserters as to
bring unwonted strength to her father.   Colonel Thirlmore
was among the Federal officers present, and he looked
up now with interest at the brave girl, never more beautiful than then, as she stood almost alone in the choir.   He
had once upon a time enjoyed somewhat more than
enough of church music; but the bearing, the exultant
voice of Myrtle thrilled him as he had not been thrilled
for a long time.

   "Oh, is n't she a beauty?" Moxy exclaimed afterward.
She could not speak of Myrtle thereafter without enthusiasm.

   "You never saw so perfect a beauty in your life
before," she often insisted to Lieutenant Van Doren, as
she saw more of the pastor's daughter.   "She acts as I
should if I were in her place.   *I* would n't have anything
to do with you Yankees!   I should be madder at them
than she is, — at least I would show it more!   How I
wish we could be friendly!" the tears coming into her
eyes as she said it.

"But was n't it funny?" the girl rattled on as they walked home from church. "How they scowled at us, — the women most of all! Did you see them draw in their skirts so as not to touch us as we went out? There was such a nice lady not far from us. When Dr. Doubleday was praying, she was leaning her head on the back of the pew before her. The instant she opened her eyes at the 'amen,' she caught me looking at her, and made *such* a face! as if she had taken a dose of oil or a pill. Still if I had been in her place I should have done the same, and boxed the ears of the first Yankee I could reach. How they must loathe and hate papa! *I* should!"

Southern or Northern, they had cause to wonder and to laugh. General J. Mandeville Gilmore, clad in his finest uniform, filling the most conspicuous seat in the edifice; conscious of being the conquering Cyrus of the small Babylon about him; fully satisfied that he was the hero of the war thus far, and was to be, in the swiftly nearing end, the Washington of final peace and reconstruction, — General Gilmore simply expressed these opinions in every line of his face, in every movement of his portly person. This is no exaggeration to those who knew the man; and who has not, at least, heard of him and his enormous vanity? The reader will accept it as rather an under-drawn portrait.

His very perfection made the poignant distress of his little wife at his side, as she glanced proudly about her with her small and eager eyes, her tremulous mouth. "Here are so many of the nicest looking people," she thought. "As long as they live, they will tell of how they first saw General Gilmore to-day. If I could but have a chance to talk to them about the General, they could n't help admiring him to save their lives; now they only fear and tremble before him. No wonder."

That first Sunday after the Federal occupation was a dreadful day for the pastor, forced to oscillate with sickening vibration between South and North. As he began his supplications for the country, every ear, Confederate and Federal, was attentive. With his audience and himself, it was as when the rope-walker essays to make his perilous trip over the Falls roaring beneath. The congregation held its breath as the pastor put forth, so to speak, first one cautious foot upon the invisible rope, and then another. It was no prayer; rather was it an exercise of verbal diplomacy, a desperate effort to beg in the same breath for a blessing upon things wholly opposite. But it was not because he was afraid of any man; it was a hopeless attempt to satisfy his judgment, and at the same time his yearning heart.

"If it were not that I was so angry with the hateful Yankees," Myrtle said to him after service, "I could have laughed. You were dreadfully put to it, you poor, poor papa!"

He was. A sudden sympathy had sprung up in him for the expelled Confederates; and yet his soul rejoiced in the advance of what he thoroughly believed to be the cause of civilization and of God; and only God knew the pain of heart, the strain of intellect in their conflict for the mastership. Although he made the sermon as brief as was possible, the pastor sank down exhausted at the amen.

"And what possessed you," Myrtle demanded as angrily as she could, "to stop behind and speak to those be-sashed and be-starred ruffians? I would have died first."

"I spoke only to Colonel Thirlmore," her father hastened to explain; "and it was he who insisted upon introducing me to his superior officer, General Gilmore. Colonel Thirlmore and I were classmates together at Old Orange. We were years together in the seminary there afterward."

"He can't be the Thirlmore," his daughter replied, "about whom you have told me so much?"

"The sensational preacher at the north? Yes, he is the man." And it was impossible Miss Myrtle should not be interested, as her father proceeded to tell her of the size and grandeur of the church of which his friend had been pastor, — for he had preached for him on a summer vacation there; of the crowded audience, the eloquence of its pastor, the salary he received, the collapse of the church, the retirement of Thirlmore. "It is natural he should go into the army," he added, "for he is a powerful fellow every way, — one of those men, pretend as he may to despise it, to whom popularity of some sort is a necessity. For him to be out of the eye and applause of people, is to die."

"I saw him," Miss Myrtle said, — "a large man in the side pews; a pompous old soul, in his buttons and shoulder stars; a conceited wretch, you can see that at a glance."

"No, no! That is General J. Mandeville Gilmore, of whom we have heard so much too. So far as I know, he is celebrated more for his vanity than anything else. No, you must have seen Thirlmore. He was on the other side of the church. A younger man, taller, finer-looking — "

"Oh, yes; I saw *him*," Miss Myrtle said. "The finest-looking man there; dark, stern. Every one of us in the choir fell in love with him, or would have done so if he had n't been a Yankee. So that is, or rather was, that great preacher? Are you going to ask him to preach, papa?"

"Hardly," her father smiled at the thought. "He never was my idea of what a preacher should be. I am too old-fashioned for that. He never should have been anything else than a soldier, a raiser of fine stock, a railway president, the head of a great telegraph company, or the like. You can see what a strong man he is; he will make a name in the war yet. Now, my child," deprecatingly, "it seems to me the wisest thing we can do, seeing he was a classmate of mine, too, — " Dr. Double-day looked so much as he did in the pulpit when entering upon the debatable prayer, that the lively girl laughed aloud. "You want to have him dine with us?" she said.

"More than that. There may be great disorder here; it will be safest. Our friends will not misconstrue it, I hope, but the most sensible thing we can do is to have him make his home with us. Don't you see — "

She did not see. She was upon her feet in a moment. Her eyes sparkled, the pallor of her cheek deepened, she flew into a rage.

"Never!" she said, "never, never! Let such a man touch my hand? Speak to such a man — a cruel slave of old Lincoln?" and a great deal more to the same effect.

She was most beautiful when at her angriest. Not an atom did she have of her father's hesitation as to the merits and demerits of the war. She was Southern as a magnolia or a mocking-bird is Southern; she would have been just as jealous for the North had she lived there; but she could not have been as lovely, — not, at least, with her peculiar type of loveliness. Her father let her talk.

When she had ceased to express her views concerning the invading horde, very little was left to be said. What had her torrent of scolding to do with the merits of the matter? As little as the odors of the magnolia, the warbling of the mocking-bird. The patient Doctor listened to it all with head drooped upon his bosom. She was merely a rose shaken by a passing gust. He recalled from his reading of the classics how Venus raved before smiling and indulgent Jupiter against the Greeks, and in behalf of windy Troy. He laughed — it was so natural in a woman — when she demanded as the climax of her vituperation, "Is he a married man?"

"Not that I know of. In fact, now I think of it, he never spoke of a wife to me when I preached for him. No, my dear, I am sure of it now; he is not married. Why do you ask?"

But Miss Myrtle had left the room. She was unusually sweet at the breakfast table next morning.

"I have been thinking over what you said," she remarked as he was rising from the table, "and I can explain matters when our troops come back and drive them out. Yes, father dear, there may be dreadful disorders; the negroes have become so insolent all of a sudden too. Perhaps it *will* be best to have your classmate stay with us. We have plenty of room, you know. You can ask him to-day if you like." She smiled so charmingly that the Doctor looked at her suspiciously.

"You have some plan of your own, Myrtle. Take care, my child, take care!"

His daughter looked up at him with the wide eyes of a little child. "Plan?" she asked, "oh, yes, I have a plan. It is to make him ashamed of himself, and go back where he came from. Better than that, — I shall try to get him

to resign and go into our ranks. Yes, I have a plan.
Ask him to come, papa; ask him to-day ! "

She was so urgent that her father could not understand
her. Why should she consent, so suddenly and un-
accountably, to having one of the hated Federals under
his roof? The distracted pastor had his ideas; but what
could she mean by so promptly waiving her objections?

"Take care, my child, what you do," he repeated;
"you may be playing with edged tools. What will Captain
Warden say? Take care ! "

CHAPTER XIV.

BROTHER AGAINST BROTHER.

BETWEEN the plans of Myrtle, whatever they were, and the desire of her father to have his classmate with him, — a classmate from the wider world outside of the South, with whom he could converse freely, — Colonel Thirlmore soon found himself a guest of the Rev. Dr. Doubleday. It was easily arranged. General Gilmore appointed him Provost Marshal, and his regiment as Provost Guard was detailed on police duty in the captured town. The good pastor long before had made a name for himself as erratic and odd, and he could hardly be more unpopular than he was already. It was a great change from the camp to the comfortable mansion which had been the home of Myrtle's dead mother, who had brought a fortune to her husband. The lawns about the house, the ample verandas, the well-trained servants, the excellent table, made the Colonel the envy of the Federal army for his pleasant quarters ; while there was hardly a soldier who did not go, sooner or later, to church to see " the parson's daughter," of whose beauty so much was said.

But even to be in the same house with her had its drawbacks. The tall, anxious-visaged host could not be still for an instant. He was unwilling to talk upon any other subject than the war, and what had brought it on. Walking up and down the veranda, his hands clasped behind him, his head drooped upon his bosom, he was glad to have some one besides Myrtle with whom he could talk, and go over and over again the old, old story to assure himself that he could not have come to any other conclusion than that the Southern movement, whatever the provocation, "was wrong, sir; radically, ruinously wrong!" He went over it all point by point, as illustrated by Scripture, history, ethics, political economy, the intuitions of the soul. From long and thorough study of the question his reasons were so lucid, his statements so clear and concise, his convictions so deep, that his guest could not avoid being greatly interested. Thirlmore had scarcely thought upon the subject; he had gone into the army because it seemed the last thing left him to do, and he was pleased to discover that, however unconsciously, he had put himself in line "with that vanguard of civilization which," his host said, "had come down from creation under the great Captain, conquering and to conquer."

Upon the whole, the Colonel was glad that he had enlisted. He liked to live in the open air; liked to be among horses by the thousand; liked to give stern orders and have them obeyed. He had been in more than one engagement. The heat of fight was what he greatly enjoyed: the hard work involved, the long and often forced marches, the rapid bridging of streams or tearing up of railroads, insured that strain upon the muscle, upon the faculty of decision, instant and irreversible, which was making him, as it made so many millions more, North and South, ten times manlier men than before. "We've got to get even with those fellows," that was his program for the future. For General Gilmore had been sadly outgeneralled, — in fact, badly beaten in one or two small skirmishes. That he had now made an advance was rather because of a falling back on the part of the enemy, than by reason of any special energy upon the part of the Union commander.

"We have made splendid progress," was the unceasing boast of the General in proclamation and in private, and his explanations of what seemed disastrous were beautiful to hear. Moreover, they were to thrash the enemy gloriously next time. But the unanimous opinion of all except the General and his wife was that there were no intrenchments so impregnable as the self-esteem behind which he lay serenely secure.

"It reminds me," Mrs. Thirlmore wrote to her husband, "of the result when Julian the apostate rebuilt the Temple of the Gods at Delphi and proclaimed to perishing heathenism an opportunity of sacrifice. You remember that the great day arrived : the Emperor and his chief officers stood by the altar in gorgeous attire ; the trumpets rang out ; and the one worshipper appeared in the person of an old, old rustic, who laid an equally aged goose upon the sacrificial fires ! General Gilmore's one adorer is somewhat like that, is she not?"

And so it came to pass that every day Colonel Thirlmore, after such a dinner as is eaten only in the Blue Grass region, had nothing to do but to listen. Dr. Doubleday held to his horror of a beard in the pulpit. Every morning he shaved himself as clean as a babe, and there was no strip of hair beneath which the play of his face could hide itself. It was the face of an over-wrought scholar. The brow was noble ; but the hollowed temples upon either side, and the long, lean, lank countenance, were plowed deeply with anxiety.

"Suppose," he argued with his guest, "that cotton, sugar, and, in consequence, slave labor had paid as well in the North as it does in the South, would you not have continued to employ it? Yes, sir. But then, on the other side, what madness, what execrable weakness, for

my section to march to battle under the devil's own
standard of slavery ! "

Never was man so distracted by contending forces within himself as this man.   Now that the Confederacy was
driven back, it had so much the greater length of leverage
upon his oscillating soul ; his sympathies were aroused as
never before.   And yet, great heavens ! could anything in
logic or mathematics be more clear than was the wholly
unanswerable argument for the Federal cause?

Had it not been for the charming daughter of the house,
Colonel Thirlmore could not have borne the wear of daily
intercourse with the nervous and distracted man.   Unable
to keep his seat for more than a moment ; hurrying up and
down the parlor, as along the streets ; button-holing now this
Secessionist and now that Union man ; questioning, arguing
for and against, conjecturing, assenting, denying, twisting
whatever news arrived this way and that, — it was plain to
all that Dr. Doubleday's fermenting soul must find rest
soon, or land in the lunatic asylum.

Meanwhile it by no means bettered the standing of
Moxy Gilmore that, aided and abetted by Lieutenant Van
Doren, she undertook to teach in a Sunday-school, which
the chaplain of the army, instigated thereto by the Lieutenant, had established in an old hall down town.   A
frightful rumor ran the rounds that colored children were
included, and the young girl walked in an atmosphere
the scorn of which, like the Egyptian darkness, could be
felt.

"It is little that I care for religious things," she remarked ; "but I had nothing in the world to do, and
the Lieutenant begged hard that I would help him ! As I
always say, I should do as these people do if I were one
of them ; worse, perhaps ; but, being what I am, I love

to horrify them ! I passed Myrtle Doubleday on the street yesterday. O, *how* scornful she looked ; but *how* I should like to know her ! She is the sweetest thing. I am sure she would come to like me. Is n't it *too* bad ? "

In the case of these two young girls, the air of the town during this existing lull of events became telephonic. Whatever Moxy said was sure to get to Myrtle ; and Myrtle's remarks found speedy goal in the ears of Moxy. They were, in fact, the belles, the queens of the rival parties ; and the war waxed fast and furious.

" Horrid thing ! " Myrtle exclaimed. " She must think that smartness can take the place of beauty. What sharp eyes ! What sarcastic lips ! They say she is to marry that dapper commissary of hers. I can understand how people can fear sùch a girl ; but love? How any man can *love* her, I can't understand. Poor thing ! "

" It is the funniest courtship I ever heard of," Moxy said, as if to the winds. " That little red-headed Mr. Warden is a perfect slave to her, they tell me. Whatever she orders him to do he does without a murmur. He is as strong as a man can be, I am told ; yet she used to insist upon it that he was a consumptive. She made him wear chest-protectors, drink cod-liver oil, go about in arctics ; and he practised a delicate cough, until one day she informed him that she detested invalids, whereupon he got well again in an hour. He was a planter when he first addressed her. To please her he gave up his plantations, moved into town, and took to selling goods. Then nothing would do but he must be a lawyer. He had hardly opened an office before she vowed that she would never marry him unless he became a minister. Would you believe it? That poor fellow — so at least I am told — was about studying under her father for the

ministry when the war broke out. Then nothing would do
but he must go into the army! What a coquette she is!
The poor fellow had a beard once, and off it must go.
Then she abominated red hair, and, if friends had not
rushed in, he would have dyed it — pea-green, I suppose,
if he thought she would prefer it. He has exhausted himself in trying to please her. She manages him like a big
doll, and makes him change his coats and neckties, at
least, twenty times a month.

"But is n't she a darling?" Moxy always ended.
"She's as sweet as sweet can be. I know I'm not
pretty; but I'm very smart, and what fun we could have
if we but knew each other. Let the horrid men fight.
Why should we girls quarrel? It's a shame and a sin!"
And Moxy cried over it in private like a child.

Myrtle graciously consented, when Colonel Thirlmore
asked to be allowed to bring Captain Grumbles to dinner
one day. The rustic officer was homesick almost to
death, and his friend at last took pity on him. An hour
or two under Dr. Doubleday's hospitable roof would do
him good, if only that it gave him opportunity to talk to
a new audience about Aurora Ann and the family at
Scrubstones.

"He is such a common creature! Our planters are not
like your farmers," Myrtle said to Colonel Thirlmore, on
the other side of the room; "they are gentlemen. I
do not see," with a winning smile, "how a person like you
can endure him!"

"Thank you."

The two had progressed, it will be perceived. The
Colonel said things to her that he had not cared to say to
any lady before; and how was it possible for a girl like
Myrtle not to be pleased with the evident admiration of a

man like this, Federal officer though he might be? Captain Warden was away in the Confederate army. Myrtle liked *him* as much as such a woman can like a lover who makes himself an abject slave to her every whim. This splendid-looking man picked up her handkerchief if he happened to see it fall, but did not put himself out of the way to do it.

"And I have known the other almost too long, too well," thought Myrtle. "Why does he persist in having red hair? And *he* has never been out of his State, much less to Europe. They say he was such an eloquent preacher, too;" but this "he" did not refer to the Confederate lover.

Captain Grumbles, on the opposite side of the room, had just risen from such a dinner as he had not eaten "since I left Scrubstones," as he boasted thereafter to his envying comrades. Now Dr. Doubleday found in him the best of listeners. It showed how deadly a hold the moral aspects of the war had taken upon the poor man, that he, a Southerner, should be willing to talk as he did to a Unionist. But he felt in an instant that the farmer and himself were fellow-citizens of a larger land than North and South combined.

"How can the Christ side with slavery, — side with the breaking up of this Republic, dedicated to Him from the outset as it has been? The Christ! No, sir. I abominate Abolitionism," the Doctor hastened to say. "I am with Henry Clay. Now, and in the awful light of battle, I see things as I did not before. But who knows," the good Doctor was riding his hobby as if it were a blooded racer, "what Christ may do? He may let Secession succeed, in view of some sweeping reaction to come after. The millenarians may be right. He may permit our Republic, the last hope of the race, the highest achievement of human wisdom, — Christ may allow our Babylon to come down with a crash ; and why? That in the hour of its downfall, when all earth has sunk into despair in the failure of its supremest effect, that then He may come "— the worn face was radiant at the thought — "may come to show man that He only is the Saviour of the world ! 'Thou art terrible in Thy doings toward the children of men ! Even so, come, Lord Jesus, come quickly !' "

Captain Grumbles began to understand how his host had won such a reputation for piety and eloquence, — a reputation so great that he could continue pastor in a Southern city and yet hold the obnoxious views he did as to the war.

In the comparative quiet which ensued in their conversation that day, Colonel Thirlmore called attention, by a smiling lifting of his hand, to what Captain Grumbles was saying ; and Myrtle heard a great deal as to Aurora Ann, Pop, Snap, Squash, Owl, and the farm. Nor did the warmhearted farmer fail of an attentive listener in the good Doctor, as he told him of orchard and field ; of Hans, his farm hand from Sweden — not even Wretch, the turnspit, was left out of the narrative.

Then the conversation took its inevitable turn back again to the one weary topic.

"Yes, ours is," the pastor assented, " in point of personal feeling, the fiercest of all civil wars. Take the English Wars of the Roses. It was only a strife after all, as to whether Lancaster or York should rule. What personal hatred to each other could the ignorant masses on either side have had? As little, almost, as the horses dashing upon each other in battle. It was far worse when Cavalier met Roundhead, a century or so later ; every man upon either side was lifted, in the advance of things, toward our days. There was a yet fiercer, because more personal, feeling in the strife of French democrat against French aristocrat in the time of Robespierre and afterward. Now, I suppose no man," Dr. Doubleday sighed, "can understand this better than I. My whole heart is with my own people ; yet there is not a Sherman or a Lincoln of you all who is more convinced than myself of the cruel wrong and madness of secession. The bitterness of the strife is in my own bosom, and never was there such bitterness before. It so happens that Cain and Abel come face to face at the altar in my church every Sunday. It is a religious strife, mind you. One party say that slavery is of God ; the other, that slavery is of the Devil. There is hardly a man or woman in church who has not lost father or brother, husband or son, on one side or the other. Their relatives are firing upon each other, bayoneting each other somewhere, while we are at worship ! How they scowl upon each other, Unionist and Secessionist, with but an aisle or the plank of a pew between them ! How long, O Lord, how long !" moaned the miserable clergyman. "If I could postpone the communion service — "

But he could not. And thus it came to pass that on the next Sabbath afternoon there were more in attendance upon the quarterly communion service than the pastor had hoped or desired to see. The general feeling upon both sides was, "Am I to stay away on *their* account ? "

"At this very moment," the pastor said to himself, as he rose to lead the services, "these communicants face each other precisely as they would do in battle. Let divine love assert itself here and now — if it can ! "

In reading the hymns and Scriptures peculiar to the

sacrament, he did what he could to aid them in melting down the embattled souls confronting each other. Still, except on the part of a few, the grim aspect of war remained unbroken.

"Surely these devout women," thought the Doctor, "will yield to things so sacred. But, alas!" His eye as it glanced around fell upon this woman and that; could they forget how and why they were clad in crape? "And *her* son, her only son," he said to himself, "is with Bragg; her brother with Kirby Smith. The husband of this poor woman is in a Northern prison. The two boys of that widow lie in a hospital, both badly wounded. You weep," he thought of yet another, "because your youngest boy, once so promising, is at your house an imbecile and a cripple for life ; and *your* son, you poor soul, is made a drunkard and a licentious ruffian by the same accursed cause."

At a certain point of the service a few persons stood up to be received into the church. "How dare you promise such things?" he was questioning inwardly, as he read off the solemn stipulations by which each bound himself. "How *can* you unite yourselves with a body of men and women where no religion is? Oh, my God, what a mockery!"

In the light of war, — war infuriating the souls on one side or the other of all there, the whole service sounded false and hollow. In prayer the minister stood on the platform near the pulpit, the communion table before him. Under the white cloth, as under a shroud, lay what to every heart was God in flesh, slain for men. "Oh, Divine Love!" the voice of the unhappy pastor wailed in its anguish, "how can we pretend by taking, eating, drinking to understand, appreciate, assimilate such food as this,

when even the individual himself is torn, himself against
himself — "

It was not long after this that the heart of the pastor
sank, in the act of giving the bread for distribution to an
officer of the church, — sank lower yet. He understood
the set face of the old Deacon. Had he not learned,
scarcely a week before, that his youngest boy, his Ben-
jamin, had been killed under alleged circumstances of
peculiar cruelty by Union bushwhackers?

"Dear brother," he whispered, as he handed the plate
to him, "as ye forgive men their trespasses!"

But the horror was too recent. With cold, hard face,
the Deacon passed by General Gilmore, his family, Lieutenant Van Doren, Colonel Thirlmore, and one or two
others. It may not have been wise in the pastor, but it
was on his special assurance and invitation that these had
taken their seats among the communicants. As the Deacon passed by as if their seats were vacant, the pastor
quietly, silently followed him with a salver taken from the
table. Colonel Thirlmore glanced up, — the worn face of
him who served was running with tears.

"Take," he said. "Eat. This is My Body broken for
you." Even General Gilmore, seated near by, his hand
before his eyes, ceased to be aware of himself, in the
glory of that transcendent love before which all distinctions,
except of sin and holiness, vanish as though they were
not. Myrtle caught the sound of Moxy's weeping across
the aisle; and as she broke into louder weeping, the soul
of the other girl gave way within her, and in their mutual
sobbing they two were one.

Yet still, when they passed each other a day or so after,
Myrtle steeled her heart to the wistful eyes of Moxy.
She omitted the scorn from her face, and did not gather

away her skirts from contact with the other; she was unaware of her existence, that was all.

"I am so sorry," Moxy said afterward. "I am not a professor, and she is. I am not a bit better than one of the wicked; but she is so lovely. I wish I could know her."

Myrtle had a sharp reply ready upon her lips when the words of Moxy were repeated to her. When she heard them she gave a little gasp, and had nothing to add. Dicey, her mulatto maid, found her weeping in her room that day. Who can tell that it was not by reason of that?

It was a very injudicious thing for Dr. Doubleday to do, but immediately after the communion service, and while still under its influence, he urged those who had partaken of it from among the Federals to call and see him again. Perhaps he regretted the invitation, when Captain Grumbles and Lieutenant Van Doren dropped in one rainy afternoon. As was natural, no allusion was made to the services, and the pastor, as they talked, came to be quite interested in his new friend; he had been told of the Plymouth-Brother portion of the Lieutenant's history, and had a hundred questions to ask him, for the South never had been the home of religious aberration.

"Oh, yes," the ex-fanatic said in the end, "I was once as long-haired, lank-faced a crank as you would care to see. I don't look like it now, do I?" He did not. His figure looked so trim in his neat uniform; he was so close-cropped of hair, so definite of mustache, so clean and ruddy of skin, that the good Doctor laughed.

"I was a sort of Lazarus," the other went on, "that is, I was sick of life, and dead to it."

"I understand you belonged to the school of Madame Guyon and Fénelon," said the Doctor. "Lazarus, did you say?"

"The buried one. When I did come back to the world," laughed the other, "I did it like a ghost. What good did it do? I went about with a corpse-like face, wrapped as if in a shroud, warning men of this and of that in a hollow voice. All I accomplished was to give healthy men the horror of me and of my kind which they very naturally would have of a ghost. Now I happen to know," with a face suddenly reverential, "who it was called me out of my self-made grave, and what He did it for. When a man gets among angels, Doctor, he will have all eternity in which to do as angels do. Till then, I prefer trying to be a man among men, like — we know whom."

Heaven, however, had used means in his case; the most successful of which, as has been said, was Moxy Gilmore. She had been the tonic which had banished his pallor, his sanctimonious tones, his general flabbiness. The shears which had shorn him of his long and lank hair had been, really, her sharp and sarcastic speeches; for at times satire is better than sermons, and ridicule than admonition. Perhaps the Lieutenant was a trifle too peremptory in business, too telegrammic in ordinary intercourse. But, then, everybody acknowledged that he was the busiest man on General Gilmore's staff, the pompous old soul taking credit to himself for things in which he was but the figure-head. We always recognize intention; Lieutenant Van Doren's intentions were as unmixed and direct as the rays of the sun; and this small, alert man, light and cheery of manner, was every day accepted to a greater degree, and next to Colonel Thirlmore he was the most popular, as he was the most efficient, officer of the brigade.

"But I am not proposing to make an idol of him,"

Moxy often laughed; "he does not stand still long enough. Besides, one idol in a household is enough!"

"My conversion finds its climax in evolution," Lieutenant Van Doren said, at the close of his visit, as he shook cordial hands with Dr. Doubleday in parting.

"Evolution? From an ape?" The Doctor, who was very old-fashioned, was alarmed.

"Take Thirlmore as an instance of what is true of every man," the other persisted. "Begin with him as a country lout, selfish to the last degree. Well, he had his development as a popular preacher, evolved by success, evolved yet more by failure. Then his wilderness of a farm, on which to meditate a bit. Then the war. Not an event befalls him, not a person touches him, but is an agent of Heaven toward the same result. We are told of the evolution of the fire-mist into a well-ordered universe; of every rock, plant, animal, driven to develop and intensify itself through all ages into something nobler. Surely all this is but a parable, a secondary instance and example of the same process in man, for whom all else exists. I try to make it my motto, '*Deus et ipse evolventes*,' — God and man conspiring together toward the development of the man into his lost likeness to his Maker;" and the commissary flashed for the moment into the prophet. "I reckon that nothing we now know is worthy to be compared to the glory which shall be revealed in us! That is the true chariot of fire and horses of fire which carry a man to heaven!" He blushed at his own enthusiasm.

Colonel Thirlmore now joined them, and the three men walked toward camp together.

"That's a fact," said Captain Grumbles; "who can know General J. Mandeville Gilmore and not be cured of conceit forever? Take this poor friend of ours, Dr.

Doubleday. No, sir; no man can be two men at one and the same moment. If I was a preacher, I would be a double darned fool if I did n't give the people either South or North. I would give myself heart and soul to one Gospel, — *that* and nothing but that forever."

The Colonel eyed him closely. "Can't you let me alone, old fellow?" he said. "Preaching? What with you and Van Doren, no more preaching is needed; you glut the market."

"Do we? Well," the Captain said gravely, "there's one head more to my sermon. You had better be careful, Colonel, about that very beautiful daughter of the house."

"What do you mean?" The other stopped as he walked, and turned on his rustic friend with wrath and wonder. "What in the mischief has she done?"

"Never mind," Captain Grumbles remarked with composure, the color stealing over his honest face. "All I say is, where she is concerned we had better be most particularly careful, that's all."

When Colonel Thirlmore was in his room an hour later he sat as one stunned. "Is it possible," he thought, "that I am such a fool as to be really in love with Myrtle?" He had been alarmed as to himself before, but now he was sincerely so. "Yes," he had to consent to it; "there never was a school-boy more desperately in love than I am — I was — am!"

He was not the first man who with his heart had lost his head also, where she was concerned. There was not a young man nor a young woman in town but could have told him that. She was so childlike, yet so womanly, — the first woman of that peculiar type that the Colonel had ever known. Her almost mother-like tenderness toward her unhappy father would itself have won his heart. As his hostess, she had laid herself out to please him ; and how could a man be so closely and continually thrown with such a woman and escape?

"It is well *she* does not know anything about it," he thought concerning his wife. "Hang it! I must get out of this, and the sooner the better. If I don't —"

He knew himself well enough to know that if he did not fly, he was very apt to stand at nothing, nothing! For he was in love ; and the love of such a man for such a woman means everything that is headlong and desperate.

CHAPTER XV.

MYRTLE DOUBLEDAY.

WHEN Colonel Thirlmore spoke to Myrtle in regard to her father, she looked all the more childlike in her loveliness by reason of the tears which moistened her long lashes as she looked anxiously up at him.

" You will excuse me," he said, with sudden increase of interest in her father, " but a lack of decided views makes little difference in men of the ordinary run. With one of your father's determined character it is different. With his judgment going one way, his warm heart the other, he simply tears himself, as it were, to tatters. He should bring his entire self into one path. It will make him happier, make him a power for whichever side he selects. As it is, if he does not take care, he will land — in the lunatic asylum, or worse," he was about to add. However interested he was in his beautiful hostess, he had learned enough from Dr. Doubleday's example to think at the moment, " Grumbles is right ; if I had but hurled myself with all my force along the one way when I was a preacher I should not have ended as I did. And I do suppose that the one way was that along which the Pauls and the Luthers swept with such tremendous force."

" It is because mother is dead," Myrtle replied. "She was a great help to him. He is apt to fly off this way and that. Some day at church," and here her smiles broke through her tears, " I will show you a place in our pew where the paint is worn away from under the seat behind which she sat. She used to laugh, and say it was where

she pressed her feet during sermons in her effort to hold
father in. I am sure I have done all I could," with a mis-
chievous glance, " to make a good Southerner of him. I
wish I could make one of *you !*"

It was amazing how Colonel Thirlmore thrilled with
pleasure under her glance. Stern and cold as he assumed
to be of late ; wrapped up, as he had always been, in a
most exalted idea of himself, — the very vigor of his health
made him more susceptible to female influence than people
supposed. While yet a greatly worshipped preacher there
was among his adorers a Mrs. Gruffden, — a blooming
country girl, the wife of his wealthiest trustee, made by
marriage suddenly rich, — his attentions to whom had made
some talk at the time. The unaccountable way in which
Mr. Gruffden turned all at once from being a friend of his
pastor to an instantaneous and almost vehement enemy,
had much to do with the collapse of the church ; and it was
whispered that Gruffden was jealous. All there had ever
been in the affair was that Mr. Thirlmore, dreadfully bored
by the many be-spectacled and over-educated women with
whom that particular city was blessed, had been intoxicated
for a moment with the milkmaid charms of one as wholly
unlike them as was Mrs. Gruffden.

And this was his first visit to the South. Myrtle Doubleday was the first girl of the definitely Southern type of
beauty he had met. Had his acquaintance with her been
but casual, it might have been different. If he had been
thrown with her in the city from which he came he would
have had her out of her simpler element and at a disad-
vantage. As it was, Myrtle's little feet were on her native
blue grass. She was at home there, and fed and throve
upon the genial air, in every curve and fold and fibre of
her being, as much as did the oleander and jessamine.

Moreover, she was his hostess. In all the wide world there are none to compare with Southern women in this one respect. A Parisienne may illuminate her *salon* with her brilliancy of dress and repartee; an English marchioness may convey to her guest his highest experience of creature comfort; a Spanish señora may be the most seductive of women, with veil and fan and perilous darkness of hair and eyes; but there is one aspect in which a woman of the Southern States of the Union is incomparable. Let her be seventy years old, comparatively poor and uneducated; let her be homely and with no special motive in pleasing, — none the less, as a hostess, she will leave nothing to be desired. But imagine her to be well educated, in a comfortable home, young and very beautiful, — let her be Myrtle Doubleday, in a word; and with an especial purpose in captivating her father's classmate, and her hospitality is irresistible.

Captain Grumbles had reasons for putting the Colonel on his guard. Except when military duty made it necessary, that officer was, of late, never away from the house which for the time he made his home. It was not enough that he sat up late of evenings conversing with Myrtle, or hearing her sing; he began to give his afternoons also, and if he could, would have devoted his mornings to her. Dr. Doubleday walked up and down veranda and parlor arguing, questioning, prophesying. To-day the papers teemed with Confederate successes, and his heart danced within him, while his irrepressible common-sense rated them as merely so many bloody prolongments of the inevitable result. To-morrow the blazing head-lines heralded Federal victories, and his heavy-laden and sinking heart was as a descending bucket which dragged, as it went down into the depths, his calm conviction up into

a yet clearer light.   But having taken the measure of the
vacillating clergyman, it required more politeness than
Colonel Thirlmore possessed for him to heed what were
but the incessant croakings of a weather-vane which veered
with every breeze.   Long ago he would have fled from his
comfortable quarters to camp, if it had not been for Myrtle,
forever fresh in the charm of her childish grace.   The
flowers beside his plate at every breakfast were not fresher
and were far less lovely.   After a while it came to be even
delightful to her guest to note her supreme contempt for
the strongest assertions upon the one hand, her exuberant
faith and rejoicing for even the least atom, and that evidently forged, of encouragement upon the other.   It gave
him a new idea of a woman's power of believing what she
loves.

   " Here are some more of those pitiful lies," she would
say, as the armies began to move with fresh vigor, and
report of Federal gains to fill the papers.   " Do you
think, Colonel, that anybody is so stupid as to believe
such trash? "   It was charming to him to watch the
way in which geography, topography, railroads to assist,
great rivers to hinder, were as nothing to her.   In vain
did the Blue Ridge or the Alleghanies lift their ranges to
heaven ; they were to her serene faith as the stone in
the mouth of the sepulchre to the women of old.   As to
argument, statistics of troops, cannon, and the like, she
disdained to listen to such trifles.   It was the same as to
the best attested Federal victories.   " That," she would
exclaim, with a rose-leaf-like curl of her lip, " is all a
falsehood !   It is done to keep up your sinking souls,
and you know it as well as I ! "

   There were mornings when her father and his guest,
seated before breakfast on the veranda, had scarcely sub-

dued their grim smiles at the wholly impossible Confederate successes as detailed in the morning papers, before Myrtle broke radiant upon them, waving a like paper over her head. "I knew it!" she would cry, "I knew it! See, we have whipped you again, Colonel! Let me read it to you," — and she would read aloud the preposterous tidings, with comments of her own, in such a joyous way as to give the news an almost credible sound. If it could by no possibility be true, it assuredly should have been so for her sake! She would pause now and again to exult over her father and his friend, to twit them with their past predictions.

"Oh, isn't it grand news — glorious news!" she would cry as she led them in to breakfast, her eyes dancing with gladness. "Hurrah for Van Dorn! Colonel, be kind enough to give us three cheers for Sydney Johnston! I know you would like to do it if you dared. We have whipped you again, whipped you, and you know it!" and she would seize upon the table-bell as they sat there and ring it for joy; or, springing to her feet, would tuck the priceless sheet in the pocket of her wrapper for another half dozen re-readings, run to her piano and make the room ring with "Dixie."

"If you would but play for me, Colonel," she would whirl around on her piano-stool to say, "I should like to dance. I can dance without music though; my heart makes music enough!" and laying hold upon her sad-faced father, she would waltz him about. "You are beaten, Colonel Thirlmore; beaten, beaten! I knew it would be so! And what will you poor Yankees try to do *now* — in this region, I mean?" with a glance of sudden sharpness.

"Wait a little, Miss Myrtle," her guest would say, taking

another muffin or batter-cake; his appetite, or the fare, was singularly good. "Wait a little, and we will show you."

"Yes, but when? and how? Your pompous old General is forever boasting as to what he is to do. When is he going to do something, and what will it be? Your people were braying on their bugles, rattling at their drums, marching this way and that yesterday. What is on hand? There's nobody I can tell;" and if Colonel Thirlmore had not been so — almost — in love with the charming girl he might have noticed the way in which she hung breathless upon his reply.

Alas, while she supposed him to be meditating a response, he was saying to himself, "Oh yes, we have the advantage of you in our female colleges, and all the humbug of higher education for women. But hang the sharp, smart females with their sciences and eye-glasses, their ologies and their isms! For pure beauty, for genuine, unadulterated loveliness, did any woman ever compare with this darling?"

"Really, Colonel, what can you do?" Dr. Doubleday laid upon the cloth the paper he had taken from his daughter, with a tremulous hand. "What with the odds against Rosecrans, the forces gathering under Pemberton," and he detailed them at length in dolorous accents, "it behooves General Gilmore to act with promptness and energy. What does he propose to do?"

Was the guest conscious of the manner in which Myrtle became all at once very still, to hear what their friend would say?

"There can be but one result, success to your cause in the end. It is the historical cause," Dr. Doubleday would add, "along which is all evolution, since in that way tend

the steps of the Almighty for human welfare. And yet he
uses means. What are you going to do? You were very
late last night in your return from the General's quarters ;
it was morning, Colonel, when you got to bed. I heard
you. I cannot sleep, as you know. I am intensely
anxious. Are matters always to be at a halt as now?
Surely there can be no traitors among you ; that you are
brave men we all know. If General Gilmore is a blather-
skite in some things, yet, surely, he is not a coward.
What are you going to do, Colonel? "

Dr. Doubleday was several years older than his classmate, but he seemed older than he was. His anxieties
were evidently deepening of late ; he was thinner, his
eyes glittered with a light painful to see from such
sunken sockets, his head was more bowed, his manner
more nervous : his guest regarded him with profound
pity. When under such circumstances such a man
could ask, even press, such questions upon a Federal
officer, it was but too evident that his anxieties were
getting the better of his reason.

None the less, all the more rather, Colonel Thirlmore
never was so near destruction as at that instant. Over-
persuaded by the eyes bent so hungrily upon him, unconsciously weakened by the charming daughter, for a
moment he was merely a man talking with an old classmate. He did know things which would greatly interest
his friend. Even if Myrtle were listening, she was no more
than a child.

Suddenly there flashed upon him a passage in a letter
received from his wife the night before.

" I am delighted," she wrote, " that you have so lovely
a hostess. But take care, Theo ! those charming Southern girls are the most determined of Confederates. If

you let drop a word or syllable, the least hint, which can be of service to the Rebels, she is sure to know how to get it to them.   Take care, Theo!"

It was as if the finger of his wife were laid upon his lips! He turned cold at the sense of his terrible imprudence.

Dr. Doubleday listened so eagerly, it seemed a shame to make such delusive answers. Except for his wife's warning, Myrtle would have been as little thought of as the wood-doves cooing in their cage on the porch. Yet her face, out of sight behind him, was very intent; her lips were parted as if she wished to breathe as silently as possible; she listened, one little hand pressed firmly upon her bosom, lest the beating of her heart should prevent her from hearing every word that was said. When Colonel Thirlmore mounted Tamerlane to ride to camp that morning, Myrtle was in her own room, the door locked, an odd-looking book lying open upon the table before her. Continually referring to it, she wrote what seemed to be a cipher despatch. She was greatly excited; her lips were as closely pressed together as such lips could be; her hair had fallen neglected about her forehead and shoulders; she trembled at every sound.

When her note was finished she folded it into as narrow a slip as possible, and sewed it into the folds of what seemed to be a satin necktie. Then she put away paper and ink, locked up the book in her jewel case, and hid it in the depths of her deepest drawer. Next she opened her door and called Dicey, her mulatto maid.

"Dicey," she said, "I want you to do something for me. You are not afraid to ride the pony, are you?"

"Law, no, Miss Myrtle." The girl looked curiously at her mistress. She must have been about the same age;

and was as pretty as her mistress in her very different type. The two had lived under the same roof since they were born.

" Now, Dicey," Myrtle said, evidently in the greatest haste, but trying to speak calmly, " if you do exactly as I tell you, I will give you my blue silk when you get báck."

" Yes, miss," and the eyes of the girl sparkled.

" All you have to do," and she tied the satin ribbon about the neck of the other, " is to take pony and ride as fast as you can to the graveyard. Inside and near the gate you will see an old man pruning the hedge. Give him the necktie, and say it is from me. That is all, and come back as soon as you can. Can you do it? "

The girl was looking almost stolidly in the face of Myrtle. " Law, miss, why not? " she said, and was in haste to be gone.

Now, herein is a strange thing. Dicey could not read, could hardly be said to think. All she could do was to love her young mistress, as she had done since she could remember, and to do what was told her. Never had she known anything but kindness from Myrtle, — or any other white person of her acquaintance, for that matter. Notwithstanding all this, she did not give the ribbon into the hands designated, until it had passed first through other hands for which it was by no means intended.

" Did you give it to him? " her mistress asked her eagerly on her return.

" Yes, miss." The face of a child could not have been more artless.

" You were gone a long time, Dicey."

" There was so many Yankees about I had to be, miss. But I tell you dat man was glad to git it. He had a horse eatin' grass outside de gate. 'Fore I could turn pony round, he was on his horse and off at a lope. It is done gone, miss."

There was a look of gleeful cunning in the eyes of her maid which made Myrtle wince a little ; but leaving her to rejoice in her new dress, she went down, a smile upon her face, into the parlor. Surely there never was a more artless, more charming girl living than was Myrtle. She was in a delightful humor, played for the Colonel, sang, talked, until, to their mutual regret, he was summoned away by an orderly.

And while Myrtle was entertaining him, Dicey was trying on her new dress. "It'll come in mighty well when we's free," she was saying to herself as she turned herself this way and that before her bit of looking-glass. Yet Colonel Thirlmore would have agreed, no man more heartily, that it was a base thing in Dicey to love anything in comparison with Myrtle.

"What was Mrs. Gruffden but a pretty idiot," he said, as he rode to headquarters, " in comparison with this charming child, who is also the loveliest of women?"

He was so full of the thought, that General J. Mandeville Gilmore came upon him, on reaching the hotel, as a specially disagreeable surprise.

. " Here is a beautiful state of things, Colonel Thirlmore !" he cried. " Come into my room, sir."

The commanding officer was fresh from parade, in full uniform, and, unbuckling his sword like another Mars, he threw it in thunder down as he proceeded to tell of what had taken place. Nothing less than an artillery of oaths sufficed him ; he perspired copiously, and was compelled to unbutton first his coat and then the protuberance of his ample waistcoat. " That it should have occurred under *my* command, sir! That *I* should be subjected to the attacks of the Northern press, sir — "

When the other could learn the facts of the case they were these : Dicey — who could conceive of transformation such as this? — had contrived, through a negro washer-woman about the hotel, to get her ribbon and its contents into the hands of Lieutenant Van Doren, who had easily deciphered them. Poor Myrtle! Her cryptogram was of the simplest. She had written what Colonel Thirlmore had said for the information of the Confederate com-mander, who was not as far away as General Gilmore had supposed.

" It was a string of — of — " the General began.

" Infernal lies? Certainly! It was an experiment of mine," Colonel Thirlmore said, coolly enough. " Dr. Doubleday *will* have information, and I gave it to him, such as it was. I hardly thought it would go beyond him ; at least not so soon. I have no doubt you have already taken steps to profit by my ruse."

" If it is Dr. Doubleday, he has imitated the writing of a lady," roared the excited commander ; " and the cipher says that the news was obtained from Captain Grumbles, and therefore might be relied upon."

" Captain Grumbles! " For once in his life Colonel Thirlmore was astounded ; when he began to comprehend, the color rose in his cheeks. It rose and rose until, for the first time in his life, he felt his face fairly burn and his ears tingle! Oh, Myrtle, Myrtle! He could not help understanding her motive.

" Lieutenant Van Doren and yourself deserve great praise, or will deserve it, sir, if I succeed ; and I am not accustomed, sir, to fail. Lieutenant Van Doren is already acting upon my order. We have got them, sir, got them !

But see to it that every possible precaution is taken."
The other smiled and withdrew.

The result became the sensation of the day. North
and South the papers were filled with the most conflicting accounts; but the simple facts of the case, now made
public for the first time, were these: —

It so happened that some weeks before, John Henson,
a muscular private in Captain Grumbles' company, was
bathing in a little lake near the Confederate lines and
was made prisoner by two mounted Rebels. It is almost
too incredible to relate, but while riding naked behind
one of his captors, Henson suddenly slipped his arms
about his captor, snatched a pistol with each hand from
the holsters, and marched back to his own camp as prisoners not merely the man on the same horse, but also the
other, who was riding just ahead along the narrow path.
When Colonel Thirlmore heard of this feat, he presented
the naked hero with a suit of his own clothes, and so won
his heart with his praise as well as his generosity, that
Henson stole out as a scout, and contrived to learn and
to report to the Colonel the intended advance of the
Confederates in time to enable him, Myrtle unintentionally
assisting, to capture the whole party. Misled by what
their guest had said to her father, she made her friends
believe that the Federal forces would be hurried off to
attack another point, and the Confederates the next
night ventured an assault upon the town, garrisoned, as
they supposed, by a greatly weakened number of Federals.
Alas! instead of making an easy prey of stores and prisoners, they themselves fell into the trap, and were captured almost to the last man!

The town is to-day, perhaps, the loveliest of the smaller
Southern cities; but there was a dreadful struggle in it

that night. Dr. Doubleday was pacing as usual up and
down his chamber when the midnight assault took place.
Myrtle, glorying in her deed, was dreadfully frightened,
and Dicey sleeping at her feet only less so, as the rattle of
small arms, the roar of cannon, the galloping of horses
increased. But Myrtle's attention was soon drawn from
the sounds by the increasing wildness of her father. He
fell upon his knees in prayer, hurried from room to room,
laughed, wept, until the poor girl knew not what to do.
Then came the distant explosion of a powder-wagon; a
house or two in the suburbs was burned.

"It was really a very trifling affair," Colonel Thirlmore
said coolly, the next day. He had been absent for many
hours, but dropped in at dinner to see that no harm had
been done.

"I am sorry for your friends, Miss Myrtle; but we
bagged them beautifully, with little loss of life, as I am
happy to say." The Colonel added, "Do you know a
Captain Warden, Miss Myrtle?"

It was an unfeeling question, for Myrtle colored vividly.
"He was in command on your side, Miss Myrtle, and we
have him as prisoner. A plucky little gentleman as I ever
saw. His hair is very red; do you know him?"

Colonel Thirlmore had evidently heard something; but
he was mistaken if he hoped to capture his hostess as
easily as the Federals had captured her reputed lover.
She was not disposed to be gay; under the circumstances
she could hardly be other than depressed; yet was she entirely mistress of herself. Never had she appeared more
beautiful, never had she been more self-possessed.

Her father sat at table, his head bowed down, white
and ominously silent. He was bewildered. Myrtle had
gathered from the servants that Colonel Thirlmore had

watched over the house, off and on, during the entire
night. He had received a slight wound also, and he had
conquered. Myrtle could understand nothing about the
situation. Federal officer though he might be, one did
not often see a nobler-looking man ; and it could not be
denied that Captain Warden was small, nor that his hair
was red,—and he a defeated soldier. On the other hand,
whenever Colonel Thirlmore recalled how his news to
Myrtle had been ascribed — for fear that harm should
come to him — to poor, unconscious, prophetic Grumbles,
his cheek and ears glowed again.

To-day he was able to see precisely how far he had
yielded to the charms of this most charming of girls. He
had not supposed it possible he could be so infatuated by
any woman. He anathematized himself, as he was about
to leave after dinner. "You are a confounded fool," he
thought, "and nine-tenths of an unmitigated scoundrel."
And what is to be thought of a lady who acted as Myrtle
had done? Surely, a girl to whom her clear-headed father
had tried so hard to show the right and the wrong of the
question between North and South might have been less
blind and unreasoning. She loved the South ; but had she
no love for her father? Was there ever a more charming
hospitality than hers? And now — As his hostess, she
had figuratively handed him across her table, and, with a
smile, a cup of coffee, into which she had dropped what
looked like a lump of white sugar, but which was really
a crystal of corrosive sublimate. He had been in the act
of taking it from her little hand, of drinking, of dying, if
his wife had not intervened ! Myrtle's childish device of
pretending to have got from Captain Grumbles the information she sent to the Confederates would have been
speedily disproved. He, her guest, would have been

convicted of sending, perhaps selling, information to the enemy. And he would have been justly cashiered, driven out as the Benedict Arnold of the war. Shot he would have deserved to be !

Colonel Thirlmore thought of all this during dinner. Myrtle, now mistress of herself again, had never presided at the table more perfectly. She was another Eve ; but her guest was thinking of the serpent also. A serpent? Very well ; but in what unaccountable way had it so happened that he had never alluded to his wife in her presence — not once !

"You are more of a villain, my fine fellow," he said to himself, realizing her great beauty as he did so, "than you have imagined. Suppose this girl, suppose my wife, saw me as I am — "

"I must go," he said, as he bowed himself out. " It is but just to myself to say that I accepted your kind hospitality hoping to be of service to you. That is why I called to-day. My orderly will come for my things this afternoon, for I cannot return."

As he proceeded with his thanks, he fancied a paleness about the lips of the girl, a quivering of her eyelashes, a something, a nothing. "The news will be in all the papers," he went on. "My people will be anxious to hear. I must give the afternoon," and he took Myrtle's hand in his, "to letters to my — wife."

But he did not look into the eyes of Myrtle, as he intended, and in another moment was gone.

He meant what he said. Leaving important matters to take care of themselves, he gave his wife, in the longest letter he had as yet written her, an account of all that had befallen. Before leaving, he had consented to her suggestions of a cipher, to be used in case they desired to

do so.   He had assented to it at the time with an indifferent nod, and had not thought of it again until now.
When he came to that part of his narrative he yielded to
the new impulse, and related in cipher how near he had
come to falling into the trap,— how he had been withheld
at the last moment by what she had written.   In thanking
her, he must have put a feeling into what he wrote, that he
had never before done.

He must have done so ; for when his wife was decipher-
ing what he wrote, her fingers tremulous and flying could
not keep up with her happy impatience.   She had prided
herself always upon being intellectual, not emotional ; but
her eyes dropped delicious tears as she read.   She kissed
the sheet as she deciphered ; when before had she done
anything but despise a weakness like that?

"She has heard good news, mother, I tell you !" Squash
remarked.   " How bright and happy she looked !   Did
you ever hear her laugh that way before?   She asked me
if I had n't better have more doughnuts at supper ; and
she must have forgot how she had kissed Pop and Owl
once or twice already, for she kissed 'em all over again
before she took her candle to go upstairs, and *I* never saw
her look so pretty ! "

CHAPTER XVI.

COUNTRY PRODUCE.

SINCE the coming of Mrs. Thirlmore into the household at Scrubstones, the even tenor of her hours had been as the flow of a deepening current through a low-lying and tree-sheltered meadow; all the more so that, up to that time, her married life had not been a happy one. Now, and for the first time since she became a woman, she was at rest. The absence of her husband was in itself a relief to her. Sure that he had chosen a path in which he could not fail, she felt that each step would bring him more into the possession of himself and of all he was formed to be. Gradually her health became as when she was a child in her country home. The old hunger was hers once again; not Squash himself, Pop, or Owl enjoyed more than she did Mrs. Grumbles' simple but excellent fare. Her sleep, too, was like that of a child who awakes with a laugh and an eagerness for the open world.

"How can I be so well, so happy, so much like a young girl who has a long and joyous future before her?" she asked herself. "Here I am, my husband caring nothing for me; likely to be killed any day, without a word or a thought about me, forgetting, if he does not hate me. It is," she answered herself, "because I am so sure of the result! I believe in it so heartily; believe in it because — because — " Not even to herself did she say why. As has been said, when on the old farm, and in the deepest depth of her despair, an experience had come to her which had been the turning-point in her life.

She had caught sight in the dense darkness of an out-stretched hand, — of a person stooping to her; and because this vision was so precious, so entirely her all, she shrank from defining it to herself. But that light, joy, a glad faith and hope were streaming into her soul from thence, she had no doubt!

There may be no such thing as an excess of apples to an orchard, or of wheat to its acres, yet with Mrs. Thirlmore's new health came what might almost be styled a new trouble. After supper, with the children clustering closely about her, she found it hard at times to stop talking to them. It was not because they were so eager to hear, but because she had so much to say. There was good Mrs. Grumbles, as profoundly ignorant of everything outside her household as she was familiar with everything inside it. She might make believe to be absorbed in the towels she was hemming, the stockings she was knitting, or the finery she was making, but she was more interested than any child there in what Mrs. Thirlmore said or read. It may be shocking to say it of one whose life had been given to scrubbing, cooking, nursing of sick children, and the mending and making of clothes for a large family; yet was Mrs. Grumbles more concerned for the fate of Cinderella than for what might happen to Anne Boleyn; Israel Putnam was much less to her than Jack the Giant-Killer, and Queen Elizabeth seemed a prosy old virago in comparison with the Fair Maid with the Golden Locks. And to her as to the rest, George Stephenson, Watt, Fulton, and Morse were dull discoverers in comparison with Aladdin and his wonderful lamp.

Squash, scrubbed as clean as though it were Sunday, was developing alarmingly into a critic as to things which his own mother took in with a childlike delight. " Did you read all that?" he asked Mrs. Thirlmore more than once; and more than once she had to confess with shame that she had not. In fact, as the months of her stay passed by, memory gave place to imagination, and her most effective stories were those which came to her lips, invented for the eager eyes about her. It was pure overflow of life.

"I can understand now," Mr. Kellogg, the minister, said to her after remaining altogether too late after supper one night, "about Mesdames De Staël, De Genlis, and the like, and Lady Blessington,— what I have heard about their *salons* in Paris. A thousand thanks. May I come again?"

"It's a great compliment," Mrs. Grumbles said, as Squash lighted Mr. Kellogg with a lantern to his buggy. "You see he's been to Paris himself; though I don't know as he called on those ladies when he was there. Dear me! what a difference there is between him and your grandpa, old Parson Van Dyke! This one may be the smartest of the two, and have seen more of the world, but your grandpa was the best. I mean he was the humblest, and most pious. Ministers did n't rush about in those days. He preached every Sunday for over fifty years. Yes, and he did it on four hundred dollars a year. How the world is changed!"

It was in the morning that Mrs. Thirlmore was at her best. When refreshed by sleep and out upon her after-breakfast walk, there came upon her such a freshness and force of thought as craved expression. Her health was so strong, her mind so trained and well-informed, she had such an excess of existence, that she would have been glad of an excuse to sing, to laugh, to put into words the things which crowded upon her.

"I wish," she laughed, "that I was Lady Palmerston, with all the Whigs and Tories of England on my hands to entertain. I do feel so well, so strong, so what Mrs. Grumbles calls ' saucy.' It seems to me," she added, with glowing cheeks, " if he were here I could, I might, — yes, I know I could — "

She had hard work to keep from writing to her husband every day. Her correspondents in the city and elsewhere fell into a way of sending her letters to their friends, they were so charmingly written. As to her husband, never had he enjoyed any reading so much. He little dreamed how she held herself in check as she wrote.

" If I only dared," she thought, " to put all that I want to say on the paper ! If he were here again, and I could throw my arms about him and tell him everything ! Yes, I know he would come to love me, if he came to know me better. To know me ? And yet we have been married all these years. Yes, but I am changed ; and I am changing ! He is changed ; is changing, too ! Those blessed days that are to be ! For I know — I know— "

Never had she been so beautiful. Mrs. Grumbles told her so. In the deepest confidence, and with a glow upon his freckled face, Squash informed her of it. People stared at her on Sundays at church. A frightful rumor ran the round of the parish that Mr. Kellogg was dying from love of her ; "anybody can see that from his sermons," was the remark. She could not deny what she could not help seeing in her glass.

" It must be the country air," her city friends said when they came to call upon her. " Or perhaps it is milk. You know how scarce good milk is in town ; half of what we get is water. If I could hope to improve so much, dear Mrs. Thirlmore, I would give up the city, risk the mosquitoes, give up public libraries, theatres, concerts, society, all, and spend my days here."

Her heart must have mirrored itself in some way upon her face, for she had at this time an experience entirely new, and which was to affect her whole after-life. For some time now, and since she underwent that subtile change from darkest despair to the tremulous beginning of another and sweeter life, the change had gone silently on, and it might have been measured by the increase of her interest in her husband. His going away had enabled her, standing apart, to get at a clearer and more loving estimate of him and of her need of him, which she, in her pride of intellect, would hitherto have rejected with scorn. One morning her thought took expression in words,— rhythmic words, — as spontaneous as is song to a bird ; and she could not refrain from writing them down as they came. A poem? Never had she done such a thing before. She had a taste of the fearful joy of a mother in her first-born. But was it a poem? Her eyes were wet as she read it over ; but would it affect others? Was it poetry? She locked her virgin lines in a drawer with a laugh and a blush ; how could she find out whether or no what she had written was tolerable on the score of sense?

Mrs. Grumbles, from some fellow-feeling for that particular flower, put all her gardening into the care of old-fashioned damask roses. She was almost as successful with them as she was with herself, so large were they, so abundant in petals, and of such crimson dyes, — cabbage roses they might well be styled. Hans, the farm laborer, was not allowed to come near them ; the children would as soon have thought of meddling with the jams and jellies, the brandy peaches and greengage marmalades on the top-shelves of the pantry, as with their mother's roses. It was a sight which the guest used to love to watch of mornings, from her window, — stout Mrs. Grumbles, rosy and rapturous, pruning withered leaves from her beloved rose-bushes, stooping over and fondling them, "as if they were so many babies, they are so plump and red, bless their hearts!" she would herself say. "Don't you think so, Mrs. Thirlmore?"

One beautiful morning Peace had been drawn from quite a distance by the fragrance of Mrs. Grumbles' largest bush. She thought that she had never seen anything so wonderfully beautiful in its way, — the green leaves and sheath, the velvet glory of the rose itself bending beneath its own excess and splendor of dewy sweetness. At first the words arose unuttered; then she murmured them half aloud; then she began to jot them down on a leaf of a book she had in her hand. She laughed at herself, but it grew upon her when, in her room, she wrote it out, re-wrote, wrote it yet again. "As I live, it is a sonnet!" she said, flushed and pleased as a girl.

Then, as before, a wonder came upon her whether it *was* a sonnet. That night after supper, and in connection with some raillery of their mother by the children as to her pet flowers, Mrs. Thirlmore repeated the lines.

"I did n't quite catch; won't you please say it over again?" Mrs. Grumbles said, her lips a little parted, holding suspended the towel with which she was wiping the cups and saucers as the family lingered about the table. Mrs. Thirlmore had always been assured at the literary parties in the city that she "read so beautifully it was a treat to hear her; she could make anything sound well."

It might be because Mrs. Thirlmore so deeply felt what she had written, but there was breathless listening as she repeated the few lines. Mrs. Grumbles was standing at her work, the moisture gathering in her eyes as she took in the melodious periods. She was as fond of good things as anybody; there were few flavors from field or orchard, from garden or kitchen, which she did not analyze as well as enjoy: but this was her first taste of the pleasure to be found in poetry. When the honeyed euphony reached its climax in the last syllables, she stood fixed for a moment.

"Please let me," she said humbly, going, like the child she had suddenly become, to the other, and for the first time she kissed her, — kissed her softly, reverentially. "Beautiful?" she almost whispered, "they're more beautiful than my roses! I wish some day I could see whoever wrote them.'

"Hoh, mother!" Squash had made a discovery. his eyes fastened upon the pleased face of their guest. "She wrote 'em herself!"

"Did *you?*" Mrs. Grumbles could only gasp it, with wondering eyes. Her friend laughed and colored and tried to speak of something else. It is very foolish; but it is surprising how foolish the very wisest are to praises of what they have written. The pleasure of creating, of writing, has the taste of the rarest of wines; the being praised for it has the same altogether peculiar and delicious flavor.

"Oh, my!" exclaimed impulsive Pop; "we didn't know you were a poet, did we, mother?" Mrs. Grumbles said nothing. Ever after, there was a new reverence in her toward her guest. "You see," she explained to her neighbor, Mrs. Sudkins, "I never saw a poet before."

Her roses were more to her after that than ever. They were hoed about and watered with religious care; yet, somehow, she had transferred to her guest whatever was most precious in them.

But Squash had an idea. Aroused by the wind of inspiration passing so near, he consulted his mother. Begging of its author the loan of the sonnet, he took it to Mr. Kellogg, who agreed warmly with the boy as to its value, and, at the request of Squash, inclosed it in his best hand to that journal in the city which was most read in Scrubstones. In his enthusiasm Squash suggested "Rose" as the best *nom de plume* he could think of, and insisted on mailing it with his own hand. Eagerly was the next number of the paper looked for. To the disgust of Squash the sonnet did not appear for some days.

"I did n't know," he complained to Mr. Kellogg, "that an editor could be such a fool! But perhaps he did n't get it; somebody may have stolen it to pass it off for his own."

Week after week each paper was almost savagely examined. But it was terror which mingled itself with his pride and triumph, when one night at table the boy exhibited the sonnet, secure now in the immortality of print. It was the first time, used to the ways of the world as she was, that anything of Mrs. Thirlmore's writing had been put into type; and what an odd sensation it was to her! The sudden publicity made her feel as if placed suddenly upon a stage and under the gaze of a thousand eyes. She was shocked, pleased, pained, pleased again. Squash produced also a note to Mr. Kellogg from the editor. He liked the poem very much; would be glad of others; hoped some day to remunerate the unknown writer. The household regarded her with awe, while she scolded the exulting boy for what he had done, was delighted, and then was angry with herself for being delighted.

Even Squash was alarmed at the number of copies of

the paper which his mother bade him procure. Some she gave to her friends ; but Mrs. Thirlmore would not allow her to mail a paper to the army, or to mention her name to any one.

All this is recorded for the sake of what came after. There are many people who never wrote a sonnet ; there is nobody who has written only one. Mrs. Thirlmore had more time than she knew what to do with : her excess of life had found an outlet ; here was an unexpected luxury wholly new to her. Writing had always been a pleasure, but writing for the press ! — there was a certain substance and solidity of enjoyment in that. And was it possible she could write anything which would produce money? It all came upon her at once. Macaulay had been paid £20,000 ($100,000) in a single check. Then there were Sir Walter Scott and Charles Dickens ! She had heard of the sums paid George Sand, George Eliot, and Mrs. Strickland ! It was not the money she cared for ; she might help her husband, who had lost everything !

She could not sleep at night ! For days she was in a species of almost delirium as to what might be. She would write a volume of poems, an epic, at least an idyl ! Who knew but she might evolve a novel? She grew silent, preoccupied, almost troubled. If she scribbled on the fly-leaf of a book, those nearest her at the moment stole away on tiptoe. No one dared to interrupt her when in her room. " She is writing something," they said to each other in solemn accents.

It was both amusing, pleasing, and vexatious. She was ashamed of feeling as if she were a young and inexperienced girl ; " and yet writers do influence multitudes of people," she thought, — " and sometimes to more than laughter or tears. Think what an effect Mrs. Browning has in moulding character. It is merely another way of having power." But if for an instant she lifted her head proudly, it was to drop it the next moment in shame at her nonsense. It was not that she had struck out a sonnet which was now running the rounds of the press ; it was a deep sense of having that in her which might result in so much greater things. All along there was a dread lest her husband should come to know of it, and so her plans in regard to him be ruined.

" For," — she said it with a movement in her like that of an incoming tide, " I would rather be his wife, loved and cherished by him, as one day he *shall* love and cherish me, — I would rather be that than the most successful woman who ever wrote ! " and with all the success which came after, the *wife* outgrew in her all other growth.

But the inevitable result came to her as to all. In the enthusiasm of her new discovery she wrote too often, too much. There had come a demand upon her from many quarters, she was so evidently a fresh force in literature. Under such pressure she failed to let her writings ripen, as they should have done, first in her mind, and afterward, as one stores away certain kinds of pears, as MSS. in her desk.

Her assumed name gave that value to whatever went with it that it was reprinted unread by the editors of most papers from the Atlantic to the Pacific. Thereupon followed a reaction. " She is not up to the mark," the critics began to growl. The blow of a clenched fist could hardly have given her more pain. To her it was like insult when the first of her MSS. came back " declined with thanks." It was followed by a despair of herself, then by a new resolve, and that by yet more marked success.

Why go into detail? She tried poem, story, essay, narrative, novel, — almost every form of literature. Her first inspiration had been in regard to her husband ; for his sake her next deepest inspiration was in regard to the war. These two, wedded love and battle, were not the only themes upon which she wrote ; but it was when in prose or poetry she touched upon these that she became most widely known. She had many a failure. But downright failure was not the worst.

"There is this outcome," her husband wrote her, " of our long-continued drill and discipline, our defeats, victories, and long waitings, and that is, — down to the most worthless bounty-jumper in the ranks, we come at last to do with mechanical precision whatever is to be done. As a rule, war is merely regular, monotonous work, like the work of a factory, or foundry, or other business."

"And so it is with me and my work," she thought of her labor with the pen ; but she wrote back to him : " Our housekeeping under command of Mrs. General Grumbles is but a variation upon yours. Monday is washing day. Tuesday we iron. Wednesday the whole house is swept, from attic to cellar. Thursday is devoted to scrubbing, as religiously as Sunday to worship. Friday the cellars and all they contain are gone over. As sure as Saturday dawns, so surely the house is redolent of baking. Our processes have the regularity of the solar system ; but there is no business in which absolute certainty is so much of an unvarying element. The *savant* may be anxious as to what will come of his experiments, the Pope as to his dogmas ; but Mrs. Grumbles is as sure of her milk, cheese, sausage, bread, pies, canned fruits, of the fatness of her turkeys, the inches of lard on the ribs of her pigs, the quality of her soap, the morals of her children,

as she is of the rising and setting of the sun over the red
barn."

But, alas! even Mrs. Grumbles was human. One day
Owl complained of a pain in her back. The next day she
was propped up in bed, her playthings spread out upon the
quilt before her; but the pain had extended to all her
bones. She had always been what the neighbors called
" a queer, old-fashioned little thing," with little to say,
but an amazing faculty for looking and for listening. She
was a dumpy darling, short-bodied, large-headed, her hair,
— " yellow, like her pa's," her mother said, — making a
funny kind of frizz, which no comb or cap could suppress,
about her singularly large and solemn eyes. It was dreadfully embarrassing to the other children to have her with
them when any mischief was in hand. " Not that she says
much," Pop complained to Mrs. Thirlmore, " but that she
keeps up such an awful looking, you know."

Sometimes the little thing seemed to the guest to be
not a member of the family, but rather a visitor, sent to
inspect matters and report elsewhere. There was not a
brighter child nor a better humored in the world, but she
did not join in the romping of the others. Seated at
table, or perched upon a chair in the sitting-room, a spectator in orchard and barnyard of whatever was going on,
clambering into her mother's capacious lap, seated on a
stool as Mrs. Thirlmore's pet, or listening to whatever was
being said, the child always had an aspect " like an old
judge," Squash declared.

" Like a parson in the pulpit, looking out for naughty
children while the singing is going on," Snap observed.

" She is an Owl, that 's what she is. When I wake up
of nights," Pop remarked, " I can see her looking at me
in the dark."

"What I think," Mrs. Thirlmore said, "is that she is the sweetest little thing I ever knew." But more than once in the midst of some story about the Singing Tree, the Talking Bird, or the Golden Water, she would be smitten in conscience, catching sight of Owl looking at her with such questioning honesty in the brown eyes opened to their utmost.

And now her eyes grew larger still as she fell away before the illness which set in. When Mrs. Grumbles knew from the doctor that it was scarlet fever, she accepted the fact and cleared decks as if the house were a ship going into action. The children were packed off to the most distant rooms ; Squash, old enough to be trusted now, was put in charge, with Hans and Maggie under him. It was in vain that Mrs. Thirlmore was urged to leave the house ; there was no place to which she cared to go. She had passed through the fever when very young, and she had formed a peculiar attachment to the child. Moreover, the doctor had told her, in strict confidence, a something concerning Mrs. Grumbles which would not allow her to think of leaving.

"I was feeling the need for a change," she thought ; and she locked up pen and paper, and made ready for whatever might come, soberly, silently.

It was her first experience of nursing. Before long, however, it seemed to her as if she had been doing nothing else all her life. The darkened room ; the hush which had suddenly come upon the house ; the sounds as from another world without, of lowing cattle, of calling voices, of wheels rolling by upon the highway ; the coming and going of the doctor ; the old-fashioned clock in the hall, persisting with its ticks through the prayer which the minister offered in a low voice by the bed, the mother kneeling on one side, Mrs. Thirlmore on the other; the light sleep snatched in chair or on lounge, — in a few days these came to seem the eternal order of the ages. And how impertinent and unfeeling looked the sunshine, stealing in through chink and crevice; how powerless the love that bent over the little sufferer, able to know so very little, able to do even less, the grown women as helpless as the child, who looked upward, now and then, but never with so much of demand in the dumb eyes as now.

If Mrs. Thirlmore went out of doors for a breath of air, the turnspit poodle, exiled as usual from the kitchen, and thus from the sole object for which he was created, was sure to be at her feet. With Websterian brows abased to the dust, writhing his ugliness into agonies of apology for existing at all, he seemed to be saying: "Yes, mistress, here is poor Wretch, more worthless than the dirt, yet well and fat, while she is upstairs dying. Yes, yes, mistress," his sorrowful gaze on hers, "it is a hard world to understand. And you? do you know so much more about it than I?"

Stealing back again she resumed her dream. Then came the moment when, lying in its mother's lap, poised between the two worlds, the child, its eyes more articulate than its moans, quietly ceased to breathe, and went forth where it would find people and things easier to be understood, tell what it had to tell of matters here, and come at last to know even as also it was known. There was profound peace in the hands clasped upon the bosom, the eyes closed, the feet stilled forever. "Surely it is," Mrs. Thirlmore said to herself, "like the sandals and shoes, the staff and travel-stained cloak, left by the Moslem outside the gate as he enters into the mosque to worship God."

For to her had been given that experience of physicians who are contemptuous in their unbelief. She was certain, as she gazed breathlessly upon the child in its last moment, of a *something* passing from it at death, leaving the body as a cast-off garment behind.

It was a strange interlude to the bloody strife of the field, the half-suppressed but more bitter conflict of South against North in the captured Blue Grass, when, one Wednesday afternoon, Captain Grumbles called on Dr. Doubleday, and desired to see him in private. It so chanced that some Federal outrage, first heard of that day, had so soured the soul of the good pastor against the invaders that it was with the most forbidding of countenances he received his visitor in his study. The Captain had made more than one visit at the house, and they had been, in his homesick condition, delightful to him. But that was when the clergyman had been in a wholly different frame of mind ; and at this moment the visitor was worse to him than a stranger, — he was one of the Vandal horde, a minion of despotism. The mood of the minister grew blacker as the ungainly officer took, unasked, a seat among the litter of books and papers, his warlike accoutrements dreadfully in his way, as they always were. For a minute or so the Captain sat in silence, his cap in his hand, his hand upon his knee. The Doctor coughed at last interrogatively ; but the other merely laid his sword mechanically across his lap, his eyes cast down.

"It is not my wont to receive any of you in my home," the master of the house remarked in crusty accents. "If Colonel Thirlmore is an exception, it is not because he is or was a brother clergyman and of the same denomination with myself, nor that he was my classmate in college and seminary. As Provost Marshal, our town is at his mercy; and I serve my people, my *own* people," with emphasis, "by having him so near. I suffer too much in the eyes of our citizens as it is, to desire anything more of the kind." His eye fell again upon the sword; he fancied he saw that upon its scabbard which caused him to add, his lips twitching nervously, "I confess, sir, I cannot imagine why you intrude yourself upon me."

The other sat silent, as if he heard him not. "Perhaps," the minister said, "you will allow me to withdraw. Was it not Colonel Thirlmore you wanted to see?" roughly.

"He never was much of a hand to comfort anybody, so I am told, not when he was pastor of a church," the other said, simply, and then broke down utterly. "Oh, my child, my little child!" He had buried his face in his handkerchief, and was weeping convulsively. "I clean forgot we were at war," he apologized in a few moments. "All I thought of was that you were a minister, a Christlike minister. Pardon me, sir, but I am a family man myself. My children are all the world to me. The telegram struck me so unexpectedly. How could I know she had been sick, even? And she was our youngest. I loved her most. But you are right. I ought n't to have come. Our chaplain is not the kind of man — you will pardon my intruding —" his hand was upon the knob of the door to go.

"What is it? Your little daughter? Not dead?" The war was forgotten. "Tell me everything;" and the pastor drew his visitor back to a seat beside him on the old sofa heaped with papers. The bosom of the farmer was full, very full. He had just heard of the death of his child. Half an hour later Myrtle, opening the door with noiseless hand, was astonished to see a man in the blue of a Federal officer, kneeling with her father and sobbing aloud, his face in his handkerchief, while the pastor poured out his heart in prayer for him, as if there were no war.

But, going back to Scrubstones and the shadow which rested upon its roof tree, it was small relief which came to Mrs. Thirlmore with the death of little Owl. A new trouble, and one which in many senses taxed her already exhausted strength to the utmost, was awaiting her. It proved to be as the Doctor had surmised ; with the death of her child, Mrs. Grumbles sank all at once into the very furnace of fever. Then followed a period of nursing, which bore heavily upon Mrs. Thirlmore. Physicians, neighbors, pressed in ; Squash had to be kept from his mother by physical force, Maggie doggedly defying the effort of Hans and the rest. It was not so much a knowledge of medicine which was needed, as that soul of despotic authority, of quiet and silent command, which rules with a lifted finger, a motion of the hand or the head.

Mrs. Thirlmore had her reward when, recovering at last, the sturdy woman trembled and wept like a babe while she tried — tried in vain — to thank her friend for the care, which, the Doctor said, alone had saved her life.

"I did n't know there were such people, — not in this world," the farmer's wife whispered. " All you want, dear, you 'll get," she added by an inspiration made perfect through weakness. "And I 'm almost glad you 're going to break down," she continued. " I 'm getting strong again, and it will be my turn now to nurse."

But Mrs. Grumbles was mistaken. A few nights of unbroken sleep, and Mrs. Thirlmore was herself again, — herself, ah, and how much more !

CHAPTER XVII.

THE CONVALESCENT CAMP.

IT was a good thing for Colonel Thirlmore that immediately after going into the army he was hurled headlong into the thickest of the fight. It was a good thing, because his first experience of the war was an almost crushing defeat. His brigade had gone in with a rush, with the flaunting of flags, the acclaim of thousands, flowers, and tears, and the waving of white handkerchiefs. General J. Mandeville Gilmore made a fitting figure-head to this enthusiasm, with his gold lace and feathers and gorgeous self-esteem ; but with the hurrahs yet upon their lips, his command, shamefully beaten, was in full retreat. The men who had been most confident and boastful were now the most prostrated. For a time, as with Milton's Satanic host, the entire army lay whelmed as in one common destruction, immeasurably disgusted with itself.

It may be that the reserves of his bodily health and strength had much to do with it, but Colonel Thirlmore, like Milton's Satan, was one of the first to lift his head and take a survey of the universal ruin. The first spark of his returning life was a fierce wrath at himself, — an anger wholly new to him, unreasonable perhaps ; but which like a living coal in his inmost heart burned up what had hitherto been an over-estimate of his own powers. The young Napoleon may have begun his career with some such a disillusionment in regard to his superiors in command ; but not even Napoleon could have had a more settled conviction than Thirlmore that he possessed powers which would enable him to supplant lesser men. The silence of this conviction was the measure of its depth. With this there came upon Colonel Thirlmore, also, such a hatred of the Confederacy as made him war upon it ever after with the unsleeping energy of a personal revenge.

Thus it happened that Colonel Thirlmore was well known before he made the advance with his brigade upon the Blue Grass region. It had long been whispered that General Gilmore left things very much in his hands. This was well known to be so when Captain Warden made his abortive raid ; and it was soon understood that the Colonel had been planning for many weeks toward the capture of this Confederate force. Since entering the army, his power of strongly attaching people to himself, young men especially, had increased ; and many of the scouts, Jack Henson especially, had gone forth and reconnoitred the country southward more from love of their Colonel than for any other reason. On their return they had reported rather to him than to General Gilmore, for whom no one cared particularly, and in whose good luck nobody had much faith. Myrtle, poor child, had played unconsciously into Colonel Thirlmore's hands, and the capture of Captain Warden and his men had got into the papers as a specially brilliant feat of strategy. The same remarkable phenomenon was true in his case as in that of Fremont, of Robert E. Lee, and pre-eminently of Napoleon, — that multitudes of men became magnetized toward a man of whom they knew almost nothing, whom they never had seen and would never see. There seemed to be a storage of force in the very name of Thirlmore, wherever heard.

Very naturally General Gilmore felt indignant at this ; and having taken the necessary steps, he suddenly sent Colonel Thirlmore southwestward to take the command

of a convalescent camp.   In one hour he was cut off from
every man with whom he had been thus far associated,
and had his reputation to make over again and from the
first.

The small town in which the camp was situated was so
surrounded on every side and hemmed in by mountains
and ranges of barren upland, as to be like a pent-up room,
of which the windows are never opened.   It was breezy
enough upon the mountain tops ; but in the bowl-like
cavity in which the town lay, life seemed caught in an
eddy : there was no current, but, instead, a pond-like stagnation to which one yielded as at the first breath.   It
chanced, also, that the people thereabout were specially
loyal to the Confederacy, and cherished a peculiarly bitter
hatred of the Union.   Every locality has some one
greatest of men ; and this had taken its coloring from an
ex-Congressman, who had been among the first to favor
secession, and who, standing high in the Confederate
Government, had long ago thoroughly saturated his fellow-
citizens with his own almost frantic bitterness.   The convalescent camp was therefore very much like an island in
an ocean of gall.   Each man, woman, and child in and
around the place embraced every opportunity to show
their hearty dislike to their unwelcome visitors.

" He must have known it ! " Colonel Thirlmore said of
General Gilmore, as he rode rapidly, at the head of a small
escort, to take his new command.

What he referred to was this.   When a city pastor,
Colonel Thirlmore had, as men who have never been
otherwise than well are but too apt to have, a hearty dislike
of visiting the sick and dying ; of attending funerals.   If it
had not been tragic it would have been ludicrous, — the
shifts to which he resorted to escape work of this kind.

"And now," he thought, as he rode ahead of his escort, "of all men living, I am selected to take charge of a hospital of four or five thousand men, more or less sick, wounded, and dying. I detest sick people ; detest them only less than I do doctors. There will be, I suppose, a swarm of chaplains, and sanitary folk, and Christian Commission grandmothers. I had rather be shot."

In the centre of the town, occupied as a convalescent camp, there lifted its vast bulk from the ground a five-story stone building, which had once been a cotton-factory. In the haste of occupancy the machinery had been pitched out of the long ranges of windows, and now lay, red with rust and mire, in heaps of wheels, shafts, pinions, rubber-belts, and broken spindles, about the walls. Down the centre of each room, running the length of the building, and along its white-washed walls, were iron bedsteads, almost every one bearing its pallid occupant. Up and down the halls and corridors men wandered listlessly about, while day and night there was the coming and going of surgeons and nurses. Upon each story was one room redolent of ether, in which men were always waiting in their shirt sleeves to give out medicine, or to take off an arm or leg, as need determined. Almost every hour, it would seem, a squad of men would pass under the windows, bearing with reversed arms some poor fellow to burial.

At one end of the ground floor was the office of the former superintendent of the factory, now assigned to Colonel Thirlmore as officer in command. The room was as cold and bare as could be, and the first morning after his arrival the Colonel awoke after a miserable night. The feeling with which he had gone into battle was hilarity compared with what he now felt. He was half ill, and overcome with gloomy presentiments. Full of disgust at himself, as he recalled the hours spent with Myrtle Doubleday, his thoughts recurred afresh to his wife. She had done her best to interest him in her letters, which she was careful not to make too frequent; and the thought of her now brought pleasure, — but it was pleasure mixed with shame, — as he lay awake long before the hour for rising. Now that there was no one to know it, he yielded to a profound depression; his career was ended.

What could he do with such a command? Suddenly the reveille began out of doors. From the first his attention was arrested by the sound of the fife. Beginning softly, its notes rose shrill and clear, with a penetrating sweetness which he had not before heard. As he dressed himself, the fife seemed to grow impatient of the loitering rattle of the kettle-drums; it ran rapidly to the front, as it were; it grew bolder, louder, sweeter, more triumphant. The Colonel paused in his dressing; the piercing yet delicious music seemed to have taken wings, and was soaring like a lark toward heaven, singing as it soared.

"Something must be the matter with my ears," he said, "or somebody has invented a new kind of fife, or there must be an echo against these hills. Who ever heard such — yes, that is it!" he thought as the melody soared and circled as if overhead and into the listening air. "It must be that fellow I have heard so much about; what is it? Yes, Ralph Jennings."

It had become a habit with Colonel Thirlmore to remember names. When a preacher he was famous for not recollecting, or caring to recollect, either a name or a face. Owing to some new purpose in him of late he had bent himself, like Cæsar, to knowing the face and name of all his men, of every man with whom he was cast. The power of growth in such a nature as his is that it has a reserve power which enables it to do, and to do well, whatever it applies itself to the doing of. Thirlmore prided himself upon it. And therefore it was that he recalled the name of a fifer who was known through all the armies in that region as, according to the current phrase, " the best fifer in the world. You can bet your life on Ralph Jennings and his silver fife ! It's the winning of a fight to have *him* on the ground ! " In the general scramble for this famous fifer, it was by a singular good chance that he should be in a convalescent camp.

" I think it must help these poor fellows," the Colonel reflected, " in their struggle with grim death." It certainly helped the Colonel.

" Jennings," Colonel Thirlmore said to him that very day, " your fife is worth all the cocks that ever crew of a morning. You are better than all the doctors." Now the fifer was a very small man, as is almost always the case with fifers ; and like all great masters of music, he so gave himself to his melodies as to be useless in every other respect. It was his entire soul that he poured into his instrument. Without his fife he was worse than nothing. What his commanding officer said was repeated by him to every one in camp ; his children heard of it after the war ; and generations must pass away before the music of that almost miraculous fife will cease' to be handed down the ages.

And thus Colonel Thirlmore entered upon his routine of work. — Reveille at six o'clock. Roll call for such as were well enough ; and the Colonel commanding was oftener on the ground than his predecessors had been

wont to be. Police of quarters. Bugle call to breakfast. Mounting of guard. Companies drilling here and
there about the grounds, — some of the men going through
it from force of habit, when scarcely able to keep their
feet. Bugle call to dinner. Men loitering about in the
sun, talking in groups as to what had been and what
would be. More drill by companies, here and there.
Bugle call to supper.

After a few weeks of this, the dulness of his days began
to drive Colonel Thirlmore almost to desperation.

"I suppose," his wife wrote to him, "that the murder-
ous monotony, as you call it, of your hospital life is something like the dense and loathsome heaviness of a South
American swamp. Yet it is just where no wind can stir
their foliage that the mahogany tree and the rosewood
develop their increasing size, their iron fibre, and the deepening richness of their color for the after uses and admiration of the world. If I were in your place I would, in
view of the future, throw myself open to every influence,
however insignificant in itself, however repulsive. Your
future is yet to be ; and I dare say Lieutenant Van Doren
has told you that all things are being ordered towards you
for that."

"Yes, he *has* told me, and with a vengeance," the
husband said, as he folded up the letter. "This idea of
evolution, — of individual evolution under the eye and
hand of God, the evolver, — how it has taken hold on the
fancies of people ! Bah ! It is the craze of the hour,
nothing more."

No man is either oak or stone. The chimes of church
bells brought tears to the eyes of Napoleon, reminding
him of those of Brienne and boyhood. Awakened every
morning by the clear gladness of Ralph Jennings's fife, it

was to Colonel Thirlmore in the dullest and most rainy of dawns like a flash of the sun through the clouds. A newer purpose shot into him from without. Unconsciously, he paid more attention to the smallest matters in making his rounds. He had a purpose in view; and his experience in the Blue Grass, and before that, had taught him the value of making a warm partisan of every man in his reach. Yielding to the urgencies of his vigorous health and of his hidden purposes, he was on foot or on horseback from morning till night. Almost every day he rode, and always slowly, through and around the town, until he knew every house, street, alley. Or he would ride more rapidly through the suburbs, noting the lay of the mountains, the points at which the roads entered the place. It annoyed him at first to be shouted after derisively by the men of the place, still oftener by the women. Once or twice articles had been hurled at him from upper windows; but as, an hour after, those houses were seized upon by his command for military purposes, this soon ceased. The hooting of the school-children ceased too, after the school-teachers had been summoned before him once or twice. As to the ladies and women, they had not the heart to go on insulting so noble-looking a gentleman, when their utmost efforts caused him merely to lift his hat — as if in acknowledgment of courtesies received.

"I have long ago learned," he wrote to his wife, "that there is no such armor against those of Southern birth as a distinguished but invariable courtesy of manner. They are too courteous themselves not to yield to it;" but this theory often required such a steady culture of patience as could not but advance that quality of character immensely.

"I am as sure," he wrote, "of the result as is my

poor friend Dr. Doubleday; and I am so sure of it that I try habitually to live, act, feel, as if the war had ended twenty years ago in the victorious establishment of such a nation as must command the enthusiastic love both of South and North. So I do believe, you see, in your idea of evolution — a very little."

" It would interest you," he wrote again, " to watch the negroes at work in the fields as I make my rounds through the country lying about the town. When there is no white person except myself in sight they always greet me with a bow and a laugh which displays all their teeth. To them we are only less than the angels of God. They are confident of the result, whoever else is not. I always smile and nod back to them. Perhaps they, too, are ' evolving,' so as to be of use to me some day."

With what breathless interest did Mrs. Thirlmore, far away in Scrubstones, read the letters of her husband. Captain Grumbles had handled plow and hoe, axe and scythe, so long that when he wrote a letter it was undertaken with more apprehension beforehand, more fatigue afterward, than the felling of a tree or the building of roods of stone fence would have required. Naturally his epistles were few and far between. All the more, therefore, did Mrs. Grumbles consider it the greatest of pleasures, when, of an evening after supper, Mrs. Thirlmore read aloud snatches from the letters of her husband. Squash and Snap listened with breathless attention, and Pop was as quiet as the redness of her locks and the tension of her nerves allowed.

There had been an indefinable something in the tone of her husband's letters during his stay under Dr. Doubleday's hospitable roof, which had filled Mrs. Thirlmore with dim apprehensions. Woman-like, she could not keep from remembering how warmly he had spoken of Myrtle Doubleday at first; how silent he had been in regard to her afterward. Then came the failure of the midnight assault upon the town, and the capture of the Confederate force. For once the papers were right in giving all the credit to Colonel Thirlmore. In his energetic efforts to disprove this, General Gilmore had aroused a storm in behalf of his subordinate which exaggerated the merits of the Colonel beyond all bounds. Wife-like, Mrs. Thirlmore believed it all. There was a banquet given in connection with it in the city in which her husband had been pastor; a handsome sword had been sent him; but his wife had resisted all importunities to visit the city, and remained where she was.

Perhaps it was this faith and pride in him which so saturated her letters that her husband would have been dull indeed if he had not been affected by them. Love is effective, however it expresses itself; but when it employs a penmanship so beautiful, a diction so faultless as hers, how should any one not welcome every letter with increased appetite? Since Thirlmore had taken command of the convalescent camp, he had more time at his disposal than when in full realization of the charms of Myrtle Doubleday; but this was not all. His wife truly surmised that the vast amount of suffering about him — suffering, as a rule, so patiently borne — was not without its influence, an altogether new influence of the kind, upon him. How eagerly she looked for his letters in those days !

"As night closes in," he wrote to her, "the men cluster about on benches, chairs, or the sides of their beds. Whatever the talk may be about in the mornings, that in the evenings, I notice, is always of home. To judge by such scraps as I can catch in passing, there never were such homes, such wives, such children, as are possessed by these men. Now and then I see some young fellow in his flannel shirt, with an arm gone, or a leg, who is telling, always in a low voice, of the girl he hopes to marry yet. You can know it by the way in which his hearers draw closer to him, by the depth of their attention. 'Bet your life she's thinking about me this moment,' I heard one say, as I passed the other evening. 'Do you think she'll have a chap with *both* legs shot off?' I overheard another time from what was left of a strapping young fellow.

"Some sit on the floor beside a candle-box, or stool, on which flickers a candle, writing letters, or reading; or perhaps it is a table, around which they are playing cards : but I allow no gambling. Let a man begin to tell a story to one hearer, in a few moments, I notice, dozens collect to come in with the laugh or the exclamation in the end, suitable to the story. Two poor fellows barely able to crawl begin an argument. It is as apt to be on baptism or predestination as upon the last battles; and waxing louder and louder, each man has before him long scores of adherents to back him up, the argument at last taking in the whole room.

"There are poor fellows here to whom the only thing left is a good voice. One of them will begin to hum to himself a tune. Growing louder and louder, in the end there will be dozens of men yearning, at the tops of their voices, after 'Annie Laurie,' or craving to be 'Babes again, if but for a night,' so that the original singer is lost. Thousands more can be heard in the evenings desiring to be, 'Nearer, my God, to Thee, nearer to Thee,' with a fervor which is not fully borne out in their daily lives."

As he had time for it, the commanding officer would

fall into talk with one man and another as to how and where the wounds were received, what battles they had been in, and the like. Conquering his repugnance, he would occasionally seat himself at the bedside of some poor fellow, to ask him of his often desperate case. He had his own plan in this; yet he could not but be touched by what he saw and heard.

"These are not ordinary invalids," he wrote to his wife. "These are men cut suddenly down while young, or in the prime of life, and while facing death for that flag which is no more to them than it is to you or me." Sometimes he went into details concerning their heroism, which brought tears to the eyes of his wife and to those at Scrubstones clustered about her after supper to hear. What he did not tell her was of his nightly rounds from picket to picket about the town. Nor did he speak of how he gave new energy to the drilling by companies and by regiments, as the men were able to go back into the ranks. He did so with a vigor which would have made him the best-hated officer in the army, if he had not secured, from the outset, the enthusiastic regard of his men. They had heard of him before he came; it was not hard to kindle their liking into a feeling which might stand him in good stead when the time came.

The one creature he loved was his horse Tamerlane. Coming into camp after midnight from his rides of inspection, he took pleasure in grooming and feeding the animal with his own hands. With his hand lovingly laid on the head of the horse, he would talk to him in a way which would have made any one but Tam think he was an idiot or crazy. Tam understood. "You are a safer friend than Myrtle," he would murmur to him.

These dull days of hospital life were rolling slowly on

toward an event. Events such as this no more arrive
without ripening processes than does an orange or a
cocoa-nut. Was it that they were conspiring of themselves toward this, or that Colonel Thirlmore was compelling them to conspire?

CHAPTER XVIII.

"FROM what I can learn," wrote the General commanding the Confederate forces nearest to the convalescent camp, "the enemy there is deplorably demoralized. The winter has been an unusually severe one, and the sick and wounded have succumbed in great numbers. Their medical staff is said to be of an inferior grade. While there has been, and is, a continual influx upon them of disabled men, — the recoveries are few. Deserters come in to me quite often, and many of them assert that Colonel Thirlmore, the officer commanding, is miserably unfitted for his place, — as is but natural, since, it is said, he came into the army from the pulpit. It is clear to me that I should not postpone what I have before suggested." The rest of the dispatch can be had among those captured after the collapse of the Confederacy.

There was one deserter in particular from whom the Rebel commander obtained much information. He was a small but athletic man ; and when shown into the presence of the officer, he told of things which justly excited the indignation of a man not so hardened to suffering as to cease to be the humane gentleman he had been before the war.

It seemed, from his story, that the deserter, a private in Colonel Thirlmore's old regiment, had fallen in love with a farmer's daughter whose home was near the town in which the convalescent camp was located. She was virtuous but poor, and proud of dress and admiration,

somewhat giddy, "but," the deserter added, with tears in
his eyes, "one of the best girls living." In an evil hour
Colonel Thirlmore had seen her. Making some errand
at a distance, he had sent the lover away. "And he
knew when he did it," the man sobbed, "that we were to
be married as soon as the war was over." Taking advantage of his absence the Colonel had seduced the
foolish girl, and then abandoned her.

"Was he not once a sensational preacher in the East?"
The Confederate commander had evidently heard of the
Federal officer before.

"He was."

"And notorious even then for his atrocious conduct?
—at least so the papers said."

"Yes, General. He is a handsome and eloquent man,
utterly unprincipled. As soon as I heard of it," the deserter added, "I came back, watched my chance behind
a tree, and fired at him. He rides a spirited horse, and
somehow I missed. I knew he would be sure enough
who did it; so I took to the woods, and here I am. As
sure as there is a God in heaven," the man said with
uplifted hand, "I will kill him yet!" And it was very
evident he meant what he said. It was from this man
that the Confederate general obtained most of his knowledge of the demoralized and defenceless condition of the
convalescent camp.

Colonel Thirlmore was informed about this time of the
presence in the Confederate camp of the distinguished
officer high in the Rebel councils whose home was in the
town, and who burned with a desire to purge it of the
enemy. He would give the Rebel general no peace until
he ventured an attack.

It must have been the fault of Ralph Jennings and his

marvellous fife. One morning it rang out clearer, shriller than before; the fifer fairly outdid himself. There seemed to be new life, too, in the drillings of the day. Men slipped out of bed when the attendants were away, to fall into the ranks. More than one crutch was dropped. for a Winchester. There was something in the air,— nobody seemed to know what; yet the ordinary routine was carried out until it was almost night. Then in an hour the entire town was in commotion. The bugles summoned every man who could bear arms into the ranks. There was a galloping of aides along the streets; cannon were being dragged hither and thither. From the hour of his coming the Colonel commanding had made preparations for such a crisis, and in a few hours many of the streets were barricaded with wagons, bales of cotton, and tobacco hogsheads. Redoubts were hastily thrown up. The magnificent maples with which the streets were lined were cut down to serve as abattis. Every man who could use a gun was on the alert. The poor fellows on their beds in the hospital dragged what was left of their bodies to the windows to see, some of them insisting upon the possession of a musket, in case " of a chance for a shot." The surgeons and their helpers laid in fresh supplies, placed their instruments in order upon clean cloths, and clustered about in groups chatting together cheerfully as to the probabilities.

And with it all there was that confidence in the commanding officer, on the part of the majority, which it is the peculiar property of men of Thirlmore's kind to arouse. General Gilmore had unlimited reliance upon himself; but there was no more infection, contagion, in that than there is in a toothache or a sprained ankle. The confidence of Colonel Thirlmore in himself was as ardent, as deep-seated as scarlet fever ; so fervent a force was it in vein and artery that it was contagious, infectious, — it might almost be styled epidemic.

At midnight the expected assault was made. The Confederate commander had not been the only one deceived by false information. Had Colonel Thirlmore known the facts he could have expected but one result, the enemy · were in so much larger force than he had supposed. But few knew this besides himself; and the men had reached that degree of faith in him which laughed at risks.

Why go into any detail of what befell upon that eventful night? Cannon opened upon the garrison from the hastily constructed batteries upon the mountains : but there were other and masked batteries, unexpectedly well located, which returned the fire. The assault upon the barricaded streets, now at one point and then at another, was made with a fury which it seemed impossible to resist. Tamerlane and his rider did the best work of their lives. Now at one side of the town and then at the other, Colonel Thirlmore seemed to be everywhere at once, commanding, encouraging, leading up fresh troops ; in more cases than one cutting down individuals of his own command who tried to fly. His language, at times, was dreadfully out of keeping with what is usual to clergymen. Now and again, as the assault continued, it seemed as if the Confederates must succeed. More than once Colonel Thirlmore, having done all he could, was compelled to give up in despair, the besiegers renewing their attacks with such fury. But he did not allow any one to know it. Wounded, and bleeding from flesh wounds here and there, he continued to cheer his men on.

For that, it may as well be remarked here as anywhere else, is said to be the difference between American troops and those of the by-gone history. Up to a certain point the battle in old times would rage, and with heroic courage upon both sides. When that point was reached, the defeated army gave way instantly, utterly, and never dreamed of anything else than flight. It was the sudden breaking down of an array, the supreme excellence of which lay in its perfect unity, its precise and mechanical movement, as in a grand machine. Being a vast and splendid machine, when it broke it broke utterly, — as does the engine, say, of a steamship, which goes on altogether or stops altogether. In these later days, and among American soldiers most of all, the efficiency of an army is shifted from the whole to the individual ; not until each separate soldier confesses himself beaten does the battle end. There are rare instances of panic and stampede ; but, as every man " goes upon his own hook " in farming, mining, merchandizing, or voting, so he does in fighting also. The hostile Hercules must slay every separate head of his hydra, or he has accomplished nothing. Even then it takes more time to mend and put a machine in working order after a crash, than it does to put the individual soldier on his feet again. It is this intense personalism which is the glory of our civilization, as it is of our religion ; and therefore is it that our Government, like our Christianity, is elastic and indestructible.

Of what avail would it have been to the commander in this fight if every man of his force had not been, more or less, like himself? But his foes were equally brave and persistent. They were picked men, too : while his was an army of invalids, more or less recovered, and greatly outnumbered. But just when the Confederates were about sweeping, with a yell, everything before them, a rocket shot out of a window in the highest story of a hospital.

As it rose into the air, a fife sounded loud and clear upon the flank of the assailants. There must have been drums with it; but only the fife was heard, soaring above the din in the very ecstasy of "Yankee Doodle." The next instant a masked battery opened upon what seemed, in the confusion, to be the rear of the Confederates; the red flashes breaking from high up the slopes of the overhanging hills, accompanied by a nearer rattle of musketry, and then a charge down hill from flank and rear. What followed was like a sudden whirlwind, the redoubts and barricades being the revolving centre !

How much can be accomplished in a moment ! One instant of hesitation, while the balance of battle hung in even poise; the next, the Southern troops, scattered to the last man, had turned and were flying in utter rout, — their enemies, in their eagerness to get over them, cursing the barricades which, up to the moment before, had been their chief security, and pursuing with a larger expenditure of shouts than of shots.

Day was breaking as the prisoners, captured cannon, horses, and flags were collected hastily into the grounds about the hospital. Colonel Thirlmore was in his room having his hurts examined, drinking hot coffee and eating by snatches, issuing his orders for as full pursuit of the defeated foe as was possible, — when his attention was arrested.

The deserter who had been so shamefully treated by him came into the room bringing in as prisoner the commander of the attacking party. Considering his misery from the loss of the girl he loved, he seemed singularly cheerful, and his kindly feeling toward the Tarquin of his Lucretia needed explanation.

"This here," he said to his prisoner, "is the man I told

you about. I wanted to introduce you to him so badly
that I kept as near you as I could while the fighting was
going on. Now, what I want," with a broad grin, "is for
you to stay with him a bit, — to cultivate his acquaintance, like."

Alas for the humane officer ! He had learned while
the kindest-hearted man and lumber-merchant of his town,
in more peaceful times, that there are those who make
shameful profit of men famous for their charity ; he had
now to learn that even war has its impostors.

"That will do, Henson," Colonel Thirlmore said. "You
have finished it splendidly ; but we have other matters on
hand. See if you cannot get Tamerlane into condition in
an hour or two. We 've only made a beginning."

He meant what he said. The result of the assault had
surprising remedial effects. Many a man too weak to stand
the day before was now on his feet, and able at least to
help guard the prisoners. Rations were rapidly served out
after breakfast ; and with a larger force than he had hoped
at his disposal, the officer in command was off in pursuit
of the flying Confederates, — Ralph Jennings fifing as if
he had not been at it for hours before.

Except that the Southern troops were more impulsive
during the war, there was not an atom of difference as to
patriotism or courage. Possibly a more deeply seated
conviction as to the right of the Union against secession
and all disintegration, gave to the one side a deeper breathing, as it were, during the contest.

"As mountaineers are proverbial," Mrs. Thirlmore wrote
to her husband, "for their love of freedom, and sailors for
their generosity, so it must be, is it not, for those who are
fighting for the whole country, not for a fragment thereof ?
It may be mere fancy, but it broadens a man to stand up

for the great Republic, I should think. Victory means more to him. Defeat must mean less, have less effect, since he has so much more to fall back upon."

And yet, as a rule, a man is more demoralized by defeat than he is exhilarated by victory. Especially when troops were as confident of success as the Confederates had been in the well-known assault just spoken of, the reaction of repulse cuts very deep. There seemed to be almost an insanity of terror in their flight. Braver men never drew breath; and yet the road was strewn with guns thrown away, wagons abandoned, cannon left sticking in the mud. These were speedily unspiked and applied to the use of the pursuers. Colonel Thirlmore was forced to give paroles on the spot, at every turn of the road, to prisoners who seemed to court capture.

"It is mighty queer," Private Henson remarked, "how many of these chaps were original Union men. 'Never believed anything in secession from the start,' — hardly one of 'em but says that."

In fact, the entire country through which the pursuing troops passed seemed prostrated by a very epidemic of alarm. It was only because the Federal commander was almost as much feared as he was loved, that excesses were not committed upon people who would willingly have compromised for escape from worse evils by the loss of pigs and turkeys.

Here and there a wild fellow had adorned himself with a hoop-skirt, an old-fashioned bonnet, or carried a captured Confederate flag trailing from the tail of his horse; but any offence worse than this would have met with discipline, sharp and to the point. It was very much like an extemporized picnic, every one was in such a jolly good humor, singing, shouting, calling to each other, and to the panic-stricken country folk who gazed furtively at them from behind barns and fences. It was very evident why the soldiers on both sides were styled " boys." It is to the earlier days of individual life, as of the world, that war carries us ; and their commander, with a heart as hilarious just then as any, was careful not to hear or see too much.

" Blessed be that law of nature," he had written to his wife long before, and concerning similar experiences, " by which the deepest weariness produces the sweetest sleep. When night comes, all we have to do is to lie down, and in an instant all our cares are ended. We may not have even a dog-tent ; our rubber clothes may be torn or lost ; our supper of strong coffee and stronger bacon may have been insufficient : the rain may be pouring down in torrents ; and we dare not kindle a fire for fear of drawing that of the enemy. All we have to do is to get under a tree ; do without a tree if there is none ; pillow our head upon a saddle or haverstack, and with our hat over our face, if we have nothing better, descend into the depths of slumber as delicious as that of a babe on the bosom of its mother."

Such were his luxuries now on this rapid pursuit. His scout Henson had brought him information which was driving him on at headlong rate. There was that, too, from which he was flying, as murderer rarely flies from the avenger of blood.

" It is the one opportunity of my life," he thought, as he urged his way on by day, and, so far as he dared, by night also.

But human nature cannot hold out forever As the hours became days, the joking and laughing slackened down into silence. His horses began to reason among themselves less favorably concerning the men they bore, and the cannon or wagons which they dragged. His men began to give out; he had to drop them at the roadside as he sped along. In virtue of having more than others of that essence of life which we call intellect, Colonel Thirlmore endured better. But, at last, things grew worse. Even his officers began to murmur, almost to mutiny.

"We are getting too far from our base," they said. "It is dangerous, this rushing so fast and so far into the enemy's country. Our ammunition may give out; what will old Gilmore think? Thirlmore is crazy!"

Still the commanding officer pressed on, until at last his subordinates made a unanimous and formal protest against it. "Our very horses are breaking down under it. Even now it will be all we can do to cut our way back to camp," they said.

"Columbus is not the one man," Colonel Thirlmore continued to himself, having refused their request, and explained matters to them as far as he could, "who has to stand by himself and against his crew, — against the world, for that matter. *You* won't go back on me, old fellow," he communed with Tamerlane that night, his arm about his neck in the darkness. Tam shook his head; but it drooped as he did so. " Hold out as well as you can, old chap," his master said to him, "because it is — don't you see? — the one chance of my life."

CHAPTER XIX.

DISOBEYING ORDERS.

COLONEL Thirlmore had not ridden more than half a day in pursuit of the flying enemy before he summoned his scout, Jack Henson, to ride by his side and apart from all others.

"Henson," he asked, "are you a married man?"

"Not much!" There was an emphasis in the tones of the man which hinted of experiences in the past, into which the other did not care to inquire.

"I am glad it happens so." Although Colonel Thirlmore said no more than that, to Henson it meant some task on hand which was not without its perils. Now, no one is going to say that the love between a man and a maid is not a beautiful thing. It may be cheerfully conceded that there are few things more charming than to see a pair of lovers straying together, hand in hand, in some sweet month of May, along a green and sufficiently secluded lane, toward the heaven of their wedding-day. Let us agree, however, that there are other aspects of mutual affection.

These two men, for instance, looked the least in the world like a pair of lovers, — the one seated on Tamerlane, and of that aspect which causes a passer-by to wonder who and what he is; the other upon a shaggy and shapeless horse, and in no way distinguished in size, face, or feature, from ordinary men. It made affection between them the more unlikely, that there was evidently greater difference of grade and blood between these two than between the animals they rode. For this very reason, perhaps, Jack Henson, small, compact, wholly uneducated, loved the other with that peculiar affection which is styled loyalty when a king is its object; and when our Maker is concerned, it is called religion. It is true that Colonel Thirlmore's liking in return was very much such as he had for Tamerlane; but it was genuine and very strong. Except that Henson was nearer the rank of a St. Bernard dog or a horse than Captain Grumbles, it was a relation such as was growing more vigorous every day between the farmer of Scrubstones and the ex-preacher.

"General Gilmore won't like all this." The scout now made the remark to Colonel Thirlmore as a feeler, and after some meditative silence.

"I fear not." But the other did not look at Henson as he made the reply.

"The General, — he'll stop it. That is, if he can," Jack Henson reflected aloud.

"I am afraid so. Perhaps," the other cast out the idea as if he were speaking of the weather, "he may send a messenger to stop me. That is all. What I wanted to say was, — You have been of great service to me. I wish I had something about me to give you. Some day I hope — "

"Don't want anything, Colonel." It was said with almost heat, as the scout drew rein and fell back. He must have taken mortal offence, for, at next roll-call, he was missing. His comrades glanced inquiringly at one another and at the Colonel, who looked as if suddenly elated at something, but made no remark.

"Jack's being away means more than his being here," was a remark quite often made; and one of the sharpest of the men created something of a reputation for himself

by saying that night at the camp fire, "Jack Henson's the
best riddle *I* know. The answer is always good, if it *is*
one no fellow can find out." While another added, —

"But it is mighty ticklish business. I ain't that fond
of rope-dancing myself."

It seemed a singular coincidence that, with a strong
escort and riding very fast, Captain Grumbles passing
along that road the next day should all at once find the
scout riding by his side.

"If you please, Captain — " It was all he said, as he
saluted the officer.

"Do you come from Colonel Thirlmore?" Captain Grumbles asked almost eagerly, half reining in his
horse.

"Me? From Colonel Thirlmore? No, sir. When
the Colonel left camp I was too sick to go. I have mighty
bad attacks sometimes. The Colonel he told me," the
scout said, with infantile innocence of eyes, "to go into
the hospital. It is acute rheumatism; and it doubles me
up sometimes so's I can't get about except on all fours.
My mother used to have it. But it's all in the weather.
It comes and goes with that. Early this morning I felt
so much better I slipped out of bed, and thought I would
follow on after the Colonel."

"Do you know where he is gone?"

Mr. Henson seemed to be searching his memory, his
closely cropped head a little on one side. A pugilist
depends upon his muscle; a sharpshooter upon the accuracy of eye and nerve; an artist upon the deftness of
his touch, answering to the beauty of his ideal, — with the
scout it was different. Very often, indeed, had he escaped
the rope of a spy by casting his sun-burned face into
the mould, so to speak, of now an artless child, then of

a stupid countryman; at yet other times of a downright idiot. To-day he was a stupid private.

"I say, Henson, you need not pretend to be a fool. Where has your Colonel gone?" Captain Grumbles demanded again.

"I should have thought somebody might have told you that, as you came through the Convalescent Camp, sir," he said doggedly.

"But they did n't tell me, except that he was gone off after the Confederates."

"That 's all I know, sir."

Captain Grumbles was in great perplexity. He had a message for Colonel Thirlmore from General Gilmore; but the General had not imagined that the commander of the Convalescent Camp would have added to his unprecedented conduct by leaving it in pursuit of anybody. The message must be delivered; he was following the culprit; how far must he go, and in what direction beyond a general southwestward, he had no idea.

"Had you heard before of the waxing we gave the Rebs, Captain?" the scout asked respectfully.

"Yes, we have heard of it! You are a slippery character, Henson. I do not know what tricks you may be up to. You like your Colonel, and I had better tell you that General Gilmore is down on him." It was said with a troubled face.

"Down on him for repelling an attack on his camp? How could he help it, Captain?"

"It 's easy to say that, Henson; but no man knows better than you do how it came about that there was an attack. The enemy were tricked into it in some way. You did most of the tricking, no doubt of that. Colonel Thirlmore and you seemed to think you were in command of an advance : it was a camp of sick men. Suppose he had been beaten? General Gilmore is very angry with him. Such a thing never was heard of before. He may court-martial him for it. Don't you see?"

Captain Grumbles would not have said as much to any man but Henson. The truth is, the scout was an exceptional character, often on terms of closer understanding with the highest officer in command than anybody else. Yet it was strange. To judge from appearances now, he was the stupidest man in the army. He had listened,— his lower jaw hung down, his eyes glassy, a lumbering and loutish booby from head to foot. He now shook his head sadly.

"People call me a fool now and then," he said ; "but I was sorry when our little fight came off. The Colonel is a mighty go-ahead man, but I know he had n't oughter got into that scrimmage. If I had a dared to do it, I would have told him so. It was such a foolish thing for him to do. That is what everybody is saying, I dare swear ; that is, if much of anything is said about it. Is anything said about it, Captain?"

"Said about it !" Captain Grumbles's broad face, in its aureole of sandy, yellow hair and whiskers, glowed like the harvest-moon at its full. In his joy and pride over his friend he forgot his rank for a moment.

"Said about it !" he exclaimed. "I should think so ! It's in all the papers, North and South. Who ever heard of a man in command of a hospital doing such a thing? Fighting fresh troops with a handful of cripples ! It's the sensation of the day ! It's the best thing since the war broke out— I mean," Captain Grumbles recovered himself, "it's the worst, the most reckless thing —and now when we get to his camp he's off after something else. He is the most dreadfully imprudent man!" The ex-farmer had to remove his military cap to wipe his perspiring brow.

The scout was chuckling to himself as he rode. As every one knew, General Gilmore had detailed Colonel Thirlmore to command the Convalescent Camp in order to put an end to a subordinate who had been too successful already. He had thus quarantined him beyond the remotest chance of doing anything; and this was the result. Still more perversely, the people everywhere did not look at that result as General Gilmore did. Worse still, the President and Congress, tired out with paper plans, abortive expeditions, and valorous generals who accomplished nothing, were but too apt to overlook anything, now that a brilliant repulse of the enemy was cheering the country, after a period of long inaction, bungling management, and official incapacity. Somebody had, at last, done something! That something was greatly exaggerated. The illustrated papers got hold of the affair, and it was ludicrously overrated. In these the hospital towered aloft into a castle, assaulted on all sides by the Confederates. Bombs were bursting in the air; horsemen dashing about on the grounds below; the invalids leaning from the windows, were waving flags of defiance, and blazing away at the foe with muskets and pistols. In other woodcuts, Rebels by the ten thousand were being repulsed from the barricades and flying in confusion, Colonel Thirlmore pressing after them with drawn sword, and on a horse which was less of Tamerlane than it was Pegasus, Hippogriff, and Bucephalus, all in one.

All this was to come after; still it is easy to understand why, at the first news of the affair, General Gilmore was so enraged at his subordinate: and here was that subordinate — insubordinate, rather — gone off, a mere corporal's guard at his heels, into who knows what disastrous attempts!

" Henson, look here ! Out with it ! " Captain Grumbles said, sharply enough. " What is Colonel Thirlmore up to now? You know where he is ? "

" I suppose so, sir: I know well enough to be glad you are come with reinforcements. The Colonel — he will be mighty glad."

" Reinforcements ! You know well enough no messenger could get to him in time to halt and bring him back unless in this way. General Gilmore," Mr. Henson's superior officer deigned to say, " had no man willing to risk being taken as a spy."

" Do you think, sir, he could trust any man to stop the Colonel and bring him in? Seems to me it would be mighty hard to find any of our men would hanker after doing that. I would hate to do it myself."

It was a weakness of Captain Grumbles, which not even the war could cure, and his color came and went; but he did not hesitate.

" Here, you ! Stop playing the fool," he said angrily, " and let us understand each other. You know I am a friend of your Colonel. Have you any idea what he is up to now? Out with it ! Do you know? "

" Yes, Captain." The scout was himself again. " I do know everything. When I tell you, I know you won't have the heart to interrupt. It 's grand, if you let the Colonel alone for a little. This is the way of it."

He went into a rapid explanation of what his superior officer was trying to accomplish. Captain Grumbles reined in his horse nearer to the other in order the better to hear. It had been one trouble since Henson had joined him, that somehow the scout could not keep up with him. "If I'm to tell you, Captain," he now complained, "you must ride slower. You see how tired my horse is. Hold in, please." The other looked at him sharply; but Mr. Henson's face was again like that of a babe.

"Go on, and as quick as you can," the other said.

But the scout took his time both in riding and in talking. Captain Grumbles forgot everything as he listened. Colonel Thirlmore had not dashed on merely in pursuit of the flying enemy. Acting on priceless information derived from the scout, — and Mr. Henson went into a painfully detailed narration of it, and of his mode of obtaining it, — the Colonel was driving on to effect a thing hazardous to the last degree, which if effected would turn an entirely new page in what had been so far, and since the war began, a volume of indecision, hesitation, and inevitable failure.

"You see how it is, Captain," the scout said, at last, slyly drawing in his horse to a yet slower gait. The other did not observe it; for he *did* see. Knowing as he did the lay of the land, the conflict of opinions in that particular region, the disposition of Confederate and Federal forces, he was deeply interested.

"I will be doggoned!" — it was the most violent expletive the conscientious farmer allowed himself. "Why, Henson," he added, "it will put another State in our arms! They never were Secesh; they'll jump at the chance! It is *grand*, by — George!" sobering himself down to that. The scout laughed aloud, reining in his horse still more.

"But if you suppose," his companion said suddenly, in a startled way, "that, therefore, I will play false with my orders — "

"Certainly not, sir!" Mr. Henson was shocked at such a thought.

"Come, there, men! have you gone to sleep? Bugler!" At the gesture of the Captain the bugle rang out for a quicker step, the Captain himself sitting more erect, riding on more rapidly. But as Mr. Henson fell back among the troops he made a sign to one or two of them. Jack Henson was in high repute, his Colonel still more so, and the column caught the hint immediately. So far as they dared they drew in their horses. Henson had already managed to check their speed; henceforth it was more than Captain Grumbles could do to urge them on. They made their halts as long as possible, were detained here and there in unaccountable ways, — the people in the farmhouses on either side of the highway gazing almost listlessly at them as they passed. The leaders were away, as a rule, in the army, at the Confederate Congress, — in Europe many of them, or Mexico, — and the commonalty were coolly waiting, with their like in every land and age, to see how the tide was to run.

It was noon the next day when the column reached the forking of roads. As a matter of course, the scout led off to the right without a word. But Captain Grumbles sent an orderly to ask a solitary negro at work in the fields near by. As the result of his information there was a halt.

"Henson!" His men did not know their officer had such a voice! While the scout looked back in seeming amazement, the bugle called the troops back, and they struck off after their Captain along the left instead. There was not a man there but felt that a crisis was at hand, as the scout galloped swiftly past the column and rode beside his superior officer.

" Captain, for God's sake ! "

" Hold your tongue, sir ! "

With everybody else, Henson had a genuine liking for Captain Grumbles, — lumbering, loose-jointed, long-legged old soul that he was, kindly-hearted as a child, always among the sick and the wounded. And none the less — so much to the scout was his colonel — that he would have shot Grumbles on the spot rather than have the plans of Thirlmore defeated. Furthermore, he would not have hesitated an instant to compass the death of every man in their rear as they rode along, could he thus have carried out the purposes of the man of whom they were in pursuit.

But the farmer turned warrior was dreadfully perplexed. He was white and red by turns as he rode along. He wiped his fevered brow more than once, cool as the day was. Confronting him in the middle of the way as he went, was the man he had induced to go into the army. He could see, as it were, every line of his face. And now he, of all men, must stop his friend upon the very edge, perhaps, of such success as would be the making of that friend. And not his making only. What vast advantage would come to the country from it ! Ought he to obey the orders of such an old goose as General Gilmore, under such circumstances?

He pictured to himself the face of Colonel Thirlmore, when he should hand him the order for his recall. It was in a breast-pocket, — a portentous document such as General Gilmore loved ; tied, sealed, the sacred embodiment of all that General Gilmore chanced at the moment to stand for. As he rode along he felt, mechanically, in his underclothing for the letter. There was no need, actually, to have it in hand ; it was so large that he could tell whether it was there or not without that. His face grew red as crimson, then white and cold; the package was gone! He checked himself in the act of tearing open his vest. The men would see it. What was the use? The document was gone. Moreover, he knew who had stolen it the night before. Henson was up to anything, as he knew of old. Any one could see he had abstracted it, if only by the face which the scout presented, as, in answer to a sharp summons, he rode up again to the side of his superior. His countenance was altogether too innocent, too blank of all wrong; it was that of an imbecile. There was no use of saying anything to him.

Now, there are men who in giving their beautifully executed note consider it as a little better than paying down the cash; and so it was with General Gilmore. The letter of recall was merely one of those military forms in which he delighted. Since he had signed it there was no fear but that it would, like his many proclamations, accomplish its object of itself. In addition, the old Agamemnon, striding up and down his room, had given Captain Grumbles such verbal instructions as themselves sufficed. No one knew that better than Jack Henson. There was nothing else that he could do, and he rode along in sullen silence. So far from intending to punish him, Captain Grumbles thought all the more of him.

"That's the difference," he reflected, "between Thirlmore and ordinary men, — like myself, for instance. Who would, or could, be as devoted as that to me?" and surely even the Devil himself must have certain of the qualities of the Almighty, if he awakens a loyalty to himself more single-hearted than that which is paid to the King of kings.

While the Captain thought of the disaster to his friend

—to the cause also — which must ensue if he reached him a minute too soon, he half unconsciously held in his horse to a slower gait.   For the instant, he could see nothing but the Colonel.

The next instant Colonel Thirlmore passed from before his eyes, had ceased to exist !   In his place there stood Aurora Ann.   How could she help excluding everything else ?   So powerful of frame was she, so blooming, her arms a-kimbo, her clear, steady eyes full in his.

" Husband ! "

Captain Grumbles lifted himself in his stirrups ; his voice reached the last man lingering in the rear.

" Double quick !   March ! "

The bugle rang out.   The men stared at each other and put spurs to their horses to keep up, as their officer suddenly shot far ahead, bending down over his horse's mane as he urged him on.

" Quick !   Quick !   Forward ! " and again the bugle rang out.   Drawing his sword as he galloped, Captain Grumbles shook it threateningly at his troops.   His cry and the peal of the bugle came to them in the same breath.

" Charge ! "

A distant sound broke upon his ear, heard faintly above the galloping of hoofs.   The road turned to the right, then turned to the left.   Before them a broad river flowed softly along.   Across it came from the distance the roar of cannon, a volley of musketry, another, yet another. The scout had now galloped ahead, his carbine lying in front of him upon the saddle.   The command had reined up at the water's edge.   The scout had halted an instant, was listening intently.   Evidently a battle was being fought, to the right.   The cannon ceased.   The musketry broke into scattering shots, coming more and more faintly upon the ear.

Jack Henson sat erect, with a hurrah.

" You can't stop him now ! " he shouted. " Don't you wish you could ? " In the insolence of his triumph his left hand was at his nose, his fingers working in derision of Captain Grumbles. He was answered by a roar of laughter from the men. Then he was tearing down stream again to the right, the gravel flying from under his horse's hoofs. " This way, this way ! " he shouted, and the troops followed him pell-mell.

At a turn of the river it broadened out into a brawling shallow, and the scout dashed in, the troops at his heels, Captain Grumbles still in advance. And — is it not the most amazing reversal of paradise ? — every man there was more eager to get to the slaughter than if they had been going to a wedding-feast !

We are all of us too familiar with what followed, to tarry for the oft-reiterated description. The news which Henson had picked up while a cruelly-wronged deserter in the Confederate camp, was this : Far away to the right, upon the Mississippi, was a town which had been held valiantly by the Rebels for many months against the Federals, besieging it by land and water. As it turned out afterward, the garrison were driven to the last extremities and were on the eve of surrender. At this juncture a large Confederate force, unexpectedly released from a yet more important point eastward, was being hastened to the relief of the beleaguered town. Its commander, informed of this, was, by desperate effort, holding his own until it should arrive. Fully advised by Henson on the night of the assault and repulse at the Convalescent Camp, Colonel Thirlmore had, wholly of his own idea, hastened southward to strike, if he could, and break the reinforcing army.

It was a most desperate enterprise. What could he do with so small a body of men, most of them exhausted by sickness and half-healed wounds, against so many thousands led by an officer of high repute? Two things were in Colonel Thirlmore's favor, — he had his reputation still to make, while the Confederate commander had already passed into the talk and camp-songs of the South as one of the immortal gods. In consequence of this, while the former was straining every sinew to do the impossible, the latter was slightly, very slightly, over-confident of himself, and careless. The officers and men of the command, trusting everything to their hitherto victorious General, were also careless; while Colonel Thirlmore's following looked to and relied upon him so far as to imitate him in his dauntless daring. It was with them that simple child's affair of, "This is the victory which overcometh the world, even your faith."

"See how things fit into each other," he wrote his wife afterward. "On the repulse of the attack upon the Convalescent Camp, I had to run for it somewhere if I was to get away for the moment from General Gilmore and what he might do by a message. Well, the only way to get away was in pursuit of the enemy; and everything else followed after and fitted into that! I'm not good at acknowledging anything, but I am ready to say that the accurate fitting together of complicated events does at least look like the process in a growing wheatstalk, or a rose. As it is true of the eyes of a fly, it may be true also of myself and all that befalls me. What do you think?"

Surely it looked like it, when he reached the river just

mentioned. There was much altercation among the Confederates then and since as to whose fault it was. There
was a bitterness among them, in comparison to which
their utmost bitterness toward the Federals was mildness
itself. And all about an unfortunate break and gap which
existed in the long line of the Confederates as they marched
to the relief of the imperilled city. The march was such
an extended one that it was necessarily engineered, so to
speak, by separate subordinates, whose pulses no more
kept exact time with each other than did their respective
watches. The disastrous thing was that the gap befell at
a point across the river where it was fordable, and just at
the moment of the arrival of Colonel Thirlmore upon its
northern bank.

There were enough men emulous of Jack Henson to
find out and report this to the Federal officer. Flashing
the joyous news through his troops, — news made doubly
electric by his way of making it known, — the Colonel
headed his men across the river. Why should he weary
himself by riding up stream to meet those who were coming toward him? Hurling his small force down stream,
and upon the rear of the advance-guard of the foe, he
swept everything before him. There is an explosive
power in surprise beyond that of dynamite. The Confederates had no thought of an enemy nearer than those
besieging the city to whose relief they were hastening, and
the effect of the attack was ridiculously out of keeping
with the numbers attacking. That accomplished, and
ambushing himself as far as he could, Colonel Thirlmore
caught the rear-guard of the Confederates as it hastened
over the gap. He had captured cannon enough, ammunition enough, Federal prisoners enough, to increase his
effective force. His men had got their second breath, and

were flushed with success; the result was reached, after
a half hour's fight, of a complete victory.

> " Surely — took a nap
> In some woman's treacherous lap,
> He was caught in such a trap !
> Oh, that gap, that gap, that gap ! "

Who of us in that region at the time but remembers the
doggerel lament springing up, as perhaps did the songs
of Homer, from soil so suddenly watered with blood?

Except, as Henson said, " to pick up the pieces,"
Captain Grumbles and his men came a little too late.
They did admirable service, however; as standards, cannon, provision wagons, a military chest or so, and prisoners in plenty were gathered in.   The well-known result
followed of the surrender to the Federals of the besieged
city, the opening of the great river, the destruction of half
a score of rising reputations upon the Rebel side.

When Captain Grumbles reached the spot where
Colonel Thirlmore was standing, he had such a wholly
unjustifiable sense of littleness that he could hardly hold
up his head.   The Colonel was busy feeding Tamerlane
out of a tent-cloth spread upon the ground, and heaped
with a prudently small measure of captured oats.   A man
was rubbing down the reeking horse, — his master taking
a bite, when he could, of bacon and hard tack, also con-
fiscated from the Confederate stores.

" Ah, Captain, that you?   Glad to see you, old fellow;
and glad you did n't get here sooner ! "   It was all the
Colonel had time to say, as he held out a cordial hand.
Herein lay the weakness of Captain Grumbles, that as
he held the hand of the other the tears were rolling slowly
down his yellow beard.

" What I liked most," Captain Grumbles wrote to his
wife afterward, " was, that, glad as he was, he was n't too
glad. I daresay he was more conceited after preaching
a big sermon in the old days to a big crowd, than he was
then. As sure as you live, Aurora Ann, war is a means
of grace ; often more than peace."

CHAPTER XX.

WITHIN a month after Colonel Thirlmore had distinguished himself at the battle, which we will here designate as the Battle of the Gap, there had been a great change.

"He should be court-martialed," General J. Mandeville Gilmore freely announced. "True, he succeeded; but if he had not succeeded, and all the chances were against him, the damage would have been incalculable. As it is, if I had my way he should be cashiered, if not shot!"

"And you are right, my dear," said good little Mrs. Gilmore. "So he should."

"He has done irreparable mischief," urged the discomfited chief; "an advance is necessitated. We are not prepared for an advance. The enemy will slip in behind. See here — " In whatsoever company he could safely do so, the General demonstrated with pencil and paper, by chart of country, river, railway, position of Federal and Confederate forces and supplies, that by Colonel Thirlmore's most rash, disobedient, and disastrous move the whole thing was up.

"Having supreme reference to himself he sacrifices the Union," groaned the old gentleman, who was visibly aged by the result. There may have been some truth in what he said. Colonel Thirlmore had, since he was born, had too single an eye to his own success.

"The Union is lost, hopelessly lost!" The disappointed

veteran sincerely believed it. Many a Federal General experienced during the war every pang of the agony which would have reached the hearts of millions had the Republic actually crumbled into a bloody dust. To each of these, confident at the outset of being the hero of a re-established Union, his own defeat and failure was an individual ruin than which nothing could be worse. Many a military man whose name was for a time the hope of the cause, can sympathize keenly with Jeff Davis. The Republic, the world, was but a wreck so far as he was concerned.

" Scoundrel ! " the epithet broke like a bombshell from beneath the white mustache of the General.

" Horrid wretch ! " re-echoed Mrs. Gilmore. She clenched her fist; every hair of her curls was alive with wrath.

Miss Moxy merely laughed. Alas for Mrs. Gilmore, the people at Washington did not agree with her. An advance was ordered along the entire line up to the position gained and held by Colonel Thirlmore. The nearest Southern city was evacuated by the enemy and taken possession of by General Gilmore, whose command was limited to that city, and military stores in abundance were accumulated within its bounds.

" Confound him ! " General Gilmore made the remark for the hundredth time one day within a week of his arrival there, dashing down, as he said it, an official document just received.

" Confound whom ? " inquired Mrs. Gilmore. It would have taken superhuman effort to keep her from following the fortunes of her husband. When there happens to be on the staff an energetic Commissary who aspires to be the General's son-in-law, it is not impossible to arrange matters.

"Not Colonel — *General* Thirlmore! Did I say confound? Blank, blankety blank him!"

Mrs. Gilmore shut her eyes, and winced as at the report
of cannon. The General was a senior warden of the
church when at home! "Yet, really, there *are* occasions,
and this is one of them." Good little woman, she could
not go quite so far at the moment; but there was no telling what she might come to feel, if not to say, for it was
but too likely that General Thirlmore would be anything
but quiet hereafter.

And thus it was that the Blue Grass region became a
thing of the past, and the same ruthless invaders were now
grouped together again in the central and handsome
Southern city, in which to be born argued gentle birth;
in which to reside was proof of wealth; an admittance
into the best society of which leaves nothing to be desired
in this otherwise undesirable and sorrowful world.

Matters here were not as they had been in the Blue
Grass. When the Rev. Dr. Glebb was pointed out to
General Thirlmore one afternoon on the streets by Lieutenant Van Doren, the faces of both fell. For Dr. Glebb
held a position similar to that of Dr. Doubleday in this, —
that each was pastor of the leading church in the place
in which he resided. There all likeness ended. Dr.
Glebb was a clergyman who was constructed upon a much
smaller pattern, in every sense, than Dr. Doubleday. He
was a native of Vermont, slight of build, swift of step, intensely single and sincere in his conviction that the South
was wholly right. Up to the time of the last Federal advance he had made perhaps the best chaplain in the Confederate army. If need were, he could pass the ammunition
during a battle; put his shoulder to a cannon stuck in the
mud; help guard prisoners, or bear the wounded to the

rear. When occasion permitted he would rush round and gather in the soldiers to worship; raise his own hymns; preach brief, pointed, admirable sermons; and put up prayers which were models of terse and intense importunity alike for the souls of his men, their success in battle, and for the destruction of the Federals in their accursed wickedness. If opportunity served, he would circulate delicacies for the sick; see to it that every man owned and read a Testament and a tract or two; write letters and take charge of photographs and last messages for the dying; rebuke as sharply for cowardice, or doubt of Confederate success, as for licentiousness and swearing; feed and curry half-a-dozen horses; or snatch up the gun from some hand suddenly made cold, and "have one crack at the Yanks." No man so popular, and deservedly so, with officers and men as Dr. Glebb.

When the Federals came down upon the city, its largest, once most fashionable church was without a pastor. It might be occupied by some Federal parson. At a hastily summoned meeting of the congregation, the chaplain, as the only available man in reach, was made pastor, and steps taken to obtain the chrism of a degree. He was but a temporary expedient as everybody agreed; but from that hour he filled, so far as he could, the capacious silk gown of the robust and distinguished divine dead just before. His sermons were only exhortations; but he made up for that in the fervor of his prayers, and in his unwearying social duties.

But he served to recall to General Thirlmore the pastor who had been his host in the Blue Grass. At the thought, his head fell upon his bosom.

"It was purely physical!" said Lieutenant Van Doren of Dr. Doubleday on the instant. It is surprising how often the same explanation was given, and by how many thousands, at the time and since.

" Purely physical ! "

But General Thirlmore was thinking of Myrtle ! Poor girl, the sunlight had fled from her face as if forever. Secluded in her home, she was shrouded in the crape of an agony beyond comfort ; her father's death had been a misery almost beyond endurance.

" Purely physical? What do you mean by physical ? " General Thirlmore said angrily. " The revolver was physical, the trembling hand which held it was physical. Do you mean that the brain, the broken brain which prompted the hand, was as devoid of soul as the hand or the revolver ? "

" Yes," the Lieutenant said gravely, " that is precisely what I do mean. The man was as really torn in two as if the oxen of the North had been hitched to his head, and the wild horses of the South to his feet. A man may continue to live, if you will allow another figure, after he has been paralyzed in the spine, when half the man is dead. What had the good Doctor's better part to do with his death? His death was the act purely of his lesser part. He was a martyr, sir. Isaiah sawn asunder was not more so."

But it was of the daughter General Thirlmore thought. For the first time he found pleasure in the society of Moxy Gilmore, who could not hear the name of her fair foe of other days mentioned without a burst of tears.

" She hated me, but I did n't blame her one bit," she said. " In her place I should have hated the daughter of a Federal General. But she need n't have hated me so much ; my father is n't half so dreadful as he looks, now is he, Colonel — General Thirlmore, I mean ? You must n't

think *I* blame you for ousting papa; I love a man who is
afraid of nobody.   I tell the Lieutenant I wish *he* had your
courage.   His business, he says, is to attend to the beef.
How could you fight, he says, without your beef?   Beef!"
The nose of the lively girl was sufficiently tilted already.
"We women love a brave man.   You know I always was in
love with you, General; don't blush!   I wrote a long, long
letter to your wife to tell her so.   What would you give to
read her answer?   In love with you herself?   I should
think she was, deluded woman!

"But, oh, Myrtle was so sweet!"   It was irrelevant,
but Moxy was weeping again.   "I know a pretty girl
when I see one, and Myrtle Doubleday was an angel.
That red-headed Captain Warden is not good enough to
be her footman.   He *is* her footman.   Let a better man
come along, and you'll see whether she does not take him
instead.   Just think of her, poor, poor thing, alone there,
crying her eyes out!   Did you ever see a girl who had
such a fresh and rosy loveliness?   She was like a rose
dipped in dew!   It was morning itself in her face!   You
lived with them; how could you keep from falling in love
with her?"   But Moxy's sharp eyes opened a little, as she
noted the color in the face of her companion.

It was because Myrtle Doubleday was so unlike herself
that Moxy Gilmore could not cease to speak of her.

"Can you imagine how she must have felt that dreadful
Sunday," she said to Lieutenant Van Doren, "when her
father was found dead by his own hand in his study.   She
lay, poor thing, in a blessed unconsciousness for days and
days.   One would have thought she would have hated the
Federals more than ever.   I know *I* should; but they say
she is meeker, quieter, more patient than ever — lovelier
she could not be.   Captain Warden, her lover, has turned

bushwhacker, they tell me, and is perfectly ferocious on her account; but it is not her fault. Do you know what *I* would have done, Lieutenant?"

"I can guess," he said.

"Yes; I should have sent for you. I would have said, 'Look here, the Yankees have murdered my father; if you don't go out and shoot and cut and kill'—what are you laughing at?"

"At you; what with your frown, your clenched fist, your set teeth, you are dreadful! And what would you have done if I had said, 'Thank you, Moxy; I love you very dearly, but if you think that to gratify you I intend to become a savage, you are mistaken?'"

"You would have said that?" Moxy asked with a stern brow. "You wouldn't do what I wanted? Not if I wanted it very, very much?"

"Be sensible, Moxy. I would do anything in the world for you; but a raider? a midnight assassin? No." The Lieutenant was standing before her, the smile gone from his lips; his face was flushed, he was very determined.

"Not if I asked you; asked you weeping; asked you as the greatest favor you could do me?" She looked him steadily in the eyes; her lover saw that everything was at stake, but he did not flinch.

"Not if it was anything wrong No."

"You dear old boy; you darling!" and to her lover's unbounded astonishment Moxy had put a hand on either shoulder and kissed him on the forehead. "Can't you understand?" she said. "Do you not know I should despise you if I could make you fetch and carry for me like a poodle, as Myrtle used to make her Captain? Remember, dear, don't you ever yield and do things when

I beg you. As sure as you live I shall ask you to do many a thing you ought not — ask you hard. But take care ; as sure as you yield I shall despise you."

" I 'll remember," laughed her lover, and they were on better terms than ever.

" It may seem strange," Moxy often remarked afterward, "and it may be because we are so unlike ; but if ever one woman fell in love with another, I have done so with Myrtle." One thing was certain ; the daughter of the Blue Grass pastor — all unconsciously — did more to change the voluble and defiant girl than any other person.

" I cannot tell why it is," wrote Thirlmore to his wife about this time ; "but I see almost nothing of Captain Grumbles these days. He is made of too honest material to whimper ; but he is growing of a deeper yellow by his increasing disgust of military life, of the war. He is perishing inwardly of home-sickness. ' Once at Scrubstones again,' he said, the last time I saw him, ' and I will not put my foot off my own soil — at least so I think now — as long as I live.' He looks at me almost as wistfully as his dog Wretch does, because I will not endure to be talked deaf about Aurora Ann and his boys. The death of his little girl almost killed him ; but if you, and the family under your control, had not hidden his wife's illness from him until she was well again, and it had proved impossible to get leave of absence, I fear he would have deserted. He has the body of a big farmer, but he has the heart of a woman, as truly as Aurora Ann herself. I am glad you are still so content with your home. Tell Mrs. Grumbles we have a pressing use for her husband in these days."

This, it is to be feared, is more than the farmer of old

had for the army. He had exhausted, apparently, the
farthest limits of his capacity in a military line.

"I am tired," he said to General Thirlmore, in the
privacy of the latter's tent during the dull period just
spoken of, "dead tired of the whole business. I ought
to be at home this moment plowing. You thrive on it;
I don't. A man can get used to knocking a beef in the
head, and in the heat of battle I go at it pretty much like
others. This shooting down of men as good as I am, or
better, I dare say, — I can stand tolerably well. What I
can't stand is having to ride over the field afterward,
spurring your horse over the dead and wounded, friend
and foe, crushing the limp and outspread hands into the
mud, tramping the poor faces. There's a difference
between men as there is between trees. You may be
oak, General, or hickory, or whatever it is; I got a softer
fibre from my mother, — poplar, cottonwood, willow, if
you say so. Raising crops is my style; fighting don't suit
me; it is n't my sort. Between you and me, there are
some things in which I doubt if Aurora Ann is n't more
of a man than I am, if it *is* a shame to say so."

Captain Grumbles's homesickness so preyed upon him
that General Thirlmore was almost tempted to fear he
might desert. "But, no," he thought, "the man has too
much of the genuine metal in him to think of it. Besides,
he knows what his wife would say and do in that case!"

CHAPTER XXI.

THE weather itself has not so many changes as has war; and now there came an alteration in thermometer and barometer. One Saturday night the Federals occupying the city were ordered southward. Dr. Glebb returned thanks to God at service the next day that they were marching to their doom.

"I am sure that I would do the same if I was in his place. But having such confidence in God, he ought not to become so dreadfully excited," thought Moxy, as she listened. "His gown is much too large for him; it will get in his way some day, and he will tear it to tatters."

General Gilmore entered a written protest against the southward march; but General Thirlmore had his own way. Jack Henson had come in, confirming the reports of other scouts that the Confederates were massing in force. A score or so of miles from the city, the General, who had his own plans, halted and threw up redoubts, a larger force being hurried on beyond his own. As it happened, Captain Grumbles was sent with the forward command.

"Remember, Captain, it is not to fight the enemy," his superior officer repeated again and again. "You are not to hold your ground. To do so is our business, not yours. You are to feel their advance and fall back. Be sure and fall back while you can do so in good order. You understand how disastrous to us in the rear it will be for you to break. Those are your orders."

"Orders must be obeyed." It was the manner in which Grumbles said this which arrested the attention of the other. It was no time for Captain Grumbles to allude to the way in which General Thirlmore had conformed to the orders of his superior while in command of the Convalescent Camp. The whilom farmer was "out of sorts," nervous, irritable, hardly master of himself. Many a month had fled since little Owl had spread her wings for a better world. Only the day before, he had written to his wife: "I cannot become reconciled to it, and I won't! I would not have Squash, or Snap, or Pop know it; but it was in her that my very heart was wrapped up. I am glad to know that we are on the eve of battle; it will turn my mind to other things."

This may account for what followed. Instead of falling back as ordered, before the first assault of the advancing foe, he behaved very much as if he had been slapped in the face by some unexpected bully. "He got mad at the first shot, and went for them!" was the comment of his men afterward. For a long time he had been boiling with suppressed disgust, weariness, homesickness, animal rage at he knew not what. Forgetting the uselessness of such a conflict with a force overwhelmingly outnumbering him, he fought until, as General Thirlmore feared, it was impossible to fall back in any order. There was a sudden panic, then a headlong rout. It was like the breaking of a dam; and in a little while Federals and Confederates poured along the highway to fall full upon the second line of Federal troops.

The ordinary assault of an enemy upon a breastwork is an easily understood thing. Here it was different. The command of Captain Grumbles were flying terror-stricken, struck down by canister and musketry, trampled by the hoofs of the pursuers who followed close behind. When the torrent of battle at last surged against the redoubts, it was a wild comminglement of Federal and Confederate, blue and gray, pursued and pursuers, intermixed. It was difficult to admit the one within the lines and exclude the other; impossible to fire upon the foe and not slay the friends. The yells and shouts, the entreaties and curses, the inferno of struggling men, could not but stamp itself upon the memory of every soldier behind the redoubts as long as he should live. How was it possible to hold the lines against such an assault? The headlong rout boiled up against the earthworks in seething fury, and then swept everything before it. The in-rushing of the Mississippi through a crevasse is the thing which best illustrates it; and for a little while the blended blue and gray poured in swollen tide up the road and toward the apparently doomed city.

The last chance of the Federals lay in the fact that General Thirlmore had anticipated what might befall, and, as far as possible, had made his preparations upon that basis. He and his men were now the only bulwark between the foe and victory, and no man knew better than he the supreme disaster it would be if the city with its immense stores should be captured. The slow results of years of battles would be lost, the key of the entire position gone. Who could tell where or when the consequent rout would be arrested?

There are moments, and this was one, when a man is measured by circumstance to his utmost limit, — measured sternly, accurately. If he has in him the hitherto uncalculated material, the hitherto unsounded strength to meet and master the event, whatever it is, it will show itself; and he will become in a single instant less than a man, more than a man. So was it now. General Thirlmore had informed his command of the emergency ; and it was as if he had done so, man by man. As a man grows toward the stature of his Maker, he, too, has the power of changing men into his own likeness ; and as the swollen stream of pursuer and pursued roared toward and upon that last barrier, it was to find that every Federal there was another Thirlmore. With the first distant sound of the coming rout, the fife of Ralph Jennings rose on the air, accompanied by the snare-drums as a king is followed by a rabble multitude ; but so far as music has power, his fife was more to Ralph than sceptre to king. Whether it is to live after death or not, there assuredly is such a thing now as soul ; and it was this mysterious, triumphant something which Ralph poured through the silver tube upon the listening force. Yes, and it proved for itself the power to shake off earth, coffin, and shroud, and raise the dust into an eternal newness of life by the way in which the shrill, penetrating, electric soul clothed in sound, lifted every man there into a tenfold manhood. It was with an exulting sense of assured strength that even the meanest there grasped his gun or handled tompion, rejoicing in the coming opportunity.

"We had this advantage over our brave fellows in the other lines," General Thirlmore said in his report, "that we had just before snatched a hurried meal, and had been well rested, while they had neither breakfasted nor dined, and were more or less exhausted by their march, and afterward by the retreat. It was greatly in our favor."

He had served long enough to know that strategy toward an enemy is not more indispensable in war than is tact in dealing with friends. General Gilmore, had he been in his place, would not have mentioned this mitigating circumstance; but General Thirlmore had reached a point in the estimation of men in general, as well as in his own, which allowed him to be generous. Whenever the Romans were in a desperate emergency, they were sure to see Castor and Pollux riding and fighting in the van; nor has Saint George been lacking, mounted on his snow-white charger, when " Merrie England " was held in the grasp of some overwhelming calamity. It is because a leader is then lifted, by the tremendous force of things, out of his ordinary self and into the ranks of the demigods, that this is so. Blessed be Heaven that such apotheosis is not confined to the field of battle !

Upon this third and last line there was the same onset, and in larger force, of the bewildering mixture of the blue and of the gray. There was the same death-struggle along the lines, and in intensified degree. Yet here was there something of the smooth yielding and obedience of things to that omnipotence which for the hour these represented. After the first dash and recoil, the flying Federals contrived in some way to glide between the defenders, and to halt and form in the rear. Backed up by these, the men along the breastworks were able at last to halt, and then to drive back their assailants. General Thirlmore and his influence were everywhere ; and surely that is the measure of a man, this wealth of silent overflow. No one afterward could say how it was done. Men spoke with almost an awe about it ; but the rout was arrested, held in poise upon the redoubts, and reversed. Slowly at first, the repulse became a run, a headlong flight, a disastrous defeat for the Confederates.

When Captain Grumbles clambered into the lines, all discipline destroyed, bleeding and exhausted, it chanced to be just where General Thirlmore could see him ; and he cursed him hotly as he did so.   If he had been beyond his own control the other would not have cared so much. But his superior officer had never seemed cooler than then.   He was master of himself because he was master, — he was confident of it even in the hurly-burly of the situation.

As if his subordinate had been a blundering horse or a stumbling ox, he put into words his assurance of his own superiority, and cursed him as he came !   Then in the heart and heat of the struggle, sore and staggering, driven to desperation by the ruin of his own causing, the farmer lost all thought of consequences.

Dimly conscious that his own men saw what was going on and would sustain him, he clubbed his rifle and turned, even amid the writhing conflict, to deal the other a blow. In the act and instant of doing it he saw a Confederate to his right taking deliberate aim across a cannon at the towering commander.   The cannon in the way, it was impossible to do more ; but with that swiftness which belongs to such an emotion, — since such emotions belong rather to another and more active state of existence, — he let fall his lifted gun and threw himself between.   To General Thirlmore's sharpened attention there was, on the instant, but those two men in the world.   The crack of the rifle was as separate from the other shots and uproar as if it were the only sound on the air, and his friend lay prostrate before him, while the Confederate fell backward down the embankment, shot by a revolver in the hand of some one to his right.

It was in that instant, with a sharp cry from the lips of General Thirlmore, that the men in gray yielded before the reinforced onset which changed and settled the fortunes of the day.

" My friend, my friend ! " The commanding officer was upon his knees beside the other, the tears gushing from his eyes, transformed into a child.

" You did n't mean it, General ; you was mightily provoked. I did n't intend to fight the Rebs ; I got mad and forgot. I can't say I 'm sorry it happened ; it 's better me than you." The cap had fallen from the sandy and dishevelled hair, the homely face was a grime of dust and sweat ; but the light-colored eyes had the wistful loving look the other had so often seen in those of oxen and of dogs, as they were lifted to the one bending over.

" If I 'd hit you I 'd have killed you, General, I was that wild, — almost crazy. Tell Aurora Ann. I 'm glad it 's me and not you."

CHAPTER XXII.

REVOLUTION.

" I DO not propose," Mrs. Thirlmore wrote to her husband, while he was still going the even round of his duties in the Convalescent Camp, before the attack upon it, " to weary you with any morbid fancies of mine. But I sometimes sit, especially of an evening, at the window of my room, and it seems to me as if it were not moments or hours which were passing over me, but ages on ages. It is so long since you left me ! Surely it must be at least ten years ago. They tell me that I never was looking younger, but I feel as if I were a great-great-grandmother.

" Could I not come on and help you in some way? Can't you appoint me matron of your hospital? You have no idea how calm I could be while the surgeons were dissecting. Won't you give me a trial? During all our sickness here I have made, I assure you, a tolerably good nurse.

" Why should you be so busy, do such glorious things, and I do nothing? You are big and strong, I am slight and frail ; but then a woman has so much more endurance than a man.

" When I read in your letters and in the papers all that you are doing, I become almost wild. It is, my dear husband, much harder to remain a spectator of the great tragedy than to bleed and die in the midst of it. I have at times so desperate a desire to be with you, if only to nurse, or help in some way, that I am like a caged tigress. Must I do nothing? *Nothing ?* "

It was not for work, it was for him she was yearning. Work?

"How glad I am he knows nothing about it," she thought. It was of her labor as a writer she was speaking. Beyond her hopes she had succeeded by her writing, had made money, and was in a position to make more every day. Taking into confidence her brother-in-law, Dr. Trent, she was investing it toward her husband's return. He should never know how she made the money; but she would surprise him some day with a house of his own. But, "Would he like that?" Her heart sank for an instant, then soared upward like a bird.

"Never mind, I will manage some way! If only I can have him again! Mine, this time as never before!"

But it was, telling on her health. There were days when she was tired of everything. Spasms of disgust came over her, — disgust of the public which could like writings as flimsy as hers; disgust of the Government, — of its army, of its plans, of its progress towards victory. There crept upon her an exhaustion of trust, of hope of herself, deepening almost to despair. It was by strong self-control that she concealed an ever-increasing irritability. The children watched her anxiously, although she was too absorbed in her own unhappiness to observe it. Squash could not eat for stealing anxious glances at her.

"Can it be the cookery?" Mrs. Grumbles demanded of herself, when her guest came down to breakfast from what had plainly been a sleepless night. "She does not care to read or write; her piano is never opened. Perhaps the children have been too much for her. It is not altogether the war, for she has buckled herself up to be braver than I am about that. If I did but dare to ask her —" Never had she been so solicitous concerning any one. But little she guessed what conflicting forces were warring in the bosom of her friend, and of how the force native to her was intrenched in her hereditary tendencies, in prejudices reaching to the foundations of the soul.

Early one gloomy autumn morning Mrs. Thirlmore returned to her room after a vain attempt at breakfast. and stood at the window looking out. On one side was the garden, — flowers and vegetables rearing their tattered and frost-blackened leaves upon the wind like the flags of a defeated army. Across the red ruts of the highway opposite stood the disconsolate orchard. She forgot how she had helped but a little before to harvest the fruit, standing upon the rounds of a ladder, and tempted, in the transient flash of a happy heart, to drop an apple now and then upon the broad back of Squash as he stooped beneath to pick up the fallen spoils. Now the dismantled trees looked as if they had never been other than an array of lifeless sticks. From another window she caught a glimpse of the barn and stables. A sudden blight seemed to have smitten the very poultry wandering aimlessly about, and all creation appeared unable to rise above the level of an ancient horse, which, scarred on back and shoulders with the marks of harness, stood, its nose upon the top rail of an unpainted fence, looking mournfully at nothing.

"It will kill me if I stay here!" she said half aloud.

As she passed out of the porch, cloaked and hatted for a walk, she was waylaid by her hostess, who said, —

"That is a good thing to do; there is nothing like plenty of exercise; look only how well I am again!" There was an aroma of pies about her, as, blooming from the kitchen-fire like an exaggerated incarnation of the goddess of morning whose name she bore, she laughed, and laid a strong hand upon the arm of her friend.

" Wait a moment," she said, and hurried away only to hasten back with a neat little basket in her hand. " There 's a piece here," meaning a lunch, " in case your walk makes you hungry. Take a long one. Won't you have Pop or Snap go with you? No? Very well, only please don't get lost; you have spoiled us from doing without you."

Beyond the pines was the hill-top on which stood the old building in which she had taught school. It was Saturday morning. No one was in miles of the spot. A profound melancholy fell upon her as she entered the one room and seated herself on the very chair she had occupied as teacher. It seemed to be ages on ages ago.

" Can I be the same slight slip of a girl I was then? I was so ignorant of myself, of my future," she thought, " so desperately eager to see, to know, to do. Now?" She laid her forehead upon her hands clasped in one upon the small, much-bewhittled table before her, and went slowly over all her life which lay between. Her marriage, her sojourn in the city, the collapse of the church, their life on the stony farm, — she lived it all over again; the hopes, fears, successes, defeats. And now the steady strain of the war; the few and brief letters she had received; what she had tried of late so faithfully to do; what she hoped to accomplish, — how vain it all seemed !

It was with a start she saw that the sun was declining toward the west. A mile or so down the hillside, brown and slippery with pine needles, ran a stream along which she had rambled one eventful morning with Mr. Thirlmore before they were married. She forgot how faint she was for want of food; and leaving her basket upon the table, walked rapidly on until she stood beside the creek. There had been a freshet the day she was there with her lover; and yonder where the road crossed the stream, they had seen a wagon upset in trying to cross water which had been fordable when it went to market early the same morning. She remembered how she had seized upon the arm of her companion when they saw that the old man who drove the vehicle was swept down with the stream. She could almost see his face now, as the poor old soul was borne past, crying to them and reaching out imploring hands in the rush and horror of the moment !

" He might have plunged in and brought him out," she thought now, as so often since then. " But I held on to him, so that he could not do it. He ought to have torn himself away, if he had broken my wrists ! He did not exert his strength to get away from me. He was all I had, and how I held on ! One minute after, and he and I would have given worlds to recall the chance ; but our first and our strongest feeling was ourselves. In the selfishness of that one minute the old man was drowned." She put a hand over her face ; she could see so distinctly in the washed-out basin below her the terror-stricken countenance of the aged farmer, as whirled round and round in the rush of the current, he sank and rose, sank and rose, and finally sank for good.

" When a strong man can and don't, it is right he should fail," she reflected bitterly. " Was it because I had hold of him? Ought I not to have forced him to plunge in? But I did urge him to go to the war ! If he is killed there, I shall still be glad I did — glad !" and she stood looking at the water rippling slowly by.

She was thinking of the country's death-struggle for existence ; of her husband fronting death for its sake ; of men pulling upon his right hand and his left as he pressed steadily on. She saw him receive a ball full in the forehead, and sprang forward as if to clasp him in her arms as he fell. His head was upon her bosom. The noble face was pallid; the eyes were closing.

"Yes, dear," she sobbed in her waking dream; "yes, darling, I never loved you as I do now; but I am glad you went, glad I did not hold you back, glad I urged you on, glad, though you have given your life, glad — glad!"

In her overstrung condition it was as if her husband lay bleeding in her arms. Her tears were all the more copious that they were unmeaning, like the perspiration which breaks through the pores from vague alarm and not from exertion. They relieved her, however. She came to herself presently; and never more deliberately did she put her heart into any thought than into this: "Yes, glad, glad! How paltry, how mean, how miserable to live only for self!" The wind moaned through the pines; the brook hushed itself as it flowed by; her solitude was as that of the grave.

And then there came back to her the old, old story of God giving himself up to death for the world. It was as though the cross was raised before her eyes; she was aware of the face bowed before her in agony. It was in vain she tried to compose, to control herself; she could do nothing but yield herself to an anguish of weeping. It was not mere feeling; it was the mind unable to resist the clearness of the historic fact, the desperate need of it, the logic, the satisfaction of coldest sense and soundest judgment in it!

And with it she caught a glimpse of herself in comparison. It suddenly broke upon her as being the essential meanness of her whole life, that, knowing since she knew anything of that Person, and of His love even unto death, she had thought nothing of Him, unless it was to despise and reject Him. And then, and as upon a refluent tide, there entered into her a joy beyond all language. She smiled at herself as she glanced at the setting sun; for she was singing in a low, happy strain, as she walked up the hill and homeward.

"I am not deranged," she said; "but I have seen something I can never cease to see."

During all the day the sun had shone in but wintry breaks, now and then. She had not observed it; but a heavy cloud rolling up from the north and east seemed as if in an instant to wrap everything in darkness. It began to rain. As she gained the top of the hill the wind struck her full; it was a storm, and so dark that she could do no more than struggle on in, as she hoped, the direction of the school-house.

It was but a confused memory to her afterward, a bewildered dream. She was weaker than she knew. It had suddenly grown very cold; she could see nothing but solid night about her; she struck against the trunks of the trees as she went; her dripping clothes clung about her person, and caught on rock and underbrush. Now and then she stopped from sheer exhaustion.

It was like a dreadful nightmare; and yet serenely above it shone that which she had seen, and would see forever. She was not terrified so much as bewildered; and she was constantly aware of that strange, new gladness, which was flowing beneath everything, as from an inexhaustible source.

"I had given up struggling on in the rain, the howling wind, the darkness," she told Mrs. Grumbles afterward, "and had sunk down on the earth, when I heard a dog bark. There was Wretch coiling and uncoiling himself all over me. He must have heard something that I did not; for he put up his nose and howled, yelped, barked, and stopped to listen. Then I heard a distant shout, saw the gleam of a lantern, and — here I am."

"I thought Maggie would have gone crazy. As to Squash, he was worse than any of us." Mrs. Grumbles said this, as she sat with all the household at Mrs. Thirlmore's bedside the next day. "I never saw children take on as they did."

"Hoh, Mrs. Thirlmore," Squash said, "mother was the worst of all. She cried worse than Pop. Snap was the most sensible; he went to the kitchen, got the lantern, lighted it."

"I did not know my boys were such men," said their mother, glancing fondly at them. "They routed out Hans to put Wretch on your track, and — "

"Wretch had gone of his own idea," Snap insisted. "We took your trail across the road, up the hill, toward the school-house."

"And he came back," Pop interposed. "Don't you remember, as you all stood there wondering which way to go, old Wretch came in?"

"Came in," Squash interposed, "all wet, and wriggled his body this way and that, as if saying, — 'Pardon my coming, please; but if you will go with me' — "

"And you threw hot water at him the last time he tried to go into the kitchen," Pop remarked indignantly to her brother.

"And who chased him last week with the mop handle?"

Mrs. Grumbles rose and put them all out of the room. "Maggie insisted on taking you in her arms when they found you," she said, "and I never saw the children so foolish. They clustered about you dancing, laughing, and crying like so many babies." Mrs. Grumbles herself

was but the largest infant of all : her eyes were full as she
spoke. "Because we love — love you so much — " and
the good soul let the tears run unchecked over her
face, which was but one large smile. "And now no one
shall say another word," she said ; "you stay quiet, my
dear, until I come back with a little something hot."

"Love? Yes," the sick woman murmured to herself
as she lay very quiet and happy ; "yes, love is the most
beautiful thing in the world." But as she lay, she was as
one who listens to catch the first sound of rolling wheels
or of galloping hoofs drawing nigh and nigher, which are
about to strike the threshold, to enter the door.

Weak as she was, they had to let her have a telegram
which came next day. Her husband had been wounded
in battle. She turned calmly to the date. Yes, it was
while she was standing by the brook that the battle was
being fought.

CHAPTER XXIII.

A JOURNEY.

"I CAN hardly believe my eyes," Mrs. Grumbles said, looking with amazement at Mrs. Thirlmore, who stood on the front porch with Maggie behind her, and a heap of valises and bundles at her feet, waiting for Squash to bring round the wagon to take her to the railroad station. "It is only a day or two since it happened, and you look now as if you never knew what it was to be ailing. When Maggie picked you up in the woods, and brought you in out of the dark and cold and wet, you looked like a poor drowned creature. We had scarcely hope enough to work over you, you were so white and exhausted. Oh, but were n't we frightened — good! And now, just see you!"

It was amazing. Mrs. Thirlmore was neatly dressed in a closely fitting and comfortable suit of some dark-gray stuff, prepared long ago and held in readiness for such an emergency. On her shapely head was a hat wound about with a veil, and seeming as much made for her as its cup for the acorn, or the calyx for the rose.

"The doctor says that your power of recuperation," — Mrs. Grumbles said it slowly, to be sure the word was right, — "is astonishing. Are you certain you 've got enough for both of you in your baskets, Maggie? The roast fowls? You did n't forget the ham? Nor the tumblers of jelly? Have you got the biscuit, — and the cheese? Ah, me! one might have supposed that I would be the one to get strong first;" and she leaned on Pop for support, as Maggie replied to her questions with a "Yes, ma'am; yes, ma'am," to each item.

Mrs. Thirlmore and her friend had exhausted the topic of the sudden journey; and the former knew that the latter was saying whatever came first to make the parting as cheerful as she could. After they were gone, Mrs. Grumbles locked herself into her room for a good cry, into which she put all the energy which would have been required for a good scrubbing, or baking, or ironing.

"One would think you had lost a sister," Mrs. Sudkins said, the next time she called. The good but somewhat slouchy old neighbor had been very much laid aside since the guest came, and could not altogether grieve at her departure.

"She is more than a sister, — a hundred times more!" Mrs. Grumbles roused herself sufficiently to say. "I do not like her husband; not if he is what he used to be. But like is no word for what we feel for her. If she is n't very religious, she's as much like an angel as I care to see. Look at Squash! He was as rough as a colt that has never been curried, and see what a man she's made of him! So of Snap. Pop never could bear to have any one look at her; and she fairly worships Mrs. Thirlmore. As to our little Owl" — here the bereaved mother broke down, "well, — she's one of those women, ma'am, such as *you* can't begin to understand!" The manner is so much worse than the tones that Mrs. Sudkins, who had intended to spend the day, took mortal offence and sailed out of the house, vowing never to enter it again.

"We have n't lost much," Mrs. Grumbles said at supper to the children, who sat there sadly enough. "Knowing Mrs. Thirlmore spoils us for everybody else." Upon which Pop burst into tears; and Squash had an errand which

called him to the barn. As to Mrs. Sudkins, she was back
again Monday night to borrow a flat-iron for Tuesday's
linen.

"At least, you've known me the longest," she said,
tearful but not apologetic. "As you say, ma'am, I am
nothing but an ignorant old woman ; but where was my
opportunities? No, ma'am, I never had one, thank you."

When Squash bade their guest good-by on the platform
as the train thundered up, she stooped down and kissed
the freckled forehead, from which the cap was lifted. Too
honestly akin was he to his father not to be of homely
visage and loutish carriage. That kiss was a baptism.
He stood there long after the train had rolled away, half
dazed under the light touch of her lips. He did not
tell his mother of it, — but it changed him for life.

"Let anybody call me Squash after this," he thought, as
he drove homeward ; "you just let 'em !" and there was
scarce an available rock or stump that he did not strike
a wheel against, lost in thinking if he could not have contrived, in some way, to have gone with her to the war.

It was not until Mrs. Thirlmore and Maggie were many
a mile away that they discovered the full magnetism of
Mrs. Thirlmore upon those about her. There was Wretch
hidden under the seat.

"It is simply dreadful ! What are we to do? " asked
his idol, as the misshapen turnspit writhed in agonies of
self-deprecation and apology at her feet. "How did he
get here? How could he get here? " But she wronged
Maggie in looking at her so suspiciously.

"I ha' no notion," the girl replied, honestly, and not
without a sympathy for the dog. There were points in
common between the two.

"But what can we do? I will have the conductor put

him off before we get so far that he cannot find his way
back to Scrubstones," said the other.

"What good will that do? He 'll follow on after the
cars tull he dies. He 'll not go back."

"If I could send him back — could pay somebody to
take him." Mrs. Thirlmore was perplexed, as the animal,
having almost apologized its skin off, crouched down, lick-
ing her feet, awaiting in dumb acquiescence his fate.

"What good will it do? Who 's he going to stay with?"
persisted Maggie.

"But it is ridiculous to take him along. We shall have
to change cars continually. It is impossible. How did
he get on the cars?"

"I don't know, ma'am ; but," suggested Maggie, "if
he got on these cars, can't he get on those, ma'am? We
can't help it. Leave him be, ma'am," and she snapped
her finger and thumb encouragingly at the poor brute
under cover of a basket in her lap.

What could Mrs. Thirlmore do? Wretch seemed, in
the absence of his master, to be possessed as by a fiend —
if such fiends there be — of devotion. During the long
journey which followed he managed, like a kind of living
corkscrew, to insinuate himself, as Maggie put it, "through
the keyhole." Whenever the conductor was inexorable,
the dog submitted to the baggage car. Everywhere his
ugliness was a sufficient passport on trains, ferry-boats, or
when trotting at last behind the army ambulance.

"The journey seems to me now," Mrs. Thirlmore said
afterward to her husband, "like a waking dream. I was
like the woman in the story, who was shut up by enchant-
ment in the heart of a ball of transparent glass. The telegram came to me like a strong tonic ; from the moment it
came, I felt as vigorous as I ever did, — sealed in, like the

woman in the story, from heat or cold, from the talk of those about me, from any interest except in one thing, safe from hunger, or thirst, or weariness. Yet all along I saw with the clearest eyes ; heard everything ; knew every least incident and interruption. During the day I took almost an enjoyment in the steady roll of the wheels, the sense of being borne on and on and on. The nights were longer than the days, harder to endure ; but then too I lay in my berth helping on the wheels. I had but one thought, one wish, — to get on. More than once the train ran beside the inclosed grounds in which men were playing base-ball, the seats crowded with spectators. It seemed to me so odd that people could be living so lightly ; could loiter on platforms, or at doors and windows to look at the cars, as if the one thing for them also to do was to give every energy to my reaching you as soon as possible.

"Maggie took the best of care of me, getting on and getting off the train as deftly as a fairy ; coming with cups of tea and the nicest of bread and butter, from I know not where ; confining her talk to Wretch when they were allowed to travel together : I really do not know what they would have done without each other.

"At one station a pleasant-faced gentleman came into the car with a cheery face and a ready tongue. He must have been on his way to get married, he was so nicely dressed and in such a delightful mood. I am afraid he thought me very churlish, for he tried in vain to enter into conversation with me. After a while he managed to fall into an easy talk with a pleasant-faced lady, while I sat there wondering that people could think or talk of anything but you and your battles."

"Why, you have become a Mrs. Gilmore," her husband laughed.

"It was not that you were enchanted into a glass ball," he went on. "When a bullet is lodged in a man it becomes, if the man lives, what the doctors call encysted, that is, incrusted, in a kind of coat to keep it from doing any more harm. You were encysted, Peace." Peace was Mrs. Thirlmore's name; and it sounded very sweetly to her, coming for the first time after so many years from the lips of her husband. What she thought on the instant was: "I was held and borne onward in the hand that was reached to me that time I was in the deepest depths on the old farm; but why is it I would n't say such a thing to him, to anybody for the world? Why is it that I shrink so from thinking such a thing? Is n't it a fact?" But this conversation between the husband and wife occurred long afterward, and when there were many matters more interesting to them to be talked of.

From the moment when she and Maggie, with Wretch worming himself furtively in at their heels, took the train from the Scrubstones Station, there had been the usual coming in and going out of the car of all kinds of people. In all the concourse there was one thing to which the wife was keenly alive. Almost from the hour she started, she could catch the name "General Thirlmore" occasionally dropped in conversation by one or another. She often could not distinguish another word of what was said, except that; but she longed to hear more. As she neared her destination she heard it more frequently. Once a portly, high-colored man in uniform made himself heard above the rattle and roar, as growing warm in conversation, he accompanied the name with an oath and a slap of his hand upon his knee.

"And he was killed outright?" she heard one ask; but a train rushing past theirs mercilessly stifled the reply.

"I tell you, gentlemen, it was the grandest thing! Whoever heard of a man — " Then the blowing off of steam drowned the rest.

"General Thirlmore!" "Grand, was n't it?" "Splendid, I tell you, sir!" "Shot, and in the groin!" "He 'll finish 'em!" "Captain Grumbles, the old codger!" "General Thirlmore, sir, and I always said of that man — "

She almost wished herself deaf, as she caught the shattered words. "I shall know in time," she thought, and turned her strength to driving the lingering wheels faster, faster. "Shall I never get there?"

Long before she reached the city, railroad travel became obstructed. The train would be run upon a siding, while cars shot past seemingly by the hundred, laden now with soldiers, now with cannon or other munitions of war. Again, and yet again, this took place. As she sat in helpless misery the detention seemed eternal. She felt afterward as if she must have wept aloud; raged up and down the car, crying to the conductors, "While we are idling here my husband is dying, is dead. For God's sake, get on!" In sober fact she remained stone still, her eyes tearless; she had not spoken a word. It was as if her imprisoning sphere of glass had come to be one of ice rather, closing upon her with a pressure which froze as it held her apart from every other.

Little as she dreamed it, there had been a mistake in the telegram sent her. It left the imperilled city at a moment of dreadful confusion. For hours the city had been smitten with the report of an overwhelming Federal disaster. This General and that were reported killed or wounded; among them, General Thirlmore. Like a vast flock of ravens suddenly let loose, the direful telegrams flew Northward far and fast, sent by operators who had yielded to the savage joy — as strange a trait in our nature as it is beyond explanation — of making sad intelligence as black as possible; and it was one of these telegrams, indited by Lieutenant Van Doren, then on commissary duty in the city, which had brought Mrs. Thirlmore.

But the long-delayed train ran into the city at last. It was like landing in the heart of a whirlwind. The station was crowded with wounded men waiting to be carried to the hospital, for it was the terminus of the road leading from the field of battle. A regiment marched through, and the music made tenfold uproar under the span of the vast roof. It was long before mistress and maid could secure an ambulance to take them to the hospital, Wretch dodging in and out of the turmoil, and keeping meanwhile his eyes fastened upon the heels of those he had accompanied so far. His mistress heard, saw everything, but dared not ask a question.

Arrived at the hospital, she would not have been allowed to go in without a permit, if, leaving Maggie and Wretch in the ante-room, she had not walked quietly past the sentries, the authority in her face more effective than anything which could have been put upon paper.

Hardly knowing what she asked, what she was answered, she found herself at last in a long hall with ranges of iron bedsteads on either side, everything as clean as soap and water could make it. Even this was a satisfaction to her as she walked up the bare white floor. When she reached the bed pointed out, she steadied herself one moment to regain self-possession. Then she advanced with noiseless foot to the side of the bed, and leaned over. The room was darkened; the face of the occupant was turned from her. As she stooped, the wounded man rolled his head over with a groan; and she started back with a suppressed scream. In the wild confusion of yellow hair and beard she recognized the countenance of Captain Grumbles!

" Mrs. Thirlmore! Thank God, it ain't Aurora Ann." The words came together in a whisper, and with a sudden gladness in the familiar face.

" I thought — thought it was — was — "

" Your husband? No; it isn't him, it's me. Disappointing, aint it?" The joy in the colorless eyes almost dazzled the looker-on. Colorless? Henceforth were they to her the most beautiful eyes in the world.

" They don't allow people to talk here," he continued in a whisper, "but I will say that I'm glad it isn't him, and glad it is me."

How could so ugly a man have a countenance so much like that of an angel?

" They're all well at home? and dear little Owl — " But here the tears dimmed the gladness of the eyes. "No, oh, no; he's not here. You heard what a glorious thing he did?" — the face brighter still. " A man like that can't afford to get himself shot. He's gone, ordered East; they've a use for men of that sort! Yes, I'm glad it is as it is, glad as glad can be!" and the wounded man had the aspect of a bridegroom.

Mrs. Thirlmore knew nothing as yet of the facts. Why was it that none the less there came to her, as she stood, a sudden understanding of simple grandeur of soul? She looked upon the freckled countenance in its mass of dishevelled hair and beard with an exceeding awe. She took in hers the large hand which lay outside the bed-clothing.

" You will let me, won't you, please?" she said: and bending over she kissed him upon the forehead, again and yet again.

But she could not see the blushes which followed each other upon the face of the stricken man. For, at best, the fountains of the great deep of a woman's heart were' broken up; the tears poured from her eyes in silent streams as she kept firm hold upon the hand of the other.

It was at this moment that Lieutenant Van Doren passing by, recognized and took her away. But she hardly saw him or heard him. She had not a word for any one but Maggie; and hastened to lock herself in her room at the hotel, and, lying upon her bed, wept and wept as if she would never cease to weep. And yet, with all the pity and the pain, her tears were more relieving to her than any laughter had ever been; until at last, with a sudden rebuke for her forgetfulness, she lighted the midnight gas, took pen and paper from her valise, and tried to say in a letter to the wife of her husband's friend a little of what she felt. Not until she had done that did she write to her husband. Then throwing herself upon her bed she fell into that deep unconsciousness of sleep which never comes to man or woman except after such experiences.

CHAPTER XXIV.

THE MAGIC OF LOVE.

"WHAT is the matter with General Gilmore?" It is Mrs. Thirlmore who asks this question of Lieutenant Van Doren, after first meeting the veteran commander.

"Matter? Your husband is the matter, madam."

The Lieutenant said it gravely enough; for was not the General the father of Moxy? That something worse than age was prostrating him would have been plain to any one who beheld him seated of a morning in his office, which he had established in a room of the hotel in which his family were staying. It was the largest hotel in the lately imperilled city; and he occupied the handsomest apartments in it, with sentinels on guard day and night at its doors. As he sat in his arm-chair at a large library-table he was dressed, as you observe, in full uniform. Since the war began, no one has seen him out of that. His broadcloth was free from speck or suspicion of dust; his linen was immaculate; his gold lace, stars, buttons, are as brilliant as if donned that day for the first time. How could it be otherwise, seeing that his wife had no object or occupation in life apart from him? Upon the table was his military head-gear, and in that his gloves, which were as fresh as newly gathered flowers. Not until he went to bed would his cream-colored belt be unbuckled. His sword, given him long ago by Congress for his Mexican exploits, lay across his knees. His left hand hung listlessly down; his right rested clenched upon the table. Everything was

in exact military order in his room, from the army volumes
and maps down to the documents, signed, sealed, and
secured with red tape, duly indorsed upon the back in
various colored inks, each of which had its own mystic
meaning, and laid in precise piles upon a stand for the
moment, — to this, too, his wife saw with microscopic care.
He was like Marius, in his own opinion, if not cast off, at
least solemnly shelved by a Government, whose blindness
was something portentous, horrible.

No one can deal kindly and fairly with the case, who
does not place himself for the moment in the boots of
this aged officer.   Euclid himself rested upon no certainty
greater than that of the General, when he drew sword for
the republic, to be its Washington.   He loved his country;
but how far it was to him the pedestal upon which he
was to be lifted, who shall say?   With his whole heart he
believed in himself.   Mrs. Gilmore began with the war a
minute diary of events as they related to him, and few were
the events which did not relate to him.   Dotted to an i,
crossed to the last t, the MS., with every corroborative
document, was ready for the printer.

· Moxy was peeping in at the door standing ajar behind
him.   She was too thin and narrow-chested, too angular
and sarcastic, to be a beauty; but there was to-day a
dewy divinity in her eyes, as they rested upon the old
man seated with drooping head at his table.   With intelligence which could not shirk the facts, her heart had
learned something more than all her education had taught
her concerning her father.   Little as Myrtle Doubleday
imagined it, altogether hostile as their acquaintance had
been, this super-refined Yankee girl had learned from the
loving daughter of the distracted Blue Grass pastor the
sweetest secret of her life; and that was to revere and love

a foolish old father, at whom she had heretofore only laughed. Her mother's silly admiration had made it harder to learn the beautiful lesson; but now she had it by heart.

"He never was the hero he thought himself," she was now saying to herself. "He has always been too slow to act, since the war began. When he did act, he always blundered; his fiercest efforts have been against his rivals. But none the less is he my father. The greater the fool, so much the greater the pity, pity of it! How little does he know that his life is ended! Except to sign this and that he has nothing on earth to do. It were better he were laid away under a last volley. Blessed delusion which binds him to this!"

Her heart swelled within her; the lashes of her eyes grew moist: she stole behind his chair, put a hand upon his stalwart shoulder, stooped down and kissed him with such affection as her poor mother could not conceive of.

"Moxy, Moxy! My dear child! But you ought not to interrupt me! Some other time, dear; but I am very busy to-day." The General dropped his pen in the ink, and drew paper toward him.

"You darling father!" It was the tear which fell upon his forehead — it was so unlike Moxy — which awoke his suspicion. Could this be pity? He looked up at her sharply.

"I am so proud to be your daughter," she said, simply.

"Proud? Proud of me? Proud to be the child of a superseded man? I cannot say, Moxy, that you have seemed proud." There was the quick suspicion which always goes with original weakness of character, which grows with the increasing weakness of age.

"That was my fun, father! You know what a perverse

creature I am ; and you have always been so good to me.
' You miserable minx ! ' I say to myself almost every day.
But, father, I do love you, love you even more than
mother can."

"Ah, Moxy, Moxy, I am very much afraid — " And
he shook his head and made ready to write. Not in a
day, a week, a year, could Moxy undo the impressions
she had made in all the past. It deepened the channel
of her tears ; she was thinking of Myrtle, so woman-like
and lovable in her devotion to her old father.

"I *do* love you," she sobbed, — "love you with all my
heart ; and I *am* proud of you ! Everybody is proud of
you. Wait a moment." An idea occurred to her, and
she ran out of the room.

Mrs. Thirlmore had been in the city for some time
now. Not long after her coming she had spent an evening in the parlors of the General, and as Lieutenant Van
Doren escorted her to the rooms in another part of the hotel, it so chanced that in the same breath they both began, —

" I am so glad — "

" I am very glad — "

" My gladness," Mrs. Thirlmore laughed and explained,
" is to see how devoted Moxy is to her father. It is a
beautiful sight."

" That is what I am glad of. Her sarcasm has done
me a world of good ; but," said the Lieutenant, " I have
feared. What I mean is, I am glad to see how gentle
and loving she is. I wish she did not see things as
they are, so distinctly."

Mrs. Thirlmore was thinking of a picture she had
lately seen of Belisarius seated, poor, aged, and blind, his
daughter beside him holding her veil for the alms of
passers-by. " What woman," she now thought, " is as

lovely as Antigone leading Œdipus blind, accursed of the gods — " which suggested something.

The fruits of this suggestion were seen now, long after, when Moxy came back into her father's room holding in her hand a copy of the leading metropolitan journal which Mrs. Thirlmore had happened to receive that day. " You doubt whether I am proud of you ! " she said. " Let the work wait, and listen, father."

Perhaps there was something of the rosy hues of poetry in the article Moxy read. A daughter can, under the circumstances, add a good deal of warmth in the way of emphasis and feeling. Standing by the General, she read a full and eulogistic article upon his life, services, personal appearance, and what was to be hoped of him in the future. It was very long since there had been anything of the kind in any journal. There had been an overplus of the reverse instead, until a gray-bearded rat could not have been shyer of a bit of cheese lying conspicuously about its cellar than was the much-abused veteran of any and every newspaper. He had lifted a deprecatory hand, had shaken his head. " I attach no value to what the lying press says," he began. " You are interrupting me dreadfully to-day," — but he listened none the less. It sent a quick pang — half pain, half pleasure — to Moxy's heart, as she saw the ashen cheek of her father grow bright, his head lifted ; he could not suppress a kindling of the eyes while she read. Perhaps the praise was too strong, or woman's heart *was* in it ; but more delicious draught the veteran had never tasted.

" I was reading it this morning ! And you say I am not proud of you ! " The journal lay on the table ; Moxy's arms were about her father's neck. She was crying like a child from pure pleasure at his pleasure.

"Foolish girl!" The old Lear patted his Cordelia on her head. "You must not believe what you see in the papers. Ahem! Has your mother seen it? No? You must not think I attach the least value to such a trifle. If you should chance to see her, you can send her to me. And now, my dear child, I must go on with my work." But the tones in which it was said were different.

General Gilmore did not disdain a bottle of champagne now and then. After a dinner party, and when flushed with the story of his Mexican exploits, the good old soul would loom up larger than life. This column of praise was more to him than a whole cellar of champagne. It took a long time for the exhilarating effects to disappear; and it is small wonder that Lieutenant Van Doren fell in love with Moxy over again. She had tasted the pleasure of filial love, as delicious to her as to father and lover. Never again could she any more be the Moxy of old.

Poor Squash, far away in Scrubstones, was as unlucky as boys of his build are sure to be, and had selected this precise juncture to break a leg by a fall from a hay-mow. Pop, too, was down with diphtheria. Although Mrs. Grumbles, on learning of her husband's hurt, was almost desperate, to join him it was impossible. As to the Captain, he showed his excellent sense by allowing his greater malady to drive out the lesser one of home-sickness, so that gradually he got the better of his wounds. But the surgeons told Mrs. Thirlmore something concerning him which held her in daily attendance until she and Maggie could accompany him home.

"No one pretends that she is to blame, poor thing," Mrs. Gilmore remarked of Mrs. Thirlmore. "They used to say in the city, when her husband was a sensational preacher, that he cared nothing for her. But we all knew that she was superior to him. It was common talk that she wrote his sermons. Perhaps she did; there was nothing in them any way. But I am so sorry, — sorry for her. Her headstrong husband will make a worse failure than he did as a preacher. Only wait awhile. But she is a beautiful woman, for one of that cold, intellectual style. You can easily see how much she has to suppress. I would n't be in the least surprised if that man is as cruel to her as he dares to be ; you can read it in her face. I tell the General, that, knowing what we do of her husband, we really ought to go out of our way to be kind to her. I was careful to send what the papers have been saying of late of the General. She may get exaggerated ideas in regard to her husband."

And thus it came to pass that Mrs. Gilmore would take her tatting, her curls, and her copious references to her hero to the neat little parlor of their rival's wife. As to her daughter, hardly a day went by that, on one pretext or another, she was not there ; and the commissary dropped in as often as business permitted, if it was only to keep Mrs. Thirlmore apprised of what her husband was doing. Thus it came about, too, that Maggie obtained a situation as nurse in the hospital. Sure of always having a little more work to do than was possible to any mortal, it crowned Maggie's satisfaction that she could see her mistress on her frequent visits to Captain Grumbles.

"And what a blessed thing it is," Lieutenant Van Doren observed, "that wherever we are thrown in the world we can always find plenty to do ; and see how things adjust themselves ! What a pleasant time we are having here !" It was in Mrs. Thirlmore's parlor that he made the remark, and to the three ladies there met. "Nice people like ourselves are like the bits of colored glass in a kaleidoscope; however the world rolls, we are sure to come together into perfect angles and patterns. And surely too there is an eloquence of living, which is as persuasive as anything to be found in speaking or writing." He added this in a half whisper to Moxy, beside whom he generally managed to seat himself. She nodded her head without looking up from her crocheting. Mrs. Thirlmore had so won upon the old General that he also was calling on the wife of his rash and headlong competitor.

"She certainly is a very superior woman, — far too valuable to be dashed in pieces, as some day her happiness will assuredly be, by that man. I was pleased with many things she said," he remarked afterward.

The General would have been puzzled to say what things. The truth is, she had opened her lips only to assent to what he advanced. Nor was there the least hypocrisy in it. Who would not have been interested in what the old veteran told her of his Mexican campaigns; interested and deeply interested in the plans, — and he was kind enough to sketch them out on a map, — by which he had purposed to crush the Confederacy? He would have crushed it long ago if he could have been allowed his way.

"And I venture to beg of you, madam," he said, before he left, "that you will go into my details to no one. It is far from impossible that I may have to carry them out yet."

Mrs. Thirlmore saw nothing to laugh at in the General. She was coming into that disposition, which sees much that is excellent, admirable, and lovable where lower natures and duller eyes would have detected folly only, and weaknesses.

"Do you know," she said one evening to Mrs. Gilmore, Moxy, and Lieutenant Van Doren, "that I think Dr. Glebb is nearer right than we may imagine?"

She was speaking of what took place in the city on the eventful day when it came so near being captured by the Confederates. It was now well known that when the second line of Federals broke, everything appeared to be lost. The city with its vast supplies was almost in the grasp of the Southern forces. An onward movement upon the North would have followed, and swept everything before it. Men raced with each other in desperate haste to get out of the city. In an hour or two the Confederates might march in. If possible, the retreating Federals must be prevented from setting fire to their storehouses, in which military supplies were accumulated in vast quantities. By telegraph and mounted messengers the news of the great victory was sent over the South far and wide. Before many days, hours even, had passed, the glorious event was known in every Southern army; in every city, town, village, hamlet, and household of the South. Everywhere, even to the remotest neighborhoods in Florida and Texas, the church bells blended their peals with those of city halls and fire departments in proclaiming the glad tidings. Men and women, aroused at midnight, sprang from their beds, and hastened to join the crowds which thronged the streets. At last, the South had achieved its independence! Illuminations were universal. People shook happy hands with each other. Union men kept close at home, or came together by night and by stealth to consider the probabilities and possibilities; and days were set apart by proclamation for solemn thanksgiving, multitudes filling the churches who never entered them except on such occasions. And then —

to the orator on the platform, to the pastor in the pulpit, to the eloquence and rejoicing — had come the sad but assured reversal of the glorious intelligence, the direful certainty that the victory was the other way. Was ever so vast a blanket, so wet a blanket, cast upon the hopes of so many!

But it was in the endangered city itself, upon which as upon a pivot everything turned, that the disappointment was worst. In his morning service, Dr. Glebb, at the utmost power of his lungs and outspread hands, had prophesied victory to the cause he so sincerely believed in. If importunate prayer could have secured it, the victory had been certain.

" I was at church," Moxy had been telling Mrs. Thirlmore, " that afternoon! And shall I ever forget it? Of course no one could be sure of the result. It was getting dark, toward the close of the service, when I heard a horse tear up the street as if for life. Not long after, an officer of the church who had gone out came on tiptoe up the aisle, and handed Dr. Glebb a despatch. His face flushed when he read it, and I dreaded what was coming. He had just given out the last hymn; but he arose again, held out a hand to stop the organ.

" 'It has pleased Almighty God,' he said, and people were leaning forward in breathless attention, — you could hear a pin drop, — 'pleased Almighty God,' he said, ' to give the cause so dear to ourselves a glorious victory. Our conquering troops are in full march; in the course of an hour or two they will be in possession of the city.' There was a murmur, swelling almost into applause; but he held up his hand. 'We will first return thanks to God,' he said, 'and then we will unite in singing the forty-fifth Psalm.' Such a prayer! You can imagine how I felt standing there; but it was grand! The man's whole heart was in it. I looked at him while he was praying, — for, of course, I could join in no such prayer as that, — and I saw the tears pouring down his cheeks while he thanked God for having heard his supplications of that morning. He was so sincere, so childlike, so overflowing with gratitude, that I felt dreadfully afterward to think that he was so mistaken. And the singing! People on every side were watching me. I kept as still as a mouse; but I was as determined as a lion. It was an awful strain. For all I knew the news was true. I never doubted it was true. I supposed we should have to fly for our lives. While I sat there so cool and smiling, I could just see Mamma in my mind's eye rushing round our rooms and piling the things in trunks. It was dreadful. All my best things were in the wash. Nobody but I knew where my evening dresses were, or my jewelry, or anything. I could actually hear her screaming, 'Moxy! Where is Moxy?' But I did not move a hair's breadth. People looked at me in wonder. After the benediction was over, I took my time in moving. Persons were hurrying out to see the Federals go, and the Confederates march in. Some were laughing, some crying, all talking. I did not have a soul to talk to; but I prided myself upon keeping as cool and quiet as if it was Sunday at the North.

"There was an impertinent young man in the pew before me, with a girl beside him. 'Excuse me,' he said, ' but are you not afraid your father will be gone when you get back?' 'Why should he be gone?' I asked, coolly. ' Did n't you hear the news?' he asked. 'The Federals are whipped, and in full retreat. The Confederates are marching in this moment!' They were excited; but I was perfectly cool. I was determined that nobody there

should see me frightened. With all the hurrying and
rejoicing, everybody in the church seemed to know I was
there. I knew that thousands of people were looking
at me and wondering. 'You had better hurry, miss,' the
young man said. 'Except what we capture, there won't
be a Federal in the city in an hour.' 'Thank you, do
you really think so?' I asked, with scorn. Then I
walked back to where I had sat, pretending to look for
something I had left.

"Would you believe it? A day or two after," Moxy
went on, "I chanced to meet that very same young man
upon the street. Our troops were marching past; the
bands were playing 'Hail Columbia!' for dear life. You
should have seen how he took off his hat and bowed to
me as he went by!"

"I do not like to moralize — "

"*Please* don't!" Moxy interrupted Lieutenant Van
Doren with beseeching eyes and hand.

"But that is what we admire," he persisted, "in your
husband, Mrs. Thirlmore, — the power of standing firmly
upon his feet when neck deep, as it were, in a swollen current. Here in the South they call it clear grit. That is
Moxy all over," he said, with a bow and a look which
brought a light to her eyes. "But it is not in war alone
one has to stand like a rock. Many a man, many a
woman, too, living apparently a dull and quiet life, has
often to breast the strongest kind of a current beating full
upon them."

Without looking Moxy knew how little Mrs. Thirlmore
relished this. "Yet in another moment I may hear that
the General is wounded; taken prisoner; killed in battle!" she said reproachfully.

"Death, madam," — the Lieutenant had been a Ply-

mouth Brother too long to be stopped in sermonizing, —
" Death, madam," he began, " is but another and higher
step in the process of evolution.   Do we not know — "
But Moxy put a determined hand upon his mouth, and
Mrs. Thirlmore was glad to leave for the hospital.

"You will see," the Lieutenant called after her, "if
the best things do not come to the General yet.   I
should take no pleasure in our dispatches in the daily
papers, if it was n't for him.   One is always expecting
something — "   .

To-day Mrs. Thirlmore, as so often before, talked to
Captain Grumbles about Scrubstones ; he took small interest in anything else.   Every least item of news from
thence she stored up against her visits, as the choicest
dainty wherewith to tempt his appetite,— the condition
of the potato crop ; the aspect of the corn ; the growth of
pig and calf ; the milk yielded by this cow and that.   He
cared more to hear how Hans was succeeding in the cider
than about what this General and the other was accom-
plishing East or West.   The President could do or say
nothing so momentous as what Hans' opinion might be
as to this or that.   As to Aurora Ann, Mrs. Thirlmore
regretted that there was nothing in the encyclopædias in
relation to her.

Once she came in with a neat basket.   " Could you not
eat an apple ? " she asked.

" Thank you ; I wish I could, you are so kind," he said,
with a sorrowful shake of his head ; " but I can't.   I have n't
a particle of appetite for anything."

" Captain," — Mrs. Thirlmore holds up the basket, —
" did you ever see that before ? "

There was something in her smile.   He lifted his head
of hair, well-ordered now, —Maggie had seen to that, —

from his pillows, and looked eagerly at it as she let it revolve by its well-worn handle.

" Basket? I do believe! Why, Mrs. Thirlmore, that is the very basket," he said, like a child, " my wife used to give me my dinner in when I went to plow or reap in the far field, — you know it, over the hill! Why, madam," his homely eyes sparkling, " I could eat a Rebel out of that basket, — could eat a crocodile — "

He was ashamed of himself; his head sank upon his pillow again.

" And she has put up with her own hand more than apples from the burnt tree in your orchard, — you have n't forgotten that tree? Your wife has sent you the very lunch she used to give you. See ! " She unpinned the napkin. " And she has n't forgotten the pepper, salt, and pickles, — here they are in little papers; as I live, a slice of pie ! — dreadfully indigestible — "

But the strong man was sobbing, the sheet drawn over his face. After she was gone he recovered sufficiently to alarm surgeon and nurse by the way in which he emptied the basket.

" And yet, love me as much as a wife can, *she* would n't have thought of it," the Captain thinks. " How is it people of Mrs. Thirlmore's sort can come to think with their hearts, to love with their brains as well? Each helps the other somehow." But herein was a physiological, pyschological fact, which the sorely weakened man was too enfeebled to think out.

There was one week of specially unpropitious weather. His wounds racked him with pain ; he could not sleep or eat. In vain Mrs. Thirlmore tried even in a low voice to sing to him. The latest news from Scrubstones did not have its usual effect. In the midst of it she was compelled to leave him in the care of Maggie. Beckoning her into the hall without, Mrs. Thirlmore told her of the emergency. Unless their patient could be soothed, inflammation might set in.

Maggie was permitted to bring Wretch into the ward. The turnspit was painfully sensible of the honor. After going through the usual convulsions upon the floor at the bedside, he sat up on his hind legs, his paws crossed upon his bosom, the intensity of his thought wrinkling his senatorial brows. Human eyes could not say more plainly than his, nor human speech either, "Oh, master, master! is there anything I can do for you?"

"Not to-day, poor fellow," the wearied man whispered ; and Maggie was obliged to drive the dog out, clad as it were in sackcloth and ashes. She racked her slow brain for something to tell him about Scrubstones. Suddenly her face lighted up, and she colored.

"You remember Hans?" she asked.

Captain Grumbles nodded his head ; his eyes closed.

"He is a good man, d'ye think, sir?"

Another nod.

"Can dig as many potatoes to the day as onny man?"

A languid assent.

"And do his stint with a cradle?"

The patient groaned and turned half away. Standing over him, Maggie hesitated. If she did but know of anything else to talk about ! She looked down at the large hands clasping and unclasping themselves upon the bedcover. The surgeons had told her that cheerful talk was better than morphine.

"An' ye think Hans is a good mon? — a sure-enough *good* mon?"

The bearded face waxed cross. She was annoying him.

Under no other circumstances would his nurse have told her secret. But she must amuse her charge. She was desperate. " Please, sir," — Maggie bent forward; she wiped the perspiration from her forehead ; her face was crimson with exertion — "please, sir, Hans and me, when I get back, is going to be — married ! "

With one sweep of his arm the cover is off the face and broad chest of the patient. He looked at her, for full a minute, in blank astonishment. Then he laughed, — laughed till sick men lying on their beds to the end of the long room sat up to see what it was. The surgeon hurried up. But the Captain laughed until he could laugh no more. Then he shook hands with Maggie. After which, often giving way to a gurgling laugh as he lay, he fell at last fast asleep, to wake hours after, feeling better than since he was shot. After that, he was impatient until he could see Maggie again, and Mrs. Thirlmore.

CHAPTER XXV.

LITTLE THINGS.

"YOU are right," Lieutenant Van Doren remarked to Mrs. Thirlmore, a month or two later, "right in getting back to Scrubstones and nature as soon as you can. It is all very well to know of the self-sacrificing deed of the Captain, and to appreciate it. You could do no less than stay and help nurse him in the hospital. Such things develop the heart for life; but did you ever think that as a man may overwork his brain, so he may overwork his heart?"

" I understand you," she said.

"That is one trouble with us, blundering boobies that we are; we will go to extremes. Selfishness," persisted the commissary, " is bad; but altruism is sometimes worse."

"Altruism?"

"Yes; that is, for me to give myself too much to somebody else. And as selfishness may grow into a disease, so may altruism. A man may be a monster with too big a head; he may make a deformity of himself by going about with too big a heart. If I think too much of myself you will despise me, and very justly; strange as it may be, you will dislike and despise me yet more if I think too much of you. Did n't I come within an ace myself of turning out a tearful, emotional, maudlin nuisance, — very sincere, but lank-haired and sickly souled! Oh, for the beautiful balance of sweet nature, without convulsive strain and reaction! Your natural devotion to Captain Grumbles for his heroic self-sacrifice for your husband is all right; but

18

if you will allow me, it may be indulged so long and so far as to weaken both him and yourself. He is no more to Maggie than the primrose by the river's brim; she can do more for him than you, and with no more drain upon her than if she were a cart-horse. I am glad you are going back to Scrubstones and nature."

"And glad enough I am to go," she laughed, entering heartily into the cheery good sense of her friend, who was adding avoirdupois to the clear color, the sparkle fresh as morning of his eyes, tones, manner; it was like a flash of sunshine when he passed briskly through the wards. Whenever he could make time for it he would read aloud to one, write a letter for another. He was the soul of his circle, and he made it a large circle. Moxy was actually proud of him, loved him, was sharply jealous of him; all, the last excepted, with excellent reason.

So it came to pass that Mrs. Thirlmore and Maggie, aided by a soldier whose enlistment had expired, and who was engaged for the purpose, took care of Captain Grumbles to Scrubstones. He was only able to walk a step or two; but Mrs. Thirlmore's name, backed by the influence of the energetic commissary, availed to secure a car to themselves; and they travelled in a leisurely way, as the wounded man could endure it. The friends they left saw to it that they were provided with books, flowers, and delicacies; while Wretch kindly undertook the office of clown and court-fool, going through his accomplishments with a gravity which Grimaldi might have envied.

"Here is a man," Mrs. Thirlmore thought, one afternoon as they rolled along, "whom we regarded not so long ago as no more than a post seen by the wayside. Now he is more to us than a brother." The Captain was bolstered up by Maggie in his berth; his face was gaunt and bony, and seamed with pain ; his hands, once so strong, now lay helpless as those of a babe upon the silken coverlet which Mrs. Thirlmore had wrought for him ; his eyes were closed, but she knew he was not asleep, by the compression of the lips when a jolt came. Her heart went out to him the more lovingly that it was for her he had been smitten down. Then like a dove it spread its wings, and fled to her husband with a flight as familiar to it as that of a dove to its cote.

At last the train arrived at the Scrubstones station. Pressing indeed was the farm-work of those of the country people around who were not there to welcome their old neighbor back. For many a long year would his story be a household possession in that region. Heretofore he had been the plainest of farmers ; now people drew rein or walked more slowly when they passed the unpretentious farmhouse, — it even took upon itself something of the reverence yielded to its owner. The worst boy in school was the more careful in hustling Squash and Snap, by reason of it, more chary of charging them with cheating at marbles and mumble the peg ; the meanest boy was not mean enough to refuse to lend them ball, taw, or popgun on demand.

People hurrahed when the train rolled into the station and stopped. Mrs. Grumbles must have been more than mortal if she had not felt herself to be in some dim way a queen, as she stood among her friends to receive her husband ; and those who helped Squash and Hans to carry the Captain to the ambulance were apt to mention it long afterward. Perhaps not a man on the ground was aware of removing his hat from his head, as their old friend, haggard, yet smiling, was borne by them ; for our deepest, truest emotions work within us as by laws of their own which we have simply to obey.

For a few weeks the neighbors flowed through the house in a quiet stream, looking respectfully at the wounded man, as if he had returned to them from an immeasurable distance and after the absence of a lifetime. Slowly the owner made the rounds of his farm, until not a spot remained unvisited, no colt or calf or ox or horse unquestioned as to how it had fared during the master's absence.

"It is so funny," Squash volunteered at table one night, "that father, *father*, turns out to be like one of the men Plutarch tells about; one of the great men you see pictures of in books, *father!*" He had become in the eyes of his own household as one of the immortals.

At last, matters settled down into their regular routine; and then, in the twinkling of an eye, it seemed as if they had been as they now were for ages, — even from the creation of the world. Mrs. Thirlmore began, after a while, to understand what she had fought against during her life among them before : that the regular life of a farmer, so void of anything but work, — hard, steady, unvarying, —explains the fact that insanity prevails so much more among them than any other class. Very rarely did she hear from her husband these days. She shrank more and more from going into the city every day, and gave herself up more and more to writing. She had larger experiences now; there was more to say. As her little savings slowly increased, so, in dimensions and style of furnishing, did the home she was aiming to secure; the home was so much in advance of the savings that it at last loomed into the air, sumptuous as to its fittings, baronial in its halls and grounds.

"I am glad the Lieutenant said what he did about altruism," she thought, more than once. "Who can tell whether these shirts I have made for him may not be too small?"

But it was not for the Lieutenant that the shirts were made ; and she forgot her fear of altruism the next week when remorsefully she dropped pen, paper, and everything, to construct a dressing-gown which might have given Sardanapalus a new idea of luxury.

" I wish," she said, as she sat at her window and quilted the rich silk, "that I could be more like her."

It was of Maggie she spoke. Some hundred yards away, but in full view from her room, and at the rear of the garden, was the tool-house, a small one-story edifice which had long ago been given up to Hans for his own. In front of it, where the afternoon sun shone fully, except as it was shaded by the vines of a morning glory, stood a bench upon which Hans was wont to sit and rest when his work was done. When, at times, he lifted his head to look at the sunset, Mrs. Thirlmore could almost imagine she saw his lips move as he repeated, *Det kan ikke vare lange nu,* — " It cannot be very long now."

But there was a change in Hans. Time had slowly sobered him into content with his lot. It sent almost a pang to Mrs. Thirlmore's heart to see that he had adopted a pipe, which had not been his habit until of late. He worked as hard, but she did not see a book in his hand, as of old. Whether Maggie were cause or effect she could not say, but the broad-shouldered maid of all work was seated upon the bench at his side. They had been gathering the turnips for the winter's use of stable and house, and were tired. So far as Mrs. Thirlmore could observe, not a word passed between them. How could it pass when neither understood more than a phrase or two of the language of the other? Sorely did it perplex Mrs. Grumbles to know how under the circumstances they managed to become lovers. But lovers they were : any one could see that in the silent satisfaction of their faces as they sat, a blue mug of Swedish beer between them on the bench, which Hans had consecrated to his new happiness by painting a brilliant green ; he pipe in mouth, she knitting at what seemed in the distance to be a man's woollen sock.

"Since they understand each other, why need they talk? They submit," Mrs. Thirlmore thought, " to not comprehending each other, as they do to the other conditions of their hard, dull lives, — to the weather, to the work. I dare say he has slowly learned to lay aside and forever all that he was, all he knew and felt, in the old days. Everything is lost to him, — money, reputation, children, wife. ' Let it go,' he thinks, when he thinks about it at all. ' I accept what I have, what is left. The past is fled ; let the future bring what it may. Maggie will help me in my labor, will nurse me if I am ill. What more do I want?'"

As Mrs. Thirlmore knew, Hans was exceedingly anxious to be married, and had been so for a long time before the secret was made known to others.

" It was the drollest thing I ever saw," Captain Grumbles told his family, " how hard Hans tried, almost before he had said ' How d' y' do,' to me, to make English enough to tell me that he wanted to marry Maggie. In Sweden he was a gentleman of family and education, you know ; but he has buried everything over the water, and now all he cares for is Maggie. How he did stammer and gesticulate and make his very fingers speak, as he tried to tell me what a good woman she was, how honest and true, and of his wish to be married. I am willing to help them in every way, and so is Aurora Ann ; but Maggie will not consent. We did all we could with her ; but no, she says she will marry him some day, but not yet ; and she won't say when."

Mrs. Thirlmore had also done what she could to persuade her. But it was useless. "I know," the obstinate woman said, "that he is a good man; he can work hard. I will marry him, but not yet;" and it was in vain that her mistress made offers of help toward the new housekeeping.

Pop, by this time, was grown to be quite a pretty girl. If her hair were red, it was also silky and abundant. Her face was a well-featured, fresh and wholesome face; and she was as straight and alert as Squash was awkward. As of old, she was very impulsive and capricious as to her tasks and employments. One week she cared for nothing but dress and visiting; the next, having "got mad" with some unlucky schoolmate, she devoted herself to housekeeping. As a rule, she preferred to be called by her true name, Peace; but at times she would refuse to answer, except when hailed as Pop. At the first mention of Maggie's new prospects she was fired with excitement.

"I want to see somebody married, *dreadfully*," she averred; "is n't Maggie too bad to put off her wedding so? I told her I would make pound-cake, cup-cake, cream-cake, cheese-cake, floating island, Charlotte-Russe, — ever so many things; and I would lend her my jet set to get married in, because Hans has had another wife, you know; and we would have such a grand time, and I would give her my heifer and a brood of turkeys — ever so many things. But the cross thing won't say when it shall be. All I could get out of her was, 'one of these days.' If there is a thing I hate," Pop exploded, "it is to hear anybody say 'one of these days'!"

Whether General J. Mandeville Gilmore would have rent his raiment and wept aloud if a cannon ball had taken off the head of General Thirlmore, who can say? It is on record in the War Office what he did do, which was to write to the Government thus : —

"I have the honor to say that I am but too well aware of the vast sums which have been lost to us by the cotton trade ; doubly lost to us since they have gone to protracting the war by replenishing the military supplies of our enemies. That no officer of the regular service has been suspected of conniving at this I am perfectly aware, and I am proud and happy to state. To prove that I mean nothing derogatory to the volunteer service, I would suggest that I know of no man upon whom Government can rely with more implicit confidence than upon General Theodore Thirlmore. Placed in command of the vast cotton region of which I am writing, he would be of incalculable service to our cause."

Whether General Thirlmore, knowing of this, would have wept or made his rival weep, no man can say ; but the result was that, within a few days after the battle before the city, he was despatched, by order from headquarters, into the cotton region referred to.

"Imagine," he wrote to his wife after his arrival there, "a vast swamp. For scores of miles in every direction is a dense forest of trees, — cypress, live-oak, cotton-wood, — each tree grown to an enormous size, and heavily draped with gray moss. Few of the trees are more than a hundred feet high ; but they make up for this in diameter. Immense limbs run out from the trunk parallel to the soil, and roots project often above the surface into those 'knees,' which seem intended by Nature, intensely and presciently practical, for that ship-building to which they are precisely adapted. Here and there are eminences of land, never over thirty feet high, and sodded with thick grass, upon which turtles, alligators, and water-snakes of all species, group themselves when asserting the land half of their amphibious nature by companionship with wildcats, panthers, and all the large family of opossums, raccoons, musk-rats, and beavers. More than half the surface of the land is water of a deadly bronze, loathsome with reptiles and reptile-like seeds and grasses. The owls and crows, the hawks and buzzards which haunt the region are in strict keeping, as to color and harsh outcry, with everything else. With sundown comes Egyptian darkness, making itself sorely felt in the mosquitoes, which are the living molecules of a malaria only less dense than the muddy water. Looking about at mid-day, the woods seem like a foul army of kobolds, stunted, twisted, writhing half in half out of the mire, with limbs hideously gnarled and knotted; the dirty white of their long and mossy beards telling of an eternity, so to speak, of gloom and rottenness perpetually renewed.

" It is part of the treacherousness of this Serbonian bog that bayous, from ten to seventy feet broad, wind in and out with serpent-like turns. None of them are apparently more than a few feet deep, and as stagnant and yellow as so much molasses ; yet there are few that cannot float a steamship. All around us are the most productive of cotton lands, worked by negroes, who are so shut in by swamps and malaria as hardly to have heard the faintest rumors of freedom and of fighting. They thrive and grow fat upon miasma as upon their native element. As you know, cotton brings fabulous prices, and it pays steamers built for the purpose to glide in and out laden with the precious commodity. A cargo of cotton escaping to the sea means a blockade runner in return from Europe with a load of arms and ammunition for the Confederacy.

" There are scores of energetic gentlemen, often of the Jewish persuasion, who are on the look-out to steer cargoes of cotton northward. It takes but a boat-load or two, and the owner is able to put thousands of dollars in gold into his pockets. The charm about it is the risk, — the excitement. It is gambling, in which the bayou pilot whirls the revolving wheel. Often the dice are cannon balls, or the consciences of those who have the power to withhold or grant permits."

To a man of Thirlmore's energetic character, this country was a living nightmare. What with the swarming reptiles, the tortuous bayous, the gigantic vines tangling the forest in their anaconda folds, life became almost equivalent to an attack of delirium tremens. The one relief from the deadly monotony was the ever-wakeful vigilance demanded in reference to the stealthy and midnight creeping in and out of the cotton-boats.

To Ralph Jennings it mattered not a straw whether he fifed for Union or Confederacy, so that General Thirlmore was in command. It was the same with Jack Henson. When the former whistled " Hail Columbia " or "Yankee Doodle," it was for the glorification of that officer ; and the General's praise was to the scout the highest reward of his most daring deeds. The Federal force in the maze of the swamp was like an enormous insect with two antennæ, the sensitive extremities of which were Jack Henson and his rival scout Luke Jarvis. Often, and for weeks at a time, the force would remain motionless in camp, while these " feelers " protruded hither and thither in search of prey.

"There was one grand time," Jack Henson said afterward. " Luke and the General and I were on the bank of the biggest bayou when our gunboat went up stream, the command marching as well as it could up the north bank. Luke and I begged the General to hold up a little after the boat and the troops had gone by. There we lay for an hour out of sight in the brush, till, sure enough, we heard a tramping and a bellowing; and along comes a big drove of cattle being driven East for the Confederate army. They were fat, — those cows. You see they had been waiting in the swamp for a chance to slip in between the gunboats; and the grass and young vines and sich was rich and plenty. Well, we lay still as mice till the last beef was safe across to our side. Then we three sprang for our horses; turned the head of the drove up stream; and before those fellows knew what was up, we was a running the drove like mad toward where we knew camp would be. Of course the Rebs let loose on us with their rifles; but that did no good. Curse? oh, how they *did* curse! It was dreadful, that perfanity of theirn. But you just ought to have seen the General! I 've been in battle with him many 's the time; but I never saw him in such good humor! He rode a splendid horse, — Tamerlane he called him; and he rode on this side and that of the drove, yelling them on. It was ' Hi! Hi! Ho! Ho!' You would 've sworn he 'd been a drover all his life. You 'd better believe the boys sprang to their ranks when they heard us coming. *They* thought it was cavalry. When they seed the drove tearing in, tails up, bellowing and cavorting, they were taken aback. But when they saw who was a driving them in, if ever you heard men cheer it was then! Fat? Those beef? I should rather think so. And then the fun of it! There is n't a man but would die for the General rather than not. He 's *my* man; and if you 've got anything to say agin him, now 's your chance. I 'm ready and willin'."

The officers of Napoleon I. did not hesitate, when at Jaffa he commanded them to kill with poison their own comrades. In very much the same way General Thirlmore stood to his scouts, — if not in the place of God, certainly as the authority beyond whom there was no appeal.

It is wholly a matter of taste as to what a man most enjoys ; but Thirlmore was never more in his element than on such an occasion. His men had never seen the General in such good humor as he was that night. Seated by a roaring camp-fire, a side of fat beef roasting before its heat, a tin-cup of coffee in one hand and a handful of hard tack in the other, he had never enjoyed himself more thoroughly.

But it was laborious work controlling the cotton-market at its source. A labyrinth of creeks, rivers, and bayous extended for miles in every direction ; and it was necessary to be in twenty different places at once, throwing up redoubts, casting booms of timber across, availing himself on the instant of reliable information, duped more than once by false news, sometimes capturing, often losing, valuable cargoes.

Then fell one of those sudden calms, worse than the " doldrums " of the seas. There was an arrest, a hush, an instant stagnation, as if the country had been smitten by paralysis. For the time there was no more cotton ; runaway negroes ceased to come into camp ; there was little coming and going of gunboats ; the mails were often intercepted ; the air was dense with disheartening rumors ; dreadful defeats were reported here, there, everywhere. To add to the depression, a general idea was in the air that a compromise of some kind was about being effected with the Confederacy ; in any case, it was impossible to conjecture what definite course, if any, the Government had decided on. There had been such periods before, when, like prize-fighters exhausted and fallen back each to his own side of the ring, the North and the South did nothing but glare at each other until their breath came again. General Thirlmore was as one who leans against a mast, wondering from which quarter the wind will blow next, and whether when it came it would blow him victoriously homeward, or break in storm.

CHAPTER XXVI.

TEMPTATION.

WHEN Thirlmore entered the army it was as a ruined man. Financially he was stripped of his last cent; not an acre of land was really his own; except his horse, he owned nothing. For a time this enabled him to give himself all the more to the war; but his poverty came back upon him with every lull in the campaign, and with new force. "What·am I to do when this thing is fought out? For what profession am I fitted; for what line of business? Whom can I compel myself to apply to for capital?" Except when sorely fatigued by a day in the saddle, such thoughts would keep him awake half the night, — a thing never true of him before.

One sultry afternoon a deeper depression than usual came on him. There had been nothing to do for a long time; he had received no letters from his wife, no instructions from headquarters. He imagined to himself a group of rough men lounging perhaps at that moment around some Confederate camp-fire, and reading his intercepted despatches aloud with many a comment. His wife's letters? It was as though she herself were in their hands. "If I had the scoundrels within range of a Gatling," he grimly muttered.

He had wandered listlessly to one side of the camp, and was lying on his rubber overcoat beneath a live oak, his weather-beaten hat slouched over his eyes. The boughs drooped down over him like those carved upon a tombstone; the heavy silence had a long and ponderous roll and heave in it like that of the sleeping ocean. Without any effort of his own the thoughts oozed, as it were, slowly through his mind.

" The war may end any day. Who can say how it will end? As to that, what difference will it make to me? Say it was over to-day, where could I go? What could I do? Occupation I must have, — but of what kind? How would it do to roast chestnuts at the corner of a street? Can I go at lecturing, preaching? Bah ! "

Falling into a species of doze, the ex-clergyman saw himself in the perspective of the past standing in his pulpit. He could see himself taking a text ; beginning in a slow and deliberate fashion ; growing warmer as he went on ; gesticulating with his right hand and his left ; demanding to know of his audience this and that ; making an appeal, both hands extended, his head thrown back, to the balconies, in which faces were banked range above range almost to the ceiling, — then to the body of the congregation below. He could see himself in the act of making a point ; could detect the white handkerchiefs being drawn out furtively here and there in readiness for the tears which were apt to come. Or perhaps the point was of another kind ; and, as then, he could see the smile dimpling as it were the faces of his audience, broadening, brightening, breaking into a general laugh. He saw himself growing more and more urgent. " Will you tell me ?" " And how dare you ?" " Is it conceivable ?" " Yes, eternally yes !" " No, never ; never shall it be said — !" " And now I close, indignantly demanding — !" " Great heaven !" he said, suddenly wide awake. " What *was* it all about? No, sir, I can starve ; but — preach? Not if I keep my wits. For what in the world have I to preach *about?* "

At that instant, as he lay on his coat, his pipe long since

gone out, his wife, in strange contrast to these faded spectres, was with him, — young, lovely, intelligent, vastly his superior, yet with her hands held out to him as impulsively as those of a girl to her betrothed. She was laughing for joy at seeing him, her aspect full of trust and glowing pride in his successes. " How am I to make a comfortable home for *her* ? " As he thinks this he feels a new affection for her, almost an ardor.

" Curse and confound it ! " he groans ; " many a fellow as poor as I when the war began is rich to-day. It is not contractors alone, nor cotton-dealers." He runs over in mind the names of officers in the army who have the reputation at least of sudden and growing wealth. " What do I care for empty praise ? Presentation swords ? I would rather have carving-knives and a certainty of beef. Not an ox have I, not a sheep, not even a dog. Oh, curse it ! "

He was not a weakling to indulge in morbid fancies ; but the malaria had undermined him. He had reached a degree of depression never touched before. " I am one of the mortally wounded in battle," he thought. " The flag is being carried victoriously over me by squadrons which trample me into the mire. Where a man has money he need not care ! "

When he got back to his tent Major Gruffden was waiting to see him. Major Gruffden ! He had been a pillar of the church to which Thirlmore acted as a preacher. A misunderstanding had terminated the friendship between them, and had done much towards terminating Thirlmore's career. Mrs. Gruffden, a country girl, brought to the city as the bride of a rich man, was an enthusiastic little person, plump and rosy. She had been in ecstasies with all she saw ; and she was enraptured with her minister, just as she was with the new organ and the Christmas festivities of the Sunday-school children. It was but another vent for her excess of health.

When the war began, Mr. Gruffden had somehow come to be Major Gruffden. He was once more a loud friend of his former pastor; had managed to get in with the people at Washington; was interested in cotton, and almost lived upon the railroads. To-day he had brought an ambulance load of things from the nearest steamboat landing, — books, papers, eatables of all sorts; and it was impossible for General Thirlmore not to be glad to see him, so weary was he of his barren seclusion. For an hour or so the Major emptied his budget of the news of the day.

"You will find flattering things about yourself in these papers," he said at last. "Here is a London *Times* which has an appreciative leader upon what you have accomplished. It predicts a splendid future for you Wait till you see the ovation getting ready for you at home!"

Major Gruffden was a prosperous man, and fairly overflowing with animal spirits. That he was rich was evident in the sheen of his gorgeous necktie, the massiveness of the chain across his vest, the rings on his fingers, the very creases in his broadcloth.

"I am tropical in my tastes," he often said; "I like things to be very sweet, and bright-colored, you know. Wishy-washy soup and puddings I can't stand. No, sir!" He had chosen his plump and rosy wife on this basis; and on the same ground he invariably pooh-poohed the dark side in everything. "Things are getting on splendidly; the war is sweeping magnificently to its ending."

After an hour or so of Major Gruffden, General Thirlmore's somewhat pallid face was flushed with more than

the choice liquors the visitor had brought ; he felt better
than he had done for months.

"I had the happiness to meet your wife not long ago
in the city.   It was," Major Gruffden got upon his somewhat dumpy legs to say it, " at the meeting in the city —
no, it was at a sanitary fair.   We had a grand time.   When
a reference was made to you, I wish you could have heard
the applause.   I had just given twenty dollars for an umbrella, and I was banging its life out on the floor, helping
on, you observe ; when I happened to catch sight of your
wife standing not ten feet off.   Do you know, General, it
touched me to the soul, not only that she was looking so
well, ten years younger than when I saw her last, — she is
wonderfully handsome ! — no, it was to see the way she
fastened her eyes on the man who was making the address.
When he spoke of you she looked transformed, fairly lu-
minous, you know ; her eyes sparkled through her tears,
she was so happy, so proud of you !   Angels look that way,
I suppose, when they see God ! "

The Major *was* very tropical, and in this instance
thoroughly sincere, or he embraced the opportunity
to be so.   But General Thirlmore grew reticent, as the
talk turned, in the most natural way, upon the cotton
trade and the very tangled question of permits.   Major
Gruffden did not seem to notice it.

"Cotton is bringing en-*nor*mous prices," Major Gruffden
said ; " but it is not that I look at.   I came to be interested
in it of late, because it is a question of life and death to
those starving factory people over the water.   They could
not obtain it from India, as I always knew.   Those Man-
chester workpeople are warm friends of the North, and it
makes my blood run cold to read of the cotton famine.
Of course, it has its business aspects also ; but I can frankly

say that I am glad to do what *I* can to supply them with cotton. Think, General, of the piles of bales as high as a house waiting ready for the torch. ' We turn it,' those Beauregard banditti say, ' either into supplies for the Confederacy, or into ashes.' It is simply horrible ! " The Major could not repress a shudder.

He had to do most of the talking, and glided off into the luxury of living which must follow upon the success of the Union. " If your wife likes handsome things as much as mine does, General, — and, bless you, all women are alike in that, — she will have a splendid time when you get back. Now that you are what you are, you will have to maintain a certain style, you know. You will pardon me for saying it, but if ever there was a lady fitted to adorn the most distinguished position — My wife is charming, of course ; but she is not intellectual. Mrs. Thirlmore is both. You will have to buy a handsome house in the city, — will have to drive good horses ; you know what horses cost. I hope you will go into something which will mint money for you. A man needs every cent he can get. After a time there will come a panic, and a man cannot secure himself too much against that."

General Thirlmore could not recall very clearly afterward half the Major had said. There was some conversation as to permits. When the visitor had driven away, and the General was locking his desk for the night, he noticed a bundle loosely tied up in a newspaper lying upon the top. As he picked it up, he remembered that in leaving the other had remarked carelessly : " By-the-by, here is a little matter which I would be glad if you will keep for me somewhere till I call."

Before the paper about it had fallen from his hands, General Thirlmore understood Major Gruffden and his

visit. It was a large roll of greenbanks, the value of which
evidently and at a glance was so great that for a moment
he stood stunned. On the instant he ran over in his mind
the names of men in a position similar to his own who were
reputed to have grown suddenly and enormously wealthy,
and yet concerning whom nothing dishonorable had been
or in all likelihood ever could be proved. He had often
heard it urged that such transactions as Major Gruffden
had in view were almost if not quite legitimate. "One
must remember it is a time of war." " If one man does n't
do it, another will." " If I do not do it in a day's time,
the cotton will be destroyed in some raid, or will go to
Confederate uses." " Everybody does it." " Such things
could never be traced." " Why should a man make a.
milk-and-water fool of himself ? " and so on.

All that night General Thirlmore lay upon his camp-bed
like one who has been cut down in battle, and left in some
obscure ditch, with the roar and rush of the hosts in the
distance, and enfeebled in every sense. Hour after hour
his thoughts buzzed and stung. By a combination and
convergence of things, he had that bewilderment of brain
as to sharply defined right and wrong, which is too
often the most painful fact concerning clergymen suddenly thrust into business. For, with many a manly quality, General Thirlmore had not been what people call
a good man. That was a pietistic something which
he stigmatized as "goody, goody," " Sunday-schoolish,"
" snivelling."

Not even he himself could have recalled what he passed
through that night and far into the next day. But there
are more incarnations of the Divine than we enroll in our
theologies ; and from the first his wife was with him, present, persistent, a silent protest, full of womanly sweetness,

yet with a joyous aspect, as of one who predicts and promises the highest human happiness now and yet to be.

Had she been there she would have known by his haggard face that the question was not yet decided. He had been held from irrevocable assent, that was all, when a gunboat brought its usual bag of letters and papers. He had hoped yet dreaded to receive a letter from her, and breathed more freely when he saw there was none.

In turning languidly over the rather belated newspapers, he came upon one which contained an account of the sanitary fair to which Major Gruffden had alluded, and at which a speaker had mentioned his name. Glancing over it, his face began to burn. He saw why his visitor had given him no paper containing details of the occasion. As he read the eulogy of the speaker he recalled what the Major had said of the enthusiasm of his wife, as she listened. There was but a passing allusion to his fighting or his victories. The entire eulogy was upon General Thirlmore as standing head and shoulders high above the least suspicion of peculation. "Like the statue of some demi-god of the antique world," the orator said, in oratorical phrase, "he lifts himself in the majesty of his stainless and enduring marble far above the rabble of gain and greed, deadlier to the Republic than Rebel hate! Thank God for a true hero like this, who brings back to our mind the incorruptible warriors of earlier days, — the men of giant mould, who have power to take by the throat and strangle whatever is base and sordid in themselves, and do so even while in the act of crushing with the other hand the bloody treason of the South."

There was more to the same effect; and the husband could see his wife, as his visitor had described her, listening with radiant face to such praise, prouder, gladder than if the orator had spoken of victory in battle.

Major Gruffden put his eulogy upon General Thirlmore into fewer words, when he received his money back in a blank envelope. "What a pity such a man should be such a fool! I could have made him rich; but what can you expect of a chap who has been a preacher?"

In olden times deserted wives or mistresses were wont to make waxen images of their lovers, place them with incantations before the fire, and as the wax melted so would its similitude consume away, though empires lay between. In this instance, Mrs. Thirlmore had made with skilful fingers an image and ideal for herself of what she would have her husband be, and the ardor of her growing love for it had its effect upon the absent General.

" If he is rising steadily," the thought half framed itself in her mind, " it is because, frail and far away as I am, I give my will — and my will never was as strong and determined as now — to lifting him ! Was there nothing in the silent will with which the Marys went, which rolled aside the stone from the sepulchre in advance of their arrival? May there not, at last, be something in what is conjectured of the power of the will to move an object without bodily contact? The sycamore-tree can be plucked up by the roots, the mountain lifted from its base, if the faith which wills be strong enough."

CHAPTER XXVII.

SUPREME OPPORTUNITY.

MRS. Thirlmore was seated at her writing-table in Scrubstones. An incident in daily life had arrested her attention, and she had been engaged for some days in trying to put it upon paper. It was work a thousand times more fascinating than if she had been a botanist, and were pressing upon the page a rare specimen of fern ; or a naturalist, pinning upon paper a curious insect, bug, or butterfly. The subject was a cruelly treated young girl ; and as she endeavored so to embalm upon the page the tortured heart, with its quivering peculiarities, that it should remain sweet and enduring for the uses of other sufferers, she grew deeply interested, — so much so that she was hardly aware of Squash, when he gave her a letter ; hardly conscious of what she was doing when she opened, glanced over, and laid the bit of soiled writing upon her own page. The paper upon which the letter was written was a fly-leaf, torn most likely from some old and well-used Bible ; and it was with great difficulty that she made out the meaning. When she did, the letter was to what she had been narrating as if a living human heart were placed palpitating upon that which was but the story of a heart. It ran thus : —

" MISSIS TURLMOR — *Mame :* The man whot written this her not is ole Budkin. Ef I wos a niggar I wos hus servent to my ole missis. Praps you mighty none her. Ebry boddy nu ole Missis Pikny ob Souf Carline. She tort me how to rede and rite, cept spellin. But whot he

wants is to be changed. 'Changed' wos wot he sed, —
changed, changed, changed; he kepped goin over it.   He
wos hurt mity bad; but He wor saf in ole budkins kabbin,
an he nu it.   He wud Haf been saf if them J Hawks had
not kum Along; that wos All He had time for to Sa.   he
begunned a letter, an i Am a riten oll roun it."   For in the
centre of the greasy page was the name and address of
Mrs. Thirlmore, " Twos then the J Hawks Runn a Russhin
in, an oll He cud sa wos, Sen this to Her and sa Changged
chang.   But I Hant got Enny mor Pape," the last word
squeezed in at the end.   With much difficulty, her hand
trembled so, Mrs. Thirlmore made out the words " Klabun
contty."   Fortunately the postmark upon the envelope
indicated one of the border States; but how the writing
had contrived to get so far on its road, who could say?

Ole Budkin had been prompt; for in the papers laid
by Squash upon her table at the same time with the letter,
was an account of a raid made upon the region occupied
by General Thirlmore, and the news that he had disappeared, whether killed or captured was not known.   With
the first word of the missive the wife had risen to her feet.
For a moment she stood dazed, yet mechanically un-
fastening her dress to prepare for travel.   Then everything became clear.   Had it been a wedding invitation
she could not have been cooler, less in doubt as to what to
do.   An hour later, and she was seated in the farm express,
her valise by her side, ready to start for the station.   ·And
there was Maggie at the gate ready to accompany her.
It was as the faithful girl had supposed : marrying Hans
was not the thing for her to do.   But to her dismay her
mistress refused to take her.   There was no time to explain.   It pained Mrs. Thirlmore even then to be obliged
to speak in words so curt to the girl, who stood, her little

bag in her hand, her head drooped, the dogged expression
deepening upon her square and resolute face. The wagon
rattled away. But Maggie seemed not to know that the
children were speaking to her. In vain they called after
her, seized upon her. Hans himself gave one look at her
face, and then stood looking after her with speechless
misery. For, settling down into a steady gait, as rapidly
as she could, Maggie followed her mistress on foot, — the
roll of a stone down a declivity not more in obedience
to the laws of its nature.

Alas for such devotion! The sound of wheels died in
the distance before her. Make what haste she could, the
sound of the whistle came, then the bell of the loco-
motive. She broke into a run, and reached the station
just as the train disappeared around a curve. For one
agonizing moment she called; threw out her hands; even
ran panting along the track. At last, exhausted, trembling
in every limb, she sank upon the ground beside the road,
and gave way to the bitterness of her desolation, weeping
with an energy of tears.

It was a relief to Mrs. Thirlmore to be by herself, when
she reached Washington; she could think more clearly,
act more promptly. At first the War Department knew
nothing, could tell her nothing beyond what she had
already seen in the papers; but the deference with which
she was received by all gave her a sharp pleasure. From
the President down, every one spoke in the warmest com-
mendation of her husband. It was an overpowering force
by which he had been attacked; and slowly it came to be
known that he had been captured; had escaped, although
badly wounded; had been captured again while lying
concealed in a negro cabin, and was now held in a well-
known prison in the far South.

"We have a bushwhacking General of theirs," the President told her, "whom we really cannot treat as an ordinary prisoner of war; and they are holding your husband, madam, as a hostage for our treatment of him. They have us there, madam! There are few men in the army, very few, who are as valuable as your husband; and they know it but too well, the rascals. That bushwhacking scamp would be in the State-prison for life if he had his deserts." The worn face of the President grew stern as he detailed a few of the deeds reported of the prisoner. "Really he should be hung, madam; but that might make it very unpleasant for your husband. We will do what we can. Passports? Permits? I assure you that you can do him no good. You *must*, must you? What a determined soul a wife is! Which reminds me of a little story — "

But Mrs. Thirlmore listened only with her eyes as the President, still holding her hand in his, stood in the doorway of his room, talking to her, laughing at his own wit. Never was the reaction of laughter more needed than in his case.

Again the cars; the long reaches of desolate country; here and there the chimneys of houses gone to ashes; new bridges pieced out with the charred timbers of those which had been burned. As she journeyed she endeavored to portray to herself the prison in which her husband lay, and what she should do. She had been in such haste; accounts were so confused and conflicting, whether she read them in the papers or heard them in the more heated statements at Washington, of this informant and that, that she had no clear idea what to expect. The picture which she drew was a terrible one, based on a long perusal of newspaper horrors.

"I am glad I would not let Maggie come," she thought, as at last, after manifold detentions and difficulties, she drew near to the place where her husband was. "I am glad not to expose her to the horrible things I am sure to see."

The train was running slowly into the dreaded yet longed-for place of General Thirlmore's confinement. She looked out with dread, rallying herself to meet the worst. It was a peaceful Sunday morning. The sky was of a celestial blue, shading into a tenderer tint where the fleecy breaths of vapor high up in the air contrasted with the depths of space. A hush seemed to have fallen upon the Pride-of-India trees which lined the broad and sandy streets, and they stirred soundlessly. There seemed to be almost no one upon the streets, except a negro man or woman here and there who were loitering by on their way to some early service. It was winter when Mrs. Thirlmore left the North. To-day she found herself in spring well advanced into summer. The air was laden with the fragrance from many a flowering tree and shrub, the yellow jasmine lording it above the rest; and the anxious wife allowed herself to revel in the perfume as she did in the laughter of the negroes, — a laughter as free as that of children, louder and more musical than the laugh of grown people. Never, in all her days, had she heard any laughter to compare with it.

"I know it is purely animal," she thought. "If I could leave behind me every sorrow, every anxiety, would I be able to laugh so?"

This flashed through her mind as she was driven to her hotel in an old ambulance drawn by mules. It seemed to her scarcely to move, the sand of the streets was so deep; her heart beat as fast as if it were the wings of the carrier-dove nearing its dove-cot.

She knew many things; there were some things of which she was as ignorant as a babe. Education, association, circumstance, had conspired with hereditary bent to make her what she was, her own will leading with resolute foot along a definite way. She was all unconsciously to come under wholly new influences now, which were bearing her, not without a struggle against it, seemingly backward toward the simpler, gentler, sweeter, more womanly, because more childlike, nature of earlier times in her life.

"I may have come down into a lower civilization," she often said to herself, during her life for the first time among Southern people; "but it is very, very charming. If it is so now with war raging and my husband what he has been, and is, how pleasant it must have been here before all this happened! Yes, and how delightful it will be when the hurly-burly is over and gone, and we are one people again."

For it was more deeply impressed upon her every day, that the war was but a tropical gust which would clear the air of all manner of malarious germs, North and South; the gust would pass, the nation would remain, the North not contributing more to its muscle than, so to speak, the South would contribute to its beauty and sweetness.

It was soon known who Mrs. Thirlmore was; and had she been a leper she could not have been much more cut off from companionship with the people among whom she lived. But, like Moxy Gilmore, she reflected, "They do what I should do if I were in their place. I am glad they cannot prevent me from attending church."

Dressed very plainly, always taking one of the least conspicuous seats, she had more than once observed an old lady looking at her from a pew not far off, first in a curious, then in a kindly manner. One evening this lady called upon her at her hotel. She was a grave-faced, benignant gentlewoman, who reminded Mrs. Thirlmore of portraits she had seen of the mother of Washington. Of commanding person, her white hair in smooth puffs upon either side of her face, which for pure white and red might vie with that of a young girl, she wore like a court-dress that gracious yet dignified demeanor so rarely seen in the last sixty years.

"My name is Mrs. Rutledge," she said, when she went in, " and I have called to make your acquaintance, if you will allow me. You are too sensible, my dear lady, not to understand why our ladies shun you as they seem to do. But I am an old citizen, and privileged to do as I please — a little spoiled I am afraid. Like all our people, I have hoped that we might succeed in this war ; perhaps it is because I am so old that I am not so bitter as some ; and then I have been severely afflicted."

The benevolent countenance of the visitor, the sweet and gentle tones of her voice, had already taken Mrs. Thirlmore captive ; and she now observed that the other was dressed in deep mourning. As she was afterward to learn, Mrs. Rutledge was the daughter of a former Governor of the State ; her husband had been a Senator in Congress, but was now dead. Of three sons, the two youngest had been killed in battle for the Confederacy. This gave her a place in the city second to none ; she was, in fact, the leader, in her quiet and old-fashioned way, of the best society, and Mrs. Thirlmore cut off from as it were the whole world, and worn with anxiety about her husband, came to love her like a mother.

"I noticed you at church," Mrs. Rutledge remarked,

before she left, "and I was glad to see that you were so much interested."

"That is because everything is different," Mrs. Thirlmore said. "Your minister seems to take everything in the Bible for granted, and I am tired of hearing things discussed. He is so fervent, too ; he believes everything ; he seems to be sure it will help those who are in trouble. Do you know," she hesitated a little, "he seems so good and sympathizing that I came near writing him a little note, begging him to come and see me ? I wanted to consult him — "

But the benevolent face of the other had changed : she seemed almost distressed. "No, my dear lady," she said, "it was natural in you ; but I do not think it would be wise to do so. He is the best of men ; but — it is war-time you know, and your husband is known to be one of your most successful generals. What does it matter, when you can go to one who is not affected by these little passing quarrels ? Yes, our minister is the most devoted of men — "

"But you cannot tell, madam, how much I have enjoyed the singing. It melts me in spite of myself. When the people come into church there seems to be a hushed expectation of something they are sure to get, — a devout hearing, which one does not always find. I can't say that I always enjoy the prayers " — she smiled.

"I dare say not, my dear. But in a little while now the war will be over ; everything will come right again. Since I lost my boys I have learned much. So that we have an unchangeable, faith, everything else is of small account."

The chastened woman spoke in so loving a manner that Mrs. Thirlmore was deeply moved.

"I am so much obliged to you," she said, as she accompanied her to the door.

"I know, of course, that it will not do for me to return your kind call; but I needed help, and I am more grateful to you than you can think," she said sweetly. She almost hesitated to give her hand to her visitor — she was not sure whether she would take it.

Mrs. Rutledge looked at the refined and beautiful face of her new friend. She saw that she was in the presence of one of those rare and lovely women to whom books and the best companionship, travel and the most developing of circumstances, are but as the cutting to the diamond. There were not three women in the city whom, after a lifetime of acquaintance, she would have so favored; but as she looked into the pure face turned up to her, this mother of the two dead boys placed a hand upon either shoulder of the stranger, kissed her with tears in her eyes, and was gone. For a moment Mrs. Thirlmore stood where the other left her, the kiss fresh upon her cheek, thinking, thinking. "Yes," she said to herself, "I had more to learn than I knew. I am glad I am here."

When, after securing rooms for herself at the hotel, she was driven to the prison armed with a permit, she found it to be a large and gloomy building. That it had been a tobacco factory once on a time was plain from the aroma with which every brick and plank, every joist and beam, was saturated. She had learned before this how her husband had been hurt, — how ill he had been, and was; but she was hardly prepared for what she saw when she entered the room at the end of a long hall upon the highest floor.

General Thirlmore was lying in a dead sleep upon his little iron bedstead. She stood over him in a tremor of

love, anxiety, passionate expectation, feeding her hungry
eyes upon him, her hands yearning like those of a mother.
The weight of a man, the height which he falls from,
makes all the difference in the hurt he receives. Because he was of so vigorous a nature, because he had
fallen headlong from a high place, General Thirlmore lay
before her more prostrate than would have been possible
of a lesser man. The wife hardly recognized in the
gaunt and emaciated object the husband of whom she
had been so proud. His hair had been left untended,
and it fell over his brow and face like the mane of a lion.
The sunken eyes; the hollowness of the cheeks showing
through the tangled beard; the arms, which seemed long
to deformity, so thin were they as they lay outside the
cover; the brown hands, upon which the blue veins stood
out like knotted cords, — it was the ruins of what had
been a man that she saw before her.

A glance about the room completed the picture. In
one corner were his well-worn boots, one of them cut
open from top to toe before the wounded and swollen
foot could be extricated. Upon the wall hung his gar-
ments, torn, muddy, cut here and there in slashes which
made her shudder; while under the table lay what was
once a military hat. Perhaps it was because there were
so many prisoners in the building, or from the inevitable
hurry and disorder of a prison, which is also a hospital,
that there seemed such an air of neglect over the whole
building. But a deadly doubt as to the final success of
the Confederacy had crept in, demoralizing everything;
and, moreover, there had been evil stories of the worse
than neglect with which Confederate prisoners had been
treated in Northern jails; and, above all, this prisoner had
been of special damage to the cause; and his treatment

was conformed to that supposed to be measured out to the bushwhacking officer mentioned by the President.

But bad as this was, there was that which was worse. The prison pen was absent; but here was something worse than that, — the stockade was within the man himself.

For a time Mrs. Thirlmore busied herself about the room. She had seen on entering that her husband was in a sleep produced by drugs which had been given by an ignorant, perhaps, or reckless hand. She sank upon her knees by his side, waiting for him to waken. Her lips touched his forehead, which looked the nobler for its hollowed temples. He seemed many years older; but her hands fluttered about him as if he were a sleeping babe. Oh, for one look into those sealed eyes! Yet she dreaded their opening. Would he know her? Into what ruins had he fallen, — disgust of himself, of everything, bitter unbelief, purpose so shattered as to be beyond renewing! She had cherished a firm faith in what he was so evidently becoming; but it had always been accompanied by a knowledge as to the unspeakable reaction and ruin into which such a man is liable to fall, if only because he is capable of things so noble.

She did not hear the door open, or heed the voice which spoke. A hand was laid upon her shoulder. It was but a common soldier, who had been sent to say that her time was up; and when she arose at last and faced him, he fell back almost in dismay.

"I 've hearn tell of angels goin' to chaps in prising," he remarked that night to his comrades, "but I 'll be goll darned if I ever saw one afore. That is, if angels can be sad like; and strong like, too, you bet! We liked to hev had a drefful time getten her out; he had n't waked up, you see. But all to oncet she straightened up; said she was mightily obleeged — and such a smile ! " The hand of the half-nurse, half-guard was in his pocket when he spoke ; but he did not think it necessary to speak of the bit of gold there. So long was it since he saw anything but Confederate notes that the coin was of diamond value to him.

The next morning, when the wife awoke out of the deep sleep which follows exhaustion, she felt strong, exultant, almost glad. She dressed herself rapidly, but with care, that she might be at the gates before they were opened. Her work lay before her, and she welcomed it with all her heart.

CHAPTER XXVIII.

DRAWING TO THE END.

THE wife did not get to her husband an hour too soon !

His capture had not taken place till after a desperate fight, in which he had been severely wounded. Within a week afterward he contrived, by the devotion of Jack Henson, to make his escape. They were pursued, the scout killed ; and for nearly a month General Thirlmore was endeavoring in vain to work his perilous way through the labyrinth of mud and water which reached in seemingly unlimited distances in every direction. Scores of men were upon his trail ; and once, if not oftener, he had to fight for his life with blood-hounds. Sometimes he slept in a negro cabin ; oftener upon a tuft of half solid ground beneath the drapery of the overhanging moss, all the time struggling slowly Northward. Sometimes his food was the bacon and corn-bread given him by negro hands at work in the fields ; at other times, he had to subsist upon such game as he could bring down with his revolver. His wounds remained unhealed ; he was shaken with chills and fever, till there seemed nothing left him at last but his will. Heart, hope, reason, were worn to shreds like his shoes and clothing. There was a steady reduction of his manhood, to that inmost and ultimate faculty, his will ; and it seemed to work as if of itself, having nothing left it but the animal instinct to get on and on, if but a mile a day.

He had almost reached the border line when, unable to

do more, he reeled into the cabin of the old negro who
had written to the wife, and there, fighting to the last with
almost insane fury, he had been captured. So reduced
was he by what had gone before, that the surgeons gave
up all hope of his recovery. It was better he should die.
How could he return to life except as a madman or a
drivelling idiot!

It was thus his wife found him. None but a wife, and
such a wife as this, could or would have had a hope of
restoring him. Strange that nothing but an unspeakable
gladness came upon her from the outset, at having such
work given her to do! It was like coming into a great
fortune. It was as if it had been allotted her to write an
epic, — an epic for which she felt herself calmly, con-
fidently competent. How she went to work, and continued to work through all variations of hope and despair,
she could not herself understand afterward. Once, twice
it was with him as if he had arrived within a mile or so
of the border line, to be there captured. Her own will
now taking the place of his, which lay seemingly dead,
she lifted him as by the strength of her mighty love to and
almost over the line of recovery, only to see him relapse
again toward death.

During wearisome days and nights, which seemed as
though they never would end, she worked over him, while
the surgeons stood back and left him in her hands, very
much as those of the Ruler's daughter may have done after
the Nazarene came into the chamber. By what silences
and half words; by what granting or firm refusing of this
and that; by what variation in medicine, and by what
subtile preparation thereof until the food was enjoyed by
the stomach; by what whispers rising into low speech,
and crooning into song yet more soothing, — she wrought,

who can describe? It was by a purely womanly influence he was saved, — an influence more restful than sleep, more nourishing than food, more divinely healing than medicine. There are things as impossible to be exercised by a man as are the processes within woman toward the unborn babe. The cooling palm upon the fevered forehead ; the absence of the nurse, as carefully ordered as her presence ; the encouragement of what he had to say ; the laughter, the tears, the rebuke sweeter than praise, the light gossip which was the mental gruel he was able to bear, — could a man have nursed him after such fashion? As he was able to endure it, she told him news of the war more stimulating than wine and less adulterated, recited poems to him, read from the papers what would divert him best. You may tell of the touches of Rubens and of Michael Angelo, of the strokes of a poet's pen ; but the woman herself was not aware of the divinity which took within her this much more necessary form of genius.

Nor was Mrs. Thirlmore without help. Mrs. Rutledge taxed her favor with her own people heavily by visiting these two. There was that in the Southern character as exhibited in her, which was more to them than the genial air ; nor did their visitor fail of something from them in return. It happened that she was in their room when the last day of the prisoner's captivity came. One thing alone had been necessary to his restoration, and that was his exchange. It was a foolishly womanly thing to do ; but Mrs. Thirlmore having secured the exchange, so arranged it that when her husband dressed that bright morning, it was in a new uniform out and out. He stood before her flushed with returning health, a larger hope in his eyes, a deeper purpose than before ; he dazzled her as

Hector did Andromache ; to her eyes he was brilliant as the morning sun.

" Dear Mrs. Rutledge," she began, for that lady was regarding him also, " do you not think — " There she stopped. It was not that her friend wore crape for her boys killed in battle. To General Thirlmore at that moment had come a memory of his victories before capture, of his sufferings while trying to escape. Again he felt the paws of the blood-hounds on his shoulders, their hot breath in his face ; and there was such an expression in his countenance, such a greed, such a purpose of vengeance, that Mrs. Rutledge grew sick at heart and turned away.

" He was elected to Congress while he was so ill," Mrs. Thirlmore faltered ; " if he could but have seen it his duty to serve his country there !" She could say no more. Had she not herself urged upon him to go to the war, when he required no urging? And now the hearts of these two were as one. But Thirlmore was a gentleman.

" Unless that scamp, Louis Napoleon," he tried to turn it off, " makes haste out of Mexico, you will see us all, madam, under command of General Lee, and fighting under him in Mexico."

A little later, and all this was over and gone. General Thirlmore, fully recovered, was in the fore front of the fighting, and his wife with the household at Scrubstones again, until the rapidly nearing end should come.

As to herself, Mrs. Thirlmore had now a renewed purpose in writing for the press ; new inspirations had come to her, and not Maggie herself with Hans worked harder in the field than she. There was just so much money to be made, and the steady pressure brought, as it always will, the due measure from the vintage. Captain Grumbles

was as well again as he ever would be, and what he had
lost in one way he had more than made up in another;
for such a thing as had occurred between himself and his
friend is something akin to an active transfusion of blood.
His wife was too strong in her own peasant nature to
change; none the less, the city lady had passed into her
as the sunshine passes into the soil. Each got from the
other that which she most lacked; and if Mrs. Grumbles
was more refined by reason of their intercourse, her guest
was of a broader, stronger fibre.

Mrs. Thirlmore had given up all hopes of making Squash
into anything apart from the farm. Father and mother
were too strong in him for that. And yet it pleased Mrs.
Thirlmore to know that the boy, when grown, would serve
as well as anything else to mark the advance of the farmer
of to-day upon the Hezekiah Grumbles of the past. So
of Pop. She was now a slender girl on her certain path
to village bellehood. One or two youths, radiant in new
neckties, had already called upon her; and one morning
she finally announced at breakfast, that if anybody called
her henceforth by anything other than her real name of
Peace he would be sorry for it. Then came such an
interest in ribbons and ruffles as alarmed her good mother.
To the indignation of the embryo coquette she was suddenly sent to a good boarding-school, where a great transformation took place. With her wonted impetuosity, she
had not been there more than a month before she announced by letter her firm resolve never to marry, or to
go into society, hollow and frivolous as it was. No; she
proposed to devote herself to science. Some day she
hoped to become a teacher herself; and with a view to
this wrote in urgent need for a black silk dress and a pair
of gold eye-glasses, — which, however, were not sent.

General J. Mandeville Gilmore resigned while General
Thirlmore was a prisoner.   Forbearance with the powers
that be has its limits.   Even in the face of the enemy one
cannot put up with everything.   He was again in the city in
which he lived before the war.   It was generally believed
that the army had lost in him its finest-looking General.
What made it worse was that the railroad of which he once
was president did not oust his successor to make room for
him, and the old soldier was compelled to fall back on his
private resources, which, fortunately, were amply sufficient.

"It is a perfect shame!"   "Nothing could be meaner!"
"Would any one have thought that those horrid wretches
could have dared to do it?"   When Mrs. Gilmore was
heard saying that, one might be sure it was of either the
Government or the railroad she was speaking.   Wherever she was, her husband, as of old, was her inexhaustible
theme.   The faithful wife never lacked material for conversation.   To a thoughtful person like Lieutenant Van
Doren, there was nothing in the good lady to be despised.

"It is the nature of some planets to have moons.   Your
father," he said to Moxy, "deserves to have one, if ever
man did.   Now there are — "

"If you expect me to be *your* moon," Moxy replies,
"you are exceedingly mistaken."

"That is what I was upon the point of observing," he
replied.   "I belong to the order of heavenly bodies which
neither deserve nor desire anything of the kind.   But you
are mistaken, Moxy, if you imagine there is anything unworthy of you, or of her, in your mother's devotion to the
General.   Take him all in all, he *is* a grand old fellow,
and everything about him proclaims it.   You are proud to
be his daughter, and so am I to be his son-in-law.   As to
your mother, remember this: You can find selfish men

and women everywhere. To me she is the most unselfish person possible. She effaces her very existence. Except as the wife of General Gilmore, I doubt if she is conscious of herself as a separate being. When people are tempted to laugh, I look at her eyes fastened upon her husband, and I respect and reverence her to the bottom of my soul."

"That is all very well," Moxy persisted; "but if you are looking forward to *my* gazing upon *you* with adoring eyes you are mistaken. I want you to be a man, as you are, with strong opinions upon every subject. That is the kind of woman I am and always shall be."

Perhaps it was fortunate for both that this conversation was not in person but by letter, for the Commissary by no means resigned when the General did. No man connected with his department stood higher; and few men were better qualified, when the war ended, for business of almost any kind requiring a clear head and a rapid step, a hand as sure and quick as his heart.

Mrs. Thirlmore had wrought so steadily at her work that the time fled almost imperceptibly. Her chief recreation was to drive over to the village post-office after breakfast every morning to bring the papers, and especially her husband's letters. Her health was not as strong as it had been, and she drove more carefully than usual one bright Wednesday morning. The horse which drew the light wagon had been exempted from all work but this, and had not been known to shy for some twenty years. Even before she reached the office, the blood began to tingle in her veins; the old horse stumbled into a feeble trot as if he anticipated something. As she neared the village the tingling in her veins increased at the sound of bells breaking into joyous peals. Obtaining her letters, she could not take time to look at them. But one thought filled her mind, — one person: it was neither Lincoln, Grant, nor Lee. She was a school-girl again, or rather a child, but with tenfold the joyous spirit she had ever possessed as a child!

"I must be careful — very careful." Mrs. Grumbles was standing on the porch, and broke into loud weeping at the radiant face of her friend, before she was out of the wagon. Then the two women ran into each other's arms, and into a rapture of weeping and exclaiming. For a moment the children stood in dumb astonishment. Then they broke away in every direction over the farm, and their cries rang through barn-yard, garden, and field, — "The war is over! The war is over!" though they had not as yet heard a word to that effect.

"Oh, Hans, Hans! The war is over!" The stolid Swede was at work as usual in an adjoining field, Maggie near by. Not fully understanding the boys who were tugging at him, exclaiming, running around like colts gone mad, he turned with wide-eyed wonder to Maggie. By way of explaining matters to him in the briefest way, she threw her arms about his neck, kissed him, and gave way to tears. Nor need she have been ashamed; many millions of men as well as women were weeping at the same moment all over the wide land!

Who of us then alive can ever forget those blessed days? What ringing of happy bells across the continent! What shaking of hands on the part of everybody! What heartfelt gladness, assuring itself of the speedy return of those who went from home, — husbands, fathers, brothers, sons, to come back heroes. There was but one thing to temper the joy, — this person and that, draped in irrevocable black, stealing away to weep over those who went forth to battle, but who would come back no more forever;

and yet the bitterness was stricken from such tears, re-membering how sacred was the cause for which the dead gave their lives.

It was a week of rejoicing at Scrubstones; but Mrs. Thirlmore, for one, was taken unawares, as we all are sometimes. Without the knowledge of her husband, she had earned enough to pay off all debts due upon their stony old farm. It was rough, out-of-the-way, stony; but then a diamond is a stone, and there was that which made the place precious to her. Had it not belonged to her husband's mother? Had he not been born there? That he had outgrown it she knew very well; but it would be the best of all halting-spots, until he could determine what he should do next. She had sufficient money, too, to buy back a part of her husband's blooded stock, and to make the needful repairs to the buildings.

When Maggie announced to Hans her purpose of going thither with her mistress, all the Swedish gentility of the man rose in rebellion against it; for in Sweden he had been a gentleman. He would not go! "Then good-by," and Maggie held out her hand. He knew what that meant, and, not knowing the English for it, put his rueful thoughts into the consternation of his square-set face.

"Say you will go," said Maggie, "and I will marry you to-morrow night. You can saddle the plowhorse and go to Mr. Kellogg now, and tell him to come, if you say so."

The meaning of her words reached him more from face and gesture than anything else. His solemn-set face slowly melted under her smile; and Wretch loitering near by could not believe his ears, for the man laughed aloud, — the first time he had laughed since leaving Sweden, and for many a sad day before.

CHAPTER XXIX

CONSUMMATION.

IT was late one September afternoon when General Thirlmore got out of the cars at the station nearest his farm. His wife had not been well enough to meet him at any point of his journey, — that was all he knew; and that she would await him there.

He had been very busy. It had taken more time than he had thought to get to Washington, and to join in that review of the whole army which, as the ages roll by, will come to be considered as an historical event unequalled in the annals of the world.

"A man cannot be forever in a condition of wonder and astonishment," Lieutenant Van Doren said to Moxy. "I dare say heaven itself will be as natural to us after the first few days as one's own home. Here I am a married man, and married to a woman such as you, Moxy; and I am not in the least enrap — no, that would be a lie — astonished, I mean."

"Neither am I. It seems so natural," said his charming bit of a wife. But her husband *was* astonished. Why had she become so gentle, so dove-like, in manner and tone? Scarce a spark of her old sarcasm was there. Like every other person, she was radiant at the shifting scenes of the great spectacle; but it was with a softened happiness which surprised her bright-faced husband while it delighted him.

"What I was trying to say," he observed, "is this: the way in which the war has resulted in freeing the negroes, and erecting this most magnificent of all possible republics, is a something I cannot accustom myself to. But we must get used to walking upon this mountain level, and take all that is to come as matter of course. Yonder rides General Thirlmore. If there is a nobler-looking man on the ground I should be glad to see him." The newly-made husband and wife were watching the march past of the seemingly unending ranks.

"My father said this morning," Moxy added, "that few men had achieved a more brilliant reputation. What is he going to do next?"

"He doesn't know himself, I suppose," her husband replied. "A dozen things are at his back. He can continue in the army if he likes to do so; he can enter Congress, or be made Governor of a Territory, or Minister to a foreign court. If he prefers business, he can be the tremendously paid president of pretty much whatever insurance or banking company he chooses."

"Do you know," Moxy said, "I had the audacity to say to him. 'If you take a church again, I'll be your organist and faithful critic.' He laughed. He didn't use to laugh like that. What a different man he is to what he once was, — deeper, gentler, grander every way! I'm so sorry I am not his wife! No, I'm not, darling," she said, like a silly girl. What *had* come over her?

"And he told me what he would like to be. He was talking to papa about it. They are great friends now. It does delight me so," the bride said, with a sudden moisture in her eyes, — "the grave deference he pays papa. Mother is as much in love with him as I am."

"But what was it he would like to be, dear?" The Lieutenant was all attention. He was seeking out a new path for himself.

"He wants to go to Dakota, or somewhere in the West."

"Not to try mining?"

"No, he had been reading of the vast wheat lands. He says there is something which exactly suits him in the boundless breadths of space; the out-of-door life; the having wheat-fields by the square mile, cattle and horses by the thousand. When he came to describing to papa what he had been told of the oceans of deep, rich grass, waving to the horizon, I begged papa to go, too. Think, darling, of the swarms of deer, the rivers full of fish, the lovely plains and mountains with snowy tops, and all as new as if it was created yesterday. That is what I like. What an eloquent man he is!"

"It would be very easy for him to get up a colony."

"Would you go?" Moxy asked, her arm in his. How had she come to grow so very pretty during these last few weeks?

"Go? Let me have the chance of going, and you shall see. Especially, if Thirlmore will head us."

But the Washington pageant faded away, as so many have done before it.

Then there was a grand reception in the city in which General Thirlmore had been a preacher, and from which he had been sent out to the war. There was a review and a banquet and a concert, festivities innumerable; and who of all the thousands cheering him and his comrades along the decorated streets would not have assented to the fact that the stern, yet genial-faced hero of the day had in some way risen to heights beyond all he had attained in the past, — heights which lay not without but within the man.

"The glory which shall be revealed *in* us!" Lieutenant Van Doren could not shake off these words that day. Some men have Shakspeare at their finger tips: how could he help it if his reading had centred upon another book instead?

One little incident befell. At the concert a song had been sung which excited almost frantic applause. General Thirlmore had heard the music of it very often since coming North. His taste was not specially in that direction; yet the words thrilled him. He was ashamed of the way in which they stormed his heart.

"You seem to like the anthem," a gentleman standing near him observed jocosely.

"Yes. I am nothing of a poet," he replied; "but I should think that, next to fighting through the war, the author of such a song is deserving of all praise. I can imagine he would make others fight. Roger de l'Isle is not Napoleon; but he is an even greater hero in his way for producing the Marseillaise. Of the two I would almost rather be Roger." It surprised the speaker himself to hear so unwonted an opinion coming from his own lips.

The gentleman looked at General Thirlmore with amazement. " Is it possible," he said, " that you do not know? "

" Know what? "

" You will pardon me, General," the other said with all deference; " but it is very remarkable! Excuse me, the song was written by your own wife — by Mrs. Thirlmore ! "

Long ago had this veteran learned to suppress all exhibition of feeling, nor did he move muscle or hair now. None the less, the words fell upon him like the flash of a cannon. Pride, pain, pleasure, regret? Which was it? What was it?

" It is but one of many noble lyrics from her pen," he heard the gentleman saying, as if from a great distance.

"Her prose, also, has had marvellous effect. We have few American women, sir, so gifted. Your ignorance is but another evidence of her modesty. It is in spite of her that she is known. You are, indeed, to be congratulated!" He spoke with sincere feeling.

One wholesome effect of the war upon this man, as upon all men, had been to cure him of too much brooding. When not looking affairs squarely in the face, planning accordingly, and then acting, he preferred to eat, to sleep, to laugh, to do anything rather than indulge in introspection. And yet as the cars bore him towards his old farm his mind drifted in this manner : —

"Knowing that I was bankrupt, is it possible that Peace can have been trying to earn something by her pen?"

But he mined, so to speak, to penetrate down to more golden results of thinking : —

"I can see that it is not mere sentiment which stirs a woman of her kind to her most vigorous work. It is not country, liberty, battle, victory, which has so wrought upon her that she, the most self-controlled of women, should have so overflowed in verse or prose. Can it be — ?" There he ceased to frame his thought into ideas ; what he dumbly but most deeply felt was, "The Republic, the war, the glorious result, — these are but names for — the man she loves." And out of that there sprang up within him a man's great love, calm, deep, to the extent of his strong capacity for loving, — a love to last as long as his being ! It humbled him ; he felt unworthy of being the ideal for such a woman's affection. Very well, let the past perish ; what he could do in the future to deserve it, should be done.

When he reached the station that September afternoon he found Hans waiting for him with the farm wagon.

"The Mrs. is at Old Farm," he said. Thirlmore stared; but telling him to follow with the trunks, he struck across the fields toward the house by a way he had often taken when a boy.

Everything was familiar to him, — every turn in the path, every bold hill, every bit of forest, every stone fence, almost every stone in it. Surely the crows elsewhere were not so familiar to him as were these, cawing from the tops of dead trees. Yonder he had gathered berries a thousand times. There he had often sat to eat his noonday lunch.

"Don't be a fool," he almost growled at himself; but he did not mean it. He rebuked himself, laughed, gave himself an impatient shake. When he had first struck within the borders of what had been his old domain, it was as if it were into an atmosphere dense with an almost oppressive cloud of memories; but as he went on, this seemed to lift, everything began rapidly to clear. There was the bare old house at last. Blue smoke curled from its chimneys, and there was a look of repair and use about it which astonished Thirlmore.

As he passed the barn-yard, Tamerlane, who had come through the war, but not unscathed, and who had been sent on in advance, put his head over the bars, and whinnied, horse-fashion, to his master: "Well, here you are. Has any new war begun? What is up next for us to do?" Tamerlane was right to ask it; his master had been at such expense and world of pains to find him, and buy him back from his captors. The time had been, and not long ago, when nothing could have held Thirlmore from stopping to stroke his nose, but no such thought came into his mind now. He could not stop to wonder or to question; all his past converged in one person. She was the gateway to all his future. To him there was at the moment no other being, not himself even, in existence.

She had not met him as he had hoped she would, in Washington. Why she had not done so he did not know; because she had not done so was itself reason sufficient. What was this dog coiling and uncoiling itself about his feet? It was a part of his home and of her; so he put it gently aside with his foot.

He was standing outside in the darkening night. Another moment and he was standing within, his wife in his arms. By mutual movement, each put the other far enough away for one hungering gaze. Nor did she remain long after that in his arms. Putting him back from her, crying, laughing, blushing, she held up a warning hand while she stole for a moment out of the room. The next, she was standing before him again, rosy, weeping, laughing, triumphant, her baby boy held high in her arms.

"And you did n't know it, Theo, — did n't dream of such a thing! Is he not a noble fellow? Look, Theo, look!"

But not even then was he regarding his child — that would come after. Now he was aware only of her.

If there are in this world supreme moments which make amends for all that goes before, what must heaven be?

THE END.

www.ingramcontent.com/pod-product-compliance
Lightning Source LLC
Chambersburg PA
CBHW060533030726
47498CB00004B/1174